EVIL
ENTRAPMENT

ALSO BY THE AUTHOR

The Demonic Indemnity Series
Demonic Indemnity
Infernal Negligence
Supernatural Peril
Evil Entrapment

Other Titles
Village Books
The Donnelly Tontine
The Hellfire Club
The International Cinema Society
Deadline
Whitechapel

Younger Readers
The Island at the End of the World

The Shadow of the Beast

EVIL ENTRAPMENT

DEMONIC INDEMNITY
BOOK IV

CRAIG McLAY

1

Zito Futchinski was just getting up from his desk to go for lunch when the buzzer went off.

"Dr. Guggendorf?" It was Monika, the receptionist. At least, he was pretty sure her first name was Monika. Or maybe it was Morgan. Zito couldn't remember her last name, but didn't think that reflected any great failure as a boss as she had only been working the front desk for a couple of weeks. Due to the highly illegal nature of its day-to-day operations, Monster Mashers Discount Necromancy & Banishment had a higher than usual rate of employee turnover.

Zito sighed and pushed the answer button. He had told whatever her name was many times not to bother him between 10 and two. Or maybe he had said that to the previous receptionist. He also couldn't remember her name. The new receptionist was a succubus, so at least he didn't have to worry about any sexual harassment complaints this time.

"I'm just heading out for an appointment," he snapped.

"I understand that, Dr. Guggendorf," she said. "But I have a client out here who would like to see you as urgently as possible."

"Have him make an appointment," Zito grunted, pulling off his white lab coat. "I think I've got some slots open next Tuesday. I have an urgent outpatient call I need to get to."

This, of course, was a lie. Zito planned to drive out to the new Greek place in the Lower Styx where he heard that you could drink directly from the breasts of the naked Bacchantae table dancers. They were said to secrete a milky wine so potent that it induced sexual hallucinations lasting for hours. Although he wasn't really a doctor, he believed that it was his scientific duty to evaluate all such claims based on experimentation and hard evidence.

"Yes, doctor," she persisted. "But I believe this client is in need of urgent servicing."

Zito paused. Something in her tone triggered an impulse deep within the core of his being. Not a medical urge to heal, of course. This was a more primal desire. "Oh yeah? How urgent?"

"I believe this case might qualify for our Dark Circle treatment plan," she said, dropping her voice to a whisper.

Zito felt his cheeks flush and his heart rate increase at the sound of those two magic words. "Dark Circle" was the not-terribly-sophisticated code name he had personally invented for their VIP clients. It applied to anyone who was clueless, heavily insured and guilty of suffering from or inflicting highly embarrassing loss or damage for which they did not want to be held personally liable.

"Really?" Zito said.

"Yes, doctor," she said.

"You know what?" Zito said, clearing his throat. "I might just be able to squeeze him in. Send him through, Michelle."

"It's Mathilda," the receptionist said a little peevishly. "Yes, doctor."

Zito stuffed his arms back into his lab coat and took a quick look around his office to make sure nothing incriminating was visible. They had just taken delivery of 500 vials of Zombidine, a powerful hallucinogenic sedative that was supposed to induce a state of trance-like calm in users. Zito had sworn he wasn't going to get hooked on the stuff, but he needed something to help him come down from all the endorphin-tainted blood he was mainlining on a daily basis.

He knew it was risky, but it was hard to resist when he had such easy access to the vast quantities of narcotics that circulated through his place of work. Besides, somebody had to be responsible for quality control.

So far, his demon Hellspawn bosses hadn't noticed that he was skimming off the top, but he was going to need to moderate his intake if he didn't want to end up tossed unceremoniously into the bottomless hot tub that Azmoda was rumoured to have in the basement of Circle 9.

Zito stuffed the loose vials in the top drawer of his desk and quickly checked his reflection using an ornate silver letter opener. He never actually got any letters that required opening, but it was always handy to have around just in case some vampire or werewolf client got shirty about some piece of fine print in the terms and conditions. The whites of his eyes were a little blue from the Narlune, but not so much that anyone not acquainted with the side effects of spectral pharmacological dependence would be likely to notice. Most of his clients did not start out as junkies, but they got there in the end.

There was a knock at the door. In the corner of the room, his pet Gogrub stopped playing with one of its three sets of genitalia and sat up on the top perch of its silver cage.

"Gazakk Tak!" the demon chirped, breaking flames from both ends and banging its claws against the bars.

"That's right, buddy," Zito said. "There's one born every minute."

Zito did not speak any of the ancient demon languages and had absolutely no idea what the tiny beast was saying. The last occupant of the office had left the creature behind after departing in a hurry. Zito kept it around because women thought it was cute, although he wasn't quite sure why. To him, it looked like the offspring of a gargoyle and a hamster, but to each their own.

"Enter!" Zito said.

The door opened and the receptionist appeared, flashing him an excited look before motioning to someone in the hall.

"Right this way," she said.

A man in his mid to late 20s stepped inside. He was dressed in a black Lucifer Delmonico suit and wearing some sort of designer glasses. In his right hand he carried a shiny black LavaGlass briefcase. Zito gave the receptionist an approving nod. If there was one thing he had learned to do when he first started dealing plasma out the back door of a low-rent blood clinic, it was how to spot a mark.

"This is Mr. Tim Davenport," the receptionist said,

"Thank you Madeline," he said, ignoring her glare as the receptionist withdrew. He motioned the man to the chair in front of his desk. "I'm Dr. Horatio von Guggendorf. What can I do for you, Mr. Davenport?"

The name had not been Zito's choice, but it had grown on him. Zito Futchiski was not the kind of name that looked impressive on a falsified medical diploma from a prestigious university, after all. The real Dr. Guggendorf had been the previous administrator, but ownership had decided to replace him. Zito had thought it best not to inquire into those reasons, especially since he was almost certain the good doctor had taken a hot tub exit.

"Thanks for seeing me on such short notice, doctor," the man said, sitting down in the chair and looking around the room carefully. His glance was so deliberate that it was almost as if he was making a mental catalogue of every single item in the place. The guy also hit the word *doctor* with a peculiar emphasis that made Zito instantly edgy.

Zito's eyes flicked to the top drawer of his desk where the Zombidine was stashed. He would definitely take a calming hit when this appointment was over. Just a small one to maintain his free-flowing, even-keeled rhythm, of course.

Who in the hell was this guy? Zito wondered. His sixth sense told him something was off, but maybe the Narlune was just making him paranoid. It was, after all, one of the listed side-effects.

"Not at all," Zito said, setting aside his doubts and getting down to business. "What can we do for you?"

The man smiled. "Ah, yes. Well, it's a little embarrassing."

"Gogrukk Suk!" said the demon.

"Please don't mind him," Zito said.

"I've never seen anyone keep a Gogrub as a pet before," the man said, turning to look at the creature.

"Gamgak Chak!" the demon hissed, grabbing its genitals and pulling them to what appeared to be painfully absurd lengths.

"He's usually asleep at this time of day," Zito said, glaring at the demon.

"Guzguk Hok!" the demon twittered. "Ginzam Sham!"

"Did you teach it to talk?" the man asked, looking strangely amused.

"Just ignore him," Zito said. "As I said, I am a medical professional. Anything you say to me will be strictly confidential. There's very little we haven't seen within these walls, believe me!"

"I don't doubt it," the man said, continuing to scan the office. "I've seen your commercials."

Monster Mashers ran three different online ads targeting visitors to websites for online gambling, pornography and bail bondsmen. The ads were each designed to appeal to a slightly different demographic. They all promised that the company's prices were so low, it was evil.

"Which one?" Zito asked, smiling. "The one with Luna Hornlove?"

Luna Hornlove was a succubus who had moved from direct-to-DeadFlix blood'n'boob exploitation flicks to co-hosting a network reality show called *PolterHeist*. The show gave contestants two minutes to locate a hidden object within a haunted soundstage before being caught and possessed by a group of wacky ghosts. The ghosts would make the contestants do ostensibly ridiculous and uproarious things, like remove all their clothing and sing the opening theme from the hit musical *The Exorcist's Wife*. The show had been cancelled at the end of its second season, after which Ms. Hornlove became a regular presence in online autoplay ads hawking everything from supernatural supplements to lupine conversion therapy.

"No," the man said. "The one with that old TV actor..." He waved his hand around in the air for a moment trying to remember the name. "Boris something..."

"Boris Craven," Zito nodded.

Boris Craven had played Count Victor Vannachomp for all 13 seasons of the vampire comedy *Bite Me*. Boris was not an actual vampire and his catchphrase-quoting response to the steadily growing movement of those advocating for more supernatural representation on screen was thought to have contributed strongly to the show's eventual decline in the ratings and subsequent failure to be renewed for a 14th season.

"Right!" the man stopped waving his hand and pointed at Zito. "That's the one."

"Googex Dex!" the demon said.

"Clawfist!" Zito snapped. "Be quiet, would you?"

"You named it after the WMMA fighter?" the man asked.

Clawfist was the stage name of Peter Cruchley, a werewolf mixed martial arts silver cage fighter who had gone 55-0 before being stripped of his title after testing positive for a performance-enhancing drug called Lunasterol. The drug had been shown to boost lupine mass and ferocity by up to 125 percent and was officially banned by both the professional and amateur werewolf ultimate fighting associations.

"Yeah, that was before the whole drug thing," Zito said dismissively. "But people sure do love those ads! I can't tell you how many people come to us just because of them. Some of them don't even need any of our services. They just want to tell us the ads are awesome!"

Zito laughed and shook his head to give the impression that this had ever actually happened, which it had not. He did know that the ad this guy was referring to played exclusively on the fourth and sixth most popular gambling websites in the country, which led him to believe that the nature of his new client's problems was likely going to turn out to be financial and not sexual in nature, although he knew better than to jump to conclusions.

"I'm sure," the man said, although his tone indicated that he wasn't entirely convinced.

"But as you were saying," Zito said, motioning for the man to get back to the matter at hand.

"Right," the man said. "It was recently brought to my attention that I–without my knowledge or awareness, I must stress…"

"Of course," Zito nodded.

"Yes," the man said. "Anyway, I apparently went to some sort of succubus wrestling event. Were you aware that this existed?"

Succubus wrestling was exactly what the name would imply. The matches were usually held in underground temples or abandoned factories. The whole thing was illegal and usually organized by criminal syndicates like the Hellspawn Triad or the Blood Moon Riders, both of whom strongly encouraged patrons to bet heavily on the outcome. Succubus vs succubus was the most common variant, but it wasn't unusual to see a succubus fighting a completely different type of supernatural entity. The list of potential opponents also included werewolves, vampires, zombies, trolls, and pretty much whatever type of corporeal entity was willing to get into the ring. The only thing guaranteed was the outcome, which was almost always rigged in favour of the organizers.

"I have heard tale of such events from clients in the past," Zito said, the false gravity of his tone pitched to indicate that he understood the horrific moral depravity of such contests. In reality, he went to the fights at least once or twice a week. The last time, he had even volunteered to get into the ring himself, where he had been painfully but not unpleasantly pinned in four seconds flat by a six-breasted demon named Hexxia the Flesh Flayer.

"I had no knowledge of this, of course," the man said. "I was possessed. It's not the kind of thing I would ever do."

"Of course," Zito purred.

"Fazzuk Fake!" the demon said.

"Well, it turns out that while I was there, I bet rather a lot of money on one of the fights," the man said. "I mean, the demon forced me to bet a lot of money on a fight. Using an advance on my company credit card."

"And I imagine that this bet did not resolve itself in your favour," Zito said. He could relate to this, having made many such wagers of his own.

"It did not," the man said.

"And I imagine your company did not look fondly upon this turn of events, either," Zito said.

"Also a no," said the man.

"Pardon me for asking this, but I assume that you're insured?" Zito asked. He tried to make this question sound casual, but in reality, it was the only thing that mattered. All other details were negotiable.

"Of course," said the man.

"And your policy includes Identity Theft coverage?" Zito asked. This was particularly important, as many insurers routinely excluded damages resulting from possession by demonic entities.

"It does," the man said.

"Goffuk Muk!" the demon cackled.

"Clawfist!" Zito snapped. "Shut it!"

"It's fine," said the man.

"I apologize for him," Zito said. "Like I said, he's usually asleep right now. Anyway, the good news is, I'm sure we can help you with your little problem! Now, when did this possession occur?"

"A couple of nights ago," the man said.

"And have you had a PKR or similar scan administered in the time since the event?" Zito asked.

A PKR was a psycho-kinetic radiograph, which was the standard test given to anyone in the immediate aftermath of a possession. Demons left traces in their former hosts that were measurable for a limited time. To be of any value, the scan had to be performed within the first 24 hours after the possessing entity had vacated the host.

"Uh, no," the man said. "I was going to get one, but…"

But you knew the result was going to be a big fat zero, Zito thought. No scan was good, however. No scan meant that there wouldn't be a previous negative result that might cast doubt on a future positive.

"Is that going to be a problem?" the man asked.

"Not at all!" Zito said, waving the question away. "Here at Monster Mashers, we've perfected some extremely advanced technology that allows us to detect PK radiation traces for up to a month after the fact!"

Zito did not mention that the "extremely advanced technology" in question was just a standard PKR with falsified numbers, a fact that he did not consider relevant to the discussion.

"And how much do you charge for your, er, services?" the man asked.

"We don't have a flat rate," Zito said. "Our charges are, like all of our services, customized for each individual client."

"And how much might that be in my case?" the man asked.

"Yours is a very tricky and sensitive case," Zito said. "Normally, most clinics wouldn't be able to help you at all. *Sorry, man! Out of luck! Just declare bankruptcy, find a new job and move on!* Am I right? Fortunately, I think our Dark Circle program is just what you're looking for."

"Dark Circle?" the man repeated with a hint of a smile. "Is that expensive?"

"Don't think of it as expensive!" Zito said. "Think of it as value for money. We provide you with a certified PKR to verify possession, a full round of post-exorcism rehabilitation and much more. All for only 50 percent of the negotiated settlement."

"Fifty percent?" the man repeated.

"I think you'll see that the difference between our fees and being personally on the hook for the entire thing will make a world of difference," Zito said. "We also provide you with your own personal claims consultant to make sure that you're getting every last cent of what's coming to you. These companies make it their business to nickel and dime honest, hard working people such as yourself out of your rightful payout. You spend your whole life handing them premiums and then what do they do when it's time for them to cough up? They do everything they can to stiff you! We make sure that doesn't happen."

"You mean by inflating the claim?" the man asked.

"By making sure that the payout matches the great suffering that you have personally endured, including reputational and loss of income damages," Zito said.

He had delivered this speech so many times that he had it down to a science. He was so good at delivering persuasive nonsense in fact, that his grade school history teacher had encouraged him to become an actor after listening to him deliver yet another tragedy-filled account of why his midterm assignment would be late. Although acting had its attractions, the young Zito had quickly discovered that a life of crime delivered a far more reliable income.

"How?" the man asked.

Zito smiled. "Take the PKR. Normally, you have to get those done in the first 24 hours or so. But with the technology we have here at Monster Mashers, you won't have any problems at all."

"And what technology might that be?" the man asked.

Zito opened a drawer and pulled out a small vial that appeared to contain a puff of swirling red smoke, which he deposited on the desk in front of him.

"All you need to do is take a tiny whiff of this," Zito said. "Then we conduct an onsite PKR right here in our top-of-the-line clinic and I'm sure the results will satisfy both you, your employer and your insurance company completely."

"What is that?" the man asked, leaning forward to peer closely at the vial.

"Just a little bit of help," Zito said. "Something to boost those remaining traces of demonic possession back up to a point where everybody is happy again."

"It looks like Stygius Acheronthicide," the man said.

"Huh?" Zito said, surprised. He had never heard the compound referred to by its actual name.

"It's probably better known by its street name," the man said. "Red Devil. A Level 2 proscribed substance known to induce powerful hallucinations in 95 percent of users. Other side effects can include memory loss, temporary psychosis, auto-consumptive cannibalism and unexpected horn and tail growth, although not always from the head or gluteus."

"Uh..." Zito stammered. He had taken the stuff himself numerous times and experienced some of those symptoms personally.

"Use or possession of the drug is illegal for anyone not certified as a Level 1 ExoSpectral Research Facility," the man said. "There are only two such facilities in the country outside of the military that I'm aware of. Is Monster Mashers a Level 1 ExoSpectral Research Facility? Do you have your government certification hanging on the wall in another office, perhaps?"

"Look," Zito said. "I don't know what you might have heard, but everything we do here is completely legal and above board. I can assure you."

"Legal in the sense of giving clients illegal and highly dangerous drugs in order to fake PKR results?" the man said. "That kind of legal?"

Zito clutched the vial in his hand and narrowed his eyes. "Look, Is something wrong here? I'm the one trying to help *you* out."

"Your clinic helps a lot of people," the man said. "So many, in fact, that I'm surprised you haven't sprung for a nicer office. Of course, that might send out the wrong sort of vibe. You certainly wouldn't want to start attracting legitimate possessions, now would you?"

Zito was starting to get an extremely uncomfortable vibe. He put the vial quickly back in his drawer and reached under the desk to push a red button that he had only ever pushed once before, and that time had been accidental.

"What are you, a cop?" Zito asked.

"No," said the man. "I can assure you that I am not."

"I think maybe our services are not for you," Zito said, pushing the button again. "I don't know who you are, but I think it's time for you to leave."

"One of us will be," the man said, smiling.

"Why in the hell are you burning my briquettes, buddy?" Zito said, standing up. "I think you need to get out of here before Lenny and Beez stick a switchfork in your ass and toss you in the ethereal waste disposal unit!"

The man looked strangely unphased. "I assume you're referring to Leonard Charmin and Beelzegrok the Masticator?" he said. "The two individuals you employ as nominal security but who also do the majority of your pharmaceutical distribution work? The ones you just attempted to summon by pressing that hidden red emergency button under your desk?"

"How did you know about that?" Zito frowned, getting down on his knees and mashing the button with his thumb. "Where the hell are those morons?"

"They're not coming," the man said.

"Why the hell not?" Zito snapped, continuing to push the button so hard that the back of the desk was lifted up off the floor. "Who the hell are you?"

"As I said, I'm not a police officer," the man said. "But the police were every bit as interested in the…*services* you were providing here as my company was, especially in light of the exorbitant invoices you've been sending to our claims department for materials and services that were never actually delivered."

There was a loud knock on the door as somebody tried the handle. "Open up!" barked a voice from the other side. "Police!"

"Who is that?" Zito said in a panicked voice.

"Maybe you missed it, but I think they just identified themselves," the man said. "You should probably open the door."

"Do you have any idea who owns this place?" Zito said, running from his desk to a file cabinet on the opposite wall. "If the cops bust me, being dead will be the least of my problems!"

"Yeah," the man said. "I'm guessing that would probably get you kicked off Azmoda's weekly fantasy Chupacabra combat league email blast."

"I get busted and Azmoda will personally feed me to his Chupacabras!" Zito said. "And then he'll cut them open and pull out my partially digested remains and toss them in his Hellfire pit!"

"Having met him once, I can say that you're probably right about that," the man said. "Although I doubt he would do it personally. He doesn't like to get anything on his custom suits. Never know when a celebrity might stop by the place and he can't exactly do his usual grip and grin selfie thing with your cerebral spinal fluid stains on his custom four-point Florsheims, now can he?"

"Open up!" yelled the voice in the hall as the door was hit by something evidently much heavier than a fist.

"I don't think they're going to ask a third time," the man said. "You should probably open the door."

"You brought the cops!" Zito said, pointing an accusing finger.

"I thought we'd already established that," the man said.

"Who the hell are you really?" Zito demanded.

"My name is Tim Lovecraft," the man said, taking out some sort of badge and holding it up.

"You are a cop!" Zito said.

"Gabuzz Fuzz!" the demon hissed.

"No," Tim said. "I work for the Special Investigations Unit at Crimson Seal Insurance."

This was too much information for Zito's overheated brain to coherently absorb. "You're what?"

The door buckled as it was hit from the outside again. Tim was surprised that it hadn't already shattered under the onslaught. It seemed like the one thing that Monster Mashers did not cut corners on was physical security.

"Aha!" Zito cackled, pulling a mug-sized silver canister out of the drawer and holding it triumphantly up over his head like some sort of championship trophy. "Well, whoever you are, now you're screwed!"

"What is that?" Tim said, leaning instinctively back in his chair.

"This?" Zito said, turning around and waving the canister at Tim. "This is what happens when you mess with a Hellspawn operation, dumbass!"

Tim got to his feet and began backing around his chair towards the door. He had seen pictures of the thing Zito was holding before, but this was the first time he had ever been in close proximity to one.

"Calm down, Zito," Tim said. He had been aware that Horatio von Guggendorf was not the head clinician's real name long before setting foot in the place. "Let's not lose our heads, here, okay? No need to pull the pin on that bad boy. Let's just calm down and talk this out."

The object, Tim was fairly certain, was a Spectrabomb. They were essentially like hand grenades except that instead of triggering a chemical reaction that caused an explosion, they instead freed an angry and extremely destructive demon that would smash and fry everyone and everything within a 100-metre radius. The weapons were supposed to be military-issue only, but many of the local gangs had somehow started getting their claws on them in the last few months.

According to police reports, the Hellspawn Triad had recently begun employing such dangerously upgraded weapons in their war with the up-and-coming Call of Ctharnak gang. News reports the previous week had been full of stories about a Spectrabomb detonation that had incinerated a warehouse in a part of town known as the Neck. The blast, which had generated a wall of Hellfire three stories tall, had incinerated a large shipment of illegal blood along with an unknown number of individuals suspected of belonging to a werewolf biker gang known as the Blood Moon Riders.

There was a bang as the door was hit again, buckling noticeably in its frame but still refusing to give. Tim couldn't see where the button was to open it. Maybe it was somewhere under the desk next to the security alarm button. He began edging around to see if he could locate it.

"Do all the talking you want!" Zito laughed. "See how far it gets you against this!"

Zito pulled the pin on the canister. There was a bright flash and a blast of scarlet smoke. In the confusion, Tim stepped back and tripped over something he couldn't see, landing on the floor. He looked up as the smoke cleared to see what looked like a large and quivering cylinder of red gelatin. It was roughly the same height and colour as a mailbox and reminded him of the way canned cranberry sauce looked right after it slid out of the can.

"What the hell?" Zito said, frowning in confusion. He turned the canister upside down in his hand and shook it, looking inside to make sure there was nothing else still stuck there. "Are they kidding me with this?"

Oh shit, Tim thought. He blinked and rolled over, grabbing at his briefcase to get at the special SIU items that were locked inside.

"Man," Zito said, shaking his head and dropping the canister on the floor. "I told them that black market source was no good. But did they listen to me? Of course they di–"

Zito stopped talking when a spongy tendril shot out of the oozing mass and clamped a gelatinous hold over his mouth, spreading quickly to contain his entire head. Tim could see Zito's terrified expression through the translucent red gelatin as he raised his hands and tried to pull the thing off. Zito's skin, flesh, eyes and skull erupted in flame and began to melt. As it did, the newly liquified contents of the former clinic supervisor were sucked down along the tendril and into the core of the creature, which began to glow and pulsate in a deeply unsettling way.

"Grossbak Blak!" the demon said, rattling the bars of its cage. "Gagrag Blag!"

Tim only knew a few words of the ancient demon languages, most of which were profanities. Coincidentally, these seemed to be the only words that Clawfist used.

Tim unlocked his briefcase and yanked out his SIU emergency kit. The demon was a Gurloth. They weren't so much like the vultures of the underworld as they were its cockroaches or maggots. They grew in the desiccant pits and oubliettes under old temple sites, feasting on the remains of ritual sacrifices after the demon overlords had harvested the parts they needed (usually hearts, guts, testicles or eyes–they rarely bothered with human brains, which they considered largely useless) for their rituals.

Gurloths were not glamorous or popular demons, but that didn't mean they were any less dangerous. Tim had encountered a few of them in his time working for his father's supernatural pest removal business and knew that underestimating them was a common shortcut to becoming the demon equivalent of the grapefruit in a juice cleanse.

The creature finished off what was left of Zito and began moving across the floor towards Tim, who grabbed his SIU bag and jumped quickly back to his feet. He knew that the demons emitted by Spectrabombs were only temporary entities, but had no idea how long they lasted before they vaporized. Ten seconds? A minute? An hour? However long it was, he was going to need to stay out of its way for long enough to avoid becoming the main course.

Tim ducked as a tentacle shot straight at his face, narrowly missing him and hitting the back of his chair with a splat. The last time Tim had run into one of these things was during his last year of high school. He had responded to a call from a vampire-themed miniature golf course that was having problems with a roving gang of teenage werewolves urinating on the roof of the clubhouse. Tim had been in the process of rigging up a motion-sensing wolf whistle, which emitted a piercing shriek on a frequency that only wolves could hear, when a Gurloth materialized quite unexpectedly from the mouth of the fiberglass monster clown on the putting green of the nearby 15th hole.

Sudden manifestations were not unusual for supernatural entities of all types on sites of known spectral turbulence. It was a bad idea to build something right on top of what used to be the site of an ancient temple or sacrificial altar or mass burial ground, which was why the city kept a record of sites for which development permits could not be granted. Tim's company, Crimson Seal, kept similar data in the form of exclusion tables for areas that they would not underwrite.

It was theoretically possible to make a tainted site usable again by bringing in a team of exorcists and supernatural remediation experts, but it was expensive and the results were never guaranteed. Demons and poltergeists often got very attached to their old haunts and strongly resisted any push for gentrification. Few investors were keen to sink millions of dollars into a health club or restaurant only to start seeing a Dybbuk rise out of the dressing tub of the all-you-can-eat salad buffet or a Banshee go rampaging through the women's change room of a high-end spa.

Cursed ground had contributed to the scattershot and somewhat schizoid development of the city as a whole. No single neighbourhood became a building hub at the expense of the others, although there were definitely some parts of town that had fewer roadblocks than the rest. People just got used to seeing a shiny new corporate headquarters or museum right next to a crumbling ruin.

On the golf course, Tim had escaped the demon by climbing onto the roof of the nearby maintenance shed. Gurloths could do a lot of things, including producing a liquid form of Hellfire that would melt pretty much anything, but they couldn't climb worth beans. Like many elemental demons, they were also vulnerable to water, which would more or less cause them to dissolve into an even less tangible form than they already had.

Unfortunately, Tim realized, there was nothing in here to climb on other than the desk, which was not high enough up off the ground to make any difference. He dodged under a shooting tendril and looked around desperately for anything else he could use. All he had in his SIU kit was some Demonex spray, which he knew would be no use in this case, and a Demon Charger, which was like a supernatural Taser but would also do him little good against this vaguely sentient red blob.

He needed liquid. Unfortunately, there was no water cooler, no bar, no fridge…not even a half-empty cup of coffee on Zito's desk.

There was another loud *blam* as the police hit the door from the other side, bringing it almost off its hinges. Tim reckoned that it had to be made of Demonite. The Hellspawn were known to use the stuff to make the doors on their secure storage facilities and clubs. It was specially tempered in Hellfire and practically indestructible. The building would give way before the door did. It meant that Tim couldn't afford to wait for rescuers to come to him. He was going to need to get out of this one on his own.

Tim scrambled past the file cabinets. He looked briefly at the windows, but they weren't really an option. The clinic was on the sixth floor. If he tried to get out that way, he would end up as a messy pile of compound fractures right in the middle of Azaxx Avenue. He cursed himself under his breath for not bringing a water bottle. He had considered it for a moment before leaving the office, but had decided against it because he was supposed to be impersonating a wealthy businessman and they generally didn't tote around two litres of portable hydration everywhere they went.

The last time he had run into one of these things, Tim had neutralized it by breaking in through the shed window and turning on the lawn sprinklers. Although it had caused some complaints from a couple of drenched foursomes on the sixteenth hole, it had also dissolved the demon. Too bad there weren't any sprinklers in h-

Tim stopped and looked up at the ceiling. Of course there *were* sprinklers in here. Two of them. Sticking out from between the tiles of the suspended ceiling. A standard commercial-grade fire suppression system. The nozzles looked old and covered in spider webs, but hopefully they still worked.

Tim looked over at the wall, where he could see the fire alarm switch. Tripping the switch would not activate the sprinklers, he knew. The switch would only set off the alarm. The sprinklers would only trigger if the wax seal around the nozzle was melted or broken off, which meant that he would need to get up there to do it himself.

"Gukruk Duk!" Clawfist yelped. "Gakhak Smak!"

Tim ducked as a tendril shot straight at his head. It flew across the room and hit the cage containing the demon, which jumped up and grabbed the top row of bars. The tendrils extended into the cage and began to wave around.

"Gixfux Yuk!" Clawfist hissed, lifting a leg and sending a stream of fiery urine down on the tendrils, which immediately started to smoke. The larger demon withdrew the tendril sharply, knocking the cage sideways to the floor, where Clawfist rolled along with it, spouting a long series of demonic curses.

Don't think I should try that, Tim thought. It probably won't react the same way to being peed on by a human.

Tim pulled out his Demon Charger. The only object in the room tall and sturdy enough to stand on was the desk, from which the nearest sprinkler was at least eight feet away. If he was going to get to it, he was going to need to find a way to distract the Gurloth, which was positioned directly between him and his objective.

Tim looked at the cage containing the angry and wildly micturating Gogrub, which had rolled to a stop near the door. Generally speaking, the only thing worse than being trapped in a space with a dangerously unpredictable demon was being trapped in a space with two of them, but the way Tim saw it, the profanity-spewing office pet was probably his best and only chance of getting out of here in a non-liquified form.

Tim ran over and picked up the cage, careful to avoid the multiple streams of green spray emanating from its occupant.

"Okay, Clawfist!" Tim said. "Ready to get out of here?"

"Fakfug Bug!" Clawfist spat, shooting a third spray of urine that hit Tim's left hand. It was freezing cold and caused his skin to immediately blister, but Tim had no time to worry about that now. "Jizpukk Tug!"

"That's what I thought," Tim said, turning the cage to face the Gurloth and opening the door. "Now go do what you do best."

The tiny demon spread its scaly wings and flew out of the cage, dodging an outstretched tendril and flying up over the pulsating red thing. Clawfist began flying in short, erratic circles as it let loose multiple streams of green fluid on its target. The larger demon began to smoke and writhe, sending tendrils shooting up in an attempt to swat its tormentor out of the air.

"Suksap Fap!" Clawfist cackled, clearly enjoying itself in a manner that suggested it didn't get let out very often and planned to make the most of it. "Cakzak Nak!"

Tim climbed up onto the desk and jumped to knock loose one of the overhead ceiling panels. The hardware in behind looked old and dusty. He grabbed hold of the metal frame, which groaned and sagged a little, but seemed strong enough to support his body weight, at least temporarily. Tim stuck the charger in his pocket and made his way unsteadily across, lifting his legs to avoid contact with either of the fighting demons below. He couldn't remember the last time he'd been on a set of monkey bars. It had probably been at least a couple of decades. He was a little heavier and less flexible now, but the basic principle was the same as it had been when he played Hellfire Sand back in grade school: if he fell off, he was dead.

Tim swung from one edge of the frame to the other. It was tougher than regular monkey bars because he needed one swing to knock the panel out and another one to grab hold. Tim had let his exercise routine slip over the last few months and was now in danger of paying the ultimate price. He hadn't been quite as motivated to go to the gym since he'd found out that his last girlfriend, Tabitha, had been cheating on him with an ex-boyfriend named Jared, with whom she had subsequently run off.

Tim took a deep breath and promised himself that if he survived this, he would find Clawfist a new home by shipping him to Tabitha and Jared as a housewarming present. It was, he thought, the least he could do short of urinating on Jared personally.

Tim swung across the last panel and pulled himself up next to the sprinkler nozzle. He was close enough to see the blue wax seal, which appeared to be intact under a thick layer of dust. Making sure he had a strong enough grip with his left hand, Tim reached down and fished around blindly until his hand found the pocket where the charger was stashed. He reached in and almost had his fingers around it when the Gurloth whipped out a tentacle in his direction.

Tim yanked his legs up to avoid it and felt the charger fly out of his hand and clatter to the floor.

"Fikfukk Wuk!" Clawfist hissed as it flew by.

Couldn't have put it better myself, Tim thought, looking down at the charger. There was no way that he'd be able to jump down, grab it, and get back into this position without getting digested.

Oh well, he thought. I'll just have to do this the old-fashioned way.

Tim swung back into position. He needed to give himself some room to make this work. Taking a quick breath, he swung both legs up at the same time, aiming his feet at the nozzle. As long as he could crack the seal, he should be able to get the waterworks running.

His first effort came up on either side of the nozzle, missing it completely. He managed to hit it with his left foot on the second and his right on the third. The sprayer was bent, but it was hard to see if the seal was damaged. He hit it again, this time more accurately with the toes of both feet. This would have been easier if he hadn't been wearing fancy shoes, he thought. A steel toe boot would have come in very handy right about now.

Clawfist flew by, pursued by a slimy red tentacle. The tiny demon was still sending three steady streams of green discharge down on its globular red target.

How on earth does that thing still have so much left in the tank? Tim wondered. Has it been holding it in for the last five years? Maybe that was why it was so ticked off.

Tim had more important things to worry about than demon bladder capacity, however. He swung himself backwards to gain some momentum and then lifted both feet up and rammed them into the nozzle as hard as he could. He heard a snap and suddenly water was gushing everywhere. The force of it was so strong that Tim lost his grip on the ceiling frame and fell to the floor, which was further away than it looked.

Tim felt all the air driven out of his lungs as he landed flat on his back next to the file cabinets. He quickly rolled sideways and pulled himself into a crouch, gasping to get his breath back. He heard a screech and looked over to see the Gurloth writhing as water poured down on it in a torrent. The air filled up with noxious red smoke as the demon began to dissolve into a lumpy red puddle on the floor.

Tim managed to get his breath back, choking on the smoke as he made his way back to the desk to avoid stepping in the spreading red mess. Clawfist was nowhere to be seen.

Tim had just managed to climb up onto the desk when the frame splintered and the door flew into the room and landed on the floor with thud. A small army of uniformed cops swarmed through the opening, all dressed in heavy tactical gear..

Once the smoke had cleared sufficiently, the lead cop removed her helmet and looked at the red puddle on the floor with evident disgust.

"Wow," she said. "I told them we shouldn't leave you alone for more than five minutes."

"Sorry, Carmilla," Tim shrugged.

Carmilla von Karn had worked in the Special Investigations Unit at Crimson Seal when Tim started there but had left shortly after winning her case against the police department, which up until then had an official policy of not hiring demons as line officers. Carmilla was a half-succubus. Her powers of attraction were largely offset by her tough as nails, no-nonsense personality.

"Where's Zito?" she asked.

"Somewhere in the middle of that," Tim said, pointing at the ooze. "Idiot pulled the pin on a Spectrabomb when he heard you guys coming. I don't think he was expecting a Gurloth to come out of it, though."

"Bomb was probably a knockoff," Carmilla said. "The Triads have been buying a lot of their heavier stuff from overseas suppliers lately. Most of it doesn't even work." She turned to one of the officers near the door. "Can we get the water shut off, Reznick? Preferably before we all drown."

"Roger that!" the officer nodded, running back into the hall.

The two of them moved away from the broken sprinkler and surveyed the room.

"Freefrik Pakk!" Clawfist chirped, zooming over their heads and flying out through the open door. "Boodbag Gag!"

"Friend of yours?" Carmilla asked, watching the other officers scramble to avoid being urinated on as the creature made its exit.

"Only insofar as we had a common enemy, I suppose," Tim said, taking off the lapel camera on his suit and handing it to Carmilla. "Did you get everything you need?"

"Sure," Carmilla said. "We were hoping to use it to get Zito to flip on his bosses, but it doesn't look like he's in much of a mood to talk at the moment."

"Oh I don't know," Tim said. "Scoop some of that up and put your necromancer to work on it and you might get something. How's the job?"

"Good," Carmilla said. "Heard your old lady quit the force and went to work for the feds."

"Yeah," Tim said. He had also heard that Tabitha and Jared had recently gotten engaged and were planning to get married at a destination wedding in the Fire Islands in the Spring. Not that he kept tabs on such things, of course.

"Sorry she dumped you," Carmilla said. "Just get drunk and hit a couple of the succubus houses on Lower Acheron. That'll perk you up."

"Thanks," Tim said. "I'll take that under advisement."

"How are things back at the office?" Carmilla asked. "Volkerps managed to cast out any of his in-laws yet?"

Volkerps the Foul was Tim's boss, a nearly 1,000-year-old demon who had been with the company since the days when policies still included human sacrifice extensions in their statutory conditions. The only thing Volkerps hated more than spending time with his extended family was having to deal with the trolls in the IT department, which he had been forced to do quite a lot since the SIU had upgraded to new laptops. Not everyone in IT was a literal troll, but there were enough of them that it didn't seem strange that their department was located under a bridge.

"He's the same," Tim said. "He'll be happy that we put this place out of business."

Tim felt his phone buzz. He pulled it out of his pocket and saw Volkerps' name on the caller ID. It wasn't possible to put the boss's face there, as he had two of them, neither of which was the kind of thing you wanted to gaze at unprepared.

"Speak of the devil," Tim muttered. "Excuse me a sec."

Tim stepped over the red puddle on the floor and walked past the other officers into the hall.

"Hey Vol," Tim said. "What's up?"

"Lovecraft!" his boss's voice boomed so loudly that his phone mic became distorted and Tim had to hold the phone a foot away from his ear to avoid injury. "Drop what you're doing immediately and get back here, pronto!"

Tim looked back into the office, where two of the uniformed cops had become stuck to the floor and one was coughing loudly after inhaling too much of the acrid red smoke. It was not a place he was especially keen to spend more time, so being ordered to leave was not unwelcome.

"Sure," Tim said. "What's the emergency?"

"I'll brief you when you get here," Volkerps rumbled. "But this is a big one. Just remember to pack your Hellfire-proof pants. You're going to need them."

2

Tim didn't have time to go back to his apartment to change out of his damp suit and had to settle for changing in the back seat of his car instead.

The suit had been loaned to him by a coworker named George Sticker, who was the SIU's resident vampire. Tim didn't have any high-end suits of his own and hadn't worn one since the funeral for his late uncle Thelonius, who had suffered a mishap on a visit to the La Llorona Hellfire Pits. Thelonius had liked to think of himself as the rule-breaking joker of the family, which probably explained why he had ignored the posted warnings and climbed over the fence to get a selfie on the edge of a geyser nicknamed the Devil's Rectum. He had also failed to pay attention to the sign warning that all posted eruption times were only approximations, as the vents were notoriously unpredictable. What had happened next, sadly, was not.

Tim pushed through the front door of Asgaroth's Relics and Ritual Supply, where the air was thick with the smell of incense. The incense was there mostly to mask the underlying smell of Essence of Mercan, an aerosol compound used to amplify consumer impulses in retail environments. Federal law imposed strict limits on atmospheric concentrations (0.25ccl per 100 cubic metres), but most merchants ignored them, confident that the likelihood of an inspector dropping by with an atmospheric gas spectroanalyzer were remote.

Tim found that he could ignore the Mercan, but the incense made him gag. Every séance joint and psychic in town used the stuff. It was so bad that you couldn't walk down the street in some districts without needing to spend an hour in a spectral decontamination shower.

The Special Investigations Unit was located several floors below Asgaroth's and not in Crimson Seal's main headquarters on Sixth Street in order to preserve its organizational independence. SIU could and did investigate anyone and anything both inside and outside the company, from clients all the way up to the CEO. It was difficult to maintain impartiality in such matters if you had lunch with some of those same people every day in the cafeteria.

Tim made his way past a familiar assortment of knockoff crystal balls, voodoo dolls, ouija boards and miniature sacrificial altars to the unmarked door in the back that was only accessible by SIU staff. He was just getting his key card out of his pocket when a familiar voice called out to him from behind the cash desk.

"Hey, Tim-bo! Long time, no see!"

Tim paused and looked over to see Madeline Ghastlee waving to him from behind the cash register. Madeline was the assistant manager. She was in her mid-twenties and studying for her Level 1 spiritualist certification, which would allow her to do individual psychic consultations and séances for groups of three people or less. She was dressed in her usual black lace robe with white face paint and bright red lips. Her curly brown hair was pulled back into a ponytail and she had so many rings on her fingers that it was a wonder that she could even lift her hands, let alone use her phone.

"Hi Madeline," Tim said, stopping by the desk. "I was on a case. How's school going?"

Tim and Madeline had exchanged a few emails in the weeks since Tim had broken up with his last girlfriend. Some of the emails had seemed to be extremely flirty, but Tim was gun shy about jumping to conclusions.

"Good!" she said, putting down her phone and leaning forward to grab his forearm. "I've got my last exam tomorrow afternoon. Summoning and banishment. I've been studying for the last, like six days straight and I'm a total wreck! My prognostication power has been just off the charts lately and I can totally see that I'm going to bomb this one!"

"Nah," Tim smiled nervously. "You'll do fine."

"Say, what's with your hair?" she said, squinting. "You look like you just drove through a carwash with the top down."

"Oh," Tim said, reaching up to pat his hair down. "No. I was just working a fraud case and the guy didn't really feel like getting busted, so he pulled a Spectrabomb and released a Gurloth. I had to activate the sprinkler system to dissolve it before it ate me."

"Ha!" Madeline laughed. "That's hilarious!"

"Yeah," Tim said, thinking that it wasn't quite so hilarious at the time. "So one more exam and then you'll be done. That's exciting."

"Yeah," she said, not letting go of his arm. "Then I can finally get out of here and open my own place."

"My mom runs a whole chain of psychic salons," Tim said. "She's always got pop-up locations opening up in different parts of town. I could always put in a word if you're looking."

"She does?" Madeline asked, her eyes getting wide.

"Yeah," Tim said. "Seer. Have you heard of it?"

"Are you kidding?" Madeline said. "I shop there all the time! Their stuff is way better than the crap we sell here, although don't tell my boss."

"I won't," Tim said. He had never met the owner of Asgaroth's, although he passed through the place almost every day on his way to work. "Actually, my mother's planning to open another one in that revitalized section of the Crypt Network when it's ready at the end of the year. If they ever finish it, of course."

The Crypt Network was an underground network of tunnels the city had introduced many years before in an attempt to draw shoppers back into the downtown core. The initial project had been a spectacular failure, but a change of leadership on city council had reinvigorated enthusiasm for the idea. Tim thought it was just as likely to bomb as the first time around, but the retail incentives had been too generous for his ultra-capitalistic mother to resist.

"Cool," Madeline said. "You know, I had a premonition that you were going to show up today with good news."

"Well then, I guess you were right," Tim said. He really needed to get downstairs to see what kind of emergency Volkerps had been talking about. "Sorry, but I've got to go."

"Actually, that wasn't the only vision I had," Madeline said, flipping Tim's hand over and studying his palm by tracing the lines with one long, black nail.

"Oh?" Tim said nervously.

"Well," Madeline said, narrowing her eyes. "I had this very clear premonition when I woke up this morning that you were going to appear and you were going to ask me out on Friday to celebrate me passing my exam."

"I was?" Tim said.

"Yes," Madeline said. "It was very lucid. One of the clearest visions I've had since I started having them."

"Well, you're an excellent psychic," Tim smiled.

"I am," she nodded. "I never get things wrong."

"Oh wait," Tim said, realizing something. "I can't do Friday. I have a kind of family business dinner thing."

Friday was the annual company dinner for his father Thad's supernatural pest removal business. Tim had tried to get out of it–he hadn't worked for his father's company in years and preferred not to spend his spare time around people who smelled like Demonex or industrial-strength garlic compound–but his parents had insisted. Thad apparently had some big announcement to make. They were being very secretive, which wasn't like them at all. Tim wasn't sure what it could be. They were still too young to retire and too old for it to be the arrival of another sibling, so Tim was stumped but also a little intrigued.

"Family business dinner?" Madeline laughed. "That sounds interesting. Is your family in the Hellspawn or something?"

"No, nothing like that," Tim said. "My father runs this supernatural remediation business. They have this big company dinner every year at Stoker's."

Stoker's was an old-school steakhouse on the east side of Morningstar Heights that prided itself on serving beef cuts so large and rare that they might as well be trotting out live cows. They had not been on the forefront of the city's culinary scene for a century, but Tim's father still considered the place to be the epitome of fine dining. Tim figured that was mostly because it was pretty much the last place Thad could still order a stuffed baked potato that was larger than his head.

"Oooh, I *love* Stoker's!" Madeline said, gripping her face in what appeared to be genuine degustatory ecstasy. "It is, *literally*, my favourite restaurant!"

"Really?" Tim said. "Uh, I mean…well, you're welcome to come along if you want."

Tim was not sure why he was suggesting this. The invitation did, technically, include a plus one, although his parents never expected him to actually bring anyone else.

"Are you sure?" Madeline asked.

"Sure," Tim said. "You know, it's a work dinner, but it's still a dinner, I suppose. Some of my father's employees are a little, uh, eccentric."

Eccentric was an understatement. As he knew from working for his father during the summers, it took a special kind of individual to make a life out of crawling through old ducts and dark basements looking for invasive demons, trespassing vampires and other often malevolent enti-ties. Thad's staff included characters like Pete "Gutter" Gorely, who had filed all his teeth down to points and had crucifix tattoos on his cheeks for every vampire he had either staked or burned, which made his face look like the side of a wartime bomber.

There was also "Multiple" Mac McPherson, who had been possessed so many times that he still experienced flashbacks to the lives of more than 200 demons. None of them were the kind of entity you wanted to encounter in a staff room on your first day on the job.

"Excellent!" Madeline said, placing a hand on her forehead. "I fore-see us having a fantastic time."

"Great," Tim said. "I, uh, should probably get downstairs before my boss charbroils me, but I'll call you later?"

"Yes you will!" Madeline said as he walked away. "I foresee it!"

Tim scanned his card and moved through the door into a clean white hallway that was mercifully free of the smell of incense.

All right, he thought. I'm getting back out there. Go ahead and get engaged, Tabby. Doesn't phase me in the least.

Tim made his way down in the elevator and into the office, which was an open-plan windowless square with a dozen or so cluttered desks. His first stop was in the back corner, where he handed the borrowed suit back to George Sticker. George tended to frequent some of the upmarket vampire clubs and was roughly Tim's size, which was why he had offered to let Tim borrow the suit in the first place.

"Thanks, George," Tim said, handing the suit back. "Sorry it got a little wet."

"Oh that's no problem," George said, unzipping the bag. "It's gotten far messier things on it than water, believe me."

Tim tried not to think about that. "I'll pay to have it dry cleaned."

"Hang on," George said, sniffing the jacket. "Why does it smell like demon piss?"

"Sorry about that," Tim said. "A Gogrub got loose when I was dealing with, uh, something else. It kind of let loose. Some of it might have splashed on me."

"Ugh," George said. "I hate those things. They never shut up."

"Like I said, I can take it to the cleaners," Tim offered.

"Don't sweat it," George said. "I know a place in the Neck I can take it to. These zombies can get anything out. Even the time I was wearing it when I fell in the wave pool at the new Red & Wild Plasma World park that just opened. Place is great, but you really don't want to be wearing your best suit if you go there for a bachelor party, believe me. Don't worry about it. I'll expense it. You get pissed on by a demon in the line of duty, it makes sense to me that the company should pay for it."

"Thanks," Tim said. He was well aware that members of SIU had to be doubly careful about what they expensed as Volkerps reviewed the reports in meticulous detail using every single one of his 327 eyes.

"Lovecraft!" boomed a familiar voice from behind a half-open door on the far side of the room.

"Speak of the devil," George said.

"Better go," Tim said, turning and heading for his boss's office.

Volkerps the Foul was in his usual position behind his desk, a massive torso floating atop a roiling mass of flickering black storm clouds. The clouds were usually a good indicator of his mood. Today, they were full of crackling jets of blue lightning, which was slightly more dismal than usual. When the clouds turned red and lighting started arcing across the office, the SIU staff knew to stay out of the room.

A towering figure with two heads and four arms, the SIU director's appearance was intimidating even by demon standards, although Tim was used to it by now. Harder to overlook was the overpowering sulphurous stench, against which no fewer than 13 different high-power electronic air fresheners waged a losing battle.

"Hey Vol," Tim said, taking a seat. "What's up?"

"Sorry to pull you off the Monster Mashers at short notice," Volkerps said. "But this is a Ninth Circle case. Red Brimstone priority."

Like all other insurance companies, Crimson Seal prioritized its clients based on a large number of factors including the total insured value of their portfolio, the number of lines of business they had with the company, their risk level and the potential for future business, amongst other things. First Circle was the lowest level. That included mostly single people with only basic Supernatural Liability coverage. Ninth Circle was at the top. It was limited to the top 100 clients, but those select few were responsible for almost 20 percent of the company's total underwriting profit.

Any case involving one of those clients was automatically assigned the SIU's top investigative priority, which this month happened to be named Red Brimstone. Volkerps was never satisfied with the code names and kept changing them. Last month, it was Green Hellfire. The month before that, it was Demon King. Everytime he changed them, Volkerps sent out a departmental memo that was the source of great mirth amongst his staff. George had even run a betting pool, but it had been discontinued because too many staffers had started sneaking their picks into conversations at meetings in an attempt to boost their chances of selection. Tim's personal favorite was Day of Reckoning, which he thought had a nice, apocalyptic feel to it.

"No problem," Tim said. "It's pretty much wrapped up, anyway. Head of the clinic pulled the pin on a knockoff Spectrabomb and a Gurloth ate him."

"What a dipshit," Volkerps muttered, shaking the head that was made up of just eyes. "Make sure you include everything in your report. But I need you to put that one on the back burner for now."

"Sure," Tim said. "What's up?"

"I assume you've heard of the Hesselthorn Puzzle Box?" Volkerps said.

Tim's jaw dropped open. He doubted that there was a sentient entity anywhere on the planet, alive or dead, human, demon or otherwise, that hadn't heard of that particular item.

"Are you kidding?" Tim gasped.

The Hesselthorn Puzzle Box was the property of one Lucifer Hesselthorn the Sixth, patriarch of one of the richest families in the world. The family had made most of its money from ancient supernatural artefacts they had unearthed (or looted, depending on who you asked) from various temples, altars and other archaeological sites located all over the world.

The Puzzle Box was famous for a number of reasons. Hesselthorn had found it about 30 years earlier during an archaeological expedition in search of the fabled Temple of Malmoroth, which was rumoured to be buried somewhere deep beneath the city. The box was supposedly made of solid acheronium, a crystalline rock-metal alloy so rare that a single gram was worth more than an aircraft carrier battle group. The stuff was highly spectroactive and supposedly indestructible. It could only be molded using green Hellfire, which meant it was well beyond the capacity of any human forge to cast.

There were only two known samples of acheronium in the entire world. The Puzzle Box was one. The other was the famous Eye of the Devil, a marble-sized centrepiece of a necklace on display behind three solid feet of demon glass and 24/7 A.M.d guard in its own secured-access wing of the Louvre museum in Paris. Anyone who wanted to see it had to submit to a full background security check, strip search, x-ray, PKR scan and pay a non-refundable $1,000 deposit just to get on the waiting list for a viewing appointment. Every year, more than eight million people applied for one of 252 viewing times. The necklace was rumored to emanate powerful spectral waves on anyone who spent more than five minutes in close proximity to it. As a result, viewings were strictly limited to two minutes per group.

Tim had never seen it, but he had seen pictures, which didn't help. The extremely powerful supernatural energy emitted by the Eye tended to distort the image in any camera used to capture it. People who had seen it in the flesh were often powerless to describe it, saying that it seemed to glow from within. No two people tended to describe it the same way. Some said that it looked like a glowing red diamond while others said that it was like stepping into the presence of whatever god or demon they happened to believe in.

The Puzzle Box was rumoured to be much larger than the Eye of the Devil. Some said it was as large as a softball while others insisted it was big enough to crush a car. The box was protected by some sort of enchantment. It was said that whoever could solve the riddle and open the box would release a Djinn. As a reward for freeing it from the box, the Djinn would then grant that individual anything they wished for.

The box was also famously cursed.

Dozens of expeditions had tried to find the box prior to Hesselthorn, and all of them had been met by death and disaster.

The first major attempt had been launched a century ago. It was sponsored by the National Spectrographic Society and led by a man named Winston Hooth. Depending on which sources you believed, Hooth was either a famous explorer and learned archaeologist or a complete fraud whose name wasn't even Winston Hooth. One account claimed that Hooth was actually a famous bank robber named Uriah "Buckshot" MacArthur, whom the author claimed had not accidentally blown himself up when attempting to dynamite a safe, but survived and went searching for a different kind of treasure.

Whoever he was, Hooth believed that the box was located in a cave network in a remote part of the Purgatory Mountains. He and his group of 13 "learned and hardy men" marched through the Pitchfork Pass on the last Saturday in August that year determined to return by the first of October with "treasure and immortality enough for all mankind."

None of them were ever seen again. A group of mountaineers hiking in a part of the Eschaton Valley near where Hooth and his expedition were last seen did discover bone fragments that showed partial DNA matches for the group's medic, a man named Heinrik Haller. The fragments, however, were too small to provide any meaningful conclusions about their fate. Some thought they had gotten lost in a storm and starved to death. More fanciful accounts posited that Hooth and his men had found the site, but had been killed and eaten by a zombie mountain tribe.

No major attempt was made again until 60 years after Hooth disappeared. The expedition was funded by an eccentric Australian billionaire named Conrad Ballser, who was best known for building a replica Marie Celeste that had capsized and sank less than 15 minutes after leaving dry dock. The expedition was widely derided at the time as nothing more than a publicity stunt designed to launch Ballser's new network, Balls TV. There were no actual scientists or scholars on the expedition. The closest thing to an expert was a woman named Henrietta Pendleton, who had studied demonology at the University of Tasmania for six months before dropping out to become an unlicensed psychic. The only thing that all the expedition members had in common was that they were all reality TV or daytime soap opera stars willing to sign almost any contract presented to them in exchange for prime time exposure.

The expedition was supposed to be chronicled on a 12-part series that would form the Thursday night anchor of the Balls TV debut lineup, although only four episodes were filmed and only two made it to air. The group were supposed to search a section of the western coastline of the Perdition Islands, which were not considered to be a likely resting site for the box by any scholar but did have the advantage of being the planned site of a future Ballser luxury resort and golf course, for which the televised hunt would provide some much-needed advance publicity.

Not surprisingly, the expedition was not a success. One of the expedition ships was hit with a freak Hellspout 37 nautical miles from its destination. The ship disappeared, taking eight cast members and most of the film crew with it. The surviving vessel got lost in a navigational disruption zone popularly known as the *Perdition Hexagon*, finally emerging 500 miles and 32 days later from where and when they were supposed to. Low on food and fuel, they stopped off at the first sliver of land they saw.

Unfortunately, the island where they dropped anchor was inhabited by a primitive tribe of cave-dwelling, pre-contact vampires known as the Buluganga (an ancient term that translates roughly as "Blood Warriors") who were not known to greet modern intruders with a smile and a cheery wave.

Unable to find anything except Bloodberry bushes and some primitive but ominous-looking rock paintings, the beleaguered expeditioneers returned to their makeshift campsite, where they were promptly slaughtered by the inhabitants as soon the sun dropped below the horizon. No further attempts were made to reach the search zone and the entire project was abandoned in a hail of litigation that was probably still ongoing. Ballser was reduced from billionaire to millionaire, Balls TV went off the air after less than six months, and the luxury resort was never built.

There had been many other attempts to locate the box over the years, each one meeting with varying degrees of failure. Each one reinforced the idea that the whole thing was cursed–a notion that only grew when the box was finally discovered.

Hesselthorn's partner on the expedition was a man named Lord Harrison Ackroyd-Jones III. A spectroarchaeologist expelled from Hexford Univeristy under controversial circumstances, he was most noted prior to that point for his role in locating the Ashtaroth Reliefs, an ancient collection of magmatic tablets that provided enormous insight into the culture and beliefs of early demonic civilizations.

Tim didn't know too much about what had happened after the box had been found. He was vaguely aware that the partners had experienced some sort of falling out, but he wasn't sure what was at the root of it. Maybe Ackroyd-Jones had insisted that the box belonged in a museum and Hesselthorn had wanted to keep it to himself? Or maybe Hesselthorn had wanted to open it and Ackroyd-Jones had thought they should leave it alone? He would need to look that up.

Many believed that the curse of the Puzzle Box was the primary cause of Ackroyd-Jones's death on a subsequent expedition several years later. None of the Hesselthorns had died, but their fate had also been shaded with ominous misfortune. Hesselthorn's wife, Ozymandia, had become the victim of demonic identity theft while pregnant with their third child. The exorcism had not gone well, leaving her in a coma and the child institutionalised.

Despite possessing the box, Lucifer Hesselthorn had made no effort to profit from it and had not ventured out on any subsequent expeditions. The family slowly disappeared from their elevated social circle and retreated to the point where they never left the grounds of their own estate, which was protected by one of the most elaborate private security systems in the world.

The Puzzle Box itself was locked in a vault located somewhere in the basement of the Hesselthorn mansion. There had been dozens of attempts to break in by a wide variety of prospective thieves, none of them successful.

"I don't kid," Volkerps said.

"True," Tim acknowledged. Demons generally didn't kid, josh or rib. Joking just wasn't in their nature.

"The box has vanished," Volkerps said.

"Stolen?" Tim said.

"Unknown," Volkerps said, studying one of his screens. With all of his eyes, it was sometimes difficult to tell what he was looking at. "But it's owner has disappeared along with it."

"Lucifer?" Tim asked. "How?"

"That's for you to figure out," Volkerps said. "Happened this morning. Notification just came in."

"Wow," Tim said. "Who'd they call first? Us or the cops?"

"Also unknown," Volkerps said. "But since that box is the second most valuable single object insured by the company and therefore comfortably exceeds our indemnity threshold, the case automatically bypasses Claims and comes straight to us for investigation."

"I see," Tim said. He thought about asking what the most expensive item was that Crimson Seal insured, but decided that could wait for another time.

"Claims doesn't like it," Volkerps rumbled. "But I could give a blue forked lightning fart about what they do or do not like. Ozgoroth can sit in his damp little cubicle and suck on Kappa bones all day, the squidhead."

"Right," Tim said. Having worked as an adjuster in the Claims department, he was well aware that they held a deep and long-standing resentment against SIU for dropping in and swiping their most interesting and glamorous cases, but that was just the nature of the job. The escalation processes were clear, and if there was one thing that an insurance company never did, it was to deviate from carefully established escalation procedures.

"Priority one is the box," Volkerps said. "You need to find out if it's legitimately missing. If so, how. If possible, get it back. We'd really rather not pay out the reserve on this one. The reinsurance would hit us for 75 points across the whole portfolio, maybe 80."

Like all insurance companies, Crimson Seal actually took out insurance of its own in the event of an unusually large claim. This secondary insurance, known as *reinsurance* within the industry, was designed to keep the company from having to pay out massive amounts on a single catastrophic event. A percentage of the overage on almost every policy was covered by it, and a claim as large as the one filed for something like the Hesselthorn Puzzle Box would trigger a surcharge that would hit every single insurable thing on the Crimson Seal books. If the estimate suggested by Volkerps was accurate, that meant premiums would essentially triple for everything they underwrote.

The last time the company had been forced to file for reinsurance was shortly after Tim had started working in Claims. An agent had entered the wrong GPS coordinates when writing a policy for a small souvenir shop and had ended up accidentally insuring the entire 756-acre Demonworld Haunted Hellride & Lavapark complex in error. The mistake was not noted and the policy not cancelled *void ab initio* as would have been normal underwriting procedure until *after* a construction team excavating the site for what was going to become the world's second-deepest pit plunge ride broke through an old altar wall and released an army of very angry headless demons.

Tired of being cooped up underground for 12,000 years, the demons let loose by taking control of most of the park's rides and food preparation machinery, resulting in 26,134 separate injury claims and 13 class action lawsuits. Tim remembered it as not the best time to start a new job in that department, as his vampire supervisor at the time had developed stress-induced spontaneous ocular hemorrhaging, or sudden uncontrollable bleeding from the eyes.

"Ouch," Tim said.

"Ouch is right," Volkerps rumbled. "It's entirely possible that the theft is fake or was some sort of inside job. We're talking about a once-rich family now rumored to be on the skids. Being in possibly dire financial straits and simultaneously in possession of a ludicrously valuable but insanely dangerous object that they cannot legally sell may have compelled them to consider other, less savory methods of converting said item into cash."

"Right," Tim nodded. The Puzzle Box was recognized by international treaty as a protected antiquity, which would make it difficult to sell. He was well aware that there was a healthy black market out there for haunted and otherwise enchanted artefacts that had once belonged to former robber baron dynasties who could no longer otherwise afford to pay the bills, but the Hesselthorn Puzzle Box was not the kind of thing that somebody could easily offload at a weekend antique market or in a local pawn shop.

"There's also the missing patriarch," Volkerps continued. "The family has significant spectral liability and identity theft coverage. So if he did let some demon out and/or got possessed in the process, we'll be on the hook for any resulting mayhem."

"Got it," Tim nodded.

"Normally, a case like this would need to be handled by a senior investigator," Volkerps said. "I would have given this to Lonnie, but he's still on leave and everybody else is already assigned."

Tim had been at SIU for just over a year and was still classified as a junior investigator. It would probably take him at least another two or three years before they would consider moving him to the intermediate level, but since he was the first human to ever hold the position, he figured that it might take longer than that.

Lonnie Fuhrman was a werewolf who had worked in SIU up until being put on administrative leave a few weeks earlier. Lonnie and his wife had recently separated and Lonnie was not handling the split well. Werewolves were limited to transforming in their homes or in designated parks throughout the city, which were known disparagingly as off-leash zones.

It seemed that Lonnie had elected to transform outside one of those areas and had gone on a bit of a rampage, breaking into the gallery where his ex-wife's new boyfriend had several art works on display. Lonnie apparently destroyed or urinated heavily on multiple installation pieces before passing out and waking up the following morning stark naked on the outdoor pickleball court of the Sleepy Hollow Seniors Centre. Lonnie had been placed on leave pending the outcome of his various civil and criminal proceedings, as some of the gallery pieces had been expected to fetch surprisingly high bids. The theme of the show was, ironically, "Transformation."

"Right," Tim said. "I'm sure he'll be back in no time."

"Between you and me, I saw the claim file on those gallery pieces and most of them looked better after Lonnie was through with them than they did before," Volkerps growled. "I don't get it. What is it about you humans that you're willing to pay a million dollars for a coat hanger if you paint it green and glue some feathers to it?"

"Sorry," Tim said. "I don't get it either."

"Anyway," Volkerps continued. "Everybody would like to get their hands on that box. Criminal organizations will not be shy about elbowing their way to the front of the line. Hellspawn Triad, Blood Brothers, were-wolf biker gangs, zombie militias…you name it. So find it, but try not to get yourself killed in the process."

"I'll do my best," Tim said. He was already starting to wish that Lonnie had not been on leave when this assignment came in.

"Excellent," Volkerps said. "I'll email you the First Notice of Loss. Claims is saying that the actual file hasn't even been opened yet, but I think that's just a load of bureaucratic altar bilge. They're just trying to slow us down and hold onto it for as long as they can. Ozgoroth would love to see this one blow up in my face."

Ozgoroth was the new director of the Claims department. As far as Tim understood it, Ozgoroth and Volkerps had been up for the same job more than 380 years before. Volkerps had gotten that job and the resulting bad blood between the two parties had not diminished in the slightest over the ensuing centuries.

Volkerps, for example, was convinced that the flaming effigy delivered right in the middle of the SIU staff winter solstice party had come from his nemesis in retaliation for an extremely realistic looking chain of decapitated heads that arrived during the Claims employee engagement BBQ a few months before. Tim, for his part, preferred to stay out of the interdepartmental politics.

"I'm on it," Tim said, trying to sound confident. This was easily the biggest case he had been assigned since he started with SIU and the involvement of the Puzzle Box meant that his boss would not be the only one paying close attention to his progress.

"You might want to change first, though," Volkerps said. "Don't take this in any HR actionable way, but you smell like the restrooms at the Lava Pits."

"Noted," Tim said, getting up to leave.

3

Tim didn't have time to drive all the way back to his apartment on the other side of town, so he just stopped in at Renfield's Quality Men's Clothing and Accessories to pick up a new shirt and tie.

Tim didn't normally shop there, but the place was just down the street from SIU headquarters and he was in a hurry. The store had a bit of a reputation as the previous owners had gotten into trouble for reselling items that had formerly belonged to victims of supernatural identity theft. The store had failed to check the donated items for leftover traces of evil presence before putting them back out for sale, where the malignant entities promptly took immediate possession of their new owners. One victim was strangled by his bow tie at his own retirement party while another came to seriously regret his decision to save a few bucks by purchasing a pair of used swim trunks.

Tim made sure that both of his items were new before ducking into the change room to switch to the clean shirt. He actually liked it so much that he bought a second one of a similar cut that he planned to wear on his date with Madeline. He really didn't know much about Madeline or what she liked. Hopefully they would be able to duck out of his father's company dinner after an hour or so. But after that, where could they go?

There was a new Count Craven movie coming out on the weekend, but somehow he suspected that she wasn't into vampire secret agent action blockbusters. He decided that he would figure out some possible options and send her a feel-out email tonight or tomorrow to gage her preferences.

Tim was just about to get back into his car when his phone rang. Thinking it was Volkerps with some last-minute update or instructions, he answered immediately.

"This is Tim," he said, tossing his old shirt into a nearby garbage can. His dad had an industrial-strength detergent that could be used to get the smell of demon urine out of most fabrics, but the problem was that it didn't leave them smelling much better than they were before.

"You have six days to live!" hissed an inhuman voice.

Tim groaned and looked at the call display, which showed "Evil Domain Beyond Death". Demon telescammers were becoming more prevalent than ever despite the introduction of a much-hyped national "Do Not Curse" list the year before. Tim had, like millions of others, registered his number on the list only to see the number of fake curse threats he received actually go up instead of down.

"Give me a break," Tim grunted.

"Unless you give me your credit card number immediately, you will be visited by a wraith at midnight in exactly six days!" the voice continued. It's efforts to sound terrifying and otherworldly were seriously hampered by the fact that it was clearly reading off a prepared script. "It will rip your soul out through your face and drag you down to the burning pits where you will scream for all eternity!"

"Does that mean you idiots will finally stop calling me?" Tim said.

"Your neverending torment can only be prevented by giving me your number plus the month and year of its expiry date and your three-digit security code immediately!" the voice continued. "Otherwise, you will roast in the hottest Hellfire pits of the lowest depths! You will writhe in agony as your entrails are pulled out by screeching m–"

"Sounds better than talking to you," Tim muttered, hanging up and blocking the number. He knew it wouldn't matter—the scammers' spectral spoofing technology was too advanced for that to work—but it made him feel marginally better than doing nothing.

Tim hopped in the car and headed out of the city on the Abattoir Expressway. Normally he would avoid it like the plague. The joke about the AE was that it was so named because most commuters died in their cars waiting to reach their exit. It was just past midday, however, and traffic was relatively light.

Hesselthorn Manor was in Ravensloft, a town occupying a narrow spit of land in the Acheron River Valley to the north. It had once been a popular location for the city's moneyed elite, who built their mansions at the foot of the ski slopes of the nearby Abholos mountains. The small town clustered on either side of the bridge at the most scenic part of the valley had once been home to a plethora of high-end, six-pitchfork restaurants, exotic Hellfire spas and pricey boutiques.

The town's fate had changed radically when a second-year crypto-demonology research student named Gorlin Penderghast discovered a species of giant Kappa, believed to have gone extinct millions of years before, was in fact alive and well and living in nearby Lake Kalkru. The lake was a 12-mile-long boomerang-shaped stretch of oil-black water that had been almost completely ignored over the years because it was also home to a series of underwater gas vents that made the surrounding air smell like the flaying room of a ghoul's flesh-drying hut.

Almost overnight, Ravensloft found itself inundated by thousands of tourists stopping off on their way to the lake to get a better look at the beast. No matter how hard the town tried to discourage them—taking away nearly all public parking, introducing crowd and noise bylaws, and hiring private security firms to patrol the streets—the masses continued to throng. And as they did, businesses began to spring up at the edges of town eager to service the crowds.

Within a year, Ravensloft found itself surrounded by Kappa-themed gas stations, museums, tour companies, rides, waterparks, restaurants and casinos. Every kind of operation that could charge money for being within a short driving distance of the beast staked out a space and threw up a billboard, rapidly converting a place once synonymous with tony elegance into a one now known the world over as a tacky grungehole. Within a year, most residents saw the bright green neon writing on the wall and left. The only ones who stayed were those too proud or too poor to move.

The Hesselthorns belonged firmly in both groups.

Tim hadn't had time to do any research, but he was vaguely aware that the family had made its money in the supernatural import/export business–shipping items of spectral value or significance out of their home countries and selling them to motivated buyers all over the world. Much of that business had gone underground and into the criminal black market in an era where modern sensibilities were more inclined to view it as looting rather than liberating. The family's fortunes had apparently dropped off accordingly.

Tim knew almost nothing about the Hesselthorn family outside their connection to the Puzzle Box. He had glanced quickly at the case file to grab the basic details. There were five listed named insureds. Lucifer was the primary. His wife, Ozymandia, was the secondary, although there was a NCM flag on her client file indicating that she did not have formal signing authority for any policy changes. NCM was short for *non compos mentis*, which was automatically applied to a client for 14 days following any supernatural identity theft or occupancy.

In Ozymandia's case, the flag had been in place for 20 years, which was unprecedented. Tim had never heard of anyone who had experienced post-possession incapacitation for such an extended period of time.

Also listed on the policy were the Hesselthorn children: Lucretia (28), Ludwig (26) and Ludovico (20). Lucretia and Ludwig had emergency signing authority, which meant that they were authorized to make policy changes in the event that their father, Lucifer, either died or was missing for a period of more than one week. Ludwig was apparently the one who had called to report that both his father and the Puzzle Box had disappeared. Tim had not had time to listen to the recording of the call, but the claims staffer who had taken it had reported that the client sounded "odd" in the notes.

Tim didn't know what that meant, but he planned to listen to the call himself as soon as he got the chance. Having worked in Claims, he knew that people often sounded odd when they were calling to report life-altering events. The disappearance of a parent and a valuable family artefact certainly qualified, but Claims staff were generally used to that kind of behaviour. For someone to have made note of it in the file was unusual. It meant that either the staff member was new or the client sounded stressed in a different way.

Tim pulled off the highway and onto a narrow road with a thick forest of Bloodoak trees on either side. Tim shivered in his seat and rolled up his window despite the warm summer breeze. Bloodoak trees were notorious for using their branches to snare small woodland creatures and birds, which they would then impale on a crown of spikes located in the middle of the main trunk and drain their blood.

There had never been any reported cases of humans being killed by them, but that didn't mean that the occasional hiker didn't get swiped if they strayed too close. The trees produced a bright red berry the size of a softball that was used in the production of a wine varietal highly prized by vampires. Tim had seen vintage bottles retail at up to $50,000 apiece, so it was generally the provenance of the ultrarich blood drinkers who clustered in an upscale part of town known as the Neck. Tim's brother Keef, who was also a vampire, could not afford such luxuries and tended to stick to cheap Blood Blast energy drinks, of which he left half-empty bottles all over their shared apartment.

Tim passed a large, colorful billboard advertising a place called Kappy's Water Wonderland. "Kappy" was the nickname given to the lake monster, and all of the local advertising was enthusiastically on brand.

Tim saw variations on the creature's smiling cartoon likeness on similar billboards flogging everything from KappyBurgers to Kappy's Adult Entertainment Warehouse & Party Supply Centre.

According to the SatMap, the lake was about a 15-minute drive from the centre of town. Tim hadn't been out here since he was a kid. His family had driven out to the lake when his aunt Medea had come to visit. She had never been to the city before and was convinced that she was going to have her blood sucked out, her brain eaten and her throat ripped out by every vampire, zombie and werewolf she saw within five minutes of stepping off the plane.

Her small-town terror of the big city did not change the fact that she wanted to see every tourist spot she could squeeze in, Kappy included. It did mean, however, that she travelled everywhere with two crucifixes, garlic spray, a silver stake and a Demon Charger stuffed in her oversized purse. The trip had not gone well. Medea had sprayed the captain in the eyes with Demonex because she thought he was a vampire in disguise and had gotten them all thrown off the tour even before the boat left the dock.

Tim turned down a private laneway, following his GPS to the coordinates that marked the location of Hesselthorn Manor. The place did not technically have a street address. After the publicity surrounding the discovery of the Puzzle Box, the family had officially delisted their street from the public registry. Even in the policy documentation, the location was listed only by its geocoordinates.

Tim wasn't sure such measures made much of a difference. Ravensloft was a small town and the Hesselthorns probably constituted the second-biggest tourist draw after the lake monster. Directions to their mansion were listed in almost every tour book and travel website, although all of them cautioned that there was very little of the place that could be seen from the street and that those who did manage to catch a glimpse of it would probably be disappointed. The place was apparently much smaller and less menacing than expected.

Tim wound slowly around the curves in the road. Every few hundred yards, he passed the gated entrance to a different estate. Many of them were surrounded by tall silver security fences, most of which were electrified and featured the latest anti-spectral repulsion technology. Not even a ghost could pass through them.

Tim rounded the final corner and saw a large number of news trucks parked in front of a gate that was blocked by a red and black police cruiser.

He could see several reporters had set up on the road and were filming segments with the cruiser in the background. He recognized Sticker Helsing, the well-known HEX-TV blowhard extraordinaire, had grabbed what appeared to be centre stage. Helsing had his own one-hour weekly show called "Raising the Stakes", most of which he devoted to sensationalized coverage of spectral-on-human crime and stories about how poor, innocent humans were being secretly cursed as a result of policy changes allowing demons to work in the post office or vampires to go to university. At least half of the show was dedicated to a Helsing monologue, the general tenor of which was always the same: supernatural forces were going to destroy the world unless they were forcibly sent back to the underworld where they belonged.

Helsing was depressingly popular. Tim's own parents never missed the show. Tim had long ago stopped pointing out all the outright fabrications, baseless accusations and exaggerations emerging from Helsing's fire hose of discriminatory nonsense and just tried to get through family functions without mentioning the subject, but it was difficult. His mother in particular seemed to love the guy, so much so that she made something of a running joke about her willingness to leave her husband should the TV personality ever set foot in one of her shops when she happened to be working.

Tim wasn't surprised that Helsing had staked out the best spot. The rumor was that he had a summer house around here, complete with its own private studio and helipad. Just because he liked to style himself as a "man of the people" did not mean that he wanted to live anywhere near them, apparently.

Tim pulled up behind the police cruiser. There were four officers standing guard at the perimeter, all of whom were large white men. The closest one approached his window.

"You can't park here!" the cop barked, waving a hand. "You need to clear the road!"

Tim rolled down his window and pulled his SIU badge out of his bag, holding it up.

"I'm with Crimson Seal Insurance," Tim said. "The family called us to notify us that some items we insure on their behalf have gone missing."

The cop squinted at Tim's badge. "Who?"

Tim repeated his introductory statement.

"So?" said the cop, looking confused.

Tim reminded himself to remain patient. The last thing he needed was to be denied access to the site.

"I'm here to ascertain precisely what was stolen and if any of it may be recoverable," Tim said. "The family requested that we come immediately."

The cop looked at Tim's badge again and then stood back up. "Hang on," he grunted, turning to say something into the walkie talkie attached to his shoulder. Tim was unable to hear much of the conversation, but whatever was said, it must have worked. "Okay," the cop said, turning back. "Give us a sec to move out of the way and then you can proceed inside. But only you, understand?"

Tim looked around to indicate that there was no one else in the car. "Thanks."

The cop signalled to the others to move the cruiser that was blocking the driveway. Tim put his car back in gear and was just rolling his window back up when another face shoved its way inside.

"Sticker Helsing, HEX-TV News!" shouted a familiar voice. "Who are you and why are you coming to Hesselthorn Manor this afternoon?"

Tim recoiled as a large microphone with the bright red HEX-TV logo was pushed through his window, almost hitting him in the nose. Up close, Helsing looked like he was made of plastic, and that included his carefully styled blonde hair, which looked strong enough to repel an RPG.

"Excuse me," Tim said, edging the car forward.

"What can you tell us about reports that both Lucifer Hesselthorn and his famous demon box have gone missing?" Helsing shouted.

"Very little, I'm afraid," Tim said. "Could you remove your microphone, please? I need to g–"

"Has the Puzzle Box been solved?" Helsing continued as his cameraman filmed the encounter through Tim's windshield. "Are humans on the threshold of immortality?"

The police car had pulled forward to allow Tim's car to pass through the open gate and onto the estate. As much as Tim wanted to tell Helsing to drop dead, he had to remind himself that he was here in his professional capacity on behalf of Crimson Seal. The company would not look favorably on one of their employees telling a celebrity to go to hell on national TV, regardless of whether said celebrity deserved it.

"Sorry," Tim said. "I have no comment and I have to go now. If you could–"

"How many bodies are on the premises?" Helsing pressed. "Are you an exorcist? Is it too early for ordinary citizens to be terrified for their lives? Should people be storming the premises even now with torches and pitchforks? Is that what it's going to take to end this reign of terror?"

"Reign of what?" Tim snorted.

HEX-TV was notorious for inspiring angry mobs. The last time it had happened was only a couple of months ago, when they had intimated that a world-renowned spectrobiologist was building made-to-order sex slaves by mixing grave-robbing with lab-grown succubus brains. The story was patent nonsense, but that didn't deter the group of a dozen or so torch-wielding conspiracy theorists who caused several thousand dollars' worth of damage in their attempt to foil this twisted scheme.

HEX-TV naturally denied all responsibility for the resulting melee by insisting that they were simply repeating what had already been alleged in other channels. The problem with that was that the "other channels" were websites also owned by HEX-TV's parent company.

One of the uniformed cops came forward to wave Helsing back to the other side of the road before he could manage to get in another question. Tim sighed with relief and rolled his window back up, edging his car past the cruiser and through the main gate. Although he was happy to get away from the glare of HEX-TV attention, he had an uncomfortable sense that it was just a taste of what was coming—and that what might be waiting for him at the end of the driveway wasn't going to be any better.

4

im drove down a narrow lane so overgrown with Bloodoak trees that the branches scraped the car windows on both sides.

Tim stared straight ahead and tried not to think about it. Many of the berries were rotting and left blackened streaks on his windshield and doors. Even with the windows closed, he could smell them. He had taken a spectrobiology elective in his first year of university where the instructor had described unmanaged Bloodoak orchards as smelling "like the viscera pits of Azaroth's sacrificial temple complex on a particularly fiery afternoon." Tim had never visited the site of Azaroth's temple, but he figured the comparison was probably pretty on the nose.

Tim emerged from the lane and into a slightly more open area in front of the house, where the gravel driveway looped around an ornate marble fountain. There was no water in the fountain, which featured a statue of a three-headed demon holding a pitchfork defiantly up into the sky. There were two more police cruisers and a black EMT van parked out front.

As he pulled to a stop, Tim reflected that the online gossip was accurate in that the house was much smaller and less grand than he was expecting. Instead of a massive mansion with stone pillars, ornamental demons and sweeping balconies, the Hesselthorn house was little more than a single storey circular stone cottage barely bigger than the one Tim's family had rented for summer trips back when he was a kid.

It didn't even really look like a house in that it had no windows, no external pipes or wires or connections, and only one door–a recessed black metal one that looked more like it served as an emergency exit for a boiler room than the gateway to the home. Especially a home belonging to one of the most famous families in the world.

"Seriously?" Tim muttered to himself. "*This* is the place?"

He almost wondered if he had missed a turn and ended up in front of the maintenance shed. The building in front of him looked more like a municipal pumping station. He pulled his tablet out of the SIU bag and double-checked the address to make sure he was in the right place.

The advisor must have seriously screwed up on this one, he thought, reviewing the numbers. According to the habitational policy specs, the home was 151,000 square feet, which made it almost three times the size of Notre Dame cathedral in Paris.

Tim blinked and rubbed his eyes. There was no way on earth that the number he was looking at corresponded with the house in front of him. Somebody in underwriting must have had a claw get stuck on the zero key when they entered the data.

Tim debated with himself for a moment before grabbing his SIU bag and getting out of the car. He could at least knock on the door and ask if he was in the wrong spot before turning around and running back through the HEX-TV gauntlet again.

Tim walked around the fountain, taking a moment to more carefully examine the statue. Although it had a demonic body, all three of the faces carved into the heads appeared to be human. Tim wondered if it was supposed to represent Lucifer Hesselthorn and his descendants. If it did resemble the family patriarch, then Tim was surprised that the sculptor hadn't taken the opportunity to cosmetically reduce his patron's oversized ears and buck teeth.

Tim rounded the EMT truck and climbed the mossy stone stairs. The door did not appear to have a handle, a knocker or a buzzer. He was trying to decide if he should just hammer on it with his fist when the door opened slowly from the inside and a figure stepped forward to look at him blankly.

"Hunnnnhgrrr?"

The figure was about five feet tall and dressed in a black suit jacket and skirt. It had grey, sallow skin and a gaping hole in the right side of its face, exposing a row of ragged yellow teeth. The left eyeball was hanging from the socket and resting against its other cheek like a forgotten decoration. A coaster-sized section of the skull plate was missing at the top of its forehead, exposing a green and decaying area of the brain that pulsated in a way that was distressingly difficult to ignore.

Tim had met many zombies in his time–Mug, the maintenance guy in his building, was one–but he hadn't been expecting to encounter one here. Based on the uniform, he guessed that the Hesselthorns employed this one as some sort of maid, which meant that they were too poor to afford human help and too proud to go without having servants at all.

"Hi," Tim said, awkwardly. He didn't speak the zombie language, Unghurr, which was hard for humans to master without developing esophageal cysts. All that grunting and groaning was hard on the voice box. Many people who did study it often lost the ability to speak anything else. "I'm Tim Lovecraft. I'm with Crimson Seal."

"Insurance?" said a voice from inside. "Well drop me in Hellfire and let the zombies eat my charred ballsack! Finally somebody I'm happy to see! Get out of the way, Ugathia! Let the man inside!"

The zombie stepped aside as a man around Tim's age emerged from the darkness. He had black hair that was elaborately styled to look like it hadn't been styled at all and was wearing a red Vlad Novecut designer shirt that Tim knew probably cost more than his car. The man was smiling in a way that suggested he found everything amusing because unpleasant things were boring. His eyes made a quick survey of Tim's far less fashionable wardrobe and bulky SIU bag, betraying just enough of a flicker of disapproval to suggest he found it hideously ugly, but no worse than the parade of police uniforms that were prowling the grounds already.

"That's what you said, right?" the man said, pointing at Tim. "Insurance? You're not a reporter. If you're a reporter, I'm going to let the maid eat your frontal lobe, FYI. Those people have been trying to get in all morning. They're like vampires who can move around in daylight! Hideous parasites!"

This must be Ludwig, Tim thought. At first glance, he didn't seem like a man whose primary concern was the recent disappearance of his father, but Tim reminded himself not to rush to judgement. He knew from his time in Claims that everyone reacted differently to stress. One satyr whose restaurant had been destroyed by a rampaging poltergeist had insisted he could keep the place open during remediation despite the fact that every dish he served sprouted jaws and tried to eat the customers instead of the other way around.

"I'm not a reporter, sir," Tim said, holding up his badge. "I work for Crimson Seal Insurance."

"Ludwig Hesselthorn," the man said, motioning Tim inside. "You brought the check?"

"Check?" Tim said.

Most clients assumed he was carrying a payout, so that wasn't unusual. Tim was about to clarify the reason for his visit, but as he stepped into the hallway, he realized something was very strange about the space he had entered.

Although the house looked small on the outside, the entryway was easily the size of his high school gymnasium. Tim could see two curving marble staircases that intertwined with each other as they made their way up at least six floors to a massive skylight. A gigantic red crystal chandelier hung suspended in the space between the stairs. It looked like an upside-down Bloodoak tree with branches dripping thousands of glittering red teardrop-shaped berries.

Neither the hallway nor the staircase remotely belonged within the physical dimensions of the building that Tim had seen from the outside.

"For the box," Ludwig said. "And my father's disappearance, I guess. I mean, I assume he's dead, but you probably need to see the actual body before you'll pay out on that part of it. So gruesome, but I guess that's the cost of doing business these days."

"The house," Tim said, staring around the gigantic interior in confusion. "It doesn't look...anything like this from the outside. How..."

"How is that possible?" Ludwig grinned. "What can I say? My great grandfather was tighter than a werewolf's pants. Something to do with the tax laws when the place was built. I guess it was based on the exterior square footage, or something ridiculous like that. He had the builders build it bigger on the inside than it was on the outside. It's a TOP house."

Tim had heard of that. TOP was short for transdimensional omniportal. Some demon temples had been built that way to allow very large beings to pass through much smaller physical spaces on their way from one place, like the 9th circle, to another, like the physical realm. Tim had never set foot inside one before.

"Unbelievable," Tim gasped.

"Pretty cool, isn't it?" Ludwig said, nodding. "Even if it does look like a waste treatment plant from the outside. Typical of this family, I suppose."

"Sorry?" Tim said.

"The outside world thinks we're nothing," Ludwig shrugged. "You have to actually step past that to see...this."

"Right," Tim said.

"So you're with the insurance company," Ludwig said. "I assume you brought the money, right? I mean, why else would you be here?"

"Your claim has been logged," Tim said. "I work for the company's Special Investigations Unit."

"Investigations Unit?" Ludwig said, looking confused. "What does that mean? Does that mean you're not going to be paying us what you owe? We have that policy for a reason, right? Why else do we pay you all those premiums?"

"That's not what it means," Tim said, aware that he had to tread carefully. "We just need to gather a little more information on the situation before we proceed to payout on any potential losses."

"Oh really?" Ludwig said. "Well then I can make it really simple for you. Some jackass broke into the vault and stole my father's Puzzle Box. Which is insured by your company. Therefore, you owe us a lot of money. Does that about cover the situation?"

"I don't think this will take very long," Tim said. He was used to people becoming confrontational as soon as they realized that his appearance did not signal an immediate payout. Ludwig, however, came off as more of an entitled trust fund douchebag than most clients he had dealt with in the past. "I'm going to need to take a look at the vault itself for starters."

"You're going to have to wait on that one," Ludwig said. "The cops have it taped off so they can get the first look. We're just waiting for the detective to arrive. We insisted on bringing in no less than Horatio Duluc himself."

"Really?" Tim said, surprised.

"Oh yes," Ludwig said, nodding with great self-satisfaction. "He's a personal friend of the family. My father insisted that if anything happened to him or the box that only Horatio could be entrusted with the case. They signed an agreement years ago. The man is a legend."

Horatio Duluc was, without a doubt, the most famous detective in the history of the metropolitan police, if not the entire country. He had risen to fame more than 30 years earlier by solving the Moor Park murders, a series of brutal slayings that occurred every full moon within the confines of one of the city's first free-roam werewolf enclosures.

The murders had been assumed to be the work of competing werewolf packs, but Duluc had discovered that they were actually being committed by an exclusive group of humans who called themselves the Most Dangerous Game Club. Members of the group were breaking into the secured parks to hunt werewolves for sport. Duluc had caught them by sneaking into the park and disguising himself as a werewolf. His plan had been successful in that he had caught the killers, but had also resulted in his being shot in the leg with a silver bullet, which meant that he was forced to walk with a silver cane.

His most famous case, however, was the notorious Butcher Block killings. Tim had only been five years old at the time, but he still remembered the palpable fear that had gripped the city that summer as the first grisly remains were discovered. Police had initially thought it was the work of just another solitary madman. It was only when the deputy mayor was found hanging upside down in front of city hall by his own intestines that police and the media started to think that something more serious might be happening.

Officially speaking, there were nine victims, although some later amateur accounts would put the number as high as 13. What made the killings unique was that, in all cases, the evidence indicated that the victim and the killer were one and the same person. Only one thing could cause a person to horribly mutilate themselves in such a fashion: demonic possession. The problem was, the demon was long gone by the time the body was found. Worse still, there didn't appear to be any pattern at all to how the creature was selecting its victims. Their selection seemed random.

The murders also seemed to serve no ritualistic or sacrificial purpose. The demon in question appeared to be committing the crimes just for malicious fun. Most spectropsychologists were reluctant even then to apply a label like psychopathic or sociopathic to a demonic entity as their brains were not built the same way and therefore lacked the framework for comparative moral equivalence.

Duluc was not even the primary detective on the case at the time. He was on medical leave following his previous investigation into a series of exsanguinations in an area around the nightclub district in the Neck. Duluc had managed to apprehend the killers, a pair of Narlune-addicted mortuary workers who were selling spiked blood on the black market to cover their gambling losses, but had been captured and nearly had all of his own blood drained in the process.

Unable to involve himself directly, Duluc had somehow discovered that the murders were not random at all. The victims were all descendants of a demonic cult who had abandoned their beliefs following a purge that had taken place two centuries before. Their patron, a Djinn named Bunenvok, had returned from banishment in the outer circle and was looking for revenge.

Although still scarred by his recent near-death experience, Duluc stretched his fragile psychic ability to its limits in order to identify the next victim and get to them before the demon did. Duluc was able to capture the Djinn, but did so at great personal cost, allowing it to possess him for just long enough to get himself tossed into a psychokinetic containment unit. The demon was not able to escape, but reportedly did a great deal of physical and psychic damage to Duluc in the process. The detective was in a coma for more than a week following the incident. When he finally woke up, he was almost totally paralysed and unable to use his once prodigious psychic powers.

Over the next six months, he managed to regain most of the movement in his limbs and returned to the police force, but he was a shadow of his former self. Some of his colleagues whispered that the possession had shattered Duluc mentally and that he should never have been cleared to return to duty. Whether or not this was true, Duluc never handled another major investigation and took early retirement less than a year later.

He didn't vanish, however. Whether it was the result of the possession or just his old skills coming back to the fore, Duluc began accepting invitations to work as a consulting civilian detective on cold cases. Those who worked with him said he seemed to have developed a new level of psychic ability that helped him to uncover fresh evidence and solve cases that his former colleagues on the force had abandoned as lost causes.

Duluc's reputation was further enhanced by the release of his two-volume autobiography, *The Psychic Detective*, which covered his most famous cases and was a massive international bestseller. Movie and TV adaptations quickly followed, along with a series of fictional mystery novels that he co-wrote with *Otherworld* author D.C. Charlemagne.

Tim had seen a couple of episodes of the original *Psychic Detective* series on DeadFlix. It was cheesy, but watchable. Duluc wasn't a professional actor, but he did have a natural charisma that compensated for his performative weaknesses.

Although he had mostly retreated from the public eye, Duluc was still as famous as ever. Tim's ex-girlfriend Tabitha had seen Duluc speak at her police academy graduation and still got starry eyed talking about meeting the legendary detective years later. Tim had actually been a little jealous of the way she talked about the guy, although he should have been more worried about the jackass in the prosecutor's office named Jared that she actually ran off with in the end.

Tim knew that the Hesselthorn family had once been powerful and connected, but he was surprised to find out that they still had enough juice to pull someone like Horatio Duluc out of semi-retirement. The guy had to be in his 60s or even 70s by now. His days of battling demons and chasing down werewolves were well behind him.

"So how long before we get the money, do you think?" Ludwig asked. "Less than 24 hours? Hopefully not more. Wouldn't look very good for your company if you withheld payout on such a well-known item. A lot of bad publicity if the word got out, methinks."

"We're going to move as quickly as we can," Tim said. He was used to dealing with people who saw him as nothing more than an annoying obstacle to a big payday, but few of them could make good on their veiled threats quite as much as the Hesselthorns probably could. "I understand that your father has also disappeared?"

"Yeah," Ludwig shrugged.

"Pardon my saying so," Tim said. "But you don't exactly seem surprised or distressed by that fact."

"And yet somehow I carry on," Ludwig said, striking a parody of a dramatic pose. "Look–sorry, what was your name again?"

"Tim Lovecraft."

"Right," Ludwig said. "Well, Tim, it's hardly a national security level secret that my family is not exactly the *Fuzz Collective.*"

The Fuzz Collective was a sitcom about an extended family of werewolves all forced to live in the same house together after two of its members are wrongfully de-lupinized following an attack they did not commit. It was mawkish, corny, formulaic and derived most of its jokes from shameless stereotyping–all of which conspired to make it the number one comedy on HEX-TV's Thursday night lineup, where it occupied a prime slot between *Exorcist For Hire* and *Vampire PI.*

"Were any of the other members of your family present at the time the box went missing?" Tim asked.

"Oh, they were here," Ludwig nodded. "But I don't think they'll be able to tell you much. My mother was in the parlour. That's where she spends most of her days. Not that she's aware of it. She's got PPSD."

PPSD was Post-Possession Spectral Disorder, which was a common side effect experienced by humans once they had been vacated by a possessing entity. The usual symptoms were memory loss, night horrors, vomiting, spontaneous levitation and joint disarticulation, but there were many other less-pleasant ones.

"I see," Tim said. "When was she possessed?"

"Back when she had my brother, Vic," Ludwig said. "So, 20 years now. She's been pretty much in a coma ever since. As far as Vic goes, well, it's like the demon jumped out of her and stayed permanently in him. We have to keep him locked in his special room upstairs."

"I see," Tim said. "Anyone else?"

"Just my sister, Lucretia," Ludwig said. "But she was locked away in her crypt and hadn't *arisen* yet when the break-in happened."

"Crypt?" Tim said. "She's a vampire?"

"No," Ludwig said. "But she likes to think that she is. Sleeps in a coffin in a custom-built, high-security crypt in the basement. Never comes out during daylight hours. Spends all her allowance on dental implants and blood shakes. She's been trying to talk our father into paying for this new entity transformational surgery. It's supposed to make her into a vampire without actually being bitten. It's crazy! Have you ever heard of such a thing?"

Tim had heard of such a thing. There were no shortage of people out there who wanted all the perks that came with being a vampire (primarily immortality) without some of the drawbacks (like only being able to consume blood and bursting into flame if exposed to the sun). Accordingly, there was no shortage of questionable medical practitioners offering dubious pathways to such an existence for those who could afford to pay for it.

"I have," Tim said. He was wishing that he'd had more time to research this family before stepping through their front door. He had only arrived a minute ago and already had a mountain of questions.

Ludwig flicked a spec of dust off his arm. "I mean, it's just–"

They were interrupted by the high-pitched screeching sound of someone or something clawing at the front door.

"What the hell?" Tim said, covering his ears and taking an involuntary step back. His first thought was that Helsing had actually convinced a torch-wielding mob to storm the house. It wouldn't be the first time.

"Ah!" said Ludwig. "Speak of the devil!"

The maid stepped forward and opened the door to reveal a demon, a satyr and a human woman standing on the front step. The demon was wearing a long black scarf and designer sunglasses with individual lenses that shaded all six of her eyes. The satyr was dressed in cargo shorts that appeared to be made mostly of pockets with padded blue moon boots and was carrying a camera on his shoulder. The woman had so many tattoos that she looked more demonic than the demon and was carrying what Tim recognized as a boom microphone on an extendable pole.

"Ludwig!" said the demon, striding forward like she owned the place and grabbing the young Hesselthorn heir by the hand. "You got my text?"

"Xetra!" Ludwig nodded. "Is he here?"

"He's outside in the car," the demon said. "He'll be making his grand entrance just as soon as we iron out a few teeny little technical details, like who the hell are you?"

Tim did not realize at first that the demon was talking to him. It was hard to tell where she was looking as she hadn't bothered to remove her sunglasses.

"This is some guy from the insurance company," Ludwig said. "Tom."

"Insurance?" said the demon. "Has he signed a release?"

"A what?" said Tim.

"A release," the demon said. "We can't have your face in the documentary without it. Otherwise we have to blur you out, which is such a pain in the ass that it's actually easier to cut around you."

"Documentary?" Tim said.

"Ugh," the demon said, shaking her head and turning back to Ludwig after having evidently decided that Tim was too much effort to address directly. "This is Torgun and Hayley."

"Kayleigh," said the tattooed woman with the mic.

"Right," said the demon with more than a trace of irritation. "Okay, so what are we looking at for secondary lighting in the vault? I'd love it if there are some nice Hellfire sconces down there."

"Well–" said Ludwig.

The demon's phone buzzed. She looked at the screen and raised a manicured claw that Tim estimated was at least 12 inches long. "Okay, let's get set, people! Mysterio is inbound! Repeat, Mysterio is getting out of the car and coming through the door momentarily!" She pushed Tim out of the way and motioned to the camera satyr. "Torgun, I want you here for his entrance! Let's not have to do this twice like the last one, okay?" She stabbed another claw at the tattooed sound woman. "Hayley or whatever the hell your name is, get behind him so we get the catchphrase! I don't want to have to ADR this again! Let's move it!"

The crew scrambled to get into position as everyone else moved out of the way. The demon grabbed Ludwig by the arm.

"Okay, Ludwig darling," she hissed. "Wait till he enters. He'll take a few steps, take off his sunglasses and say his catchphrase. Then give it a beat and you step in when I give you the signal. Got that?"

Ludwig nodded and straightened his suit jacket, coughing a couple of times to clear his throat.

"What the hell is this?" Tim asked in a hushed voice. He had to duck to avoid being hit with the boom pole as the woman extended it and swung it into position.

"Horatio's filming a documentary about his return to detective work after his time away," Ludwig whispered. "Part of his new three-picture deal with DeadFlix. Said our case would be the perfect hook. Maybe the subject of a whole movie of its own! Can you imagine?"

Ludwig shivered with excitement. It was as if he couldn't imagine anything more glamorous or exciting than being the subject of a criminal investigation–provided that investigation was televised.

"A what?" Tim said.

"Shhhh!" hissed the demon. "We're rolling!"

Everyone fell silent as the door opened and a tall, silver-haired man in a black leather trench coat strode into the hall. He was wearing mirrored sunglasses and carrying a cane with an elaborate silver handle molded to look like a wolf's head. He was limping slightly in a way that seemed to favour his right foot, although he moved so purposefully that it was barely noticeable.

Tim couldn't help but let out a small gasp of recognition. He had seen this man numerous times on TV, but this was his first time seeing the legend in the flesh.

Duluc stopped just in front of them, reached up with his free hand, and removed his sunglasses with practiced ease. His left eye was covered by a shiny red eyepatch and there was a scar on his right cheek. It was difficult to guess his age. He looked younger than 60. Like a politician or movie star, the glamour subtracted years in some places and added them in others.

He narrowed his good eye and seemed to sniff the air.

"I sense great evil here," Duluc said in a raspy whisper.

There was a brief pause before the demon elbowed Ludwig in the ribs. Ludwig cleared his throat again and stumbled forward, holding out his hand like a fencing foil.

"Horatio!" he said. "So good of you to come!"

Duluc regarded Ludwig for a moment before extending his cane.

"Mr. Hesselthorn," he said, nodding in a way that Tim guessed was supposed to look grave but that actually looked slightly dyspeptic. "Please forgive me. But I may not make physical contact with anyone. It would be extremely dangerous, mostly for you."

"Oh," said Ludwig, who reached out and shook the handle of the cane awkwardly. "Of course."

"I understand that both your priceless and legendary Puzzle Box and your father have recently gone missing," Duluc said, looking around the hall.

"Yes!" Ludwig said, smiling like this horrible turn of events was the greatest thing that had ever happened to him. "That's correct!"

"Cut!" yelled the demon.

"What?" Ludwig said, looking around with a confused expression.

"Ludwig, darling," said the demon. "Try to keep in mind that your beloved father is missing and your priceless family treasure is gone. Try not to look like you just won $500 on a Devil's Bingo scratch card."

"Oh, right!" Ludwig said, trying to adopt a more serious expression.

"Do you need me to do the entrance again?" Duluc groaned, putting his sunglasses back on.

"No," said the demon. "Let's just cut straight to the vault. Ludwig, show us the way. And try to look more bereft this time."

"Will do," Ludwig nodded, dropping his voice. "Why didn't you tell me he doesn't shake hands?"

"It's more dramatic if you don't know," the demon said. "We just needed to emphasize it to get the right reaction for the initial meeting."

"I still wish you'd told me," Ludwig muttered. "Now I look like a putz. Can you cut that out?"

"Absolutely not," the demon said. "And you already signed the contract, so let's move this along. The vault?"

"Right," Ludwig said, turning to Tim. "This might take a while. Can you come back first thing tomorrow?"

"Sure," Tim said, looking dubiously at Duluc and the film crew. "Provided nothing is disturbed."

"Great," Ludwig said. "See you then. This way, everyone!"

Tim watched them disappear down the hall. He made a quick note of the time before turning to let himself back out through the front door. Although retired, Duluc was still a cop who was conducting a criminal investigation. That technically gave him the legal right to secure the scene before access was granted to any third party, which unfortunately included any representatives of Crimson Seal. There was nothing Tim could do about that. All he could do was hope that nothing was disturbed before he could get in there to look for himself. In the meantime, he would head back to the city and start going through the file on the family, which he was sure would make for some interesting reading.

Tim made his way down the steps and across the cobblestone drive. He was just about to get back into his car when a voice spoke up from behind him.

"Ah, so you're the thief!"

Tim stopped and turned around to see a woman approaching from the other side of the driveway. She looked to be in her mid-twenties, with short red hair and some sort of tattoo on her neck. She was dressed in a black camo pattern windbreaker, torn cargo pants and steel-toed combat boots. She was twirling an object in her left hand that he recognized as a Demon Charger.

"Excuse me?" Tim said, wondering who this woman was. His first guess was that she was a reporter looking for a scoop or some distant member of the extended family here to cash in on whatever chunk of inheritance might be up for grabs.

"Actually, I don't think I will excuse you," she said, waving the charger uncomfortably close to his face. "This one is mine! You understand? You stole it!"

Tim reached into his SIU bag and grabbed his spray canister of Demonex.

"Whoa!" he said. "How about we calm down and point that thing somewhere else? Who are you? What are you talking about? I didn't steal anything!"

"Who am I?" she asked. "I'm the one you stole this case from, you grave-robbing dickbrain! That's who I am."

"Sorry?" Tim said.

"You will be!" she said. "You're pretty slow on the uptake, mister star of the Special Investigations Unit! Are you this stupid all the time or just when you're working?"

"Wait a minute," Tim said. "You work for Crimson Seal?"

"Look at that!" she shouted, throwing her hands up in the air in mock amazement. "He solved it! Oh, you are a clever boy, aren't you? And all it took was me giving you all the information with written instructions outlining what to do with it. You're a regular damn demon Allfather of brainpower, you are."

"Have I done something to offend you?" Tim asked.

"Offend me?" she said. "You want to know what offends me? What offends me is that they took my case away from me before I had even gotten started and handed it over to another one of Volkerps' little golden boys to grab all the credit and the glory. That's why I'm in the remarkable state of good humour and equanimity in which you find me today, you demon dong."

Tim sighed and relaxed his grip on the Demonex.

"You're with Claims, right?" he said. "Look, this wasn't my choice, okay? I got the call less than an hour ago. I used to work as an adjuster myself. I got cases taken away from me and handed to SIU all the time. The important thing is not to take it personally."

"Well, that's the difference between you and me, isn't it?" she said. "That and the fact that I'm not some privileged little corporate ghoul looking to screw everyone who gets in my way. You take something from me, I actually do take that personally, you understand?"

"I'm sorry if they took the file away from you," Tim said, fishing around for his keys. "But I had nothing to do with that."

"You know what else you're going to have nothing to do with?" she said, leaning forward. "Solving this case. You know why?"

"Because you plan to solve it first?" Tim said.

"Exactly!" she said, poking him in the shoulder hard enough to make him take a step back. "I'll have this figured out before you even unlock your car. And then they'll realize that you're an idiot. And then I'll get promoted. And then the first thing I'll do is fire your sorry ass."

"I look forward to it," Tim muttered, unlocking his door.

"You better," she said. "Because I'm not kidding. I've worked with this family before. I know them better than anyone. I already know exactly what happened here. You know how many files I've had stolen right out from under my nose by your stupid department over the years?"

"I'm guessing at least one," Tim said, tossing his SIU bag on the passenger seat and climbing in.

"Yeah, well this is the last one," she said, shoving her face in the window much in the same manner that Sticker Helsing had done. "So stay out of my way, you got it? This one is mine. You get under my feet and I'll–"

"You'll what?" Tim said. "You're not about to threaten a fellow employee with physical violence, are you?"

"You'd love that, wouldn't you?" she smiled. "Go running back to your boss and rat me out to HR, you little zombie."

"Right," Tim said. "Well, I must say it's been an absolute joy meeting you. Sorry, I don't think I got your name?"

"Giallo," she said.

"Is that first or last?" Tim asked.

"Giallo is all you need to know," she said.

"Okay then, Ms Giallo," Tim waved. "If you'll excuse me, I have to get back to work. But I must say that it's been a pleasure making your acquaintance."

She stepped back as Tim started his car. As he was pulling out, he saw her point to him and then wordlessly draw her finger across her neck like an imaginary knife. She followed the gesture up by blowing him a kiss.

Well, Tim thought, maybe it's not so bad. It looks like there are at least two other people determined to get to the bottom of this before I do. As long as they manage to do it without killing me, that's fine.

Tim pulled up to the gate, which began to open automatically. He was relieved to see that the police had moved the HEX-TV crew back out of the way. The way things were going, it would be just his luck to accidentally run over Sticker Helsing on his way home.

The only plus was that working in insurance, he knew how make it look like an accident.

5

Tim got off the elevator and was surprised to encounter a group of three people in ill-fitting suits trying to get what looked like an oversized coat rack through the open front door of his apartment.

Tim's first assumption was that they were delivery people who had gone to the wrong address, but couriers didn't tend to wear three-piece pinstripe ensembles. The Decameron, where Tim lived, was notoriously haunted, so it wasn't out of the ordinary to see strange figures moving through its halls and walls. Many of its deceased residents still considered the place home.

For example, the headless ghost of the late Henrik von Hapsdorf was notorious for popping out of the garbage chute into which his freshly detached head had been tossed 213 years earlier by the husband of the woman he had been gracing with his semi-royal presence in unit 2110. There was also the notorious Screaming Mimi, a former opera singer who had thrown herself out of the window of room 1812 after a poorly received performance in *The Vampire of Lisbon*. Her ghost still jumped out the window from time to time, singing the entirety of the notoriously difficult aria, *Você drenou meu sangue,* as she plummeted slowly to the sidewalk.

As he got closer, however, Tim could see that these figures were not ghosts. There were two women and one man, none of whom looked more than 20 years old. The thing they were trying to get through the door looked like a cross between a weight bench and a coat rack. Whatever it was, it appeared to be both too tall and too wide to fit through the opening.

"Can I help you with something?" Tim asked, stopping to survey the scene.

"Are you Hink?" asked a blonde woman with her hair pulled back in a bun so tight that it seemed to stretch her face. "Did you bring the screwdriver and wrench from the cupboard under the sink in the kitchen?"

"No, I'm not Hink." Tim said, bemused.

"Then where the hell is he?" demanded the other woman, stabbing angrily at her cellphone. "I texted that pit slag, like, a hundred times!"

"Hey Hink, give me a hand with this!" said the man. He was trying to grab what looked like the base of the metal frame and nodding his head at Tim to take hold of the top bar and angle it sideways. "I think we can get this in without taking it apart!"

"I think you have the wrong door," Tim said. "I'm not Hink. This is my apartment."

"Is that my hanging rack?" boomed a voice from inside. "What is it doing in the fucking hall? I need to get some goddamned blood to my brain before I pass out in here! Ideas, darlings! Do you understand? My brilliance is drying up as I speak! My brain is the dick of my genius! You understand? Without blood, it just doesn't function!"

"Look buddy," said the blonde woman. "I don't know who you are, but unless we get this thing inside, Killian's going to be pissed. Do you have a screwdriver?"

"Unfortunately not," Tim said. "Who's Killian? Is that the guy with the dick brain?"

"Shhh!" hissed the woman with the cell phone. "Hell's your deal, Hink? You *wanna* get fired?"

Tim sighed and stepped around the metal contraption and into his apartment. Once inside, he found a short, fat, bald man pacing in the living room talking on a cell phone. The man was dressed in an expensive-looking suit that seemed slightly too large for his frame. His shirt tail was hanging out on one side and he appeared to have food stains on his cuffs and tie, which had been pulled down so far that it looked more like a noose. He had a scraggy, three-day growth of beard and his skin looked flaky and sallow.

"I don't care if they already hired Gorestein to do it!" the man shouted into his phone. "If that satyr-grabbing ghoul doesn't shitcan that altar pit dwelling bag of bones and hire my guy like he said, I'm personally going to pay every Serrabluk I have ever represented to shaft his dead grand-mother live on the set of *Count Popula's Magic Castle*, you understand? Oh, and sincerest congratulations on your niece's wedding. Wonderful girl. I'm sure they'll be very happy, darling."

He hung up the phone and grabbed an open Blood Blast energy drink from the coffee table which he chugged enthusiastically. "Ah, that's the life! Who the hell are you?"

"Tim Lovecraft," Tim said, looking uncomfortably at the rivulets of blood running down the man's chin to soak into his shirt. Humans did not normally drink blood-based beverages and this man did not look like a vampire, so he wasn't sure exactly what was going on here. "This is my apartment."

"Ah!" the man said, darting across to grab Tim's hand and shake it awkwardly in his large, clammy mitt. "Killian Costigan. Your brother Keef hired me as his new agent-slash-familiar. So very pleased to meet you."

"Sorry, hired you as his what?" Tim said, extricating his hand from the man's sticky grip.

There was a groan and the sound of a door opening. Tim looked over to see his older brother Keef emerge from one of the bedrooms, yawning widely to display his prominent canines.

"Speak of the devil!" Killian said, clapping his hands.

Keef was a vampire who had been living with Tim for almost two years, largely because of his inability to acquire or maintain any form of steady employment. Tim would have kicked him out, but there was nowhere else for Keef to go. Their parents lived in a condo complex that did not allow vampires, for whom housing options were severely limited.

"Hey bro!" Keef said, stretching. "You just get home?"

"Yeah," Tim said. "What is, uh, all this?"

"This is Killer," Keef said, gesturing at the bald man. Keef was dressed in his usual unbuttoned shirt, black leather pants and bare feet. He grabbed an open bag of *Scabs* off the couch and tossed a reddish-black lump in his mouth, which he began to chew enthusiastically.

"Killer?" Tim asked, wincing. He hated *Scabs*, which he considered the most disgusting of all vampire snack items.

"Ah, that's my nickname, darling," Killian said. "In the industry."

"Industry?" Tim asked.

"Show biz," Keef said, popping another lump. "Killian here is gonna make me a star."

"A what?" Tim said, confused.

"Mock if you will," Keef said. "But he's the real deal. You're looking at the next *Blood Stalker*, buddy!"

"Speaking of which, master," Killian said. "I just got off the phone with Headless Pictures and we're very close to getting you locked in for one of the supporting leads in their upcoming *Hellspore* sequel!"

"Cool!" Keef said. "All the even-numbered ones have been shit, so it looks like I'll be in lucky number 13!"

"Master?" Tim asked.

"Yeah," Keef said. "Killian's my new agent and my new familiar."

"Is that why those people are out in the hall trying to move some sort of playground apparatus into my apartment?" Tim asked.

"Killian just needs to set up his office here while we get my career off the ground," Keef said.

"Office?" Tim said. "Are you kidding?"

Sensing trouble, Keef pulled Tim into the kitchen to continue their conversation in private.

"It's just temporary," Keef said, lowering his voice and waving his fingers in front of Tim's face. "You will have no problem with this new living arrangement!"

"Don't try to hypnotize me, you idiot!" Tim snapped. "You have about as much talent for that as you do for turning yourself into a bat!"

Keef had little to no facility for any of the additional skills that vampires were supposed to possess, like transformation or hypnosis. Many of them required a great deal of effort and practice to master and Keef had a spotty track record with anything work-related.

"Sorry," Keef said, dropping his hand. "You can't blame me for trying, though. I knew you'd react this way."

"Of course I can blame you for trying!" Tim said. "You can't use mind control to try to get me to let even more people move into my apartment! You're the one who's supposed to be moving out! You're not supposed to be moving even more people in!"

"It's just temporary!" Keef said. "He got kicked out of his other office."

"Why?" Tim asked.

"No reason," Keef said. "Some former personal assistant with a grudge accused him of trying to drink her blood or something. You know, the usual HR bullshit."

"Drink her blood?" Tim said. "Is he a vampire?"

"Not quite," Keef said. "He just has this, like, condition that makes him crave a little blood every now and then. No biggie."

"No biggie?" Tim said in disbelief.

"Well, actually, it is *kind* of a biggie," Keef said. "He's gonna die in, like, six months or something? That's why he asked me to turn him into a vampire. It's that or the disease kills him."

"You're joking," Tim said.

"No," Keef said. "I met him when I did that commercial for the Scream Factory last month. You remember? I told you about that. Anyway, we kinda got to talking. He explained his situation and we sort of came to an agreement."

The Scream Factory was a tacky tourist trap of a haunted house where Keef had worked up until a few weeks previously, having been fired for getting caught naked with two young female trainees in the ball pit of Count Yorga's Party Crypt.

"Is that why he looks kind of like his skin is falling off?" Tim asked.

"Yeah," Keef said. "But don't worry. It's not contagious. At least, I'm pretty sure it isn't."

"You're *pretty sure*?" Tim said, thinking about the fact that he had just shaken the guy's hand. He began searching his SIU bag for hand sanitizer. He always carried a tube of the stuff just in case.

"It's not!" Keef said. "I'm sure, okay? Only maybe don't make actual physical contact with him. You know, just in case."

"Ugh," Tim shivered. He found the sanitizer and squirted a larger than usual amount onto his hands. It was supposed to eliminate 99% of topical curses. "Look Keef, I don't care what kind of an arrangement you two worked out, okay? He can't live here."

"He'll be setting everything up in my bedroom!" Keef said. "You'll never even see the guy!"

"But I've already seen him!" Tim said. "And heard him. The guy yells loud enough on the phone that everyone in the building can probably hear him. Including the ghosts."

"I'll tell him to keep it down," Keef said. "I'm his master. He has to obey my every command."

"It doesn't matter!" Tim said. "This apartment is already crowded enough! You understand? Max capacity has already been exceeded! The last thing we need is your new familiar moving in with his entire staff or personal assistants!"

"They won't be moving in, too," Keef said. "They'll just be coming and going during regular office hours. He's setting up a place of his own in a building downtown. Faustus Talent International. Cool name, eh?"

"Why would you think I care about the name?" Tim asked.

"I'm just saying," Keef said. "He's the real deal. He saw me do the commercial. He told me that I have genuine talent."

"The guy whose life depends on you turning him into a vampire told you that you have genuine acting talent?" Tim said, not bothering to keep the sarcasm out of his voice.

"Yes!" Keef said. "He can open doors for me! He's already got gigs lined up. You keep telling me that you want me to get a real job and move out, right?"

"Yes," Tim said through gritted teeth.

"Well, this is it," Keef said. "I think we can both agree that the regular nine-to-five thing and I do not harmoniously coexist. I can't handle the kind of mind-numbing, soul-sucking corporate torture that you do every day. This might be my best shot and Killian thinks I have what it takes to go all the way to the top."

"The top of what?" Tim asked.

"To the top of the A-list, smart ass!" Keef said. "Six months from now, you're going to be able to brag to everyone that we're related! Tabloids are gonna be coming to you for the inside scoop on what it was like to live with the great Keefer Lovecraft for all those years."

"Is that so?" Tim said. "In that case, you're going to have to pay me a fortune to keep my mouth shut."

There was a crash from the living room. Tim and Keef ran back out to find that the attempts to get the metal contraption through the door had finally succeeded. Not only had they made it through, they had made it all the way across the room and punched a hole in the wall next to the TV.

"What the hell is this?" Tim yelled, rushing to inspect the damage.

"Relax!" Keef said. "It's just a scratch. Besides, you're insured, right? I mean, you work for an insurance company for crying out loud."

Before Tim could respond, two demons in *Speed Demon* courier uniforms showed up at the door carrying what looked unmistakably like a golden coffin.

"Where d'ya want this?" grunted the first demon whose name tag identified him as Haarg. He was a large Serrabluk and appeared to be having a much easier time with his share of the load than his partner, who was a much shorter and thinner Aylith named Mikey.

"Ooh, nice!" Keef said, his eyes going wide. "Is that my new bed?"

"Not yet, master," Killian said. "That's for me. I want to start getting into the headspace of my new life right away. I'm also switching to a nocturnal schedule, but a lot of my meetings are still during the day. Good thing I've got these *Blood Blasts* to keep me going."

Killian tipped the energy drink up and guzzled the remaining contents in a single chug. Overconsumption of *Blood Blasts* could lead to a variety of unpleasant medical side effects ranging from oozing red facial boils to displodocardia (a condition where a vampire's heart quite literally exploded in their chest). A tiny legal warning printed on the underside of every bottle advised consumers not to ingest more than 275ml per day. Naturally, the smallest commercially-available bottle was 600ml.

Killian finished it off and tossed the empty bottle. It was caught by an assistant who was sitting on the floor next to the metal rack nursing his elbow, which had apparently gone through the plaster as well.

"Nathan!" Killian barked. "Stop mincing around and order me another four cases of *Blood Blast*! Make sure it's virgin cherry flavour this time! You get the O Neg again and I'll drain every last corpuscle out of your body and piss you straight into the toilet, understand?"

"Yes, sir," said the assistant, staggering back to his feet and pulling out his cell phone.

"The coffin?" grunted Haarg.

"Yeah, hurry up!" hissed Mikey struggling to hold on to the other end by alternating his tentacles. "This damn thing weighs a ton! Is it real gold or something?"

"Just put it in there for now," Killian said, pointing to Tim's bedroom.

"No way!" Tim said. "Uh uh! That's my room! None of this stuff is going in there!"

"All right," Killian groaned, pointing to the dining room. "Just put it in there."

"That's my dining area!" Tim protested.

"It's the perfect size for my office," Killian said as the demons carted the coffin across the room and dumped it on the floor with a thud. "Where's the stand?"

Haarg shrugged and held out a tablet for a signature. "Beats me. We didn't get no stand. Just the box. Sign here."

"Nathan!" Killian erupted. "Where the hell is my coffin stand? Do you expect me to sleep on the damn floor?"

"Sorry, sir!" the assistant said, reaching into his pocket and grabbing a second cell phone while simultaneously involved in a conversation on the first. "I'll track it down immediately!"

There was a knock at the open door as a group of five women all arrived at the same time. They all looked to be between 16 and 25 years old and were dressed in skin-tight clothing that left little to the imagination.

"Hi," said the first one. "Is this where the auditions are happening?"

"Excellent!" Keef said, smiling.

"I don't believe this," Tim muttered.

"All right, ladies!" Killian said. "Are you all here for the audition for Ol' Horny Bastard's music video for *Suck Me Dry*?"

The women all nodded in unison.

"I was in the last one he did for *Fang Fan Fun*," said one.

"I was a featured extra in *The Offering*!" said another. "I have a line in the big climactic scene at the end where the head demon gets butt-speared with the pitchfork. I say: '*I think he got the points!*' It's really hilarious! It didn't make the final cut, but the assistant director said I had real comic timing."

"I'm sure," said Haarg, grinning at her.

"Now all of you have read the listing," Killian said. "So you're aware that this will feature real and not simulated fang penetration, right?"

"Totally," said a blonde woman, pulling back the strap of her dress to reveal a bite mark on her neck. "I just got bit for a *Scabs* ad. I heal, like, instantly. You know, for callbacks."

"Me too!" said another, pulling up her skirt to reveal a similar mark on her right thigh. "Mine was for a Blud Pop video. It got over a million views!"

Tim was aware that Blud Pop was an online parody channel that featured comedic reenactments of famous historical events, but had never actually seen one. The star was a 15-year-old kid who seemed to film most of the segments in his backyard and had quickly attracted a depressingly large fanbase, probably because many of the women who appeared in his show weren't wearing much.

"Excellent," Killian said, clapping Keef on the shoulder. "Ladies, meet your co-star, Keefer Darklove."

"Darklove?" Tim snickered.

"Shut up!" Keef hissed. "Killian came up with it. I like it. It gives me an aura of sinister attraction."

"Oh, it gives you an aura all right," Tim said. "The aura of a mail-order sex toy."

"Normally, we'd bring you in one at a time," Killian said. "But since you're all here, why don't we just try all of you at once?"

There was general agreement for this suggestion amongst Keef and the auditionees.

"Let's just set up in here, shall we?" Killian said, grinning. "Nathan! Where the hell is the camera?"

"Getting it, sir," the assistant said, tripping over his feet and crashing back into the wall as he stumbled for a plastic case.

"Ugh," Tim groaned. "If anyone's looking for me, I'll be in my room."

Tim went to his bedroom and closed the door. He had just powered up his laptop to start some research on the Hesselthorn file when a familiar voice piped up from behind him.

"Tim Tub!"

Tim spun around to see a small form fluttering towards him through the air. He tried to get out of the way and fell off his chair onto the floor as the thing landed on the desk next to his laptop. Tim was reaching into his SIU bag for his Demonex when he looked up and realized that he recognized the intruder.

"Clawfist?" Tim said in disbelief.

"Chik Chak!" the demon chirped, bouncing up and down on its tiny hooves.

"What on earth are you doing here?" Tim said. "How did you get in?"

"Freek Fruk," the demon said. "Flig Frag."

Tim and the demon just sat staring at each other for a moment. Tim had no idea what the demon was doing in his apartment and was about to try and shoo it out when he remembered something from all the way back in his first year of demonology studies at university.

Clawfist was a Gogrub, which was a species of microdemon so small that they were originally classified as pets, but their size wasn't the only determining factor in their spectrotaxonomy. Tim pulled out his laptop and quickly logged into the university archive using his alumni account. Only a small portion of the school's records were digitized, but he was pretty sure he would be able to find what he was looking for in the *Fulgate Daemonaerum*, one of the largest and oldest records of supernatural creatures ever compiled.

Modern scholars regarded the work as an antiquated relic of an igno-rant and colonialist mindset as it was largely responsible for perpetrating some of the most spectralist and damaging stereotypes of non-humans in academic and popular culture, but it also happened to be the only one with a keyword search and Tim was in a hurry.

He found the entry on Gogrubs and skipped quickly past their ori-gins and spectrology to their behaviour, which was the entry he was most concerned with:

> *Like many luminarecornutumbelu, the Gogrub was a common altareprodigium in the time of the Sextus Diabolus Regnum (5660-4820). A known demonopophagus, stewardship was transferred most commonly by consumption of the former demodominus.*

In plain language, this meant that Gogrubs had existed thousands of years ago as the altar pets of the once mighty demon Allfathers, who kept them around to help keep the place clean by eating the remains of sacrificial offerings. Ownership of these minor demons was transferred when their former master was in turn killed and eaten. This was exactly what had happened to the late Zito Futchinski (aka Dr. Horatio von Gug-gendorf). It seemed that since his former master had been consumed, Clawfist had transferred his loyalties to the individual who had in turn destroyed the creature that ate Zito.

"But I didn't kill and eat him!" Tim said to the demon, which was making itself comfortable on his pillow.

"Bid Bed!" Clawfist said, closing its eyes and wrapping its scaly wings around its body like a blanket.

"I'm not your new master!" Tim said. "You can't stay here!"

"Seep Keep," Clawfist yawned. A moment later, it was snoring con-tentedly while tiny jets of blue flame sparked from its nostrils.

"Great," Tim grumbled. If it isn't bad enough that I have to put up with my freeloading brother and his new entourage, now I've got a pet demon?

Tim watched the demon sleep for a moment before turning back to his laptop. The creature had evidently decided to live here at least for the short term, so he figured that he'd better find out as much about them as he could. If he could get Clawfist to eat Killian or at least set the agent's coffin on fire while he was in it, maybe this wouldn't be so bad.

6

Tim returned to the Hesselthorn mansion the following morning. There were no news reporters blocking the driveway this time, which was a relief. Tim was also relieved that he had not featured on the previous day's HEX-TV broadcast, as the arrival of Horatio Duluc had received far more attention.

This had not stopped Volkerps calling, texting and emailing roughly every 15 minutes for an update on the status of the case. Tim figured that was probably easier to do when you had three arms and two heads. The SIU boss was not remotely surprised by Giallo's appearance on the scene and had some extremely unorthodox suggestions on how Tim should handle the situation.

"She shows up again, feel free to use the Demon Charger," Volkerps said.

"You're kidding, right?" Tim asked.

"I told you, I don't kid," Volkerps said. "Especially not when the audit committee is pouring liquid Hellfire down my shorts!"

"You wear shorts?" Tim said. He had never seen his boss's lower half, which had led him to believe that the old demon simply didn't have one.

"Only to the lava pits," Volkerps said. "If Claims finds this thing first, our department is gonna look more useless than the contestants on that stupid zombie baking show!"

"Right," Tim said. He assumed Volkerps was talking about *Zombake!*–a reality TV show in which the undead contestants routinely set themselves, the set, and sometimes the studio audience on fire. "I'm on it."

Tim had looked up the combative claims adjuster in the company's intranet and found that her name was listed as G Giallo. He had no idea if the G was short for anything or if the single letter was the totality of her first name, but it was all that was listed on all of the departmental records he checked. According to her HR file, she was 26 years old and had worked for the company for nearly eight years.

She had started in the call centre before moving quickly up to Policy Processing and then getting the adjuster job, which she had been doing for just over two years. She had started working for Crimson Seal straight out of high school, which was extremely unusual, as a university degree was the minimum requirement for most humans coming in the door. Her professional certifications showed that she was doing an online diploma in supernatural remediation–one of the requirements for anyone studying to be an exorcist–but had completed only three of the eight required modules.

She had no other family members listed on any of her own policies. Her listed address was an apartment in Little Carpathia, a part of the city with a lot of derelict industrial buildings, most of which were occupied by homeless vampire squatters.

As a rule, Tim did not do this kind of research on another employee unless they were under investigation, but since she had threatened both him and the outcome of the case he was working on, he thought it was a good idea to get a better sense of who he was dealing with. Having worked as an adjuster, he knew how it felt to have a case taken away by SIU, but had never taken the matter quite as personally as Giallo seemed to be taking it. He had always tried to stay out of office politics, even though internal feuds were often as unavoidable as the smell of microwaved brains in the break room.

I just need to put it out of my head and focus on the case, Tim told himself as he waited for the gate to open. If it becomes a serious problem, I'll kick it up the chain to Volkerps. It would be nice to have his fiery attention directed at someone else right now.

Tim parked at the side of the house and knocked on the door. There was no answer. He counted to 30 and tried again. They had to know he was here, because somebody had buzzed him in at the front gate. He was about to give up and try calling when the door was finally opened by Ugathia, who grunted and motioned him inside. Tim could hear music coming from somewhere as he stepped into the hall and was almost knocked to the floor by a woman in an elaborate black gown who went careening past him.

"Excuse me!" Tim said, staggering backwards.

The dancing woman did not reply and gave no indication of even being aware of his existence. She looked to be in her 60s and was dancing with the furious intensity of someone less than a third of her age. Her eyes were closed. She must have some sort of photographic memory of the room, Tim thought, because she didn't open her eyes as she wheeled around tables, chairs, statues and other potential obstructions.

Tim knew very little about ballet, but he knew enough to recognize that this woman moved like a professional. Her every sweep and skip and gesture was executed with laser precision and in perfect sync with the music. She didn't stumble or hesitate once as she moved around the room, dominating it as purposefully as the stage at the Infernal Centre on opening night.

"Quite a sight, no?"

Tim turned to see Ludwig approaching from the stairs. He was wearing a red dressing gown and puffing on a gold-plated vape, the smell of which reminded Tim of wolfsbane. Was Ludwig a werewolf? It was hard to tell, as he was wearing blue-tinted glasses. There was nothing about it in the policy file, but that didn't mean much. A lot of people just assumed that the standard spectral liability covered werewolf damage, but it did not. They needed to get the Lupine Liability Extension to pay for any damage or injury they caused while in such a feral state.

"Very…artistic," Tim said, not sure how else to respond.

"Ozzy was once a great dancer," Ludwig said, sending out a reddish black cloud that hung in the air around his head. "Lead dancer of the Bacchana Company, back before it was bought out by that tribe of godforsaken, nouveau riche bloodsuckers."

Tim was aware that the bloodsuckers Ludwig was referring to was a small group of ultrarich vampires with luxury penthouses in The Neck. They had been steadily expanding their presence in high society circles over the last half century by financing various exhibits and performances at the city's premiere museums and concert halls. This had generated much anger among the waning human dynastic classes, who resented their loss of societal dominance. Since he didn't move in those circles, however, it wasn't something that Tim felt like he was in a position to comment on.

"Is she even aware that we're here?" Tim asked.

"Oh no," Ludwig chuckled. "No clue. The PPSD, you know. Exorcists said it was one of the worst cases ever documented."

Tim had never heard of uncontrollable ballet dancing being listed as one of the side effects of chronic PPSD, but he wasn't an expert on the subject. He was familiar with the more standard ones, like paradermal hematoma (demons loved leaving behind nasty messages on the skin) and green projectile vomiting. The more serious ones included uncontrollable levitation and spontaneous *spectrasubcutanic infuria*, where the victim literally erupted in Hellfire without warning. Most aftereffects lasted only a day or two, but Tim had read about edge cases where victims experienced them for months and even years afterwards.

"So she's been dancing like this for 20 years?" Tim said incredulously.

"Oh hell no!" Ludwig said, almost choking on his own smoke. "For 23 hours of the day she sits totally catatonic in her wheelchair or in bed.

Totally unresponsive. About as self-aware as the furniture. It was only a little while ago that we discovered…this." He gestured to the dancing woman. "Totally by accident."

"By accident?" Tim repeated.

"Yes," Ludwig said. "Ug had wheeled old Ozzy upstairs for midday brunch when father decided to put on some music for a change. Next thing we all knew, she had hopped out of her chair and was flying around the room like a succubus on Narlune."

"Anytime she hears music?" Tim asked.

"Not just any music," Ludwig said. "We tried a few different things and It seems she only dances to the *Necronomicon*. Specifically act two, scene six. *The Psychopomp*."

"Really," Tim said, still not sure if this was some sort of elaborate practical joke.

"Yep," Ludwig said. "Doesn't seem to care if it's the Gezwurdhardt or Bellinari recording, though. Anything else, she just sits there like a stump. Tried almost everything else in the family library. Not a twitch."

"Amazing," Tim said.

"Her exorcist thinks there must be something about that particular piece," Ludwig said. "Triggers a deep, lizard brain muscle memory of some sort. She probably danced to it when she was young. Ah, here comes the grand finale."

The three of them watched as the dancing woman flittered up the stairs and then launched herself into the air, somersaulting backwards down them one by one. Once she reached the bottom, she rose up to complete a graceful pirouette and then bowed as the music swelled and finally stopped.

Tim felt an almost overpowering urge to clap, but suppressed it as Ugathia shuffled over and helped the now limp woman back into her nearby wheelchair. It was a sad thing to watch. It reminded Tim of a marionette that was hung on a hook at the end of a performance.

"So what can we do for you?" Ludwig said, doing nothing to help as the zombie maid lifted his mother back into the chair. "You've brought the cheque I assume?"

"Not quite yet," Tim said. "I need to inspect the safe and do an inventory of all the insured items covered under your policy to make sure nothing else is missing. Then I'll need to interview everyone who was present at the time the object was taken."

"Right," Ludwig said. "Well, I can show you the collections room and the safe. As far as the interviews go, it's pretty much just me, I'm afraid. My sister Lucretia was in her crypt at the time. As I said before, she never pokes her pasty face out during daylight hours. You won't get much out of dear Ozzy, as you can see. Or Ug, for that matter, unless you speak in grunts."

"I have software that can translate back and forth between Unghurr," Tim said. "I believe your younger brother Ludovico was also here when the box was taken?"

"Ye-es," Ludwig said. "Unfortunately, Vic is in rather a similar boat to Oz."

"Unresponsive?" Tim asked.

"Not quite," Ludwig said with the air of a man measuring his words carefully. "In his case, the aftereffects were somewhat more unpredictable and, er, violent. I'm afraid he's been required to remain permanently confined to his room for his safety and that of others."

"How long?" Tim asked.

"Since birth, I'm afraid," Ludwig shrugged.

Tim couldn't believe this. What kind of family would lock their child in his room for 20 years?

"What about a clinic?" Tim asked. "The Crowley or…"

"None of them would take him," Ludwig cut him off. "And besides, father refused. Didn't want to make the family's private shame a matter of public record, he said."

"Has he ever attacked anyone?" Tim asked.

"Not with anything that could be described as intent," Ludwig said. "We try to look after him as humanely as possible."

Ludwig's tone gave Tim an ominous feeling, but he reminded himself that the investigation was his first priority. He was here on behalf of an insurance company, not Family and Children's Services.

"Okay," Tim said. "Well, let's start with the safe and go from there."

"Of course," Ludwig said, gesturing for Tim to follow. "This way."

The two of them walked around behind the main staircase to a large pair of silver doors that looked like they led to a closet or pantry. Ludwig paused next to the door to type a six-digit code into a keypad on the wall. The keypad flashed green and the door slid open, revealing not a room or a hallway but an elevator.

"The safe is in a separate room underneath the main collection," Ludwig said, motioning for Tim to step into the elevator first. It was larger than a standard passenger elevator. Tim reckoned he could easily park his car in the space and get in and out without hitting the door on the wall. That made sense considering this was probably the primary route to move large artefacts in and out of the family collection. Tim had read through the schedule of insured items the night before and knew that some of them were much bigger than the missing Puzzle Box.

"How many people have the keycode for the elevator?" Tim asked.

"Just the immediate family," Ludwig said as he stepped inside and the doors slid silently shut. "Myself, my sister. Ug goes down there to clean, of course. And father."

"No one else?" Tim said.

"I suppose Ozzy might have known it once upon a time," Ludwig shrugged. "But no one would ever get it out of her now."

"You don't change the code regularly?" Tim asked. It was buried in the policy documentation that the insured agreed to maintain basic security protocols, which included changing the access codes on all secured entrances and storage units at least once a month. He knew that this was a nitpicky point. The company would never actually deny a claim on that basis, mostly because they would never be able to legally prove that a client had failed to do it. It also wasn't great publicity to develop a reputation for denying claims on such a flimsy pretext. About the only way a client could run into trouble would be if they voluntarily and knowingly handed the code over to the thieves. That was surprisingly common in cases of claims fraud, where clients would partner up with a third party who would commit the actual theft.

"Oh no, father changed the code about every month," Ludwig said, smiling in a way that gave Tim the distinct impression that he had just finished reading his client policy documentation carefully. "Ozzy is just so completely unaware that you could tattoo the numbers on the inside of her eyelids and she wouldn't know any more about it than she does what day of the week it is or what she had for dinner last night."

"Anyone else?" Tim asked.

"No," Ludwig said. "He didn't dare tell Ludovico. The way his mind works, there's no telling how the information might find its way out."

"And what about the rest of the security system?" Tim asked. "Cameras? Motion sensors?"

"That was one of the first things the police asked about," Ludwig said. "The cameras are all on the outside of the house. Father didn't trust having them anywhere within the walls. He was convinced somebody would hack into them and spy on him while he was working."

"I see," said Tim. His active hypothesis was that the theft of the Puzzle Box was most likely an inside job. The theft had been committed either by a member of the family acting alone or in collaboration with an outside third party who could provide ostensible cover for a fake break and enter. It was a lot easier to steal the family jewels when you already had the key to the safe.

Based on his disappearance, Lucifer was the most likely suspect, but that didn't rule out the involvement of any of the kids or the maid. It was also possible that Ozymandia was faking her condition, so she couldn't be ruled out, either. By reporting the box stolen, the family would be able to collect 100% of its listed value from the insurance as well as whatever cut they might get from any subsequent sale, which would put them well ahead of where they started, financially.

Assuming they didn't get caught, of course.

The elevator doors opened to reveal almost total darkness. Ludwig stepped out and waved, causing motion-sensing overhead lights to flick on, each one spotlighting a different artefact.

"Hardly anyone ever comes down here," Ludwig said. "Until yesterday, I don't think I'd even been down here in at least five years."

Ludwig continued through the room, waving his arms disinterestedly over his head like a minimum-wage summer student playing a ghost at a roadside haunted house. Tim recognized many of the items on pedestals and displayed behind spectre-proof glass from the Scheduled Personal Items list in the file.

There was the disarticulated skeleton of Gregorovich Poliokovsky, whose organs and muscles had swelled so badly during his possession by the demon Oxzlthet that he had lived the rest of his life with the unfortunate nickname of Balloon Boy. Next to that was the onyx skull of the Magda, which was used as an initiation rite for the 12th century cult known as the Brotherhood of the Broken Blood. Prospective members were forced to wear the skull while having sex with what they were told was a succubus named Huxt but were later informed was actually a goat carcass. Not surprisingly, this did not do much for their recruitment efforts and the cult died out.

Tim continued along, spotting the infamous portrait of Johannes Volk. A series of unfortunate coincidences involving previous owners had caused some to speculate that the painting was haunted, but a forensic examination had revealed that it was just a really ugly painting. He also saw the resurrection cabinet of Dr. Eusebio de la Fantasma, which only brought the dead back to life for long enough for them to sign over all their worldly assets to the notorious Spanish con man. Next to that was the mummy of prince Akamunset the third, who was best known for breaking out of his sarcophagus and attempting to strangle an entire 8th grade class on a field trip, something the lumbering long-dead pharoah might have been able to pull off had one of the supervising teachers not crushed his skull with a nearby fire extinguisher.

"Wow," Tim said. "Why didn't you ever send any of these out for public exhibition? I'm sure people would have lined up around the block to see some of this stuff."

"I suggested it many times," Ludwig said. "Father always refused. Said it would trivialize their scholarly importance. Whatever the hell that means."

Ludwig did not mutter the last sentence under his breath, which made Tim wonder just how harmonious things were in the Hesselthorn household prior to Lucifer's disappearance. Tim's research on Ludwig showed a long trail of failed business ventures, some more outlandish than others. Ludwig had tried his hand at crypto currency, real estate, exotic creatures and medical technology over the years. Ludwig had even called himself a movie producer at one point, although the movie he was associated with–a musical biopic of adult actress-slash-spy Chestity Bon-exx–had never been made.

Ludwig reached the end of the room and entered the code on a key-pad next to a large demonite door. The door rumbled open to reveal a clear spectraglass partition, on the other side of which was a crumbling stone well that rose up from in the floor.

A pale, claw-like hand with ragged black fingernails rose up out of the well and grabbed the edge, gripping the stone so firmly that it looked like it might crumble. It was followed by a wet clump of stringy black hair and a skeletal face with sunken eyes and a mouth hanging wide open in a permanent scream. The creature's skin looked like rotten cheese and it was wearing a ripped white hospital gown. It rose up out of the well one painful step at a time, its joints grotesquely disarticulated and moving with the herky-jerky motion of a remote control spider.

Once out of the well, the thing plastered itself against the window and let out a horrific scream. The sound generated no natural echo, travelling straight through everything in the room.

Tim shivered and took an involuntary step back. The creature was an Akumamizu, an extremely powerful type of demon found in cursed bogs, lakes and, in some cases, even swimming pools. Just as some demons could create Hellfire, the Akumamizu turned any body of water it inhabited into the liquid equivalent of the same. The scientific name for liquid Hellfire was *gelidospectranate*. Anyone getting too close would quickly find themselves pulled below the surface, where they would suffer all the physical sensations of being instantaneously burned up and frozen solid but without the release of actual death.

"Wow," Tim gasped. He had never seen an Akumamizu outside of a textbook and the few photos that existed did not really communicate just how unsettling the demon's movements and sounds truly were.

"Pretty cool, no?" Ludwig said, smiling. "Only one of its kind in the world!"

Tim knew that the well that housed the demon was not, in reality, a well. At least, not strictly speaking. It was, in fact, a safe. Despite Ludwig's claim, Tim knew there were at least two other secured storage vaults like this one in existence. One belonged to the notorious Hellspawn Triad underboss Gozo Gormaw, who supposedly used it to store his collection of celebrity cadavers. The other one belonged to a Russian casino owner who, according to rumour, used it for his extensive collection of demon sex robots.

The safe was a marvel of simplicity. The demon was conditioned to respond only to the designated owner. The owner would command the demon to take or retrieve any item they wished to keep safe down in the well. If anyone else tried to access it, the demon would take them down instead. Although technically a relation of the water variant of demonic elementals, the Akumamizu did not share their vulnerabilities to opposing powers. It could not be weakened by fire in the same way as a water Djinn, for example. If the creature escaped, there was almost no limit to the damage it could do.

With metre-thick demonite walls that were reinforced with an unbreakable curse, no amount of explosives or drilling would penetrate the safe's exterior. Like the house that contained it, the safe itself was a transdimensional field generator, which meant that its storage capacity was, in theory, infinite. The safe was rare largely because it was unlikely that anyone would have anything to store in it that cost more than the safe itself.

"So who in the family had access?" Tim asked, taking a couple of cautious steps forward.

"Just the old man," Ludwig said. "He warned me, on threat of disinheritance, to never, ever, under any circumstances, enter the collections room and attempt to access the safe. Which naturally only made me rush down here at the first opportunity. Saggy here gave me nightmares for months."

"Saggy?" Tim asked.

"It's what I call her," Ludwig said. "Bit of a long story, I'm afraid. Named after an old ex-girlfriend of mine. She tried to drain me of all my money and lifeforce, so it seemed appro at the time."

"I see," Tim said. His opinion of Ludwig was shifting in inverse proportion to the time he spent with him. A little more digging would probably reveal whether or not Ludwig had a drug or gambling problem. Either one would immediately move him up to top spot on the suspect list.

Tim opened his SIU bag, took out the SpectraVision attachment and clipped it on to the front of his glasses. He then got out his cell phone and opened the company app, which would allow him to tune the spectrum display to a variety of different frequencies. He started with standard IS, which would show any active sources of spectral emanation.

Other than the demon, the room was surprisingly clean. If anything supernatural had come and gone, it had left no visible trace of itself. The only thing showing the faintest hint of spectral energy was Akamunset, but even that wasn't much. The late prince of Egypt had evidently lost most of his mojo after his grade school misadventure.

Tim swiped his thumb on the phone screen to dial the filter up to UHIS and did another sweep of the room. This would pick up any older trace signs of low-frequency supernatural presence. It was standard procedure to start with IS before moving up to UHIS to avoid blowout. If a demon or ghost had walked down this same hallway admiring the exhibits, Tim might be able to see trace foot- or hoofprints where it had stepped or reached out to touch things. In reality, most of those traces disappeared after as little as 15 minutes, but he needed to check as a matter of protocol. Nothing in the main hall was lighting up.

Tim knew the Puzzle Box wasn't anywhere in the room because it had a pair of special Crimson Seal tracker tags attached to it, The tags were ID units with micro transmitters that could be used to track just about anything. Every high-value scheduled item had one. The ones attached to the missing Puzzle Box were the most advanced type available. They could be used to locate the box anywhere on the planet with an accuracy of plus or minus 2 microns. If even the temperature around the box dropped by so much as a tenth of a degree, the tag would register and, if programmed to do so, trigger a notification to the Crimson Seal asset security department instantly. The tag was practically indestructible and couldn't be removed by anyone other than a Crimson Seal technician.

As far as the Puzzle Box was concerned, that should have made finding it no problem. Tracking records, however, showed that the box had been removed from the safe and then immediately disappeared. None of the safe alarms had been triggered, which to Tim meant that whoever had removed it had been authorised to do so. Since the signal had immediately dropped off, Tim was also fairly certain that the Puzzle Box had been placed in a Croatoan Cage, a specially insulated container that would prevent it from sending or receiving signals of any kind. If the box did pop up anywhere, however, an alert would be triggered on his cellphone and Tim would know where it was within seconds.

The lack of evidence to suggest a break-in and his recent disappearance made Tim fairly certain that Lucifer Hesselthorn had removed the box and disappeared with it. The only questions to be answered were why he had done it and where he had gone. Tim doubted that the safe would provide many answers, but he needed to check it anyway.

Tim knelt down next to the service panel and plugged his laptop into the secondary service port. This would not allow him to activate or deactivate the safe, but it would give him access to transaction and diagnostic data. According to what he could see, the safe was in perfect working order despite the fact that it hadn't been serviced in almost 18 years. Although these models were guaranteed for life, it was a good idea to stick to the bi-annual service schedule in order ensure that the curse hardware keeping the Akumamizu in check didn't fail. If that happened, the creature could get out, and they weren't known to look fondly on the puny humans who kept them locked up in service industry purgatory.

A quick check of the activity logs showed that the safe had been accessed by an authorized user 27 hours and 46 minutes ago. The log did not identify the user, but Lucifer was the only one registered. The contents of the safe had been removed and another item was placed in the safe three minutes later.

"Do you keep anything else in the safe?" Tim asked.

"Not that I know of," Ludwig said. "Why?"

"The safe shows one item stored down there," Tim said. "But it's not the Puzzle Box or anything else on the scheduled articles list."

"Huh," Ludwig said, his face twisting into a confused expression. "No idea what that could be."

"The police didn't tell you this?" Tim asked.

"No," Ludwig said. "Horatio didn't even look at the safe."

Tim stopped. "Excuse me?"

"Nope," Ludwig said. "Not once."

Tim wondered if Ludwig was putting him on. His sense was that the middle Hesselthorn child was telling the truth.

"So you're telling me that your house was broken into and one of the most valuable items in the entire world was removed from this safe and the lead detective on the case didn't even bother to look at it?"

"I thought it was odd, too," Ludwig said. "He spent most of his time with Ozzy."

"Your mother?" Tim said. "Doing what?"

"Communing, I suppose," Ludwig said, making a swirling motion next to his forehead. "Not much point in that, though. You might as well try to read a rock. There's nobody home."

Tim considered this. What on earth was Duluc doing? The guy was a legend, so he must be on to something. Was Ozymandia not what she appeared to be? Did she know something that only a psychic could get out of her?

Tim did not have psychic abilities, but the company had lots of them on contract that he could call in if needed. He made a mental note to talk to Volkerps about scheduling a consult. The family was not obligated to undergo psychic examination–that would be a violation of the statutory conditions–but since they had already requested a famed psychic detective to investigate, they probably wouldn't object.

"Is anything else missing?" Tim asked. "Any household items or any other part of the collection?"

"Not that I know of," Ludwig said, scratching his head. "The safe doesn't tell you?"

"No," Tim said. "Only that something new was added."

"Maybe it's the box!" Ludwig said.

"Unlikely," Tim said. "The tracker shows that the box was removed before it dropped off the scanners."

"Maybe the scanners stopped working," Ludwig said.

"Unlikely," Tim said. Functional redundancy was the reason there were two trackers attached to the Puzzle Box. That way, if one stopped working, there was always a backup. The tracking system showed that both had gone silent at precisely the same time, right down to the millionth of a second.

"Or maybe somebody removed it?" Ludwig suggested.

"Also unlikely," Tim said. Unfortunately, without an authorised individual who could open the safe, there was no way to know what might be down there. "Was your father the only person in the family with access to the safe?"

"As far as I know," Ludwig said.

"It's usually recommended to have another party with access to act as a backup in the event of unexpected events or accidents," Tim said. "Are you aware of any such party?"

"No," Ludwig said. "I mean, it's probably in the old man's will. I talked to the lawyer yesterday, but we can't actually unseal it without a death certificate or at least a declaration. Which she said could take *five years* if they don't find his body."

"Right," Tim said. The emotional impact of his father's disappearance didn't exactly appear to be taking a devastating toll on the son. "Hopefully it won't come to that."

Tim wasn't able to read all of the safe data. Some of it appeared to have become corrupted, or was somehow encrypted with a security protocol that he had never seen before. He downloaded the scrambled data and made a note to send it to the trolls in IT. Maybe they would be able to make something of it. He didn't like dealing with IT. Most of them would rather turn to stone than deal with end users. Not that it would have any effect on their responsiveness.

"You're sure there are no security cameras for the vault?" Tim asked.

"Positive," Ludwig said. "Unless the old man had them and he never told us about it. Cameras don't really work in a TOP, from what I've heard."

"I've heard that too," Tim muttered. There wasn't a lot of information on the subject since there were so few trans-dimensional buildings that were used as living spaces.

"So how long before we get the payout for the box?" Ludwig said, trying to sound innocuous. "Day or two maybe?"

"Once I've completed my investigation and filed my report," Tim said. "First, I'm going to need to interview all of the relevant parties."

"Well, that'll be easy!" Ludwig said, raising his arms like a game show host introducing a new segment. "You're already talking to them."

"Sorry?" Tim said.

"It's just that nobody else in the family is in any kind of position to really tell you anything," Ludwig said. "Ozzy's about as self-aware as an umbrella stand. If you get a single word out of her, you'd be the first person in 20 years to manage it. It would be a miracle of parapsychology! Ug doesn't speak a word of English. Barely even seem to understand it, either, aside from a few rudimentary commands. I ask her to make me a martini and she'll come back with a hard boiled egg and a bottle of disinfectant! Useless, really. But she's been with us for years and she's so used to Ozzy's needs and habits that we just can't get rid of her now. Lucretia was slumbering away in her crypt as usual. And Vic was in his room. I'm afraid none of them will be able to tell you much of anything."

"Be that as it may," Tim said. "It's procedure."

"Of course," Ludwig shrugged. "Horatio said that the solution to the puzzle was right under our noses."

"Oh really?" Tim asked, thinking that the solution might not be quite that close, but was probably within the grounds and possibly even inside the room.

"Yes," Ludwig said. "Man is brilliant. I have no doubt he'll find the missing box before the end of the week. And the old man, too."

Tim spent several more hours at the house. He double-checked the security system. As Ludwig had said, the cameras were all external. There were six cameras altogether. Five of them covered the areas immediately around the house while a sixth was trained on the driveway just inside the main gate. Backing them up to the time of the theft showed no one entering or leaving the property. The coverage did not appear to be comprehensive, however. Tim was pretty sure there were slight gaps in the northeast and southwest corners.

It was possible that somebody could have snuck up to the house from those directions, Tim thought, but they would have to make their way through a thick growth of Bloodoak trees to do it. Not many would be keen to crawl through a tangle of bloodthirsty vegetation, and even if they did, they would still need to find a way into the house, which would be difficult as all the doors and windows were covered by cameras.

Although Tim knew it was too early to rule out a third party, the absence of external invaders on the surveillance strongly reinforced his belief that the theft was committed by somebody who was already inside the house.

After that, Tim had moved on to the formal interviews, which he recorded. Ludwig claimed that he had been in his private office in a separate wing of the building working on a funding proposal for some sort of holographic crystal ball. Tim had made the mistake of asking what that was about and had been treated to a 20-minute pitch about how HoloBall was going to completely disrupt the entire psycho-services sector.

Once Tim managed to steer him back on the subject of the theft. Ludwig said he had no idea anything was amiss until he went downstairs for dinner and his father wasn't there. He had then gone to his father's room and found his father not there, either.

"To tell the truth, I didn't even suspect that it had anything to do with the Puzzle Box at first," Ludwig said. "My first worry was that Vic might have escaped, but when I checked, he was still in his room, thank Belial!"

It was only after ensuring that his brother was not out and roaming the house that Ludwig had thought to go and check the vault, where he found that the Puzzle Box was gone. That was when he had called the police and notified Crimson Seal. Having already checked the call log, Tim knew that Ludwig had called Crimson Seal first, which was interesting. Most fire extinguishers did not have instructions that read IN CASE OF FIRE, CALL CUSTOMER SERVICE printed on the front because that was not usually somebody's first instinct in an emergency.

"Honestly, the vault is just not a room that anyone in the house ever goes into," Ludwig said. "Father sometimes goes down there to look at some of his old relics, but that's it."

Tim had to be careful about how he broached one key element of the discussion and tried to do it as tactfully as possible.

"It seems that the family doesn't have quite the resources that it used to," Tim said. "Did you ever consider selling any of the artefacts at any point? There certainly wouldn't be any shortage of potential buyers."

If Ludwig was insulted by this line of inquiry, he did a good job of hiding it.

"The old man absolutely refused to even consider the idea of selling anything," Ludwig said, shaking his head to indicate that this was a topic of conversation that he had raised many times with his father in the past. "Especially the Puzzle Box. He said it was far too dangerous to ever allow it out into the world. I thought he was crazy. I mean, it's just a box, right?"

Tim knew that there were no real pictures of the Puzzle Box anywhere. Acheronium emitted far too much spectral radiation to be photographed by even the most advanced cameras, which showed either a giant red blob of distortion or nothing at all. There were a few drawings of it, but they were little more than sketches made at the time it had been recovered. Based on those, the box looked like a red crystal ball engraved with hundreds of rune-like letters and shapes. That was the only image that Crimson Seal had in the scheduled item attachments, at least.

After Ludwig, Tim had tried to interview his older sister, Lucretia. But, as Ludwig had warned, she was locked away in her private crypt and refused to answer when he pressed the buzzer.

"If you want to talk to her, you'll need to do it at thVrst," Ludwig said.

Tim had heard of thVrst. It was a private and highly exclusive vampire club in the Neck that was open from sundown to sunrise every night except for Tuesdays, when it closed to run decoagulant through the pipes supplying blood to the sauna and spa areas. All of the richest and most glamorous vampires in the city went there. Werewolves, demons, zombies and other spectral beings were not allowed. Humans were allowed in only if they were willing to become part of the menu, which rotated seasonally (summer was Greeks and Italians).

"But you said she's not actually a vampire, right?" Tim said.

"Right," Ludwig said. "But it's not for lack of trying. She's been begging father to pay for this new surgery that'll turn her into a vampire without actually being bitten. He would never agree."

Tim had heard of this new procedure. It was supposed to grant vampiric abilities but allow those who went through it to continue doing many of the things that ordinary humans took for granted, like going out in the daytime without bursting into flame or eating garlic bread without vomiting a geyser of arterial blood. It was only available from a private clinic in Switzerland and was reputed to be obscenely expensive. Tim did not know of anyone who had actually undergone the surgery, but there were no shortage of rumours in the tabloid press.

"So if she's not a vampire and she's not a victim, then how does she get into thVrst?" Tim asked.

"Beats me," Ludwig said. "But she's got her own private room."

Tim next tried to talk to the youngest sibling, Ludovico, but this too was a non-starter. When Ludwig said that his brother was "in his room" however, that didn't provide the full picture. Ludovico didn't have a room so much as a cell. The youngest Hesselthorn was locked in a secured spectral containment unit behind a door made of two solid feet of demonite with a tiny demonglass viewing portal no larger than a coaster.

"Is this really necessary?" Tim asked, peering through the glass. He could see a figure in what looked like a black prison jumpsuit sitting cross legged and floating about two feet off the ground in the middle of the room. Ludovico had long black straggly hair and a thick beard covering his face. His claw-like hands swept back and forth through the air like someone in the midst of a prolonged hallucinogenic experience.

"Unfortunately," Ludwig said. "He really should be in the secured possession wing at the Crowley or even Xanadu, but father refused, so we built this special room for him here at the house."

As Tim watched, the figure disappeared and suddenly reappeared right in front of the door, screaming and shooting red bolts out of his eyes. Tim jumped back in surprise. He had seen many people in various stages of possession before, but nothing quite like this.

"Whoa," Tim gasped. "How long has he been like this?"

"His whole life," Ludwig shrugged. "We've had him seen by the best exorcists there are, but none of them can do anything for him. Most of them won't even set foot in the same room. The last one took one look at him and fainted right where you're standing."

Tim risked another glance through the window. Ludovico had gone back to floating in the middle of the room.

"Incredible," he gasped.

"Still want to talk to him?" Ludwig said. "I can punch in the code and let you in if that's what you want."

Tim decided against it. Instead, he spent five minutes posing questions to the mute Ozymandia, who simply stared back vacantly from the confines of her wheelchair. She gave no indication that she was aware of him or anyone else in the room. Tim knew the only way to even begin to get any possible answers out of her would be to hook her up to an SNA machine (aka a spectraneuroanalyzer) and try pulling the answers directly out of whatever part of her brain might still be working, but he didn't have immediate access to that kind of equipment.

The maid, Ugathia, was his last option. He had a translation app on his laptop that could take his questions and convert them to Unghurr and then do the same with her answers, but it didn't seem to be working. Either she was speaking in some exotic zombie dialect or the program just didn't work. Unless of course the words "elbow grater command prize" had some secret meaning beyond his comprehension.

Tim continued with the questions for about 20 fruitless minutes before packing up his laptop and calling it a day. He thanked Ludwig for his time and promised that he would be in touch.

"Don't forget the cheque next time!" Ludwig said as Tim put on his jacket. Tim again promised that the claim would be processed just as soon as the investigation was concluded.

"Good luck with Lucy," Ludwig had said. "She might not be a real vampire, but that doesn't mean that she doesn't have a taste for the red stuff."

Tim wasn't sure what Ludwig meant by that and decided not to ask. The Hesselthorns were easily the most unusual family he had ever encountered, so he had no reason to suspect that the oldest sister would be any different. Tim checked his phone as he walked down the driveway to his car. Volkerps had called three times looking for updates on the investigation, of which there were none to report.

Tim's mother had also called to remind him to wear his best suit to his father's company dinner later that evening. Tim groaned inwardly. How had he allowed himself to be talked into having his first date with Madeline be at a family event? He did not claim to have Madeline's psychic abilities, but he did not believe it was a decision that portended good omens for anyone involved.

7

As it turned out, Tim wasn't able to wear his best suit because Claw-fist had peed on it. At least, he hoped that it was Clawfist. With Keef and Killian turning the apartment into a makeshift production office, there were so many people and creatures cycling through the place that it was hard to keep track.

Tim raced to his closet and pulled out a dark blue suit that he hadn't worn since he interviewed for the SIU job. It was a little tight–he had gained weight since Tabitha left, mostly because he'd gotten out of the habit of going to the gym and into the habit of sitting on the couch eating junk food and watching *Real Vampire Brides of Hollywood* with Keef–but it would have to do. Once he had showered, shaved and made some sort of attempt to do something with his hair, he knocked once and stumbled into the darkness of his brother's room. He felt around in the candlelit darkness and found the lid of Keef's coffin, which he yanked open to find Killian chatting on one cell phone while typing out a text message on another.

"Finally!" Killian barked, not even looking up. "I thought I ordered a wake up call for one minute after sunset! What the hell time is it? Make yourself useful and get me a cafe sangre, would ya? Heavy on the froth."

"Ugh," Tim said, closing the lid and turning to find the coffin that his brother was in. It was further back next to the window.

"I'm not going!" Keef grunted. His eyes were more bloodshot than usual and his cheeks were covered with red crumbs. "You can't make me!"

"Arise, already!" Tim snapped. "Or I'll call mom. You look terrible, by the way."

"I'm undead!" Keef said, climbing out. "How else am I supposed to look?"

"What's he doing in here?" Tim asked, pointing at the other coffin in which Killian could still be heard issuing muffled orders to whomever was on the other end of both of his phone conversations.

"He wanted to get used to the lifestyle," Keef said. "But I swear the guy only sleeps for like, 20 minutes a day. It's been a tough adjustment."

"Is he paying rent?" Tim asked.

"No," Keef said. "But he did get me a commercial!"

"A commercial?" Tim said. "For what?"

"For *Scabs!*" Keef said. "They're rolling out this new tainted blood flavour. I'm going to be the face of the campaign!"

"Well, I guess that makes sense based on how many bags of them you eat in a week," Tim said. "And the fact that you look kind of tainted yourself."

"They sent me three whole boxes as part of the deal!" Keef said. "But that stupid demon of yours pissed on two of them."

"He's not my demon," Tim said, thinking that Clawfist's destruction of two of the boxes meant that the creature did actually have a positive side, as it would mean fewer sticky red crumbs accumulating between the couch cushions. "He's just another presence in this apartment that, for one reason or another, I can't seem to banish."

"Just you wait," Keef said. "As soon as I land my first big movie role, you'll be begging to be part of my infernal entourage."

"Uh huh," Tim said. "You look like you just woke up in the alley behind a blood bank, so you might want to brush the crumbs off your shirt before you pose for your head shots."

He pushed Keef towards the closet, where he grudgingly began pulling on a pair of ripped leather pants and a cape.

"Why do we have to go to this thing?" Keef moaned. "We haven't worked for dad's stupid extermination business in years. All of his staff are creepy, antisocial weirdos who live in their parents' basements and spend too much time in Infernachat conspiracy threads about how the government is sneaking wolfsbane into the water supply. I hate it."

Tim thought the complaint about a creepy weirdo who lived in a relative's house was a bit rich coming from Keef, but that didn't mean it wasn't true. Most of the employees of Thad's Supernatural Remediation Services *were* creepy weirdos. It took a certain kind of person to make a career out of crawling through dank basements and haunted attics looking for poltergeists and demons. They were not the kind of person you usually wanted to spend your Friday night with.

"We have to be there," Tim said. "Dad's making some big announcement about something. He insisted we be there."

Tim had no idea what the big mystery announcement was about. Normally his parents were incapable of keeping the lid on any kind of big news, but he had been unable to pry this latest one out of either of them. That meant that it had to be big, but what? His father was still too young to retire. As much as his mother complained about the stink of industrial-strength Demonex on the furniture, she would undoubtedly complain even more if Thad packed it in to spend more time around the house. Regina was actively expanding her psychic spa business, so she wasn't stepping down anytime soon, either.

"I'd rather they just send me an email," Keef said peevishly, switching the cape he was wearing for one with a bright scarlet lining. "Unless he's selling it and giving me my inheritance early, I don't need to know."

"Maybe he is," Tim said. "At least it's only once a year. Now hurry up! We have to pick up Madeline in ten minutes."

"Oh right!" Keef said, his eyes narrowing in a predatory way. "The new girlfriend!"

"She is *not* my girlfriend," Tim said. "She just works at the supply shop upstairs from SIU, that's all. It's sort of a date, I guess."

"And you decided to ask her to the annual dinner for dad's ghost roach business for your first date?" Keef said incredulously. "You thought a romantic evening spent surrounded by the ectoplasm-encrusted dregs of society would really impress her, did you? Smooth one, Casanova. Where are you gonna go for date number two? Maybe take her to one of your sexy risk management conventions? Or you could throw caution right to the wind and opt for the sensual bacchanalia of a zoning committee meeting the next time the Decameron's historical designation is up for review. You naughty boy."

"I didn't actually plan to invite her to the employee dinner," Tim said. "She kind of asked me out and sort of insisted that it had to be Friday because she'd had a psychic vision that that's what we were going to do."

"A what?" Keef said, his smile growing even wider.

"Nothing," Tim said, aware that he had already said too much. "Could you just pick a cape already? We're going to be late."

"Wait!" Keef said, closing his eyes and putting a hand theatrically to his forehead. "I'm having a vision of my own! I can see it so clearly!"

"Just shut up and get dressed, would you?" Tim said.

"I see a man," Keef said. "A very boring man with tiny genitals! He is a man with great power! The power to instantly repel all women of breeding age who come within 100 yards of his presence!"

"Breeding age?" Tim said.

"His very existence makes their ovaries shrivel and their libidos crumble like a vampire in the noonday sun!" Keef snickered.

"Are you by any chance talking about the same guy with the strange and mysterious power to toss your lazy, goldbricking ass out on the street?" Tim asked.

"Geez," Keef said, looking hurt. "No need to get personal."

Tim finally managed to get Keef dressed and into the car. By taking a few judicious short cuts, they arrived only five minutes later than he said he would at the front door of Madeline's apartment. They might have actually been on time, but a Hellhole had opened up at the intersection of Beelzebub Avenue and 665th street and they were forced to divert the long way around Repulsion Park by a city works crew.

"It's always the same in this part of town," Keef grumbled as Tim drove down a seldom-used maintenance path that ran through the park. On their right was the Lugosi Amphitheatre, which hadn't been used since a musical performance of *The Exorcist and Me* was cut short when the lead actor became legitimately possessed (instead of pretending to be) and started vomiting exploding organs onto his co-stars. "You can't get anywhere because of all the damn construction. And if it's not the construction, it's the friggin' protestors."

It was true that the Oubliette neighbourhood was a popular gathering spot for protestors. Rents were cheap and Beelzebub Avenue offered a straight shot downtown for marchers headed to city hall. The vampires only marched at night, so they were easy to avoid. Werewolf packs were too small and combative to organize on a large scale, so they were rarely a problem. The zombies were the ones you really had to avoid. They moved so slowly that it sometimes took them days to assemble and march the mile and a half to civic square carrying their largely illegible signs and placards.

"You look...great," Tim said as Madeline emerged. She was dressed in a spangly purple robe and what looked like a wizard's cap. He was pretty sure that he had told her the event was formal attire, but she evidently had a different definition for that than most people.

"Thanks!" she said. "I bought this for my sister's wedding last year. But then her fiancé ran off with his exorcist and I never got a chance to wear it."

Tim decided that he would ask about that later. Or maybe not at all. They headed for the car and he introduced Keef, who was sitting in the back seat.

"Sup?" Keef said, sticking his head out through the open window and smiling. "Nice threads."

Madeline stopped. "You're a vampire!" she gasped, eyes wide.

"Huh," Keef said, feeling his elongated canines. "I guess that would explain what happened to my teeth. And why I suddenly started drinking all that blood. And why I get those really bad sunburns no matter what level of SPF I'm wearing."

"You never told me that your brother was a vampire!" Madeline said, turning to Tim in an accusatory fashion.

"Uh, no," Tim said. There were a lot of things they hadn't talked about. "Is that a problem?"

Madeline tapped her foot and seemed to think for a minute. Tim had a strong feeling that this date was not getting off to a good start. Like a rocket failing to clear the launchpad, that did not usually bode well for those on board.

"Would you mind maybe moving to the front seat?" Madeline said. "I'd just feel a little more comfortable that way."

"Not at all," Keef said, getting out of the car and shooting Tim an angry look as he changed seats. Madeline took two large steps back, giving him a wide berth as he moved past. "After all, my whole reason for being is to make humans more comfortable with my existence."

"Thanks," Madeline said. She made a point of checking the back seat to make sure there were no other unpleasant surprises hiding back there before tentatively getting into the car and reluctantly pulling the door shut. It didn't really close the first time and Tim had to re-open it and close it again more firmly to make sure it didn't fly open en route. As he got into the driver's seat and checked the rearview before pulling out, he saw Madeline fumble in her purse and pull out a large silver crucifix.

"Okay," he said, trying to sound jovial. "This is going to be fun, right?"

The dinner was happening at Stoker's, an old-school steakhouse located on what used to be known as Bloodthirsty Row. The Row consisted of a block of mausoleum-style townhouses that had once housed some of the richest and most notorious vampires in the city before they decamped to the luxury black condo towers in the Neck. Stoker's had stubbornly refused to change its menu, décor or dress code requirements for more than 200 years, which probably explained why most of its regular patrons were only a few months shy of the century mark themselves. Their business was quite literally dying off, but the ownership either didn't care or intended to go into the ground with the same aura of decaying and slightly tacky elegance they had always espoused.

Thad had apparently been taken there by his own father when he had graduated from high school, an experience that had evidently left a permanent culinary mark. In Thad's mind, all office parties and family celebrations worth marking had to take place at Stoker's. Tim himself had been dragged there after graduating high school and would probably have been forced to go there after graduating university as well if Regina hadn't put her foot down and insisted Tim should be allowed to pick his own spot for once.

For Thad, Stoker's was a place of mystic rituals. He always wore the same suit, ordered the same meal (Cadaver Blue Ribeye with baked potato and mushrooms), had a snifter of the same brandy (Cushing '91), and smoked the same foul black Diabolo cigar. Regina insisted that it made his clothes smell worse than a double shift spent removing transient ghouls from a wastewater treatment facility, but Thad would not budge where his yearly traditions were concerned.

The place was as stale and tacky as an old wax museum, but Tim didn't begrudge his father his annual Stoker's fix. Thad didn't get many chances to feel like a high-rolling master of his domain, so there was no harm in granting the old man the indulgence at least one day a year.

Thad and Regina were standing in their customary spot near the door greeting people as they arrived. Thad was dressed in a tuxedo that was only one year older than Keef. The cuffs were worn thin and it was at least a size too small for Thad's expanding middle aged frame. With skin pale from days spent creeping around in dark spaces and his hair shellacked into place, Tim's father looked like a sickly, overweight kid on school picture day.

Regina, in sharp contrast, was wearing the latest Elsa Guignol designer dress, her hair styled in a glittering updo that made her appear at least 18 inches taller than she was. Tim could see she was wearing her best ruby necklace and matching brooch, her arm held out and wrist inclined just so as to ensure it was visible to everyone who walked in. As the proprietor of one of the most fashionable chains of psychic salons in the city, his mother firmly believed that she couldn't afford to be seen out in public looking anything less than spectacular, even for an audience as downmarket as her husband's employees.

"There are my boys!" Thad said, spotting them as they walked in. He shook Tim's hand and waved his smouldering cigar around the room at a cluster of tables occupied by mostly single men who shifted uncomfortably in cheap suits and regarded them warily. "Don't it look great? What a night!"

"What happened to your tuxedo?" Regina said, looking at Tim's suit like it was a plastic coroner's bib covered in entrails.

"Small accident back at the apartment," Tim said. He did not want to get into an explanation about how he had somehow inherited a tiny demon that loved nothing more than flying around peeing on things. "So what's this big announcement?"

"All in good time!" Thad said, grinning. "I'm savin' it for my speech!"

"Ah," Tim said. Thad's speeches were also something of an unfortunate company tradition. Thad always waited until after dinner, by which time he'd usually had at least four and often as many as a dozen brandys. This tended to make him think it was a good idea to try out some of what he liked to call his "classic standup" material. If this happened, it was imperative to cut off his microphone before he got to the succubus jokes (example: "How many succubuses does it take to screw in a lightbulb?" [Short pause to glance around the room with mouth open in anticipation while failing to notice that you are dropping cigar ash on your wife's dessert plate.] "Just two. But good luck getting 'em into the lightbulb!" [Laugh uproariously while failing to notice that your wife is now using her phone to call for a taxi.])

"And who is this?" Regina said, spotting Madeline. Her expression was uncomfortably similar to a large snake laying eyes on a sleeping hamster.

"This is Madeline," Tim said. "Madeline, these are my parents, Thad and Regina."

"Delightful to meet you!" Regina said, eyeing Madeline's necklace. "I see you're wearing the eye of Axznar! Are you by any chance a seer?"

"I am!" Madeline said. "I just graduated! My specialty is summoning. I love your spas by the way! I swear I must shop in the Seer near my apartment, like, every day!"

"How nice to meet a regular customer," Regina said. "Where are you working now?"

"Nowhere yet," Madeline said. "I was just working at Asgaroth's while I finished school. That's where I met Tim."

"How fortuitous!" Regina said. "I just opened a new shop in the Dungeon district! I'm always looking for good psychics. Especially ones with a talent for summoning the dead."

"That would be awesome!" Madeline said. "It's so strange. I had a premonition that something like this might happen!"

Tim saw Keef shoot him a look, the meaning of which was eminently clear to both of them.

"Oh, I like this one, Timothy!" Regina said. "So much better than that meter maid who dumped you!"

Tim smiled thinly. He was well past the point of continuing to correct his mother on his ex-girlfriend Tabitha's actual position within the police department. That did not mean that it didn't continue to irritate him just as much every time she did it.

"I heard you met Sticker Helsing!" Thad said to Tim. "You get his autograph? Or one of those phone picture things? Y'know, a self-me? Selfer? Is that what the kids call it?"

"I think the word you're looking for is dick pic," Keef said. "And yes, he did. It's true what they say about celebrities. They really are so much smaller in person than they look on TV!"

"Keefer!" snapped Regina.

"I *love* Sticker Helsing!" said Madeline, seeming to rise up off the ground and grabbing Tim's arm to keep herself earthbound.

"It's a 'selfie,'" Tim said. "And for the record, no, I did not."

"He's so handsome!" Madeline gushed. "I love the way he just tells it like it is. Not like those SNN phonies who are always complaining that we're not being nice enough to werewolves and satyrs. Uh, I'd rather be able to walk down the street in a city where I don't have to worry about being torn limb from limb or raped, thanks!"

"I work with a werewolf," Tim muttered. "And so far, all my limbs are still attached."

"It's just their nature," Madeline shrugged. "It's like Sticker says on his show: you can take the demon out of the pit, but you can't take the pit out of the demon."

"That guy is such a douchebag," Keef muttered.

"Keefer!" Regina snapped. "I will not tolerate such language on your father's special night!"

"Well he is," Keef said.

"I think he's a hero," Madeline said. "I heard a rumour he's gonna run for mayor!"

Tim groaned inwardly. Was it too late to fake a migraine or a work emergency and bolt? Probably.

"This is gonna be a big one!" Thad said, clapping his hands and steering the conversation back to the matter at hand. "Biggest thing that's happened since I started the business! I gotta tell ya, it's all down to Harry!"

"Who?" Keef asked.

"This guy I hired a few months ago," Thad said. "Best employee I've ever had!"

Tim and Keef exchanged a look.

"Dad," Tim said. "You remember that Keef and I both used to work for you, right?"

"Yeah, but this guy's incredible!" Thad said. "He's relentless! And totally fearless! He'll take on jobs that the other guys wouldn't touch if I paid them triple overtime!"

"I'm not insulted," Keef shrugged. "I used to sleep in the back of the truck. Unless I was using it for something else, of course. There was this one time I responded to a call at that pole dancing club in the Pitchfork? Manager was this super-hot succubus who couldn't afford to pay the removal fee, right? But they had this awesome bungee–"

"We've all heard this story, Keefer," Regina said, cutting him off. "No one needs to hear about your shameful sexual misdeeds."

"Maybe *you* don't," Keef grumbled. "Everyone else I know thinks it's awesome."

"Who is this Harry guy?" Tim asked, looking over his shoulder to do a quick scan of the restaurant. All he saw were the familiar faces of his father's senior staff, each one looking more wanton, pale and bedraggled than the next.

Tim recognized Bobby Borschardt, a 45-year-old college dropout who still lived in his mother's basement with a disquieting number of department store mannequins he bought directly from a manufacturer in Little Hades. Sitting next to Bobby was "Cannibal" Clive Halpern, a man who had been kicked out of the police academy after making his own nightstick out of a human femur. His explanation that the weapon had been ethically sourced apparently did not serve as a mitigating factor. Across from them was the familiar bald dome of Sadie Lachinglas, a former exorcist who spent her weekends fighting demons in an underground MMA circuit. She had been impaled, roasted, chewed and cursed so many times that she was mostly scar tissue by this point, although no one would dare say as much to her face.

"Yeah," Keef said. "I gotta meet this super exterminator."

"Should be here any…" Thad said, looking around the restaurant before breaking into a broad grin and pointing at the door. "Ah, there's my Monster Killer!"

Tim turned and felt his jaw drop open in surprise as a man with wraparound sunglasses and a black mohawk walked through the front door. The man was wearing a long black leather trench coat and carrying a green canvas backpack slung casually over his left shoulder. He had added a pair of large silver crucifix earrings and cross-shaped neck tattoos since Tim had last seen him, but was instantly recognizable nonetheless.

"Stake?" Tim said in disbelief.

"Oh no," Keef groaned. "Not this asshole."

"Everybody, this is Harry," Thad said as Stake approached. "Harry, this is–"

"Don't bother," Keef said. "I've met this dipshit already."

"Keefer!" Regina hissed. "You apologize immediately!"

"That's okay, Mrs. Lovecraft," Stake said, smiling. "I've met these guys before. Hey, Tim!"

"Hi Stake," Tim said, shaking Stake's hand. "How long have you been working for my father?"

Tim had first met Stake shortly after he started work in SIU. Back then, Stake had been working as a security guard by day while he prowled the streets as an amateur spectral vigilante by night. Stake saw it as his mission to rid the city of what he considered the horrific scourge of creeping supernatural evil–otherwise known as perfectly ordinary, law-abiding vampires, werewolves, demons and other non-humans.

Stake had started his own security company after inheriting money from a recently deceased relative, but that business had gone bankrupt after one of Stake's employees had been impersonated by a demon and murdered one of the city's most powerful money managers. The resulting flood of lawsuits and bad publicity had been more than Stake's fledgling business could stand, and he had been forced to shut down operations shortly after.

Tim had lost track of Stake after that. They weren't really friends in any official capacity. Stake was a deeply odd guy with some rigid beliefs about how humans and spectral beings should coexist. In Stake's mind, humans would only be able to live in harmony with supernatural beings if all of those supernatural beings were destroyed.

"A few months," Stake said. "Best job ever!"

"And you're the best employee I've ever had!" Thad said, coming over to pat Stake on the shoulder. "Tonight's big announcement is almost totally down to this guy right here."

"Sorry I'm late," Stake said. "I just wanted to stop by the Renfield Clinic on the way over to make sure they weren't having any more problems with those vampire scum breaking in to steal lab samples out of the basement refrigerators."

"Vampire what?" Keef said, tonguing one of his prominent canines.

"They were Baggers mostly," Stake said, using a common term to refer to black market blood dealers. "A sun bomb and a couple of garlic emitters did the trick."

"I love your earrings!" Madeline said. "And your tattoos! Where did you get them done? Stigmattack or Crypt Strips?"

"Thanks," Stake said. "Actually, no. A friend of mine in the Brotherhood has his own shop in the East Purg. Talismania. Got it there."

"Brotherhood?" Tim asked. "What brotherhood?"

"The Brotherhood of Light," Stake said. "We meet at least once a week at an undisclosed location. I'd invite you along, but It's kind of a members-only deal and they're real picky about who gets selected."

Tim groaned inwardly. The Brotherhood of Light was a group of bumbling anti-supernaturalists who believed that humanity needed to arm itself to fight the impending war they believed was coming between humans and non-human beings. Like most things, it had started as a discussion thread on InfernaChat and had rapidly mushroomed into a growing underground movement. No one knew exactly how long they had been around or how many of them there were. They had risen to national mockery around a year ago, when a small group of them had turned out to protest the opening of a Narlune clinic. One of them had brought a homemade garlic bomb that detonated unexpectedly in his backpack, covering himself and his fellow protestors in a cloud of foul-smelling toxic gas. A similar rally in front of city hall a few months later had seen eight of them force their way through a construction barricade and fall down a Hellhole from which they had to be rescued by emergency services. To Tim, it made perfect sense that Stake would join a group like that.

"I know all about them!" said Madeline. "My cousin's a member. He told me they wouldn't let me join because I was a woman."

"It can get rough out there on the front lines," Stake said, grabbing hold of his belt in a way that was supposed to look macho but really looked more like he was worried that his pants might suddenly fall down. "Wouldn't want an attractive lady such as yourself to be injured or disfigured in any way by some foul and evil beast of the night."

"Oh my!" Madeline giggled. "You are so brave!"

"Yeah," Keef said. "It takes guts to leave the house every day looking like that. Especially when you've got a baggie of wet dogshit where your brain should be."

"Keefer!" hissed Regina. "Apologize!"

They took their seats at the table. Tim, Madeline and Keef were seated with Stake and another employee named Lizzy Barker, who had worked as the company receptionist since Thad first opened. Lizzy was in her early 60s and quiet as a water demon–unless she'd had one too many brimstone and selzers, of course. When tipsy, Lizzie behaved like she was possessed by a satyr on spring break. The dinner hadn't started yet, but Tim could tell from Lizzy's ruddy cheeks and wobbly demeanor that she was only a few sips away from her annual bacchanal.

"Hello boys!" she said, drooling dark droplets on her décolletage. "Which one of you is coming home with me this year? I got my hoverbed fixed!"

She broke into a wheezing laugh punctuated by a loud belch. Tim tried to sit as far away from her as possible, but Keef and Stake cannily grabbed those chairs first.

"Hi Lizzy," Tim said, sitting down. "Having a good night?"

"I am now!" she said, grabbing Tim's leg under the table. "Why don't you buy me another fireball and soda? Your dad tells me you're single again, you poor baby. Tell Aunt Lizzy all about it!"

Much to Tim's relief, the food arrived a few minutes later. Stoker's didn't offer many options for non-humans, meaning Keef was limited to the soup.

"It's not even human blood," Keef grumped, pushing it away. "Maybe the bumpkins in the country don't mind sucking on cows, but I think I'll pass."

Stake spent most of the dinner talking about times he had nearly died on the job while Madeline gasped and shrieked and asked the same question over and over again.

"Were you scared?" she asked as Stake regaled them with the tale of his encounter with a banshee in the stock room of a party supply store. Stake had apparently lured it out using a whoopee cushion and then immobilized it by sticking a self-inflating werewolf balloon in its mouth.

"Can't afford to be scared in a job like this," Stake said, filling his own mouth with vast quantities of scalloped potatoes. "They should be afraid of me, to be honest."

"That is so cool!" Madline said. "Isn't that cool?"

"Very cool," Tim muttered. He was acutely aware that he and Madeline had barely said a word to each other since they arrived. As far as dates went, this was rapidly making its way into his all-time worst list. It was currently running just behind the dental hygienist who had turned out to be possessed by a Djinn. Tim had only realized the truth when the sommelier had approached their table to offer a wine recommendation and she had tried to remove one of his eyes with his own corkscrew.

Tim pushed away his half-eaten steak. It didn't matter how you asked them to cook anything in this place, it always came out extra-rare. Stoker's was the kind of place that believed that if it couldn't serve great food, it could at least make up for it by serving too much.

Once dinner was over, Thad got up to deliver his annual speech. It always started with jokes he had found online, evidently after having done a search for the remarks that had yielded the most human resources complaints of the last five years. ("Lady, if you're tired of finding naked men in your backyard, maybe you shouldn't hire werewolves to mow your lawn!") Regina had long ago made it abundantly clear that she had zero enthusiasm for his "disgusting" work stories at home, so he tended to save them all up for special occasions.

Next up were the awards. Stake won employee of the year, which Thad semi-jokingly suggested should be changed to "All Time" in light of his unrivalled dedication.

"What the hell is the deal with this guy?" Keef hissed as Stake got up to accept the award, which looked like a gold-plated garlic bomb. Thad ordered them from a discount trophy shop in Lower Purgatory that gave him a bulk discount. This meant that he had more awards than he had staff, so some of the categories seemed a little tacked on. For example, Tim still had no idea what "Chud of the Year" was for.

"Maybe you're just jealous because even your father thinks he's better at the job than you ever were," Madeline suggested tartly.

"Or maybe I'm just mad at myself because I didn't eat him when I had the chance," Keef said.

"Vampires," Madeline said, shaking her head. "I bet you think that's the answer to all your problems. Just bite it."

"I don't have any problems," Keef said. "I'm gonna live forever! Unfortunately, that makes nights like this feel sooo much longer."

The finale of the evening was Thad's big announcement. It turned out that Thad's company had landed a big city contract to clear out a large underground cave system as part of an ambitious plan to reinvigorate the long-neglected Crypt Network.

The Crypt Network was a failed development project that had been started many years ago as part of an attempt to boost commerce in some of the city's dying retail districts. The thinking was that if people didn't want to walk the streets of certain neighbourhoods because of poverty, crime, or rampant poltergeist infestations, then maybe they would be willing to walk under them. A network of tunnels was dug with plans to install retail and restaurant space to lure consumers back. Only a small fraction of it was ever built before the project fell apart as the demon and vampire gangs found the prospect of moving below ground far more attractive than the customers that were the project's target demographic.

In the years since, the Crypt Network had become so haunted and dangerous that not even the metropolitan police's armed spectral response units would go down there. The last election had seen a change of attitude, however, with a new mayor and city council coming to power on a promise to completely revitalize the project. Major contracts were put out for bid, and it appeared that Thad had managed to land one. The company was going to be responsible for remediating five kilometres of caves at the north end of the network in a part of town called the Pitchfork, which was so named because it was crosscut by old shipping canals.

Below that was the main entry point to a large network of caves that ran under much of the city. The caves had never been fully mapped as they were far too cursed to allow human exploration. It was one of the least developed sections of the original Crypt Network and would consequently be one of the most difficult to purge of supernatural presence.

Thad looked more animated and excited than Tim could remember seeing him in years as he pointed to the area on a large map mounted on a metal stand. The company would need to go on a hiring spree that would see it double in size over the next three months. Most of the people in the room would be moving up to team supervisor roles and receiving significant pay increases in the process, an announcement that not surprisingly received a far more enthusiastic response than any of Thad's jokes. Stake was being promoted to site supervisor, which made him the overall second-in-command.

Watching the faces in the crowd, Tim sensed that not everyone was happy about the last part, but the pay increases seemed to be enough for them to overlook that for now. He wondered what all of this might mean for the future. Thad had never considered applying for big government contracts in the past. It had to be Stake's idea.

No matter who came up with the idea, it certainly seemed like Stake was going to play a central role in the business—and by default the family—from now on.

Thad was in the middle of outlining his corporate restructuring plans when Tim felt his phone ping. He dug it out of his pocket, assuming it was just another email from Volkerps demanding an update on the Hesselthorn case and was surprised to see that it wasn't his boss. It was an automated notification from the Crimson Seal High-Value Scheduled Items Tracking System.

The Hesselthorn Puzzle Box had popped up.

"Holy shit!" Tim gasped, double-checking the reference number to make sure he was looking at what he thought he was looking at. Based on the geo-coordinates, the box was in a part of town near the docks known as the Muzzle. It was a rough-and-tumble area best known for its wolfsbane clinics and werewolf biker bars. It was considered a no-go area for humans after dark, especially during full moons.

"What?" Keef said, noticing Tim's reaction.

"Sorry, but I have to go," Tim said, standing up and turning to Madeline. "It's a work emergency."

"Oh?" said Madeline, not looking terribly upset.

"Can you make sure Madeline gets home okay?" Tim asked Keef.

"Can I what?" Keef asked, looking like he had just accidentally swallowed a handful of communion wafers.

"Maybe you could give me a ride home?" Madeline asked, turning to Stake.

"Uh, sure," Stake said, looking uncertainly at Tim. "I mean, if that's okay and everything…"

"Totally okay with me," Keef said.

"Sorry to eat and run," Tim said. "It's just this case I'm working on. My boss has been on me every five minutes about it. I can call you a cab if you prefer."

"Thanks," Madeline said. "But I'd just be more comfortable if I went with Harry. There are so many ghouls driving taxis these days. I'm sorry, do you prefer Harry or Stake?"

"Normally I go with Stake," Stake said. "But you can call me Harry if you want."

"Stake, then," Madeline smiled.

"Looks like somebody's getting staked," Keef muttered under his breath.

"Great," Tim said, grabbing his jacket. "I'll, uh, call you tomorrow?"

"That's okay," Madeline said. "I foresee that I may be busy tomorrow."

"Right," Tim said. He wasn't sure how to handle this, but was mercifully in too much of a hurry to have to think about it. He turned to Keef. "Tell the folks I had to run."

"Tell them yourself," Keef said peevishly. "Hey, can you drop me at Circle 9?"

"Sorry," Tim said. "I'm going in the other direction."

"Nevermind then," Keef said. "I guess I'll just *walk* the 13 blocks."

"Can't you turn into a bat or a dog or something?" Madeline asked.

"I don't like bats," Keef grumbled. He had never mastered the ability to turn into a daemonic anthromorph, largely because he couldn't be bothered to do any of the required study or practice. He had managed to turn himself into dust once, but had been unable to turn himself back and had been vacuumed up by the building maintenance zombie. It had taken him several hours of banging on the door before someone had come to free him from the collection tank in the basement. The Decameron was a Class 2 haunted building, so its inhabitants were largely accustomed to unexplained thumps, screams and other noises.

Tim headed for the door. He hoped that he had remembered to put his SIU bag in the trunk. If the Puzzle Box had surfaced, there was no telling who–or what–might have popped up along with it.

8

T im raced across town. The signal had dropped out almost immediately after it had been registered. That suggested that either the tracker had malfunctioned or had been disabled almost as soon as it had started working, which was odd.

According to the GPS, the location of the signal was a place called the Torn Throat. The Torn Throat was a bar that was notorious as a hangout for a werewolf biker gang known as the Howlers. They were in a semi-perpetual state of war with another werewolf gang called the Blood Moon Riders for control of the city's Narlune and Wolfsbane trafficking business. The Howlers were also aggressively pursuing a bigger chunk of the Moondog trade. "Moondog" was a slang term referring to humans who liked to have sex with werewolves in their animal or feral state. Organized criminal gangs made a lot of money bringing often underage werewolves into the city and setting them up in what were referred to as "doghouses", many of which were located on the same block as the Torn Throat.

Tim did not know if the Torn Throat was itself a doghouse, but he didn't imagine that it could look any scuzzier if it was. The sign out front was so faded that it was almost illegible. One of the front window panels looked to have been smashed from the inside and had been roughly patched with a torn piece of cardboard that had come from a case of Werebeer Light.

Tim checked his phone. The box had pinged at exactly 21:05:13 and disappeared again at 21:05:19, meaning that it had been active for only six seconds. The coordinates showed that it had appeared somewhere inside the Torn Throat. Based on the map, it looked like it was close to the northwest corner, less than ten metres from where Tim was parked.

Tim wasn't sure why the box had pinged and then immediately disappeared, but he could think of a few possibilities. The trackers were almost impossible to disable, but there were devices that could be used to block the signal. A Croatoan Cage or a Goreham Sarcophagus would probably do the job if the lining was thick enough, but those things were rare and expensive. A unit the size of a tissue box cost almost as much as a Demon 666LM sports car. The only people who tended to use them were the military and certain high-end exorcism clinics.

Tim had triple-checked the signal ID and even ran a diagnostic check on the claims app to make sure the alert had definitely come from the Hesselthorn Puzzle Box. There was no doubt it was the box, but what was it doing in a dive bar located in one of the most notorious neighbourhoods in the city?

There was only one way to find out.

Tim got out of the car. The smell of werewolf urine hit him immediately. It was so overpowering that he staggered and almost tripped over the curb. There were several different were-gangs active in this part of town. They tended to mark their territory in the way that ordinary wolves did, which meant that it was impossible to walk down the street in this part of town without gagging. Even werewolves could barely stand it.

Tim covered his face with his inner elbow. He could smell less of the wolf urine, but his jacket was infused with the blood and cigar smoke smell of Stoker's, which wasn't much better.

I'm going to have to do so much more laundry this week, he thought bitterly.

Tim realized that he wasn't dressed like the regular clientele of a werewolf biker bar. He yanked off his tie and loosened his shirt, but that had minimal effect. Checking his reflection in the driver's side window, he still looked like a bank manager heading out for lunch on casual Friday. Even if he'd had time to go home and grab a leather jacket, some torn jeans, and insert a pair of yellow contact lenses, it probably wouldn't matter. He wasn't a werewolf and would never be able to pass for one. He wished that Lonnie were here. This was exactly the kind of assignment for which his fellow investigator would have been perfect.

Tim tossed his tie in the passenger seat and grabbed his canister of Demonex and a Demon Charger out of his SIU bag. He had no idea who or what he might run into once he got inside, but it was better to be safe than to end up looking like the disemboweled villager on the ad for Mauling Mickey vodka. He took a few loose bills out of his wallet and stuffed them in his pocket, locking his wallet in the glove compartment. Hardly anyone ever used cash anymore, but he wasn't about to hand his credit card over to anybody in *this* place.

The street was deserted, which wasn't unusual for a Friday night in this part of town. Most of their customers were bikers or werewolves who worked on the commercial fishing boats that came and went from the docks, which were located two blocks east. The boats usually worked three-week round trips that coincided with the moon cycle. It didn't make sense to have half your crew transform in the middle of retrieving a six-mile-long Kappa line, after all. The boats usually returned early in the morning. Many of the bars in this part of town opened at four or five a.m. in order to accommodate the sudden influx of fisherwolves coming ashore with money to spend in the short time before they went back out.

Tim jogged across the street and hopped onto the sidewalk. The front door of the bar was covered with claw marks, dents and a colorful assortment of graffiti, most of which was about someone named Wanda and the fact that she liked to be mounted from behind. Some of them were supplemented with crude illustrations.

Tim took a deep breath through his mouth and pushed the door open. It was lighter than he had been expecting and as a result he practically flew into the bar and almost sprawled across a pool table where two large werewolves in white leather jackets were playing a game of Evil Eye. The Howlers always seemed to wear white, although Tim was never entirely sure why.

"Sorry!" Tim said, just narrowly avoiding sending the Eye ball into the centre pocket with his elbow.

"Watch where you're going, meat!" growled the larger of the two. He had gray fur styled into a mohawk and had a row of moonstone piercings through each ear and one in his muzzle. Tim could see a silver combat knife strapped to one leg sticking out from under the jacket. A lot of werewolf gang members liked to carry silver weapons even though they were themselves allergic to them. The knives were cheaper and easier to obtain than silver bullets and worked just as effectively in close quarter combat with rival gangs. Although he couldn't see any, Tim had no doubt that these guys probably had guns, too.

"Sorry," Tim repeated, backing away. Werewolves were legally prohibited from assuming their animal form outside off-leash areas, but the Torn Throat was clearly not the kind of place where those rules were enforced.

"What's wrong with ya?" said the second werewolf. He was smaller than the first and was wearing a bright red neckerchief. In gang circles, that meant he had killed at least ten victims, although Tim didn't know if that included just humans or rival gang members. His brown fur was patchy and his gums were receding from his long yellow teeth, which Tim recognized as a classic sign of Wolfsbane abuse. "You almost cost me a hunnerd bucks!"

"Sorry!" Tim said, backing away.

Tim had no desire to get into any kind of argument with drugged-up gang wolves. He turned and looked around at the rest of the bar. The only other individuals in the place were the bartender and a grossly obese individual sitting at a table in the back corner studying his phone. Both of them were also in wolf form. The bartender was wearing a faded Lycanthrocide concert shirt and moonglasses while the obese wolf was decked out in a sleeveless white leather vest with the Howlers gang crest emblazoned on the back.

There were a couple of tables and a booth tucked in at the front of the bar, all of which were empty. Based on the coordinates generated by the claims app, Tim was pretty sure that the signal had originated from the booth. He strolled over and looked at it as casually as possible, even going so far as to drop his car keys on the floor so as to give himself an excuse to take a closer look.

There was definitely no sign of anything or anyone there now and nothing to indicate that anyone had been seated there recently–no crumbs, stains or puddles caused by condensation dripping down off cold glasses. The floor, however, was filthy. It was covered in brown stains that looked uncomfortably like dried blood as well as other vaguely organic matter that Tim did not care to try to identify.

Tim was about to get up when he spotted a couple of tiny objects on the floor next to one of the table legs. He reached under and picked them up, dropping them onto his palm for closer examination. He recognized them instantly.

They were Crimson Seal claims tags.

He could see that the demonite casing had been melted on both units and the transmission circuit had been cut in half, rendering both of them inactive. Demonite was not an easy thing to cut through. Whoever had done this had known exactly what they were doing and had used some seriously advanced tech to do it.

"You want somethin', buddy?" the bartender barked, looking at Tim with a mix of curiosity and disdain.

"Sorry!" Tim said. He stuffed the tags in his pocket, got quickly back to his feet and approached the bar.

Tim didn't have time to check the registration number on the tags, but had no doubt they would turn out to be the same ones attached to the Puzzle Box. That left no doubt that it had been in this room only minutes ago. It was close. He needed to find out as much as he could about who had been in that booth and where they had gone.

"I, uh, was supposed to be meeting some friends here," Tim said. "But it looks like I missed them."

"Friends, huh?" said the bartender. "These friends a' yours spend most of their time on the floor, do they?"

"Can't hold their liquor," Tim said, chuckling. He took a seat at the bar. "Asked me to meet them here. They love this place."

"Whoopee fuckin' doo," said the bartender. "What'll ya have?"

Tim studied the taps. He had never even heard of most of the brands. "Uh…Brimstone Lager?"

The bartender grabbed a chipped and milky-looking pint glass from under the bar and filled it with a viscous-looking red liquid from the tap at the far end. He deposited it in front of Tim, who took an exploratory sip. The stuff tasted like a combination of burned motor oil and blood.

"Ah, that hits the spot!" Tim said, trying not to gag. He needed to try to get as much information out of this guy as he could, which meant that he had to keep him talking by any means necessary. "Nice shirt. You a fan of Lycanthrocide?"

Tim knew almost nothing about Lycanthrocide other than that they were a werewolf death metal band that had enjoyed a fluke top ten hit with their song "Fuzzbox" after a remixed version was used in a truck commercial.

"My cousin used to be their lighting technician," the bartender said.

"Cool," Tim said, trying to take another sip of his drink without actually getting any of it in his mouth.

"He quit after they dropped the moon on his leg," the bartender said.

"Sorry," Tim coughed. "The what?"

"They had this big disco ball moon prop," the bartender said. "It was supposed to descend from the rafters at the start of the chorus for '*Floss With Sinew*'. I guess they didn't attach it properly or whatever and it fell on him when he was rigging a spot."

"That's terrible," Tim said.

"Thing rolled across the stage like a giant pinball," the bartender said, wiping the counter with a grey rag. "Took out two drum techs and the bass player before it rolled off. Pretty awesome."

He went back to wiping the bar. Tim guessed that meant he had reached the end of his Lycanthrocide story.

"Busy night?" Tim asked, trying to keep the conversation going.

"Oh, insane," said the bartender. Tim was pretty sure that he was kidding, but it was hard to tell. Werewolves were not naturally predisposed to irony. "Had to put two guys on the door just to keep out the undesirables. Ever since we got that write-up in the Times, man. Damn hipsters just won't leave us alone. So many satyrs that I started to grow horns myself. Place is actually booked solid but you just caught us between the eight and ten o'clock seatings."

"Right," Tim said, smiling to suggest that he found all of this terribly funny. "Speaking of seatings, you didn't happen to notice anyone in here about 15 minutes ago, did you? Maybe in that booth up front?"

"These your *friends* we're talking about?" The bartender said. "What'd they look like? Maybe that'll help jog my memory."

"Hmmmm," Tim said. "It's been a long time since we've seen each other."

"No doubt," the bartender nodded. "I forget people all the time. Why, yesterday I even forgot what my wife looks like!"

"Right," Tim chuckled, not sure if this was the payoff of a joke or just part of the setup.

The bartender leaned over and dropped his voice to a low growl. "Thing is, I've got a good reason for that."

"Oh yes?" Tim coughed, pretending to take another sip and actually taking one by mistake.

"Yeah," said the bartender. "See, I don't got a wife."

Tim felt himself grabbed from behind by two enormous, furry arms. One arm wrapped around his midsection while a large and sweaty claw clamped over his mouth. He couldn't see who it was, but he could sense instantly that he wasn't going to be able to break free.

"What's the deal with all you people comin' in here askin' all these questions?" the bartender growled, leaning in so close that Tim could smell the Wolfsbane on his breath.

What did he mean by '*all you people*'? Tim wondered. He tried to work a hand into his pocket to get to either the spray or the charger, but both of his arms were locked firmly in place.

"Mrrrgggh!" Tim said, unable to speak.

"Guy looks like a cop," growled the bartender. "Search him."

Tim felt hands push into his pockets and pull out the Demonex and Demon Charger.

"Looky here!" said a squeaky voice from behind. Tim guessed that it belonged to the smaller of the two werewolves who had been at the pool table.

"Well, well," said the bartender, taking the items and holding them up in Tim's face. "Expecting trouble, were ya?"

"No wallet," said the squeaky wolf, checking Tim's other pockets so forcefully that he tore the fabric with his claws. Tim winced in pain as he felt the nails scratch his legs. He was glad that he had left his wallet in the car and just brought the small bills, some of which the wolf tossed on the bar.

"So who are you?" the bartender said, picking up a ten and sticking it in his pocket. "A cop? The hell are you doing here?"

Tim tried to speak, but his mouth was clamped shut and so all that came out were unintelligible grunts.

"Let him talk, Marty," the bartender said.

Tim felt the claw lift off his face and took a deep breath just in the off-chance that he might not get the opportunity to take another one. He obviously couldn't tell these guys the real reason for his visit, but he couldn't think of a single other reason that would sound remotely credible. Humans didn't just stop by dumpy werewolf gang hangouts on the spur of the moment to renew old acquaintances.

"Take it easy, guys!" Tim said in the calmest and most reasonable voice he could manage. "I'm not a cop! I'm not here to arrest anybody or report on any possibly illegal activity! Which I'm sure absolutely does not take place in any form within these premises at any time!"

The claw re-clamped itself over Tim's mouth.

"Doesn't sound like a cop," growled the large werewolf.

"You're right," said the bartender. "Guy sounds like a friggin' lawyer."

"I hate lawyers," said the small werewolf. "My ex-wife's bloodsucking lawyer cleaned me out in the divorce. She even took my Growler. The bitch doesn't even ride! She just took it so she could roll it off a cliff and into a quarry. Posted the whole thing on InfernaChat just to make me suffer."

"Whaddya wanna do with this one?" asked the big werewolf.

"Stick him in the lounge," the bartender said. "Loop's on his way in. He'll know what to do with the professor here and his little friend."

Tim felt himself lifted out of the chair and carried through a beaten door marked "Staff Only" in the back of the bar. They continued down a poorly-lit hallway stuffed with dented kegs and torn boxes full of snack-sized chew toys. Tim glanced through one half-open door and caught a glimpse of a dozen or so naked female werewolves standing in groups around two long metal tables. They were using scissors to rip open werewolf plush toys and remove bags full of white capsules, which they were then sorting into smaller bags.

Tim had heard all about operations like this, but had never actually seen one in person. The fact that they didn't seem all that concerned about letting him see their operation did not strike him as a good sign.

They continued down the hall and stopped in front of a metal door at the back next to a stairwell. The werewolf stopped and pulled up a set of keys attached to a chain on his belt. He found the right one, unlocked the door and stepped through. Tim heard a screech as the other wolf grabbed a folding metal chair and dragged it over. Tim was placed in the chair and quickly tied in place using frayed black nylon rope.

"I'm telling you, this is totally unnecessary!" Tim said as the wolves finished securing him and turned to leave. "I was just meeting a friend!"

"Hang tight, little buddy," the big werewolf said as he pulled the door closed. "It won't be long."

"Yeah," said the small one. "Maybe the chef'll put you on the menu! Been a long time since we had some of those tasty sweetbread crostinis, eh Marty?"

The two of them rumbled with laughter as they closed the door and locked it. Tim could hear them talking as they made their way back down the hall, but the sound was too muffled to make out what they were saying.

He looked around. The room was about 20 by 20. Most of the middle of the room was taken up with a sunken circular pit that at first glance looked like an empty inground pool. It was about six feet deep and eight feet in diameter. The inside walls and floor of the pit were covered in scratches, dents and dark brown stains.

It was a wolf fighting pit. A lot of bars like this had underground ultimate werewolf fighting competitions. The network was so well organized, in fact, that it even had ranking tables, undercard bouts and copious betting. It also had the copious match fixing that went along with it. The fights were often brutal and bloody affairs, many of which ended in dismemberment or death. Werewolf fights were most common, but there were all kinds of other variants: demon vs demon, human vs wolf, wolf vs demon, human vs zombie, zombie vs zombie–on and on. The zombie fights weren't as popular because they mostly involved stumbling and gnawing. Some of the bigger matches were even broadcast live on secured-access darknet channels. Tim had little doubt that he was in one of those secret locations now.

The most striking thing about the room, however, was that he was not the only one in it.

9

"Oh shit, not you."

Tim immediately recognized the person tied to the chair next to him. It was Giallo, the claims adjuster who had harangued him the first time he walked out of the Hesselthorn mansion.

"What are you doing here?" Tim asked.

"Oh, you know," Giallo said. "I was sitting home alone with nothing to do on a Friday night, so I decided to head out to a doghouse biker bar for some kicks. It's just how I roll. Drop some 'bane, get sold into sexual slavery, maybe catch a couple of UWFC matches. Looks like you had the same idea."

"You used the claims tracker!" Tim said. "You knew that the Puzzle Box pinged in here!"

"It's not my fault that IT never disabled my access," Giallo said. "I'm just doing my job."

"It's *my* job!" Tim said.

"And yet, here I am, doing it better than you," Giallo said. "How do you explain that? Could it be that you suck? That really seems like the simplest explanation. And, as you know, the simplest explanation is almost always the right one."

"What do you mean better?" Tim asked. He knew that Giallo had not found the claims trackers, which meant that she had not searched the booth as carefully as he had. Or maybe the wolves had grabbed her before she got the chance. Either way, he figured this was a point in his favour, competency-wise.

"I was here first," Giallo said. "I've been sitting in this room for *ages*."

"Ages?" Tim said. "The alert only pinged 15 minutes ago!"

"Okay," Giallo said. "Maybe that was a slight exaggeration. But I still got here before you did."

"And got yourself captured, too," Tim said. "You didn't last long before you got tied up back here, either. How much beer did you manage to drink?"

"Ugh," Giallo said, making a face. "Even I know better than to drink the stuff they serve in a place like this. You know they piss in it, right? Werewolves piss everywhere."

"I can't imagine that makes it taste any worse," Tim said. "We need to try and figure a way to get out of here."

Tim began trying to work at the ropes that were coiled around his wrists. He could move his elbows, but the ropes cut into his wrists when he tried to twist them free. He tried pulling his arm out, but that caused the chair to rock back. He was right on the edge of the fighting pit and didn't want to risk falling in and breaking his neck.

"I heard them say they were calling some guy named Lou or Loop," Giallo said. "I'm guessing that must be the boss."

"I heard them say the same thing," Tim grunted, straining to try and reach the knots. "These guys evidently aren't smart enough to figure out what to do with us on their own."

"There's a lot of things these guys aren't smart enough to do," Giallo said, reaching her left hand inside the right sleeve of her leather jacket and fishing around. "Like check for weapons in anywhere other than the most obvious places."

Tim watched as she continued to fish around for a moment before pulling out a small silver object that looked like a cigarette lighter.

"What is that?" Tim asked.

"This?" Giallo said. "This is my ticket out of here."

As Tim watched, she carefully spun the object between her fingers and held it out underneath the ropes attached to her left wrist. Once it was in place, she flicked a button on the side a couple of times and a tiny blue flame emerged. As soon as the flame made contact with the ropes, they melted.

"Is that Hellfire?" Tim asked in disbelief.

"Sure is," Giallo said, pulling her left hand free and spinning around in the chair to use the flame to melt the ropes on her right. "Got it in a little place down in East Hades. It's come in handy a few times, believe me."

"That's fantastic!" Tim said. "Hurry up! Do mine!"

Giallo melted the last of the ropes and stood up, stretching her arms and back. "Ah, that's better!"

She turned to Tim, smiled, and tucked the lighter into her jacket pocket.

"What are you doing?" Tim hissed. "Get me out of here!"

"Sorry, hotshot," Giallo said. "See, if I let you go, that will marginally increase your chances of finding the box before I do."

Tim couldn't believe what he was hearing.

"Are you insane?" he said. "These werewolves are gonna kill me!"

"Well, I'm sure you were aware that there was an element of risk involved when you took the job in SIU," Giallo said. "So you can't say that you weren't given the opportunity to put a more robust mitigation strategy in place before something like this happened."

Giallo cracked open the door and peeked out into the hallway.

"You can't do this!" Tim said. "We work for the same company!"

"If you do get out of this, then I'm sure you'll fire a very comprehensive report on me with the zombies in HR," Giallo said. "It certainly wouldn't be the first time."

"You're a monster!" Tim said.

"Typical," Giallo said. "The first time a woman shows any hint of ambition, some mediocre dude comes along and says something like that. Good thing I don't let such patriarchal negativity get the better of me. Now do me a favour and keep your mouth shut while I make my escape."

"But…" Tim sputtered. "But…"

"Good luck!" Giallo said. She gave him a wink and then slipped through the door and disappeared.

Tim couldn't believe that she had managed to free herself only to leave him trapped here. Who would do something like that? He tried to think about who he might leave trapped in the backroom of a dumpy werewolf bar–or any other foul-smelling and dangerous place–and was surprised to realize that there actually were a few that immediately popped to mind, but he needed to focus.

Okay, Tim thought. I need to figure out a way to get out of here before this Loop guy arrives, which could be any minute.

He tried pulling on the ropes again. He could sense some give in the one wrapped around his left wrist. With a little more force, maybe he could get it loose enough that he might be able to get to the actual knots.

Tim yanked upwards, feeling the legs of the chair pop up off the ground as he did so. It seemed to be working. Just a few more…

Tim heard a muffled rumbling sound. Was that a motorcycle? Maybe it was the boss. Being stuck in a windowless room with cinderblock walls, it was hard to tell. All he knew was that the more time he spent in here, the lower the chances of his ever getting out again were. Now was not the time for half measures.

Tim pulled harder on the ropes, lifting the legs of the chair higher and higher off the ground with each successive attempt. He could feel it. He was almost there. The rope had edged down off his wrist and was stuck around the base of his hand just below the thumb joint. One or two more good yanks and he would be free.

Tim was so focused on getting his arm loose that he had lost all awareness of his proximity to the pit. He did not become aware of the pit again until the moment when he yanked on the rope and only three of the chair's four legs landed back on solid ground. He felt the chair tilt backwards, his legs pinwheeling wildly in empty space as his view shifted from the floor to the ceiling and back again.

"Yeeaaargh!" Tim screeched as he tumbled through empty space.

Tim closed his eyes and felt himself do what felt like a full backwards somersault before the chair landed at a 45 degree angle on the dank concrete of the pit floor. There was a loud crack as the back part of the chair broke in half. Tim's arms suddenly came loose as his weight came down painfully on his right hip. He pitched over and rolled sideways, coming face to face with an eyeball lying caked in a pool of dried blood. It had a yellow iris and was larger than he would have expected.

"Ugh!" Tim gagged, sitting up. He spun around to see that the moulded plastic chair back had cracked and broken loose from the metal frame, letting his left arm slide off. The bracket on the right side was still attached. Tim tried pulling at it, but it didn't budge, so he immediately set to work on the knots with his free hand. It took him a minute or so before he was able to loosen it enough to get his right arm loose.

"Yes!" Tim hissed.

He was breathing fast. Had his captors heard the crash? Were they already on their way to investigate? There was certainly no point in hanging around down here waiting for them.

Tim looked around. He didn't see a ladder or steps or any easy way to climb out, but that wasn't entirely surprising. It was an illegal fighting pit, after all. It wasn't like they were going to be overly concerned with safety or fire regulations.

Tim put his hands on the edge at the point with the fewest blood spatters and boosted himself back up. He made his way over to the door and cracked it open to peer back down the hall. The coast appeared to be clear.

Tim slipped through the door, closing it as quietly as possible. He could see the open door leading to the Wolfsbane lab. He didn't want to walk past that again if he could avoid it. Somebody in there might spot him and alert the guys who had tied him up. He turned and headed the other way to a metal door that led out through the back, but it was locked and he couldn't see any way to open it. On his right was a half-open door leading to a stairway, but he definitely didn't want to go up. He wanted to get out.

How in the hell had Giallo gotten out? Tim wondered. She must have done it somehow. Just wait until I get out of here, he thought. I have no idea what I'm going to do in terms of revenge–the company probably frowned on employees murdering or maiming each other–but I'll think of something.

Tim heard low voices approaching and saw the handle of the front door starting to turn. It looked like the big boss had arrived and they were coming back to deal with the hostages. If he stayed where he was, they would spot him as soon as they came through the door. He needed to get out of sight.

With no other option, Tim turned and ran up the stairs. He rounded the landing in a single jump and made his way up to the second floor, where he poked his head carefully through the door.

He saw a long hallway with about a dozen doors, most of which were open to reveal tiny rooms with cheap, foldout massage tables in the centre. Each room had a plastic desk stacked with bottles of what Tim assumed were body oils and hand sanitizer. He couldn't see anyone through any of the open doors or moving around in the hallway. Some sort of howling trance music was emanating from speakers mounted in the ceiling. The music was not loud enough to drown out the weird growling sounds coming from behind some of the closed doors. They weren't angry growls, but

Tim had no doubt they would quickly become so should he open any of those doors to confirm his suspicion about what was going on inside.

Looks like quite the vertically-integrated criminal operation here, Tim thought. These werewolf biker gangs are better organized than they look.

Tim stepped out into the hall and began making his way towards the front of the building. He could see a window at the far end that looked like it might open and figured that might be his best bet. He checked each open door before going past. He didn't want to be spotted.

He was almost at the end of the hall when he checked the last door and saw that it wasn't a service room, but something else. There was a desk in the corner with a computer hooked up to a bank of monitors. The chair in front of the desk was unoccupied. Next to the desk was what looked like a safe, which was closed. Beside the safe was some sort of storage unit.

Tim paused. It looked like he had stumbled on the Torn Throat's security operations room. Unable to stop himself, he pushed open the door and stepped inside. He recognized the security system they were using. It was a SpectroSite XC–not top of the line, but not the cheapest thing out there, either. A lot of blood banks and Narlune clinics used it because it could identify individual werewolves or vampires when they had transformed into their animal or beast form. That was a necessity when it came to minimum evidence requirements for prosecuting thefts, which were common for those types of businesses.

Tim approached the monitors and leaned in for a better look. Each screen was linked to a different camera, of which there appeared to be one in almost every room in the building. He could see the bar, the pit room from which he had just escaped and the drug room full of the naked werewolves. He could also see inside each of the massage rooms, as well as the front and back of the building looking out at the street and an alley.

The alley cam showed an image of two large werewolves in white leather jackets getting off enormous motorcycles while the bartender and the other wolves who had grabbed Tim waited. Tim figured that was probably Loup or Loop or Lupe or whatever the hell his name was. The big boss. The monitor for the bar showed that part of the building was empty and the lights had been turned off.

Maybe they had closed up shop temporarily while they decided what to do with the trespassers, Tim thought. Even in a place like this, it wasn't a good idea to have potential witnesses hanging around right before something nasty went down.

And speaking of nasty things, Tim could see that at least four of the massage rooms appeared to be occupied. In one of them, a small silver werewolf was handcuffed to the table and being jolted with shocks from a long metal prod held by a bored-looking woman in a white leather bikini. Similar activity was taking place in the other three rooms, although the method of stimulation varied.

Tim could see a flashing red dot in the corner of each image. It appeared that the Torn Throat was not only filming the activity that took place on the premises, it was recording it, too.

All the better to blackmail them with, Tim thought.

Tim's gaze drifted back to the bar. If they were recording what happened upstairs, maybe they recorded what was happening down in the bar, too. Which might mean that he could rewind and see exactly who had been there and what happened when the Puzzle Box tracker alarms went off.

Tim leaned forward and began typing. He was familiar with this system because he had taken a course in security systems back when he was still a claims adjuster and this wasn't one of the more complicated ones to use. He quickly isolated camera six, which was the only one for the bar area, and brought it up on the main screen.

Tim rewound the footage to the time that the box alarm had gone off, backtracking past the images of his own arrival. He winced as he watched himself emerge through the back door in the clutches of the bikers, sit at the bar and disappear out the front door in quadruple reverse time. This was followed almost immediately by footage of exactly the same thing happening to Giallo, which was somewhat more satisfying to watch.

Tim backed it up to the key moment and stopped. In the corner of the image, he could see two shadowy figures sitting in the booth near the front of the room. They were both leaning forward and looking at something on the table in front of them, but the image wasn't good enough to tell what it was or who they were.

Tim did a quick scan through the feeds. Camera six appeared to be the only one that showed the front room, but it seemed to focus mostly on the bar and didn't bother with what was happening at any of the tables. Tim guessed that the owners of the Torn Throat weren't terribly interested in what actually happened with the legitimate side of their business and only focused their attention on the parts that made them real money.

Tim backed the image up slowly. The two figures seemed to have all their attention focused on something on the table between them, but try as he might, Tim was unable to zoom in and get a better look at what it was.

Tim checked the timestamp in the top right corner of the image. The ping on the box appeared to have occurred exactly when the closer of the two figures lifted something up with his hands.

Tim continued to rewind slowly. A waitress arrived at the table with two drinks, neither of which the two figures touched. One of the figures appeared to be wearing a hat while the other one was in a hooded jacket or cloak. Tim wondered if the cloak was a vampire's cape. Lucretia, the oldest of the Hesselthorn kids, was a vampire wannabe. A lot of vampires and their familiars wore capes these days. Was that her under there?

The image continued to roll back. Tim saw the waitress arrive at the table again, presumably to take the drink orders. He recognized her as one of the workers in the massage rooms. The bikers had probably told her to split right after Giallo showed up.

Tim saw the figure in the hood get up and walk backwards out of the bar. That person had arrived after the first one, but not by much. Based on the timestamp of when the one in the hat arrived, the two figures had both walked through the front door of the bar within two minutes of each other.

The hood was black and hung down so far over the individual's face that no matter how much image manipulation Tim tried, he couldn't get a better look. Even height and weight were tricky, as the angle on the lens gave the image a slightly distorted effect. Maybe if Tim was able to get a copy of the raw footage and bring it into IT, they would be able to do something with it, but he didn't have that luxury. He could see that the hooded individual was carrying something close to their body under their right arm. Was that the Hesselthorn Puzzle Box?

Tim watched carefully as the figure in the hat got up and walked backwards out of the bar. Tim slowed it down to the point where he was looking at the image frame by frame. The figure had their head down for most of the short walk from the door to the table, but there was one point–just a flicker–when they raised their head and looked around to see that the other figure had not yet arrived at the designated meeting point.

Tim froze the image at the moment when the figure was looking almost directly at the camera. The image quality wasn't the best, but it appeared to be a satyr. He was probably in his mid 50s or early 60s, but it was hard to tell. Tim had a hard time gaging the age of satyrs in particular, as they always looked older than they were. This one had some sort of mark on his left cheek and was wearing a patch over his right eye.

Tim squinted at the monitor. It wasn't anyone he recognized. He zoomed in on the face and looked down at the controls. There wasn't a printer and there didn't appear to be any way to get a better angle or enhance the image.

Tim heard a muffled roar from somewhere on the floor below. There was no time to dwell upon his discovery. He pulled his cell phone out of his pocket and snapped a quick photo. The quality would be terrible, but it was better than nothing.

Tim checked the monitor for the pit room and saw that the leather-jacketed boss and his goons had discovered that he and Giallo were no longer tied up and helplessly awaiting their fate. The boss had picked up the bartender and shook him like a rag doll before tossing him into the pit in a rage.

"Okay," Tim said. "I think that's last call for drinks, folks."

Tim ran back out into the hall. One of the doors opened and the waitress with the cattle prod stuck her head out.

"What was that?" she asked, giving Tim a quizzical look. "Who are you?"

"Uh, new IT guy," Tim said, running towards the front window. "I was just checking on your router. You should be all good to stream those werewolf fights again!"

"Say what?" the woman said.

"Nothing!" Tim said, reaching the window and pulling it open. "Just, you know, go back to your werewolf sex torture!"

Tim leaned out the window and looked down on the street at the front of the bar. There was no fire escape, but there was a metal rod that held up one side of the bar's sign. It appeared to run almost all the way down to the ground.

"You're not the IT guy!" the woman said, pointing the werewolf prod at Tim in an accusatory fashion. "He's in there with me!"

"I'm just filling in!" Tim said, climbing through the window as the woman advanced towards him. "I just need to check on your external HDMI cable!"

"My external what?" said the woman, but Tim was already out the window and on his way down the side of the building.

im arrived at work early the next morning. He was hoping to get in before Asgaroth's was open. He needed to talk to Volkerps. Plus, the dinner date with Madeline had not been a rousing success and he was hoping to avoid any awkward encounters.

It just wasn't possible for him to date somebody who was a fan of HEX-TV or its most loathsome correspondent. But that wasn't the only thing. There was the way she treated Keef like a walking disease. Granted, Tim often thought of his brother that way, but that had more to do with the fact that Keef was a lazy, freeloading slob. Not because he was a vampire. Keef had been a parasite long before the guy started drinking blood, which was a small but important distinction.

Tim had gotten back to his apartment after his near miss at the Torn Throat to find Keef demonstrating proper feeding techniques to Killian with the assistance of a group of four attractive young female volunteers. All of the women were dressed in short-sleeved green hospital gowns that went down to just above their knees.

"What the hell is this?" Tim had asked.

"He needs practice," Keef said, removing his fangs from the arm of a woman with poofy blonde hair.

"Practice?" Tim said.

"Right," Keef said. "You remember the mess I made of mom's Persian rug the first time I brought a victim home? She freaked! That was a big part of the reason they kicked me out!"

"But this is exploitation!" Tim said.

"They all signed releases," Killian pointed out.

"Yeah," Keef said. "And we put down a drop sheet and everything!"

Keef pointed down at the square white sheet the women were standing on. Tim recognized it as the embroidered damask tablecloth he kept in the linen closet for special occasions. He had gotten it as a housewarming present from his grandmother. Its pristine surface was now covered with dozens of blood spatters.

"That's my best tablecloth!" Tim said.

"Relax!" Keef said. "We'll get it dry cleaned, for crying out loud! Like you ever have anyone over for fancy dinners anymore anyway! Sheesh! Would you rather we just did it right on your precious hardwood floors?"

"I would rather you did it somewhere else!" Tim said, spotting an arterial spray that had gone all the way across the room and hit the fridge. "Or not at all."

"We're almost done," Keef said. "He's getting the hang of it."

"Yes," Killian said, leading a brunette woman with a bandaged arm into the middle of the sheet and getting down on his knees. He inserted a pair of gold fangs in his mouth and took hold of her knee. There was dried blood all over the front of his shirt. "I jutht need thome more practithe with legth."

"Just don't take more than a pint," said the woman. "I have a commercial audition first thing in the morning and I don't want to pass out in the middle of it."

"You're getting us on the *Blood Stalker* audition list for this, right?" said the blonde woman.

"Of courthe!" said Killian. "The cathting director and I have a great perthonal relationthhip! Further to that point, I'm thinking thith might be a bit eathier without the thcrubth. How doeth everyone feel about that?"

"I'm fine with it," said the brunette, taking off the green smock to reveal that she wasn't wearing anything underneath. "If it's, you know, central to the role. Everything starts with story and character. It's all about getting to the truth of the scene for me."

"Yeth," Killian said, eyes and fangs gleaming. "That'th better."

"Just no bites anywhere visible," the brunette said, wagging a warning finger. "They'll never hire me if they need to FX anything out."

"Oh man," Tim groaned. "For the sake of the inevitable future depositions about all of this, let the record show that I was in my room the entire time."

Tim went to his room and closed the door. He was exhausted, so he put on his noise cancelling headphones and climbed straight into bed. There was no sign of Clawfist anywhere in the apartment. For a minute, Tim thought the tiny demon had finally gone back to wherever it came from, but realized that was not the case when he found the Gogrub sleeping in his SIU bag the following morning.

"You can't live in here!" Tim said, scooping the demon out of the bag. "I need it for work!"

"Bag Blug," Clawfist said, fluttering across the room to settle on Tim's pillow, where he curled up and started to snore. "Nag Nrug."

Tim pondered the idea of chasing the demon out, but it was late and he had to get going. He drove to work and used his ID badge to enter through the staff door on the side of Asgaroth's Relics and Ritual Supply. He was relieved to see no sign of Madeline in her usual spot behind the cash desk. It was Saturday, so the office would be largely deserted, but he knew that Volkerps would still be in. His boss hated spending any time with his family and used that as an excuse to be at work as often as possible.

Tim was just holding out his card to open the secret door in the back that led to SIU headquarters when he heard a familiar voice from behind him.

"Tim! I had a premonition that you'd be coming in this morning!"

Tim turned to see Madeline get to her feet. She had been restocking a shelf of Door Demons, which were cheap magnetized figurines that people attached to their front doors in the belief that they prevented malevolent entities from gaining access to their homes. They didn't work, but that didn't stop people from buying them. That was the case with most of the things that Asgaroths sold.

"Hi…" Tim said, trying to frame what he was about to say in his head.

"I had a lot of fun last night!" Madeline said.

"You did?" Tim said, surprised. She had not seemed to be having much fun, but psychics could be notoriously difficult to read.

"Oh yeah!" Madeline said. "Your parents are hilarious!"

"They are?" Tim said, not at all sure what she could be referring to. He didn't remember her drinking a lot of wine, but maybe she'd had more of it after he left.

"Totally!" Madeline said. "Your mother invited me over for dinner tonight."

"She what?" Tim said.

"We got talking about this idea I've got for a new line of psychoactive face creams," Madeline said. "She loved it!"

I'm sure she did, Tim thought. *Almost as much as she enjoys interfering in my personal life.*

"Uh huh," Tim said. "Ummm…"

How on earth am I supposed to break this off now? Tim wondered. Maybe he could say that he had to go away for a few days for work. No, that wouldn't fly. Madeline's job was on the floor above his office. What was he going to do? Wear a disguise? He couldn't call in sick. Not when he was on a case like this.

"Listen, Madeline," Tim said. "I was thinking…"

Tim was interrupted by the sound of the phone ringing behind the front counter, which caused Madeline to perk up immediately.

"Sorry!" she said, jogging back to the desk. "Gotta grab that! We have a big shipment of runes coming in for the next blood moon festival and the boss'll curse me if I miss it!"

"Sure," Tim said, waving. "We can, uh, chat later."

Tim headed for the SIU entrance and took the elevator down where he found Volkerps fulminating in his office.

"Lovecraft!" Volkerps rumbled. "Where are we at with the Hesselthorn case?"

Tim gave Volkerps a quick summary of his adventure in the werewolf bar, complete with the presence of the unwanted claims adjuster.

"She just left you there?" Volkerps said.

"Yes!" Tim said. "If I hadn't gotten out before they came back, those werewolves would probably have ground me into Moon Bites."

Moon Bites were a brand of highly processed wolfsbane-infused snacks. Tim had never actually tried them, as they looked and smelled almost exactly like dog kibble.

"Let that be a lesson," Volkerps said. "Always be prepared. And never trust anyone from claims! That pit sucker Ozgoroth has been gunning for my job for more than 300 years. If he can get a few of my employees brutally murdered in the process, then that's just the eyeball on top of the organ pile as far as he's concerned."

"Right," Tim said, shifting slightly in his seat to hide the sudden onset of queasiness. Demon colloquialisms were nothing if not colourful. "But this Giallo is interfering directly in the investigation. Isn't there any way to get them to officially back off?"

"Sure," Volkerps said. "I could schedule a meeting with the entire board of directors and formally ask them to ask Oz to stop trying to do my work better than my own department can do it. But I don't really feel like doing that. Any idea why I might not feel like doing that?"

"I get the picture," Tim said.

"Good," Volkerps said. "Because Xena's just wrapped up the Van Haarken poltergeist case and I'm giving serious consideration to transferring this file over to her."

"Wait!" Tim said, sitting up and pulling out his phone. "I did get a picture of one of the individuals on the scene at the time the claims tracker was triggered. Well, it's a picture of a picture. It's not the best image quality. I was just about to run it through recog."

Volkerps took the phone in one of his massive claws and studied it closely. All of his eyes widened at once.

"Don't bother with recog," he growled. "I know who this is."

"You do?" Tim said. "Who is it?"

"This is Damien Ugarte."

Tim got the feeling, based on the way Volkerps said the name, that it was supposed to mean something, but he had never heard of the guy before.

"Who?" Tim said.

"He used to work here," Volkerps said, handing the phone back.

"Here?" Tim said. "As in…SIU?"

"Correct," Volkerps said. "One of the best investigators in the department. Had a truly supernatural talent for spotting fraud, which was unusual. Not to dig on satyrs. Usually, the only thing you expect them to spot is an orgy club on half-price night–and Ugarte certainly didn't shy away from that–but there also wasn't an angle or a scam he hadn't heard about. It's like the guy was spawned for the job."

"Okay," Tim said. The face in the security footage did not look to be all that old. Satyrs actually tended to age faster than others because of their ultra-hedonistic lifestyle, but he knew better than to indulge broad generalizations. "Let me guess: the reason he was so good at identifying fraud was because he was also quite good at committing it?"

"Astute," Volkerps said. "He started working with some of our, shall we say, less ethical clients to falsify claims. When they came through to us, he would get the investigation and then close it as legit in exchange for a cut of the payout. Appetites got the best of him. Ended up owing a lot of money to gangsters. Hellspawn, Blood Brothers, Satyrites…you name it."

"And so he was fired," Tim said.

"We spent almost a year on the investigation," Volkerps said. "Had to go back through every case he had ever worked. Azag, what a mess."

"Charges?" Tim asked.

Volkerps shook one of his heads. "The board preferred that the whole thing be handled as quietly as possible."

Tim was not surprised by this. No company liked to publicize cases of massive internal fraud. It was bad for business. Many perpetrators were quietly let go, often with generous severance packages and a nice letter of recommendation included in the terms of their nondisclosure agreement.

"What does he do now?" Tim asked.

"He runs his own supernatural artefacts and consulting business," Volkerps said. "He's got a place down in Little Purgatory. Markets himself as a respectable trader and import-export specialist, but it's just a front. He really makes most of his money as a high-end fence."

"So if somebody did happen to get their hands on an item like the Hesselthorn Puzzle Box, then Ugarte might be exactly the kind of guy they would approach if they wanted to try and sell it on the black market," Tim said.

"He would," Volkerps said.

"And if Ugarte worked here for all those years," Tim continued. "Then he might even know how to deactivate our tracer alarms."

"Before he worked at SIU, Ugarte worked in Claims Tech and Logistics," Volkerps said.

"So not only did he know how those alarms worked," Tim said. "He actually built and programmed them."

"That he did," Volkerps said. "There are few beings inside or outside this building who know more about how we work than he does."

Tim sat back in his chair. "Sounds like I need to have a little chat with Mr. Ugarte."

"Indeed," Volkerps said. "And not to belabour the point, but be extremely careful when you do. Chances are, with an object of this kind of profile, if Ugarte is involved, then he's not alone."

"Right," Tim said.

The werewolves had taken his Demon Charger and Demonex, but he figured that he might need a little more in the way of self-protection, under the circumstances. He decided that he would stop by his father's shop and pick up a replacement charger as well as something with a little more kick before he went over to Ugarte's place. Technically, he still had his remediation certification and could claim to be part of his father's operation, which would allow him to move around with more...*persuasive*...anti-spectral tech than the general public was permitted to carry without a licence.

"I would suggest you give Ugarte's file," Volkerps said. "There might be something in there that proves useful."

"Will do," Tim nodded, grabbing his laptop bag and getting up to leave. "Thanks."

He headed back up to Asgaroth's, where Madeline was showing a selection of crystal balls to a short woman wearing a black kaftan and more bracelets and necklaces than seemed humanly possible. Tim didn't have time to wait around, so he just waved and headed out to his car. As soon as he was inside, he called his mother.

"Yes, Timothy?" she said. By the background noise, he could tell she was at one of her salons. They were all tuned to the same mystical electronica satellite radio station.

"Hey ma," Tim said, checking to make sure the lane was free before pulling into traffic. "What time should I show up tonight?"

There was no point in grilling his mother about why she had invited a woman Tim was not enthusiastic about dating to a family dinner. Regina did that sort of thing all the time. Resistance was futile.

"Show up where?" his mother said.

"At your place," Tim said. "Madeline said you invited her over for dinner tonight."

"Oh, that," Regina said in an odd tone.

"What?" Tim asked.

"I'm hiring her to work at one of my salons," Regina said. "She has a wonderful idea for a new skin cream we're going to discuss."

"Okay?" Tim said.

"What I mean is that it's a *working* dinner," Regina said.

"Okay," Tim said. "So what does that mean? Does that mean you don't *want* me to show up?"

"Don't be silly," Regina said. "You know you're always welcome. Along with your brother provided he isn't covered in the blood of yet another poor, demented young girl with a death wish."

Something strange was going on here, Tim thought. He just couldn't put his finger on what it was.

"What I mean is you haven't orchestrated this as some sort of set-up or potential girlfriend vetting process like usual," Tim said.

"Don't be ridiculous," Regina said. "I have long ago given up on trying to help kickstart your love life."

"Ma, you tried setting me up with your new receptionist just last week," Tim pointed out.

"Well, those days are over," Regina said. "If you want to continue to hide away in your little dungeon and pout over that heartless security guard who ran off on you, then I won't interfere."

"What do you mean dungeon?" Tim said. "Are you talking about my apartment?"

"Everyone knows the Decameron is a seedy flophouse for deadbeat ghosts and low-rent ghouls," Regina continued. "I don't know why you continue to live there. Anyway, I really don't think that Madeline is the girl for you. Don't forget, I'm one of the most trusted and experienced seers in the city and I don't see any future there. As your mother and your psychic advisor, I would strongly urge you to let that one go and move on to explore other paths."

Something truly and deeply weird is happening here, Tim thought. His mother had spent practically his entire post-puberty life attempting to pair him off with deeply unsuitable women. The only possible explanation for her current behaviour was that she had just become the victim of a supernatural identity theft.

"Are you feeling okay, ma?" Tim asked. "You haven't suddenly started levitating or developed an irresistible urge to transfer everything in your bank account to some unknown entity, have you?"

"Don't be ridiculous, Timothy," his mother sniffed. "I'm simply saying that I have only ever had your best interests at heart and I truly believe that this is not the woman for you. Tonight's dinner is merely a welcoming gesture for a new employee and nothing more. Now I have to go. We've got the entire cast of that new haunted house reality show coming in for full packages and we have to prepare. Ciao!"

The line went dead. Tim stared out the window and tried to figure out what in the world was going on. No matter how many times he turned the conversation around in his mind, the only logical explanation was that some sort of demonic entity had taken control of Regina Lovecraft.

She had never invited one of her staff over for dinner before just to talk business as far as Tim could remember. And warning him *not* to date a psychic with whom he had practically nothing in common? That was upside-down bizarro territory.

Maybe dad will have some idea what's going on, Tim thought as he pulled up in front of Thad's shop.

When he went inside, however, his father wasn't there.

"You just missed him," Stake said, pointing to the door that Thad had evidently just walked through. "The big man went out to pick up some special gear we're gonna need for the new job."

"That's okay," Tim said, walking around the front counter and through the staff door into the supply room. "I just stopped by to pick up a couple of things."

"How did things go with your emergency mission?" Stake asked, following Tim into the back where Thad kept most of his high-end gear and dangerous chemical agents in a locked storage room. The room was always open during the day, which meant that the smell of the concentrated Demonex and other anti-spectral agents seeped into every corner of the place.

"Fine," Tim said, flicking on the light. "Just part of a case I'm working on."

"Confidential matter," Stake said, nodding in a knowingly conspiratorial way. "Roger that."

"Pretty much," Tim said, not keen to get into the details of what had happened at the werewolf bar. "You seem to be doing well. Landed on your feet after the whole NightStalker thing."

"Things are great!" Stake nodded. "Working with your dad is the best job I've ever had. Even better than when I had my own thing. I mean, come on! I get paid to take out the worst of the supernatural worst! Demons trying to horn in and take over people's houses or appliances? Vampires sucking around breaking into pet stores and labs? Werewolves marking their territory in private gardens? And they call me to take them out? Come on! It just doesn't get any better than that."

"Yeah," Tim said. "The place hasn't changed much from when I worked here."

"Oh, but it will!" Stake said. "This new contract is gonna put us on the map big time! We're even bidding for defence contracts, although I'm not supposed to say anything about that yet."

"Uh huh," Tim said. He didn't care for the way Stake referred to his father's business as "we". He had no idea how a character like Stake, with his criminal past and various diagnosed personality disorders, would ever pass the kind of high-level security vetting process required to work with the federal government, but he had also learned never to underestimate the guy.

"So I guess things with you and that Tabitha chick didn't work out," Stake said, scratching the shaved part of his scalp next to his mohawk. "Your mom said she ran off with some ex-boyfriend or something?"

"Yeah, something like that," Tim said, having no wish to get into the matter.

Tim scanned the shelves and picked a few items off. He knew a wide variety of entities would be interested in the Puzzle Box, so he made his choices accordingly. He grabbed a mini sun gun, which shot a beam of high frequency light that would deter vampires. Next he picked up a silver sprayer, which was a canister that shot a concentrated jet of a compound that repelled werewolves.

The last thing he took was a Devil Stick. The Devil Stick was like a Demon Charger except larger and more powerful. Where the Demon Charger was a contact weapon, the Devil Stick fired a bolt of heavy phased energy at a target up to 500 metres away. It was also capable of incapacitating larger demons, like Serrabluks and Ornithons, against which the Charger barely registered.

"Uh, are you authorized to use all of that?" Stake asked, looking at the Devil Stick as Tim loaded it into his SIU bag. "I mean, the big man knows you're taking it?"

Tim paused. He hadn't actually told his father that he would be stopping by or mentioned that he would need to borrow anything, so technically, on some level, he probably shouldn't be helping himself. On the other hand, he didn't think his father would have any issues with it. Thad was always bringing home the latest gear to show off or try out.

Tim recognized that it went beyond that, though. He had taken very little to do with the family business since he finished college and got the job at Crimson Seal. He hadn't really thought about what would happen when Thad decided to step back or retire. Would Thad sell the business? Or would he just hand everything over to Stake to run the show? It was a little alarming how quickly the former nighttime vigilante had inserted himself into the operation. The other times Tim had stopped by the place, nobody said boo to him or questioned why he might be there. Stake, however, was a different matter.

It wasn't that Tim didn't trust Stake, it was just that Stake had never struck him as an entirely stable guy. If he were to open the news one day and find out that Stake had been arrested for walking into the middle of a vampire neighbourhood association meeting and pulling the pin on a sun grenade, Tim would not be remotely surprised. Stake was a true believer. It just so happened that what Stake believed was probably going to get him–and several others–incinerated.

"He's aware," Tim said, making a mental note to call his father and let Thad know that he had stopped by to borrow some equipment.

"No problem," Stake said, making notes on a clipboard that he seemed to produce from nowhere. "I'll just record everything so that the inventory numbers match up. Did you grab one Devil Stick or two?"

"Just one," Tim said through gritted teeth.

"Yeah, those are pretty badass," Stake said. "You should see the new repulsor packs we're getting, though! Strong enough to blast a Djinn straight back into the ninth circle on a single charge! We ordered a load of them at the last SpectraCon. Serious, military-grade hardware. We're gonna need it for this new Crypt Network job."

"Oh yeah?" Tim said distractedly. He did not share Stake's fascination with anti-spectral tech.

"Give me three good men with those things and I could clean up this city in a single night!" Stake said, his eyes drifting into a far off expression. "Couldn't let you walk out with one of those, obviously!"

"Oh no?" Tim said.

"No way!" Stake laughed. "You'd burn your face off before you'd even picked it up! You need a level three spectral device licence, minimum. Definitely not for civilians. Although, the stuff you've got there is probably fine for the kind of thing you have to deal with on a day-to-day basis. You know, for around the office or whatever."

"Never hurts to be prepared," Tim said, grabbing a replacement canister of Demonex as well.

"True that," Stake said.

Tim thought about grabbing some garlic bombs, but decided against it. A couple of them had accidentally detonated in the trunk of his car once and he had never really been able to get rid of the smell. Tabitha had always joked about it whenever they went anywhere in his car instead of hers. She called it the Stankmobile.

"Congrats on your employee of the year award, incidentally," Tim said. "I worked for my dad for three summers and never won anything like that, so he doesn't hand it out to just anybody."

"Thanks," Stake said. "Your parents have been great. They even invited me over for dinner tonight."

Tim was just reaching for a battery pack used to recharge the Devil Stick when he stopped. "They what?"

"Yeah," Stake said. "Your dad said he wanted to sit down and go over some of the details on the upcoming job."

"The upcoming job?" Tim repeated.

"Yeah," said Stake. "He said it would be like a working dinner."

"Oh he did, did he?" Tim said.

"Yeah," Stake said, looking confused. "I wasn't going to bring the schematics, but now I'm thinking maybe I should. What do you think?"

Tim smiled. "Oh, I think you can probably leave the schematics at the office. They probably have…other things they're going to want you to focus on."

"Really?" Stake said. "Like what?"

"You'll see," Tim said, heading for the door. "Tell the big man I stopped by."

Tim made his way back out through the shop. So that was it, he thought. His mother wasn't trying to push things along with Madeline. She was trying to set Madeline up with Stake. That was why she had said all that stuff to him about Madeline not being a good match.

Tim felt a mix of anger, confusion and guilt. Sure he didn't think things were going to work out with Madeline, but that didn't give his mother the right to try and set her up with somebody else! As far as Regina knew, he and Madeline were still dating. Where the hell did she come off playing matchmaker with another guy? Especially when the other guy in question was Stake of all people?

Tim's mind was reeling as he stepped outside. How ironic was it that his mother was interfering in his love life in order to break him up with exactly the kind of woman she used to set him up with? And she had the guile to try and do the whole thing behind his back! Well, she wasn't going to get away with this.

Tim pulled out his phone and was about to dial when he spotted a dark figure in the alley across the street. The figure was crouching down behind a stack of empty crates next to an old vampire bar called the ArtLine. It was the middle of the day and the place was closed. As Tim stopped and looked directly at the figure, whoever it was ducked down and ran the other way.

"What the hell?" Tim muttered. Was somebody actually following him?

Tim shoved his phone back in his pocket and jogged across the street. By the time he reached the entrance to the alley between the bar and the building next door, whoever had been there was gone.

Tim debated whether or not to try to follow. There was a dumpster next to the bar that showed many of the classic signs of homeless vampire habitation. The vent openings had been crudely covered up to block out any possible sunlight and the ground around it was covered with broken keg valves, which desperate vampires broke off to suck out the last dregs of leftover plasma.

If he did venture in, there was no telling who or what he might run into. Even though it was daylight, the alley was almost totally shaded, and he had no interest in stumbling straight into the middle of a ravenous nest of thirsty bloodsuckers. He had almost been spiked by baggers once before and knew there was no shortage of them in this part of town.

Tim dropped the idea and headed back to his car. He needed to talk to Ugarte. Volkerps was getting impatient with his lack of progress on the Hesselthorn case and openly talking about replacing him. He was chasing down an item that could potentially bankrupt his company. He didn't have time to go running down dark alleys in pursuit of shady figures who would probably turn out to be nothing more than smelly pigeon suckers.

As he got behind the wheel and started the car, he reminded himself to be careful. If somebody really was following him, they were probably after more than his blood. He decided that he would deal with his mother later.

Right now, he had more devious fish to fry.

11

The Blue Demon occupied the first floor of a narrow blackstone building on Lower Brimstone Avenue between a tattoo parlour and a zombie nightclub called Carpe Callosum.

There were heavy silver bars mounted in front of the window and a thick silver plate welded to the front door to deter both human and supernatural intruders. A sign written in faded red script above the window promised: "Expert Consultations and the RAREST Artefacts Bought & Sold!"

Tim paused to look at the artefacts mounted in the window, which included two funerary urns, a worn copy of Clythe's *Demonomicon* and the ugliest clown doll he had ever seen in his life. None of them were labelled. At first glance, the urns looked similar to the ones used in sacrificial altar pits, but Tim could see the handles had been glued on with ordinary adhesive instead of being melted into place with Hellfire, which was a sure sign that they were fake.

The *Demonomicon* was the infamous "lost" volume of Professor Johannes Clythe's *Infernal Perambulations* cycle. Every known copy had supposedly been burned shortly after its publication as it was rumored to contain curses so horrible that not even the demon Allfathers had dared use them. Every year, at least a dozen copies were "found" and put up for private sale or auction and every year almost all of them turned out to be forgeries, some more skillful than others. Tim had no doubt this one was no more legitimate than the urns.

Tim turned his head and looked at the clown, which turned its head and looked back at him, its mouth twisting up into a horrible rictus of a smile.

Okay, Tim thought. It's probably not really possessed, but it's still creepy as hell. I'll give it that.

Tim glanced up at the camera mounted on the wall next to the sign. He recognized it as a SpectraCam XD. The place might look like a dump, but it had top-of-the-line security.

Tim stepped up to the door. Attached to a brick on the right was a silver plate with a button that may have at one time lit up but no longer did. Pasted at an angle above the button was a cheap black strip that looked like it came out of an antique label maker that read, simply: "Service". Tim pushed the button. He did not hear any corresponding buzz from inside to indicate that it was working. He counted to 15 and pushed it again.

"How may I be of assistance?" crackled a surprisingly plummy voice. Tim couldn't tell if it was a real accent or a fake one, but he was guessing the latter. Ugarte's file said he came from East Necropolis, and Tim knew the people who lived there did not sound like that.

"Hello," Tim said. "I'd like to speak to Mr. Damien Ugarte."

"I see," said the voice. "And whom should I advise Senor Ugarte is calling upon him this afternoon?"

"My name is Tim Lovecraft," Tim said. "I'd like to discuss an extremely rare item of great value."

"Indeed?" said the voice. "Then do come in, Mr. Lovecraft."

Tim heard a click and the door swung open. Tim stepped inside to find himself in a long, narrow space illuminated with two banks of overhead fluorescent lights. The lights gave everything a sickly green pallor. Some of them were flickering with an audible crackle, like bug zappers.

The walls on either side were lined with cheap wooden shelves stacked with a variety of items similar to the ones in the window. Tim saw worn Vandoo dolls, a row of smudgy crystal balls, and a selection of dusty and chipped Ouija boards. None of the items looked like they had been moved in decades.

Tim's initial impression was that the place did not feel like the home of a high-end artefacts house. It felt like a pawn shop.

At the far end of the room was the sales desk, behind which stood a satyr in some sort of purple cloak. He was wearing the eyepatch that Tim had seen in the security footage, although Tim was almost positive that the patch was now covering the other eye. His beard was woven together with a strand of red and gold beads and he sported a jaunty red fez on his head. He didn't look sophisticated. He looked like he should be performing at children's birthday parties.

"Welcome to my store, Mr. Lovecraft," Ugarte said. "How may I be of assistance?"

"Damien Ugarte?" Tim said, walking towards the counter.

"That I am," said the satyr, giving a slight bow. "No more, no less. Now which extremely rare object of unimaginable value did you wish to ask me about? As you can see, I have many mysterious items of great value and terrible power here on my shelves. All of them have stories. Some will terrify you! Some will amaze you! Some will thrill you! And some, if you are not careful, will kill you."

Tim could tell by the way Ugarte finished speaking with a practiced flourish of his manicured claws that this was a carefully rehearsed speech. He probably gave it to every potential sucker who stepped through his front door.

"I'm sure," Tim said. "I'm here to ask you about the Hesselthorn Puzzle Box."

Ugarte's beaded eyebrows shot up so fast that his eyepatch almost fell off.

"Excuse me?" he coughed.

"The Hesselthorn Puzzle Box," Tim repeated. "The one that recently went missing from the vault of the Hesselthorn estate. Along with its owner, Lucifer Hesselthorn."

"My good man," Ugarte said, smiling. "I'm afraid that I wouldn't have the slightest-"

"The same Hesselthorn Puzzle Box that you saw only last night in a werewolf bar called the Torn Throat?" Tim said.

"Who are you?" Ugarte said, standing up straight. Like most satyrs, he was surprisingly tall when not in his normal hunched position. "A cop?"

"I am not," Tim said.

"Then beat it," Ugarte said, dropping the accent. "You've got no proof that I was anywhere other than here last night."

Tim took his cell phone out of his pocket and held it up to show the screenshot from the Torn Throat's security video. He had done as much as he possibly could to clean the image up and remove some of the blur.

"As you can see from the timestamp in this screencap of security footage of the bar at the Torn Throat, it looks like you *were* somewhere other than here last night," Tim said. "You're kind of hard to miss."

"How did you get that?" Ugarte said with a note of alarm. "If you're not a cop, then who are you?"

Tim put the phone back in his pocket and pulled out his SIU badge. "I work for the Special Investigations Unit, Crimson Seal Insurance. I imagine you're not entirely unfamiliar with it."

'You're kidding," Ugarte said, his jaw dropping. "You work for Volkerps?"

"I do," Tim said.

"Don't remember them ever having a human in that department," Ugarte said, giving Tim an appraising look.

"I was the first," Tim said.

"Well, well, well," Ugarte said. "So how is the old gang? Lonnie still there?"

"He's on leave right now," Tim said.

"Not surprising," Ugarte said. "That guy was so tightly wound. Always knew he'd snap one day. And how is Volkerps? The old bastard finally plug in one too many room deodorizers and blow the grid?"

"No," Tim said.

"I bet he told you all about me," Ugarte said, smiling.

"I read your file," Tim said. He had read the copy that Volkerps had emailed to him in the car before driving over. He almost got a parking ticket because it had taken longer than he had expected. It was a big file.

"I'm sure you did," Ugarte said. "It's not what it seems."

"It was quite comprehensive," Tim said. Ugarte's record of under-the-table kickbacks, fraud, skimming and outright theft covered almost the entire duration of his employment with Crimson Seal.

"I'm not saying that I'm innocent," Ugarte said. "But I wasn't the only one working both sides of the street. My game was nickel poker compared to what was going on over in Claims."

"Uh huh," Tim said. Moral relativism was a popular defence. Almost everyone he had investigated eventually resorted to it.

"You're probably new, right?" Ugarte said. "How long you been there? A year?"

"About that," Tim said.

"Right," Ugarte said, nodding. "You're still too green to have any idea what's really going on. Well, allow me to let you in on a little secret, okay? They're all doing it. Especially in SIU! Are you kidding me? You take a group that knows fraud better than anybody and stick 'em in a place with no real oversight? What do you think's gonna happen? The only reason they didn't try to put me in jail was because they knew they'd all end up in the same cell block! I know things. A lot of things. The kinds of things that your flaming devil fart of a boss doesn't want getting out, believe me!"

Tim put the ID badge back in his pocket and strolled to the side of the counter as Ugarte talked. Leaning against the wall was a black cane with an elaborate silver handle in the shape of a naked and extremely buxom sea nymph.

"Wow," Tim said, picking it up and bouncing it in his hand to test the weight. "This is impressive. Yours?"

"Yeah," Ugarte said, looking confused. "Why?"

"Do you actually need it?" Tim asked, turning the cane around in his hands to examine it more closely.

"What do you mean?" Ugarte asked, narrowing his eyes.

"As in, to walk," Tim said. "Do you have an actual physical impairment or is it just an affectation? Like your accent or your hat or your eyepatch or just about everything else about you?"

"A lot of people don't trust satyrs," Ugarte said. "A few small refinements here and there helps to put them at ease."

"Well, that's one way to do it, I suppose," Tim said, putting the cane back down where he had found it. "It's pretty heavy, too. So I imagine it comes in handy when some of those same people figure out you ripped them off."

"As I was saying," Ugarte said, pointing towards the door. "You need to get your ass out of my store. I have nothing to say to you. And you can tell that two-headed hornsucker you work for he can kiss my ponytailed ass."

"Oh I will," Tim said. "Just as soon as you tell me who you were meeting with at the Torn Throat last night."

"I dunno what you're talking about," Ugarte said, coming out from behind the counter to reveal a large pair of glitter-studded hooves. "Now I'm only gonna say this one more time. Get out of here before I stomp you into paste."

Tim casually pulled the Devil Stick out of his SIU bag and leaned it against his shoulder, causing Ugarte to stop in his tracks.

"What the hell are you doing with that?" Ugarte said, taking a half step back. "Those things are illegal!"

"Only if you're not licenced to carry one," Tim said. "But, as it happens, I have completed all the courses in order to receive the necessary Class 2 permit, and so I am legally allowed to use such a device for spectral remediation and self defence. In a strictly professional capacity, of course."

"Are you threatening me?" Ugarte said.

"Not at all," Tim said. "I think you were the one who said you were going to attack me. I was just asking you a question. But since you seem reluctant to respond, how about I give you my theory?"

"How about I cut your balls off and mount them in my window display?" Ugarte hissed.

"At least they'd be genuine," Tim said. "Which would be more than could be said about any of the other junk you have in there. Except for the clown. That thing is legit creepy."

"It's an antique," Ugarte said, dropping momentarily back into sales mode. "It was found in the ruins of the Poordam Orphanage. It contains more than two dozen individual spectral entities!"

"I got that impression," Tim said. "But as I was saying. My theory is that whoever stole the Hesselthorn Puzzle Box was aware that the item had a claims tracking device on it."

"So?" Ugarte shrugged.

"So that strongly suggests the theft was committed by a member of the Hesselthorn family," Tim said. "Probably Ludwig or Lucretia. They knew the tracker was there, but they didn't know how to disable it, so they stashed the box in a blocking container. Probably a Croatoan Cage. They're expensive, but certainly not out of the reach of a trust fund baby like one of them."

"Again, so?" Ugarte said.

"So they needed help disabling the tracker," Tim said. "Somebody with inside knowledge of how such a tracker worked and, more importantly, how to shut it off. Somebody with highly specialized knowledge and a willingness to look the other way. Somebody, in other words, exactly like you."

"I don't know what you're talking about," Ugarte said.

"They give you a call or more likely drop you an encrypted email," Tim said. "You agree to meet in a neutral location. Somewhere off the beaten path. The kind of place where they're used to looking the other way on extra-legal matters. Someplace like the Torn Throat."

"That's bullshit," Ugarte said.

"You meet," Tim said. "You agree to deactivate the tracker for a cut of the proceeds. You know there are a lot of buyers out there who are willing to pay just about anything to get their claws on an item like that. You probably even offer to broker the sale."

"You're in fantasyland," Ugarte said.

"The problem is, you don't quite disable the tracker in time," Tim said. "Who knows why. You are getting old. Rusty. Slow. Losing your touch."

"Bite me," Ugarte spat.

"Pass," Tim said. "The tracker gets a beep out. Just one. But it's enough. You and your new business partner clear out. Only you're not quite as smart as your companion. You show your extremely recognizable face to the camera, beaded eyepatch and all."

"You can't prove anything!" Ugarte said, throwing his arms up and laughing. "I used to do your job! And I know that you've got squat!"

"On the contrary," Tim said. "I have your smiling face at the scene."

"Maybe I was there and maybe I wasn't," Ugarte said. "Doesn't mean a thing. Go ahead and call the cops if you like. Won't make any difference!"

"Oh, but it's not just any cop who's been assigned to this case," Tim said. "Haven't you heard? They brought the great Horatio Duluc out of retirement for this one. The great psychic detective himself."

"That guy's a phony," Ugarte sneered. "Everybody knows he just plays a psychic on TV. He hasn't got any real ability."

"Still," Tim said, looking around. "I notice that roughly half of the stock on these shelves is stolen and the other half is fake. How closely do you want the cops looking at that?"

"Go ahead and rat me out if it makes you feel better," Ugarte hissed. "It won't get you any closer to the box!"

"But I'm not the only one looking for it," Tim said, stepping closer and pointing the Devil Stick at Ugarte. "You should know that better than anyone."

"What do you mean?" Ugarte said.

"Are you kidding?" Tim said. "That box is a legend. Everyone wants it. The Hellspawn. The Blood Brothers. Every criminal organization in this city is looking for it. Should word reach the street that you have the box? Or even that you know where the box is? How long do you think you'd get to perambulate around swinging your cane and sporting that tacky little bucket on your head before one of them snatches you up and gives you a few dozen more breathing holes?"

"Go ahead!" Ugarte said. "I'm not afraid of those guys!"

"Then you must be a lot braver than you look," Tim said. "I've heard the Hellspawn have a particular fondness for satyrs. Especially slow-roasted with some allspice and a little fenugreek on the side."

"You don't understand!" Ugarte said. "She told me she'd kill me if I said anything!"

"She?" Tim said. "As in Lucretia Hesselthorn? Is that who you met with?"

Ugarte grabbed his cane and waved it at Tim.

"You stay away from me!" he said. "Just get out of here!"

Ugarte darted behind the counter and disappeared through the back door, slamming it loudly behind him. Tim took one last look around before heading back out the front door. The place really was a dump and he didn't want to spend any more time in here than was absolutely necessary.

He had a lead, though, which was good. The problem was, he was going to need help to follow it up, and it was not the kind of help he would enjoy asking for.

12

Tim drove back to his apartment. He needed to talk to Keef, whom he found dozing under the dining room table next to a half-empty bottle of Old Nosferatu 80 Proof O Negative Whiskey.

Tim shook his head and knelt down to put the cork back in the bottle. He didn't care for regular whiskey, but just the smell of this stuff was enough to make his stomach lurch. Fortunately, all of the blinds were closed, which was the only reason that his brother hadn't passed out and immolated himself.

"Keef!" Tim said, shaking his brother's shoulder. "Wake up!"

Keef snorted and let out a belch that made Tim recoil. He looked around the room. There was no sign of Killian or any of the women who had volunteered to have their blood sucked out as part of Keef's half-assed vampire training camp.

"Keef!" Tim said, shaking his brother more forcefully. "Arise, you putz!"

Keef let out a gurgling sound and opened his eyes. "Ugh. Where am I?"

"You're under the dining room table," Tim said.

"Our dining room table?" Keef squinted.

"*My* dining room table," Tim said.

"What the hell am I doing there?" Keef asked, rubbing his forehead. "What time is it?"

"Just after seven," Tim said. "I need you to do me a favour."

"Seven?" Keef said. "Morning or evening?"

"Evening," Tim said. "What the hell have you been doing?"

"It's kinda fuzzy," Keef groaned. "The girls wanted to go to Circle 9, so I think we started with a few drinks and a bite. After that, I kinda lost the thread. You know, the whole timeline of events becomes cloudy."

"You're lucky you didn't charbroil yourself," Tim said.

"What can I say?" Keef said. "I live a charmed life."

Keef crawled out from under the table and leaned against the couch. "Man, I need a drink."

"I think you've probably had enough," Tim said, shaking the whiskey bottle.

"Yuck, not that stuff," Keef said, wincing. "I was up half the night barfing because of that stuff. No, I mean fresh blood. Where's my phone? I need to order something from Blud2go. Have them send over a nice, fat, juicy O Positive with ruddy cheeks and soft skin."

Keef began padding his pockets looking for his phone.

"Before you do that, I need your help with something," Tim said.

"You need my help?" Keef said. "With what? You want me to set you up with one of the audition chicks? Between you and me, I'd steer clear of show business women, man. Take it from me. Lot of impurities in those veins."

"It's not that," Tim said. "I need you to get me into thVrst."

"Are you kidding?" Keef said. "Why in the hell do you need to get in there? That place is exclusive with a capital X."

"It's for a case I'm working on," Tim said. "I need to have a chat with one of the members."

"Well, ask me in like a year from now when my movie comes out and I'm top of the A list," Keef said. "Because right now, there's no way they'd let either of us through the front door."

"What about Killian?" Tim suggested.

Keef thought about this for a moment. "Yeah. I mean, I guess he could. Guy's got connections out the wazoo. But…"

"But what?" Tim asked.

"I dunno," Keef said. "It's just…I'd feel weird asking him for something like that. You know? It's like asking a celebrity for a selfie. It's just kind of, well…lame."

"What are you talking about?" Tim said. "He's your familiar! He has to do everything you ask him to do!"

"Well, yeah," Keef said. "I mean, *technically* that's true."

"He doesn't do everything you ask him to do, you don't turn him into a vampire!" Tim said. "Correct?"

"Well, yeah…"

"Are you his master or not?" Tim said. He didn't like applying so much pressure, but this case was important and he needed to follow up this lead if he was going to have any chance of solving it.

"I mean, I guess I am…" Keef mumbled. "You know, despite the fact that I find the whole master-slave dichotomy thing to be pretty retro in a deeply uncool way, if you know what I mean. We modern vampires look at it as more of a symbiotic deal than they did back in the day. Not so woke."

"All right then!" Tim said, pulling Keef to his feet and straightening out his wrinkled shirt. "Then march right in there, pull him out of his coffin and command him to get us into thVrst tonight else he face your righteous wrath."

"Okay," Keef nodded. "I'll, uh, see what he says. While I'm in there, you think you could order me something? My head is killing me and I could really go for a nice, chubby virgin right about now."

"I'll get you a Blood Blast from the fridge," Tim said.

"Okay," Keef said. "I guess that'll tide me over. I'll be right back."

Keef headed for his bedroom. Tim decided that he should probably change if he was going to try to look like somebody who could pass for a member at an ultra-exclusive club and headed into his room, where he was greeted with yet another unexpected sight.

"Tig Tag!" said Clawfist, fluttering past Tim's head as Tim stepped through the door and stopped in his tracks. "Par Pat!"

The tiny demon had not, it seemed, relocated to Tim's SIU bag. And not only was he back, he seemed to have brought half the parademons in the city back with him.

"What the hell?" Tim gasped.

His bedroom was filled–from floor to ceiling–with tiny demons. There were eight of them on his bed playing what looked like some sort of elaborate board game that involved colored smoke pots and animated skeletons. A dozen more were lined up along the top of his desk doing choreographed dives into a flaming bucket on the floor. A pack of them were racing back and forth across the ceiling chasing a glowing green ball. Another group was sprawled out on the floor around some sort of miniature barbecue pit. A fat demon with a single green eye and a body covered in so many horns that he resembled a cactus was standing next to the pit rotating a spit upon which was the blackened husk of what Tim desperately hoped was not a cat. Especially not the cat that belonged to one of his neighbours and featured prominently on a sad Lost Pet poster taped up in the lobby.

"What is going on?" Tim squealed as the green ball bounced past his face and crashed into the ceiling light. "Clawfist!"

"Freg Fig?" Clawfist said, offering Tim a charred piece of something that was furry and still smoking.

"I don't want whatever that is!" Tim said, waving his arms and stepping carefully towards his closet. He opened the door to find a gang of purple demons hanging off his best suit, which they were in the process of eating. Tim grabbed the suit and shook them off. "That's mine!"

"Sut Sat?" Clawfist said as Tim examined what was left of his wardrobe. The suit was covered in hundreds of tiny bites that looked like cigarette burns. Many of his other jackets and shirts had received similar treatment.

"Oh, you've got to be kidding me!" Tim hissed. "I step out for five minutes and I come back to find my bedroom turned into some sort of pint-sized demon resort?"

"Part Put?" Clawfist said, landing on Tim's shoulder and appearing to examine the remains of Tim's suit.

"No!" Tim said, causing Clawfist to jump off and hover near the ceiling out of attack range. "This is not a party! This is my bedroom!"

"Bast Bat?" Clawfist said.

"You need to clear out!" Tim yelled, waving his hands at the demons. "I already have too many people living here! Do you understand? I don't have room for some sort of demon frat party in my bedroom!"

The demons paid no attention to Tim's efforts to disrupt their fun. They simply jumped or swooped out of the way, although some of the more aggressive ones burped tiny fireballs or lightning bolts in his direction. Tim spent another fruitless few minutes trying to shoo them out before giving up and stomping out of the room.

He would need to do some research and find out the best way to banish an infestation of parademons from a residential space. If he couldn't find anything in the Crimson Seal manuals, he might have to resort to calling in his father. The only thing that gave him pause was that the thought of having to call in Stake to take care of such an embarrassing problem was too galling to contemplate.

In the meantime, however, he was going to have to find something to wear to thVrst. Since his own clothes were trashed, he had no alternative but to borrow something from Keef. Everything Keef owned looked like it had been stolen from the lost and found bin of a goth swingers club, but Tim figured that he didn't really have any other choice.

The last time Tim had been forced to borrow clothing from his brother was when they had snuck into Circle 9, which was a packed and pulsing nightclub. This would also be a stealth operation, but one that would call for a much more muted wardrobe. Once inside, they would need to blend in to the point of invisibility.

He was definitely drawing the line at capes, though. Even if there was a dress code, there was no way he was wearing one. Even vampires looked stupid in them. He didn't care that they were supposedly back in fashion. If fashion liked capes, then fashion was stupid. Capes were for bloodsucking wannabes and cosplayers. Tim didn't have anything against anyone from either of those groups, but that didn't mean he had to look like them.

13

ThVrst was located in a surprisingly anonymous-looking cinder block building on Renfield Street right in the middle of the Neck.

The name of the neighbourhood had been shortened from "bottleneck", which was how commuters had long referred to the 3-mile-wide choke point that formed the closest geographical convergence point of the Acheron and Styx rivers. It had been home to a seemingly endless daily traffic jam for much of the north-south traffic on the city's west side until the Morningstar Parkway had been built to route commuters over and around the area.

That was also when the demographic shift had started, with many of the old factory and warehouse businesses moving out and a whole new population moving in. The new arrivals were almost exclusively vampires, many of whom were drawn to the area mainly because it had the fewest churches, temples and altar sites per square mile in the city.

The new owners quickly went about transforming what had once been a grimy industrial zone into one of the most exclusive, desirable and expensive chunks of real estate in town. Factories became luxury lofts where units routinely went for sale prices in the middle seven figures. The same thing happened to most of the warehouses, which were quickly sub-divided up and converted into townhouses and apartments.

The Neck was also attractive to vampires because it contained one of the few sections of the Crypt Network that had been completed before the project was abandoned. The tunnels allowed Neckers (as they called themselves) to move around below ground, which was a huge advantage to a demographic that was deathly allergic to the sun.

"Man, I am *definitely* getting a place out here as soon as I hit it big," Keef said, his face plastered to the rear passenger side window as Tim made his way through traffic to their destination. "The loft units out here are just *insane*."

"I have many clients who live out here," Killian said from his spot in the passenger seat. Tim wasn't super-familiar with this part of town and Keef's agent had taken the shotgun seat in order to help with directions. "As soon as you book *Blood Stalker*, we'll make it happen."

"You have other clients who are vampires?" Tim asked.

"All the big ones," Killian said. "You name it, I get a piece of it. At least until they forced me out. Damn ghouls."

"Ghouls forced you out?" Tim asked.

"They're buying up everything." Killian said. "Flesheating scumbags. They'll even eat each other if they get the chance."

"We have a fair number of ghouls at Crimson Seal," Tim said. "They seem to be mostly in legal and finance."

It was an unpleasant stereotype that ghouls were only interested in making money. HEX-TV had recently run a story claiming that ghouls made up 90 per cent of the hedge fund managers at the six major in-vestment banks responsible for the last financial crash, but Tim treated anything that came out of Sticker Helsing's mouth with more than average skepticism.

"As soon as they found out about my diagnosis, they turfed me out." Killian said, making a flicking motion with his right middle finger.

"Diagnosis?" Tim said. "You mean the blood-drinking thing?

"Yeah," Killian said. "Found out last month I've got Cthuluthremia."

"Oh," Tim said. Cthuluthremia was a nasty parasitic condition that altered a victim's cellular reproduction process, slowly changing them from human into something more closely resembling a horrifying monster space squid. As far as Tim knew, the condition was only spread by eating (or coming into contact at a metabolic level) with cursed or possessed demon flesh. There was no known treatment and the condition was always fatal as most victims did not possess the financial means to launch themselves into space. "That's…uh, a tough one."

"No biggie," Killian said. "I had just got the news when I ran into your brother at the club one night. That's when we struck up our deal. I make him a star, he makes me a vampire. Everybody wins!"

"Right," Tim said.

There were, broadly speaking, two distinct groups of wannabe vampires. The first was made up of horny teenagers who had read too many of bestselling author Rianne Starch's *Bloodlust* series romance novels. The books, which Tim thought were formulaic and pulpy, portrayed vampire life as an eternal celebrity afterparty of glamorous carnal and consumer frenzy. The heroine, Mircalla Sangre, is turned into a vampire on the night of her high school graduation by a mysterious billionaire rock star named Vincent Nero, who then promptly disappears. Mircalla had so far spent 22 books and three movie adaptations searching for him with only limited success. Tim had been dragged to the first movie by a high school girlfriend and had broken up with her shortly afterwards because she kept pressuring him to let her stab him with a metal straw and suck his blood (her braces prevented her from the more traditional biting).

The second group, known as Grave Dodgers, was made up mostly of senior citizens and the terminally ill. They were understandably afraid of death and had decided that life as a vampire was better than the alternative. They tried desperately to get into vampire clubs and placed ads in online forums and message groups looking for a vampire willing to do the deed.

Killian, it seemed, was one of the latter.

What neither group seemed to understand was that vampire life was not what Rianne Starch or a million other movies or shows made it out to be. Even if you were rich, being a vampire did not mean a life of consequence-free decadence. And the vast majority of vampires were not rich. Vampire or not, you still needed a place to live and a steady supply of real or synthetic blood to survive.

If you couldn't go out in the sun, that seriously limited the kinds of jobs you could get. Vampires made up the largest percentage of the city's unemployed and homeless populations. Stroll past any blood bank in the city and you would find scores of them in the alley hiding under make-shift cardboard sunscreens and sleeping in dumpsters, subsisting largely on a diet of pigeons and rats. Glamorous it was not.

"I've heard this place is off the rails," Keef said.

"It is," Killian said.

"You've been inside?" Tim asked.

"Just once," Killian said. "Couple of years ago for Fang Bloodly's birthday party."

Fang Bloodly was the stage name of Cristos Necrostolus, host of a popular children's show called *Count Fang's House of Horribleness*. The show mixed animation with cornball sketches, most of which revolved around Count Fang's near destruction by a comedically incompetent vampire hunter named Beauregarde von Dumkopf. It was one of the longest-running shows on TV and somewhat groundbreaking in that it was the first network production to cast a real vampire in a lead role.

"He's a member?" Keef said in disbelief. "I used to watch that show every day when I was a kid!"

"Any vampire who's anybody in this city is a member," Killian said.

"Really?" Keef said. "In that case, I better get myself signed up."

"Don't hold your breath," Killian said. "The waitlist was 215 years last time I checked."

"Then it's a good thing I don't breathe," Keef said.

"You need at least three current members to sponsor your application," Killian said. "They're pretty selective about who they let in."

"That won't be a problem once I'm a big star," Keef said, waving this away.

"Of course not, darling," Killian said. "Let's just do one thing at a time. This is it up here on the right."

Tim passed the building, made a quick U-turn and parked half a block down on the other side of the street. The club did not look at all the way he had expected it would. Most night clubs announced their presence with neon lights, pumping music and caged succubus dancers dangling on either side of the entrance. In comparison, thVrst looked about as glamorous as a dentist's office. There were no lights, no dancers, no velvet rope and no visible security.

"Put these in," Killian said, handing Tim a set of fangs.

"Say what?" Tim said.

"It'th vampireth only," Killian said, inserting his own custom-designed set of diamond-studded gold teeth. He was still getting used to them and they tended to make him speak with a noticeable lisp. "Other-withe they won't let uth in."

"What about familiars?" Keef said.

"They have a theparate entranthe in the back," Killian said, checking his reflection in the rearview mirror. "They're not allowed into the main part of the club."

"If it's vampires only, I'm surprised they let in somebody like Lucretia Hesselthorn," Tim said.

"Don't be too thurprithed," Killian said. "Her family'th loaded. Be-thideth, I heard they won't let her into the party roomth. Hath to thtay in her own private VIP thuite."

"Any idea where it is?" Tim asked, inserting his own set of false teeth. They pinched his upper molars uncomfortably and tasted like tin foil. He decided that he would take them out again as soon as they were inside.

"No," Killian said. "My gueth ith thomewhere in the bathement."

"Okay," Tim said. "Once we're inside, you guys just quietly mingle. I'll make my way down and see if I can find Lucretia."

"Be careful," Killian said. "Thith ith a plathe where the motht powerful vampireth in the thity do thingth they can't do anywhere elthe. If they catch you, I won't be able to do anything to help."

"Thanks," Tim said as they got out of the car. "I'll keep that in mind."

Tim adjusted his leather cape as they approached the entrance, trying his best to wrap it around himself to hide the silver shirt and uncomfortably tight leather pants he had been forced to borrow from Keef on short notice. He felt like an idiot. It was bad enough having to wear a cape, but the fact that Keef hardly ever did laundry made it even worse. The shirt had bloodstains on the collar, which might actually be an advantage when it came to sneaking into a place like this, but was still gross.

Tim had stowed the sun gun in one of the cape's inner pockets and was strongly hoping that they wouldn't be searched on the way in, as a weapon like that would be impossible to explain away. Still, he didn't want to risk sneaking into a place like this without it.

They were greeted at the front door by a skinny vampire who was dressed in black leather overalls studded with hundreds of tiny gold spikes. Tim wondered how it was possible for this guy to sit down without leaving a grid pattern of holes in every chair. He had an elaborate tattoo of a bat on his left cheek and a row of metal piercings where his eyebrows would normally be. As they got closer, Tim could see that the piercings extended straight up the middle of the vampire's forehead and over the top of his skull, where they disappeared down the back of his neck.

"Welcome to thVrst, gentlemen," he vampire said. "What can I do for you this evening?"

"Let me handle thith," Killian hissed out the side of his mouth to Tim and Keef before turning back to the oddly dressed attendant. "Yeth, good evening! Name'th Cothtigan. My dear friend Fang Bloodly invited uth down here to vithit him."

"Are you members?" the vampire asked.

"Not yet," Killian said. "Fang thought we might want to check the place out firtht. Thee what it'th all about."

"I'm afraid this is a private club, sir," the vampire said. "We don't allow guests. Unless of course, you are here in a supply capacity."

He looked directly at Tim as he said the last part, which made Tim think that perhaps his disguise wasn't quite as good as he thought it was. He wished that he'd had more time to spend on makeup before they left the house. He had a feeling that the grey pancake makeup he was using didn't give him quite the right deathly pallor.

"Of courthe not!" said Killian, laughing so much that his fangs nearly fell out. "We are here at Fang'th perthonal invitation. Now, I can only imagine that he would be none too pleathed if our planned meeting did not protheed due to thome thilly little bit of confuthion."

"No *confuthion*, sir," the vampire said in a mocking tone. He smiled, revealing his own row of long, gold-plated ivory fangs.

"I mean, I would hate to have to call him and bring him all the way out here," Killian said, pulling out his cellphone and brandishing it like some sort of detonator. "We're going to be talking about hith role in the new HellBlathter movie. We're thtill cathting that one, by the way! And not to be too life-changing, but there'th a role I think you'd be perfect for! Have you ever done any acting before?"

Tim was starting to get worried. Before they had left the apartment, Killian had conveyed the impression that getting into the club would be no problem whatsoever. Now that it was turning out to be more than no problem, Tim was having serious doubts that Killian's fading industry connections were going to work.

"No," the vampire said. "I'm afraid I'm going to have to ask you and your party to leave the premises as you are not formally invited to enter."

Vampires did not have to be invited in to enter a building of course–that was a long-debunked superstition–but trespass laws were applicable to everyone regardless of supernatural affiliation. And vampires had more options to defend themselves against intruders than most.

"Okay!" Killian said, waving his hands. "Don't thay I didn't give you a chanthe to keep your job! I'll just get my good friend Fang on the phone…"

"Mr. Bloodly has not been a member of this club for several months," the vampire said. "His membership was terminated shortly after his destruction."

"His what?" Tim said.

"Yes," said the vampire, appearing to be enjoying himself enormously. "The story I heard was that he had new blinds installed in his condo. There was some sort of malfunction. Opened unexpectedly right in the middle of the day. Cleaning lady vacuumed up his remains without even noticing."

Killian stabbed at his phone with his finger before turning the screen towards the vampire.

"Not pothible," Killian said. "I jutht got a methage from him thith morning!"

The vampire squinted at the screen, which flashed green. The vampire's eyes went wide just before he fell forwards and face-planted on the floor between Killian and Tim.

"What the hell!" Tim said, jumping out of the way as the vampire hit the floor with a thud.

"Hurry!" Killian said, pulling out his fake fangs and bending down to grab the vampire. "Let's stick him under the desk!"

"Did you really not know that Bloodly guy was dead?" Keef said, looking at Killian suspiciously.

"Who cares?" Killian said, grabbing the vampire by the ankles and beginning to drag him towards the reception desk. "His career was over. That's practically the same thing!"

"What did you just flash in his face?" Tim asked, bending down to help while looking around nervously for security cameras. He knew that just because he couldn't see them did not mean they didn't exist.

"Latest self defence app," Killian said, stuffing the unconscious vampire's head into the open space under the desk. "It just scrambles his brain for a couple of hours. Shouldn't be any lasting damage. Although as a bonus, there's a good chance he won't remember what we look like. Or anything else he saw or did in the last 48 hours."

"But you said that Bloodly guy was your client and you didn't even know he was dead!" Keef said.

"I have a lot of clients!" Killian said. "I can't keep track of all of them! That's what assistants are for!"

"Those were just some kids you hired to help you move!" Keef said. "Do you really have any industry connections or not?"

"Of course I do!" Killian said, struggling to push the vampire's body out of sight. "Like I said, I am *this* close to lining up that audition for you."

"Lining it up?" Keef said. "You said it was set!"

"It is set!" Killian said. "It's just not quite set-set."

"Set-set?" Keef said. "What in the hell does that mean?"

"I'm taking care of it!" Killian said. "Now instead of complaining, I need you to work with me to get this bloodsucking pervert out of sight before anyone else comes in or security shows up!"

"Are you even really an agent?" Keef said. "Or was that all just a bunch of bullshit to get yourself turned?"

"Of course I am!" Killian said. "I just have a couple of tiny little niggling licence bumps to sort out and everything'll be fine."

"Licence bumps?" Keef said. "What the hell does that mean? Am I gonna be in the next *Blood Stalker* or not?"

"Of course!" Killian said, rolling the vampire sideways. The vampire's piercings made a melodic tinkling noise as his body moved across the stone tile. "I talked to the casting manager myself! Well, her assistant. And they are very excited about having you come in to audition for the role of Background Thug Number Three."

"Background Thug?" Keef said in disbelief. "But I'm supposed to be the star! That's what you told me!"

"Yes, and you are absolutely going to be the star of the scene that you're in!" Killian said. "You're going to have the opportunity to give a *very* significant look to camera."

"Look to camera?" Keef said. "You mean I don't even get any lines?"

"Will you two knock it off!" Tim hissed. "We can talk about this later! Right now, we need to stow this guy so we can sneak downstairs!"

Tim got down on his knees to help Killian hide the unconscious vampire out of sight. It wasn't easy, because the vampire's exposed skin was covered in some kind of exotic moisturizer that made him extremely slippery. It occurred to Tim that he would probably have been better off with his original plan to sneak in through the back door, but there was no turning back now.

14

Once they had finished stowing the bald vampire under the front desk, the three of them made their way through the door and into the club.

Despite everything he had heard in advance, Tim was still not prepared for the scene that greeted them once they had stepped through the dark red curtains.

On their left were six semi-private jacuzzis sunk into the stone floor. There were curtains set up around each one to screen it from its neighbours, but only one set up curtains had been pulled closed. There were vampires in three of the other units, which Tim noticed appeared to be filled with blood instead of water. The blood bubbled and boiled, sending dark steam up into the air and making it difficult to see more than a few feet in any direction.

Tim could see the occupants of the nearest tub were a male and three females. The male appeared to be human. He was sitting on the edge of the tub and bleeding copiously from dozens of bite wounds all over his body. Tim could see tubes plugged into both of the man's arms that snaked up to a large red intravenous bag hanging from a stand next to the tub.

I guess that's to keep him from bleeding out, Tim thought as he watched the vampires feeding. But wouldn't it be easier to just drink the stuff right out of the bag?

On their right was a large hexagonal pool which was also filled with blood. There were about a dozen vampires in it, some swimming lengths and others just floating on the edges. The swimmers were naked and so pale that they looked almost spectral. Tim watched as a fat vampire he recognized as the host of a popular renovation show did a backstroke across the pool, opening his mouth to swallow large quantities as he went.

"Ugh," Keef muttered. "Even I know better than to drink pool blood. Still, this place is pretty cool!"

One of the vampires lounging by the side of the pool looked up at them with a slightly suspicious frown. Tim pretended to cough and quickly reinserted his fake teeth. He didn't want to be recognized as a human in a place like this.

"Come on," Killian said, reinserting his fangs. "The VIP roomth are downthtairth."

They continued on through another set of curtains and emerged in a room that looked like a cross between a museum exhibit and a torture chamber. Elaborate blood draining devices were set up almost randomly on the floor. Pumping bass music played as seizure-inducing lights flashed on and off from the ceiling and the corners. The effect was nightmarishly disorienting, and that was even before Tim got a better look at the machines.

The first one featured a naked woman being slowly lowered onto spikes that went into her arms, legs and throat. Blood drained down the spikes and onto a much older looking naked female vampire who lay underneath, soaking the red droplets in through her pale skin. Another contained a naked man hanging in what looked like a clear disco ball made of razor wire. As the ball rotated, the blades sliced hundreds of cuts into his skin. His blood then sprayed out through holes in the side of the ball onto a group of vampires who appeared to be doing some sort of pagan dance ritual.

Tim knew that there was a whole subgroup of humans who volunteered to be vampire victims. Some were gig workers who did it for money, like the ones who showed up at vampire homes for parties and other events and allowed themselves to be drained of a pint or two. Those with rarer or more desirable blood groups tended to make more (an AB negative donor got paid roughly three times as much as someone who was O positive), but the pay was still pretty minimal, especially since sanguinary sector labour laws prevented them from working more than one shift every three days.

Another group did it because they wanted to become vampires themselves. If you didn't want to put in the years of service required of a familiar, working in a Suspension & Draining club like thVrst was another possible pathway to bloodsucking immortality. Tim couldn't imagine ever voluntarily climbing into any of the devices in this room, but that didn't mean there weren't a lot of people who would.

The third group did it simply because they got a kick out of being drained by vampires. They weren't much different than the ones who craved sex with werwolves or got off on being possessed by demons. A recent study published by Necropolis University had found that as many as 18 percent of psychics admitted to getting into the business because they enjoyed the feeling of having a foreign entity in control of their body.

Tim had never quite understood such urges. He was rather possessive of his blood and preferred to keep as much of it inside his body as possible. He was not attracted to werewolves any more than he was attracted to ordinary wolves, which was to say not at all. Having majored in demonology and seen the aftereffects of malevolent supernatural identity theft, he also had no desire whatsoever to be taken over by something else. The majority of possessions were committed by small-time scammers looking to get their claws on their victim's banking information or credit card numbers, not to engage in kinky adventures.

They continued through the room, with neither the vampires nor their victims paying them much attention. At the back, they found another set of red curtains leading to a spiral metal staircase. A handy sign next to it indicated that up led to the bar while down would take them to the VIP area.

Tim started down the stairs. He knew from her InfernaChat feed that Lucretia had a private room somewhere in the basement. Although she was evidently forbidden from posting any pictures from inside the club, her channel was full of images that looked like they could have come from nowhere else. Each one carried a caption that was both cutesy and vague enough to avoid spelling this out explicitly. She didn't have many followers–at least not when compared to celebrity members of the S&D community like "Bloody" Mary Danniken, who had more than five million–but Lucretia clearly aspired to vampinfluencer fame, posting pics of the latest high-end home blood juicing gear and extraction devices.

Tim had been able to piece together enough clues to know that Lucretia had a smaller room and went by the alias of Mircalla, which was written on the door next to a stencil of a child with bat wings and fangs. The stencil was also one of the most common tattoos amongst familiars and wannabe vampires.

They reached the bottom of the stairs and found themselves in a hexagonal landing with hallways leading off in six different directions. The tiles on the floor were a checkerboard pattern of red and black.

"Man, I think they're overdoing it with the sixes," Keef said. "I mean, I get it. It was in, like, two years ago. Now the whole mark of the beast thing just looks old, you know?"

"It's true," Killian said, taking out his teeth. "Now everything is zombie chic. I don't see that lasting long, though. Those splatter patterns are just too hard to accessorize."

"Okay," Tim said, removing his own fangs and sticking them in his pocket. There didn't appear to be vampires wandering the halls down here and he figured he probably wouldn't need that part of his disguise. "Maybe we should split up and look for her room. She's under the alias 'Mircalla' and has a Bampy stencil on the door."

"Seriously?" Keef said. "What is she, like 12 years old?"

"If you find it, don't go in," Tim said. "Just come and find me so I can talk to her."

"Why do you need to talk to this chick again?" Keef said. "She owe you money or something?"

"No," Tim said. "It's related to a case. It's a work thing."

"Fair enough," Keef said. "But should I accidentally stumble in on some rich widow who wants me to suck on her extremities for big bucks, don't be surprised if I get somewhat waylaid."

"I would expect nothing less," Tim said. "Let's go."

The three of them each selected a different hallway and started walking. Tim picked the one on the left, as it was closest to where he was standing. He had no idea how large the basement was or who else might be down here. It was only a matter of time before somebody figured out what happened to the vampire at the front door and some sort of alert went out, so they needed to move quickly. Tim pulled the sun gun out of his cape pocket and held it firmly in his right hand. If security did come after him, he did not plan to throw up his hands and go quietly. Based on what he had seen, he doubted that they would just call the cops.

Most of the doors he passed were closed. It was hard to tell if there was anyone inside as the rooms appeared to be soundproofed. He was more careful with the doors that were open, checking each room to make sure that there was no one inside before going past. The first room had a couple of leather-upholstered armchairs positioned in front of a raised platform that Tim assumed was supposed to be some sort of stage. In the middle of the stage was a golden pole surrounded by dangling chains, each of which had a shiny metal hook attached to the end. Tim didn't want to think about what kind of performances might feature on it.

The next room looked like a nursery, only the crib had spikes instead of bars and a rocking horse that definitely should not be ridden by anyone who had a strong desire to go through life without perforations.

Tim shivered. This place made the worst extremes portrayed in the late night blood 'n boobs movies that Keef loved so much seem downright innocent and wholesome in comparison.

Tim reached the end of the hallway. He could hear chatter coming from one of the rooms to his right and decided to go that way. The door was open a crack, allowing red light to spill out into the hall. He couldn't make out words, but one of the voices sounded angry.

He crept up slowly. The reflected red light was just enough for him to make out the image of the winged vampire just below the handle.

Bingo, Tim thought. He tightened his grip on the sun gun and pushed the door open just enough to see inside. He saw a figure that he recognized as Lucretia. She appeared to be struggling to get out of a coffin on a platform in the middle of the room. Stopping her from getting out was a tall figure in a black robe. Tim couldn't see the robed figure's face, but he could see that whoever it was appeared to be holding some sort of knife or metal stake in their right hand while using the left to restrain Lucretia.

"I told you I have no idea where it is!" Lucretia shrieked. "Now let me out!"

Tim quickly deduced that things were not good and were quickly about to get worse unless he did something. He pulled open the door and held up the sun gun.

"Hey!" Tim shouted. "Let her go!"

The figure paused. Lucretia turned to look at him, her face a mixture of fear and confusion.

"Help me!" Lucretia said. "I–"

That was all she managed to say before the figure in the robe pulled their hand free and drove the stake straight into Lucretia's chest. It made a dull crunching sound as the tip went through her breastbone and straight into her heart. Lucretia opened her mouth to scream, but all that came out was a gush of blood.

Tim was so shocked and surprised that he pulled the trigger on the sun gun as a reflex, sending a blazing jet of blue light straight at Lucretia's attacker. The bolt hit the figure right in the chest, but seemed to have no effect. Instead, the figure pulled out another stake, vaulted over the coffin, and ran straight at Tim.

Tim staggered back out of the door, tripping over his own cape and falling backwards into the hallway. The figure missed him and instead crashed into the wall as Tim struggled to get back up. He could see Lucretia manage to get out of her coffin and collapse on the floor as blood fountained out of the hole in her chest. She might not be a vampire, but she was certainly dying like one. With a wound like that, there was nothing anybody could do. She would be dead in seconds.

Tim got off another shot with the sun gun, this time right in the attacker's face. The figure in the robe staggered sideways, momentarily blinded. Whoever it was, they weren't a vampire. A vampire would be mostly melted or at least on fire after two direct hits, even with the best sun armour available on the market.

Tim wondered if the figure in the robe was the same one he had spotted in the alley across from his father's shop. This individual seemed taller, but it had been hard to tell from far away.

"Who are you?" Tim yelled. "Are you following me?"

The figure staggered for a moment and put a hand to their eyes, shaking their head to clear their vision. It occurred to Tim that this was not the first time he had encountered someone in a long black robe.

But that's not possible, he thought. It couldn't be one of them. All of the Sons of Darkness were caught and put in jail.

The figure lunged blindly forward, knocked Tim aside and staggered down the hall. Tim struggled back to his feet, tripping over his borrowed cape. Yanking it aside, he chased the figure down the hall and around the corner. Whoever it was appeared to be heading for a staircase at the far end. Tim had lost all sense of where he was in the building relative to the elevator, but supposed that even vampire-owned buildings weren't exempt from fire code bylaws that required an alternate exit.

"Stop!" Tim yelled.

The figure paid no attention. As Tim was running, he saw Killian emerge from a junction just up ahead, evidently drawn by the commotion.

"Stop that guy!" Tim yelled, pointing.

Killian looked momentarily confused before spotting the hooded figure and giving a quick nod. He stepped into the hall to intercept them.

"Hold it right th–" Killian started to say, holding out his arms to block the route. He only got part of his command out before the figure pulled something out of the inside of it's cloak and swung it at Killian's head. Killian let out a surprised squeak before he was knocked up against the wall and slumped to the floor in a heap.

In almost the same movement, the figure spun around and threw whatever it was carrying straight at Tim. Tim managed to duck to one sideas the figure turned and ran up the stairs.

Tim turned to see what he had dodged and saw a three-pronged silver pitchfork lodged in one of the doors, which was opened a moment later by an elderly-looking vampire in a red velvet robe. The robe looked like it had been put on in a hurry and did not cover up as much as Tim thought it should.

"What the hell is going on out here?" the vampire hissed. "Who are you?"

Tim didn't think he had time to explain, so he jumped back to his feet and continued the chase, reaching the stairs right behind Killian, who had also gotten back to his feet in a way that was surprisingly nimble for an older guy with a terminal disease. Was he lying about that, too? Tim decided that he didn't really care.

"What's going on?" Killian asked as they made their way up. The stairs were made of volcano glass tile, which made the clacking echo of their footfalls seem infinite and surprisingly loud.

"Whoever that is, they just killed my prime suspect!" Tim said. "We can't let him get away!"

"Right!" Killian nodded, picking up the pace.

They reached the top of the stairs and pushed open a door to find themselves in the middle of what at first looked like some sort of casino. A group of vampires were standing around a table with an oversized roulette wheel in the middle of the room. Tim could see a naked man had been strapped to the wheel. He appeared to be impaled on a large golden spike through his midsection. As the wheel came to a close, the blood that had pooled under the body was released and filled up one of the numbered compartments on the board.

Everyone in the room appeared to be a vampire. A massive figure that Tim immediately pegged as a bodyguard leaned over to help an ancient-looking figure up off the floor with the help of a woman in a croupier's uniform. Tim got the impression that the old vampire had been knocked to the ground by the robed figure they were chasing. Two more bodyguards rounded on them menacingly.

"Are you all right, Ravie?" said the first.

"What the hell is going on?" hissed the older vampire as he got unsteadily back up. "I can't even play some roulette in my own damn place?"

The bodyguards took a step forward. Tim saw bright red tattoos on each of their exposed and bulging forearms. The images were identical–a pair of fangs with the middle teeth replaced by a sideways letter B. The image identified them as members of the Blood Brothers, which was the largest and most fearsome vampire criminal syndicate in the city.

Tim assumed that the old vampire who had been knocked down was none other than Count Illyich von Ravelstien. Known on the street as "Bloody Ravie", he was one of the six heads of the organization and, if the rumours were to be believed, the most sadistic and ruthless. He had a bald head, large, bat-like ears and glowing red eyes. He was rumored to be at least 600 years old and to have committed dozens of massacres, the most notorious of which was the Bloodfeast of Prague. Not even the rats had survived that one.

"Who the hell are these blood bags?" the second bodyguard said, pointing at Tim and Killian.

"I bet they're with that other guy," said the first bodyguard, baring his oversized fangs with a practiced sneer.

"No!" Tim said. "We were chasing that other guy! Did you see which way he went?"

Tim saw a door on the far side of the room that was still swinging slightly, but his path to it was blocked.

"Whaddya think, boss?" the second bodyguard said, looking back at Ravelstein.

"You believe this?" Ravelstein said, straightening his suit. "Who the fuck are you guys? What are you doin' here? You ain't vampires!"

Tim and Killian looked at each other, both realizing that they had forgotten to reinsert their fangs during the melee.

"Uhhh…" said Tim. "Well, not strictly speaking, no."

There was a moment's pause while they all looked at each other.

"Bah!" Ravelstein's dark red eyes narrowed. "Bleed 'em."

The two bodyguards lunged at Tim and Killian. Tim gave the nearest one a blast from the sun gun, causing him to scream in pain and fall to the floor. Killian tried to turn around and go back down through the door behind them, but the bodyguard grabbed him by the cape before he could make it through. Tim tried to shoot the second bodyguard, but was attacked by the croupier, who hit him with an appetizer tray covered with blood sausage canapés. Tim staggered sideways and tripped over an overturned stool.

"Help!" said Killian, as the bodyguard sank his fangs into the agent's neck.

Tim struggled to get to his feet. He had dropped the sun gun when he fell and was in the process of making his way across the red carpeted floor to reach it when Ravelstein stepped in front of him.

"Think you can come into my club and blast my guys?" Ravelstein said. "You have no idea who you're messin' with, you stupid juice box!"

Ravelstein reached down and was just about to grab Tim by the neck when a dark mist suddenly appeared in front of him and appeared to launch him backwards across the roulette table. Tim felt himself grabbed by the shoulders and hoisted unceremoniously to his feet as the mist congealed into a recognizable form.

"Keef!" Tim gasped in surprise.

"Time to go!" Keef said, pushing Tim towards the exit.

Keef grabbed the other bodyguard and pulled him off Killian, who wobbled on his feet. Keef grabbed his agent around the midsection and picked him up effortlessly, slinging Killian's limp body back over his shoulder like a value-sized bag of *Scabs*.

The second bodyguard rolled off the table and lunged at Keef. Tim grabbed the sun gun and squeezed the trigger, careful to make sure that he didn't hit his brother. The blast missed, but did reflect off an overturned bottle and hit the bodyguard in the leg. The bodyguard let out a shriek and went down clutching his smoking thigh.

"Come on!" Keef yelled, grabbing Tim by the cape and propelling him out.

Tim's feet barely touched the ground as they raced around the table and out of the room. They moved back past the pool area with supernatural speed and out through a side door into an alley, where they cut through the receiving entrance of a dry cleaners on their way back to the car.

"Why didn't you tell me you were mixed up with the Blood Brothers?" Keef said as they jogged down the street.

"I'm not!" Tim said, looking anxiously back over his shoulder to check and see if they were being followed. "I didn't know they owned the place!"

"Yeah?" Keef said. "Well, the next time you get the bright idea to break into a place that's run by the mob, do me a favour and get somebody else to help you get in the door, okay? This insurance stuff is dangerous!"

"Thanks for getting me out of there," Tim said.

"No problem," Keef said. "You find who you were looking for?"

"Sort of," Tim said. "But somebody else got to her first."

"Who?" Keef said. "The Blood Brothers? But they own the place! I thought you said you were looking for somebody who was a member?"

"I don't think it was them," Tim said. "Whoever it was, they were dressed like they belonged to a different group. One I've run across before."

"Who?" Keef said. "The Hellspawn?"

"No," Tim said. "Worse."

"Are you kidding?" Keef said as they arrived at the car. He tossed Killian in the back seat and got in. "Nobody's worse than Azmoda, man! Didn't they almost drop you in a bottomless jacuzzi?"

"Yeah," Tim said, getting behind the wheel and starting the engine. He took a quick look at the unconscious agent. "Is he okay?"

"Oh yeah," Keef said, waving a hand. "A quick snack on an assistant or two and he'll be fine. Just drive!"

Tim didn't need to be told twice. He started the engine and peeled out onto the street.

15

Tim was not remotely surprised to see nothing about Lucretia's murder on the news. Humans died in vampire-owned establishments all the time, but most of those deaths were never reported. That was doubly true of any business owned or operated by the Blood Brothers, as thVrst appeared to be. The general attitude amongst the non-supernatural community was that anyone other than a vampire who knowingly walked into a vampire establishment deserved whatever they got.

Lucretia, despite her blood-drinking ambitions, was not a vampire. But she hadn't been killed and drained by one, either. Tim was sure that whoever had killed her had been looking for the Puzzle Box. But who had done it? Was it Ugarte? Had he been so worried that he'd blown his connection that he had decided to try and take matters into his own hands?

Tim thought that was possible, but not likely. Lucretia might have brought Ugarte in to help sell or even steal the box, but killing her wouldn't get him any closer to getting his hands on the thing.

Ugarte was a middle-man. Based on what was in his file, the satyr seemed to go out of his way to avoid actual danger. He was more likely to be acting on behalf of a third party. Tim doubted that the self-aggrandizing pawnbroker was the one who had broken into thVrst and killed Lucretia, but he might have been working with whoever had done it.

As Keef had mentioned, the Hellspawn was a possibility. The city's most powerful group of demon gangsters would be extremely keen to get their claws on something like the Hesselthorn Puzzle Box. Not for its cultural or historical value of course–demons were remarkably unsentimental about their past–but for its financial value.

The Hellspawn, however, did not dress in long black robes. Hellspawn assassins tended to wear flashy Kraken-skin suits with Mark of the Beast brand designer sunglasses and Firewalker shoes. They were hard to miss. And even if they did try to blend in, they were immediately recognizable courtesy of the Mark of Azazel brands on their cheeks. Their preferred weapons were easily concealable switchforks, not bulky, single-use stakes.

The only people Tim had encountered who did dress that way and showed few qualms about ritualistic murder was a group that called itself the Sons of Darkness. He had run into them during his first case in SIU, when he had thwarted their plans to resurrect an ancient demon named Belial. Many of them had been in positions of power in city government and in some of the biggest companies in the city. That had included Crimson Seal, whose new vice president of Claims, Lilith Warwick, had turned out to be their high priestess.

They had all been arrested when a police tactical unit swooped in and cut their resurrection ritual short, preventing them from doing likewise to Stake, whose presumably virgin blood they required to bring back their big bad demon daddy.

Or had they?

Part of the problem Tim had with being able to report what had happened at thVrst–to the police or anybody else–was that he, Keef and Killian would immediately become the prime suspects. They had been spotted both sneaking in and then escaping from the place. The fact that they were wearing disguises was probably the only reason that Metro was not knocking on his door already with an arrest warrant.

Things would be different if Tabitha was still around, he thought grimly. She might violently disapprove of his methods and involvement, but at least he would be able to tell her what really happened and know that she believed him.

Security cameras had probably caught Lucretia's killer entering and exiting the place as well. Considering thVrst was owned by the Blood Brothers and there had been no mention of Lucretia's murder on any news sites, it was evident that they were keeping the whole thing quiet. It was a good thing they didn't know who he was, either, or the cops wouldn't be the only ones looking for a follow-up chat.

Tim also had no way of knowing who was under the hood. The Sons of Darkness certainly weren't the only ones who might wear one to hide their identity. It could have been Ludwig under there for all he knew. Or Ugarte. Or any one of a million people who might be willing to kill to get their hands on what they thought was a priceless treasure. Lucretia's membership at thVrst was no secret. Lots of interested parties might think she had the box or at least knew where it was.

If the Sons of Darkness really were back, though, then what did they want with the Hesselthorn Puzzle Box?

Tim had turned the question over and over in his mind for hours before finally giving up on sleep and heading to the kitchen to do some research. Although some of the members of the Sons of Darkness had gotten jail time, this mostly applied to the minor, rank and file types. The ones further up the chain had seen their charges reduced or dismissed entirely. Some had argued they had been blackmailed into membership. Others claimed they had been possessed or cursed. And some saw their charges dropped with no explanation whatsoever. In total, of the 148 individuals who had been arrested on the night of Belial's failed resurrection, less than a dozen were doing any time. Many of those would be eligible for release in less than six months.

Nevermind a comeback, Tim thought, sipping a mug of coffee. It looked like the Sons of Darkness never left.

Suspicion, however, wasn't proof. For now, it made sense to stick with the scumbags he knew about and not lose focus. If Lucretia was out of the picture, that left only one functioning adult member of the Hesselthorn family: Ludwig.

Tim finished his coffee, took a shower, got dressed and packed his SIU bag. He planned to drive out to Hesselthorn mansion and conduct another interview with Ludwig. He wanted to see how Ludwig had reacted to the death of his sister, assuming he had even heard about it yet. While he was there, he might also take another shot at decoding the safe, as the trolls in IT hadn't gotten back to him yet about the data extract he had sent them. Even Volkerps' most violent eruptions of rage and threats of eternal damnation had not been enough to get them to move any faster. This was totally in line with Section 13.4 of the IT department's Basic Standards of Minimum Service, which clearly stated: "We will process all requests in order received if and when we feel like getting around to them. Or not."

They would sometimes expedite requests in exchange for under-the-table bribes, of course. Tim had heard rumours of them completing password resets in exchange for brain cheese or Kappa jerky, but that stuff was so rancid that not even demons could stand to be within 100 yards of it. Tim's new laptop still smelled unpleasantly funky, and he had even taken it to his father's shop to have it cleaned in the decontamination fogger. Twice.

When Tim arrived at the Hesselthorn house, he was surprised to find the gate was already open. Not only was it open, but it looked like it had been battered in by something much larger and heavier than an ordinary car.

Tim idled at the entrance for a moment, debating what to do. Maybe Ludwig had just gone out and gotten drunk and then forgotten the gate code when he got back. Or maybe Sticker Helsing had finally fomented a torch-wielding mob into storming the place. It certainly wouldn't be the first time that HEX-TV had caused a riot. Tim remembered the time when he was in university and they had reported that a satyr-owned charcuterie located just off-campus was using human children for their sausages. Three employees had been hospitalized and the entire building burned down in the resulting melee.

Tim tapped the wheel. The other possibility was that whoever had killed Lucretia had gone directly to the source because she didn't have what they were looking for.

Tim edged forward slowly. There were no other cars parked in front of the house and no one visible on the grounds. He thought about calling the police immediately, but if the gate really had been damaged by accident, then he would be stirring up a kerfuffle for nothing. He needed to get a better sense of what was going on before he pushed the panic button.

Tim circled the drive and parked so that his car was facing the back towards the gate. If he needed to get out of here in a hurry, it would be easier if all he needed to do was jump behind the wheel and mash the accelerator. He turned off the engine and unzipped his SIU bag, pulling out the Devil Stick and Demonex. The sun was blazing overhead. If the Blood Brothers had been the ones who had broken into the place, they would have fled back to their coffins long before now.

He walked slowly up to the house. The curtains were all drawn and there was no sign of activity, although Tim was pretty sure that he could just make out the sound of music being played from somewhere inside. The music got louder as he got closer to the door, which was open. Tim used the Devil Stick to push it open further and leaned in.

"Hello?" he called. "Anyone home?"

Tim stepped tentatively into the hallway. The lights were still on over the grand staircase and in the main hall, which meant that it didn't take his eyes as long to adjust.

"It's Tim Lovecraft," he said. "From Crimson Seal In–"

Tim's words died in his throat.

Ludwig was lying on the floor just in front of the stairs. A large black pitchfork protruded from his chest.

Tim stepped closer. Ludwig's eyes and mouth were open in an expression of surprise. There was a darkened pool of dried blood under the body. Based on the blood, it looked like Ludwig had been dead for several hours, but Tim was no forensic pathologist and didn't want to jump to conclusions.

The pitchfork was a strong indication that Ludwig had been killed by the Hellspawn Triad, for whom it was the preferred method of assassination. Granted, there were a few famous cases of other criminal organizations using it as a murder weapon in an attempt to frame the Triads for something they didn't do, but criminals were lazy and tended to stick with what they knew.

Tim crouched down for a closer look. Whoever had killed Ludwig had driven the pitchfork straight through his body and right into the Styxian tiles underneath, which would have required a tremendous amount of force. Tim knew that ordinary street demons wouldn't be strong enough to do that, but a Serrabluk would.

Serrabluks were massive creatures, usually standing between seven and ten feet tall and weighing roughly the same as an SUV. The Hellspawn used them primarily as bodyguards and debt collectors. It also wasn't unusual to see them working security on the front door of some of the more exclusive nightclubs in town. Nobody in their right mind would ever try to force their way in past a Serrabluk. Even vampires and werewolves treated them with caution.

Tim sensed movement on his left and turned around quickly, raising the Devil Stick in front of him. Maybe whoever had killed Ludwig was still in the house. If that was the case, the last thing they would want was a witness left alive to identify them.

Instead of a massive demon, however, Tim was greeted with the sight of Ozymandia dancing back and forth in front of the parlour. As before, she gave no indication that she was aware of either Tim's presence or that of her son's dead body lying on the floor less than 20 feet away.

Tim relaxed his grip on the Devil Stick and approached her carefully. The music appeared to be coming from speakers controlled by a unit mounted on the wall next to the stairs. Tim walked over to the box and examined it closely, trying to figure out how to turn the music off.

He pressed what he thought was the power button and only succeeded in changing the music from the swirling orchestral ballet of the *Necronomicon* to another track. This one was so different from the elegant dance opera that it was almost impossible to imagine that it could be broadcast through the same speakers. Instead of the prancing lilt of horns and violins, Tim was suddenly subjected to a battering ram of angry, down-tuned guitars, muffled drums and the most anguished shrieking imaginable.

"Ugh!" Tim said, covering one ear while trying to find the pause button. He recognized the song as one by a demon metal band named Hammer of Hell. They produced sounds at such a frequency that ordinary humans could actually become sick and even die if exposed to it for prolonged periods.

The music was so bad that it was literally fatal in a live setting. Humans were banned from most demon concerts, but that didn't stop the crazy or suicidal superfans from trying to sneak in anyway. Every year, between eight and 15 humans exploded or spectrally combusted in the stands. All of Crimson Seal's life policies had performance exclusions embedded in their statutory conditions.

Tim was so busy trying to figure out the panel that he didn't notice Ozymandia had stopped dancing until she was standing right behind him.

"What the hell?" Tim said, jumping at the sight of the comatose woman, who was looking at him with a strangely expectant expression. "Mrs. Hesselthorn! Are you alright?"

She gave no indication of having heard him and continued to stare. Tim gripped the Devil Stick a little tighter. Was Ozymandia aware of her surroundings? Had she somehow killed Ludwig? What the hell was she doing? Was she going to attack him?

"Mrs. Hesselthorn?" Tim said again, louder. "Can you hear me?"

Nothing.

"Who killed Ludwig?" Tim said. "Is there anyone else in the house?"

Nothing.

Tim looked from the control box to the woman standing in front of him. Had the music somehow triggered her response? She had been dancing to the ballet, so why had she stopped when the demon death metal started? He had heard of people who claimed to have been possessed when listening to demon music—one man had even claimed that his copy of *Bloodgorge* by Bacchantae Bax had caused him to strip naked and sexually assault the mannequins in a department store window display—but this was different.

"Mrs. Hesselthorn?" Tim said. "Blink your eyes if you can hear me!"

Ozymandia blinked. Tim felt a momentary thrill of connection. Was this woman desperately trying to communicate with him?

"Did you see who did this?" Tim asked. "Blink once for yes or twice for no."

Ozymandia blinked once, and then, after a pause, blinked twice.

"Which is it?" Tim said, exasperated.

Ozymandia stared back at him.

"Of course," Tim said with a sigh. He spotted Ozymandia's wheelchair parked in the corner next to a statue of somebody he assumed was a distant Hesselthorn descendant. He wondered where Ugathia was. Was the maid hiding or had she been killed, too? "Let's see if we can get you back into your chair until I can figure out what's going on here."

To Tim's surprise, Ozymandia turned around and walked back across the hallway to her chair, which she sat down in and stared back at him expectantly. Tim found the button on the control to shut off the music, at which point her head dropped and she sat staring at the floor instead.

Tim dug into his pocket and pulled out his phone. Unlike the situation at the vampire club, he had no doubt that this was a situation where calling the police was the only option.

16

It took 15 minutes for the first police cruiser to arrive, which was somehow 10 minutes longer than the first news van.

Tim had no idea how the reporters had been tipped off that something had happened in the house, but they showed no compunction about pulling straight into the driveway and trying to push their way inside. Tim actually had to stand in front of the door and pull out his Devil Stick to stop Sticker Helsing from barreling past with his camera crew.

"How many of the Hesselthorn family have been massacred?" Helsing asked, shoving his oversized HEX-TV microphone under Tim's nose. "Do you believe this is the work of the same group of Blood Brothers believed to be behind the disappearance of Lucretia Hesselthorn?"

"I have no comment at this time," Tim said, trying to maintain his composure. He could see other camera crews from different news outlets circling the house trying to get shots through the windows. One was even trying to climb a drainpipe to reach a second-floor balcony. If there was a back door, Tim hoped that it wasn't open.

"Is this the work of the Hellspawn?" Sticker continued, undeterred by Tim's evident truculence. "Or the Blood Brothers? Or the Wolfpack? How many supernatural monsters are still present in the house?"

"Please step back," Tim said, pushing the microphone away. All indications were that Ludwig Hesselthorn had been murdered by the Hellspawn Triad, but Tim certainly wasn't about to admit as much to this jackass.

"The question on everybody's mind right now," Sticker said, giving a dramatically-timed look straight to the camera. "Is where is the Hesselthorn Puzzle Box?"

Tim had no idea where the box was, but he certainly wasn't about to admit that on live TV either, not his boss almost certainly watching.

"As I said, I have no comment at this time," Tim said. "As per statutory claims custodianship, I am going to need to ask you and your crew to remove yourselves and your van from the Hesselthorn property immediately or face legal action."

Tim knew that this wasn't strictly true. Claims custodianship was a liability condition related to the obligation of due care and consideration for insured items transferred to third party possession during inspection, valuation, change of title or repair. It had nothing to do with trespassing, but it was the most official-sounding thing that he could come up with on the fly. As he expected, it had absolutely no effect on the reporter from HEX-TV.

"Okay," Helsing said, motioning for his cameraman to temporarily stop filming. "How about this? We'll give you ten thousand cash right now to let us in."

Tim was stunned. No one had ever offered him such an absurd sum of money for something so blatantly unethical.

"Are you kidding?" Tim said.

"Nope. Got it right over there in the van," Helsing said, flicking his eyebrows in his trademark manner. "All you gotta do is move."

Tim raised the Devil Stick and pointed it straight at Helsing's nose.

"No," Tim said.

"How about fifteen?" Helsing said, grinning. He was apparently used to being threatened with dangerous weapons. "Tax free!"

"You need to leave," Tim said.

Helsing opened his mouth to say something else, but was interrupted by the sound of a police siren. Tim looked up and was relieved to see the cruiser pull into the driveway and weave between the news vans before screeching to a stop just behind the HEX-TV truck. Tim was even more relieved when he saw the door open and Carmilla get out

"All right!" she yelled. "This entire property is hereby designated a crime scene! You all need to get back into these vehicles and back out onto the road immediately! Anyone still on the property in two minutes is going to be arrested for obstruction! Am I making myself clear?"

"A demon cop?" Helsing sniffed. "Is this some sort of joke?"

"No joke, sir," Carmilla said, walking up the stairs to face the reporter. "You and your crew need to leave the premises immediately."

"You know who I am?" Helsing said, smirking. "Maybe I'll just wait for your boss to get here. I'm sure he won't have any problem letting me inside, sucky."

"Sucky" was a common slang term for a succubus. It was used most often by the kind of human men who thought of them as nothing more than prostitutes or strippers.

"I do know who you are," Carmilla said. "Which is the reason I recommend that you voluntarily exit the premises before I am required to remove you by force."

"Yeah, right!" Helsing laughed. "You wouldn't dare!"

Carmilla grabbed Helsing by the neck and the belt, lifted him into the air and began to carry him down the stairs.

"Hey!" he screeched. "You can't do this! This is police brutality! Bruno, get this on film!"

The cameraman was stopped from filming the spectacle by Carmilla's partner, who took the camera out of his hands and grabbed him by the shoulder, forcefully escorting him in the same direction as his on-air talent.

"This way, sir," the cop said. His nametag identified him as Officer Trentino.

Tim watched as Carmilla tossed Helsing through the back door of the HEX-TV news truck and kicked it closed.

"Now get this thing off the property before we impound it along with the asshole inside," she said to the cameraman, who quickly jumped behind the wheel, started the engine and took off.

"That was awesome," Tim said as Carmilla came back up the stairs.

"Not gonna lie," Carmilla smiled. "I did enjoy that. This job does have its little perks, sometimes."

"He offered me cash to get inside," Tim said. "Two more minutes and I think I would've had to shoot him."

"Helsing's the worst," Carmilla said. "Guy has a rep for using curse apps to get people to tell him what he wants. He's been caught a few times, but the network always settles out of court."

"He must have forgotten his phone, I guess," Tim said.

"So what have we got in there?" Carmilla asked as two more cruisers pulled into the driveway, lights flashing.

Tim gave a quick summary of what he had found when he arrived at the house. It was a little difficult to explain Ozymandia's odd behaviour, but he did his best.

"Okay," Carmilla nodded as the other officers exited their vehicles and ran up to join them. "You wait out here while we do a quick sweep of the house. Duluc's apparently on his way. He was shooting some stupid promo out in Gorgon Rock."

Gorgon Rock was a barren expanse of terrain to the north of the city that was popular with hikers and production companies looking to shoot an alien planet without a special effects budget. It was especially popular with fans of the show *Quasar Quest*, a few hundred of whom trudged out there every year to photograph themselves in front of the same rock formation from which that show's villain, Tylo Vexx, had fallen to his death in the series finale. Park rangers had closed the site after a dozen or so of the show's more ambitious fans had met a similar fate.

"I see," Tim said, moving to one side as more officers followed Carmilla inside.

One of the remaining cops eyed Tim's Devil Stick suspiciously.

"You got a licence for that thing?" he asked.

Tim nodded and produced his contractor's licence from his wallet, which the cop examined closely before handing back.

"You don't look like an exterminator," he said, eyeing Tim's shirt and dress pants.

"It's my dad's business," Tim said. "I help out on evenings and weekends when he's busy."

Carmilla emerged five minutes later and called in a group of EMTs.

"We found the maid semi-conscious in the kitchen," she said. "Sometimes it's hard to tell with zombies if they're actually awake or not. No idea if she saw anything, but she seems okay. We'll need an interpreter."

"That might not help," Tim said. "She seems to speak some rare dialect. Even the latest version of my translation software had no idea what it was."

"Did you see anyone come or go on your way in?" Carmilla asked.

"No," Tim said. "Based on the pitchfork, it looks like the Hellspawn. And maybe it is. But I think another interested party may be involved."

"Like who?" Carmilla asked.

Tim motioned Carmilla away from the front door and out onto the lawn, where there were fewer people likely to overhear their conversation. He told her about what had happened at thVrst and the appearance of the familiar figure in the black robe.

"You think the Sons of Darkness are back?" Carmilla asked, dropping her voice. Carmilla had still been working at SIU when Tim had encountered the mysterious, demon-worshipping cult the first time.

"I don't know," Tim said. "Have you heard anything?"

"Nothing official," Carmilla said. "But I'm not on any of the OSC task force units. Most of the ones who ended up in jail from the last time were the lower-level schmoes. Guess you can't ask your ex about any of that, huh?"

"No," Tim said. "We don't really keep in touch."

"Lucretia hasn't even been reported missing," Carmilla said. "We just haven't been able to track her down to get a statement on the break-in that led to the theft or her father's disappearance."

"I had the same problem," Tim said. "That's why I had to try sneaking into thVrst. Unfortunately, somebody else got to her before I did."

"Still," Carmilla said. "You're making more progress than we are. Any luck tracking down Lucifer?"

"No," Tim said. "I have absolutely no idea where Lucifer Hesselthorn is. Although, given what's happened to the rest of the family, I'm guessing he's either been dropped into a grinder in a Blood Brothers-owned energy drink factory or some anonymous Hellfire pit by the Triads. How are things going with Duluc?"

"Terrible," Carmilla said. "We have to do every briefing three times so that his camera crew can get it from the best possible angle for this stupid documentary he's making. At first, I was genuinely excited when I heard that he was going to be involved. I mean, this is supposedly the guy who solved the Moor Park murders, for crying out loud! But having observed him in action, I can state that this moron couldn't find brains in a zombie delicatessen."

"You think he's a fake?" Tim asked.

"Not sure about that," Carmilla said. "But he definitely doesn't follow standard investigative procedure. At first, I thought it was because he was this great psychic genius. But the truth is, I think that he just doesn't know what the hell he's doing."

"Well, we both know how important following procedure is to us law enforcement and insurance types," Tim said.

"True," Carmilla said. "You're going to need to come in to give a statement about what you saw at thVrst. Even though the Brothers will have no doubt gotten rid of all the evidence. We need to have something on the record and you might be the only one who saw anything."

"I will," Tim said. "But I want to find out who I might be dealing with first. The Blood Brothers are bad enough, but if the Sons of Darkness are back, that's a whole new level of trouble."

"We can seal it," Carmilla said. "No one outside the investigation will know."

"And you and I both know that'll last for about 30 seconds," Tim said, shaking his head. "The Brothers and the Hellspawn have almost as many sources inside Metro as they do at city hall. Right now, they don't know who I am or what I know and I'd like to keep it that way for a little longer. If I uncover something I think you can use, I'll let you know right away."

Tim remembered the dark figure that he had spotted in the alley across from his father's place. It was entirely possible that one of the gangs was already following him and had even tailed him all the way out here.

"You better," Carmilla said. "Because I don't think this is going to get solved, otherwise. Not by this clown."

"Speak of the devil," Colin said, watching as a black van pulled into the driveway and stopped just a few yards from where they were standing. The doors shot open and the documentary crew jumped out like soldiers out of a military landing craft in an active fire area. Two of them were carrying cameras. The first ran out and dropped a tripod into place on the driveway to get what Tim assumed was an establishing shot of the house. The second raced around the van to get a shot of Duluc emerging from the passenger seat.

"Ugh," Carmilla said as the door opened and Duluc stepped out. He was quickly approached by a woman who began to simultaneously comb his hair and pat his cheeks with a makeup pad.

"We rolling?" Duluc asked, checking his reflection in the side mirror.

"Rolling, Mysterio," said a demon standing next to him holding a tablet. Tim assumed she was some sort of director or producer.

"Mysterio?" Tim whispered. As far as he was aware, Horatio Duluc was not a member of any royal line, but SpectraPedia entries were known to be notoriously unreliable.

"That's what he insists we call him," Carmilla shrugged. "People have different names for him off-camera."

Duluc approached them followed closely by his crew.

"You're the one who called it in?" he asked Tim.

"I am," Tim nodded.

Duluc took Tim's hand and, instead of shaking it, enfolded it between his palms and closed his eyes. Tim, aware that the B camera was pointed directly at his face, did his best to maintain a neutral expression and avoid reacting in a way that suggested this was not something that happened to him every day.

"You have seen much," Duluc said, appearing to quiver with concentration.

"Uh, not really," Tim said, not sure how else to respond. Duluc was not a large man, but he was squeezing Tim's hand with an uncomfortable and clammy force. "I kind of got here after everything had already happened."

"You are followed by the Dark One," Duluc said.

"Dark One?" Tim said, somewhat taken aback. Was Duluc actually talking about the figure Tim had seen in the alley? "What Dark One? Did you see a face? Who is it?"

Instead of answering, Duluc dropped Tim's hand and opened his eyes to look towards the house.

"A great evil prowls within these walls," Duluc said, arching one eyebrow in a dramatic fashion. "And it fears no one…but me."

Duluc turned and began walking towards the door as the crew hurried after him.

"What the hell was that?" Tim asked.

"Relax," Carmilla said. "He does that a lot."

The two of them stepped inside after Duluc, who stopped in front of Ludwig's body before circling it slowly counter-clockwise.

"Who did this to you, my dear Ludwig?" Duluc said. "Tell me who entered your house and snuffed out your essence with such violent ferocity!"

Duluc did a full circuit of the body before kneeling down and taking one of Ludwig's hands in his, just as he had done with Tim outside.

"Tell me your secrets, my friend," Duluc said, closing his eyes and bowing his head. "Help us in our quest for justice!"

Tim watched with a mix of skepticism and genuine curiosity. He had seen enough genuine psychics at work to know that it was sometimes difficult to tell the legit ones from the fakers. Some of them went all in on the clichés of the job–crystal balls, turbans, robes, incense and loads of tacky paraphernalia–while others looked and acted no differently than a lawyer or accountant.

Duluc seemed to be an uneasy mixture of both. But just because he was followed by a camera crew and indulged in lame catch phrases from his days on TV didn't necessarily mean he was a fake. The guy had legitimately solved some supposedly uncrackable cases in his time. There had to be *something* underneath it all, didn't there?

"I'm listening, Ludwig!" Duluc said, trembling. "Reveal to me the face of your killer!"

Duluc began to bounce up and down on his knees and arched his back, twisting from side to side as if Ludwig's dead hand was a live wire and he couldn't let go. He clenched his teeth and began to make a growling sound from deep in his throat that varied wildly in pitch and volume, looking to all those assembled like a man in the process of trying to self-exorcise some sort of demonic baboon.

"Hrrrrrrgggggghhhhhrrrrr," Duluc growled. "Grrrruuuuuunnnngghhaaaa!"

"You've seen him do this before?" Tim whispered to Carmilla.

"Are you kidding?" Carmilla hissed back. "The guy can't order lunch without speaking in tongues."

Duluc rolled around for another 20 seconds or so before suddenly sitting up straight and letting go of Ludwig's hand.

"I know who it is," Duluc huffed, his chest heaving. "I know...the identity...of the guilty party!"

"Really?" Tim said, unable to hide the doubt in his voice. "Who?"

Duluc jumped to his feet and ran up the stairs as everyone rushed to follow. Nobody told Tim to stay back, so he figured he might as well tag along for the big reveal, too. They reached the top of the stairs and made their way down a corridor to a door Tim had visited before.

"There!" Duluc said, stopping and pointing through the glass at a solitary figure on the other side. "There is the killer!"

Tim couldn't quite believe his eyes. Duluc had stopped in front of the door to Ludovico's cell. Peering inside, he could see the youngest Hesselthorn asleep and hovering over a bunk in the corner.

"Ludovico?" Tim said. "Are you serious?"

"I have seen it!" Duluc said. "Before us lies the master manipulator at the root of all the evil in this house!"

"But he's been locked in there the whole time," Tim observed. "He can't even leave his room. How exactly did he orchestrate all of these murders and disappearances and thefts?"

"My inner eye sees only truth!" Duluc said. "Arrest that man."

"Hang on a sec!" Carmilla said, stepping forward to block the door. "We have no evidence on this kid."

"I have all the evidence right here!" Duluc said, holding his hands up on either side of his head.

"Maybe so," Carmilla said. "But I think a judge is going to need a little more than that to cough up an arrest warrant, don't you?"

"This is outrageous!" Duluc said. "Do you know who I am?"

"Yeah," Carmilla said. "You're not the first person to ask me that today."

"I solved the Moor Murders!" Duluc said. "I alone cracked the Savini Kidnapping! I am a legend in the force! I will not be questioned in this way by some succubus patrolwoman!"

Carmilla's partner shrugged. "I guess we can at least bring the kid in for questioning."

"Yes!" said Duluc. "We must bring this evil fiend downtown! Once I have him in the box, I will get all the evidence you need!"

There was a general murmuring of agreement. One of the cops began to open the door.

"Wait!" Carmilla said. "He's gotta be locked up in there for a reason! We should wait for the tactical unit!"

Duluc was about to object again but was interrupted by his producer.

"Actually, I think that's a good idea," she said. "The guy will look more threatening if he's led out by four huge guys in full spectral body armour."

"Hmmm," Duluc considered this for a moment. "Very well. Although I would have preferred to have led him out myself."

"Not to worry, Mysterio," the producer said. "We'll cut it together so it looks like you're right at the front of the line."

There was a brief delay while they waited for the tactical unit to arrive. It rolled in 10 minutes later in three large APCs.

"I don't believe this," Carmilla whispered as they watched the heavily armoured officers open Ludovico's door and head inside.

The officers got Ludovico up off the bed and put him in a full body spectral restraint. It was similar to the ones Tim had seen used at the

Crowley Clinic to secure possessed individuals, but this one had much more bulky plating. Ludovico offered no resistance. He seemed less aware of what was going on than Ozymandia.

"Is he nuts?" Tim whispered.

"He's famous," Carmilla said. "The two are interchangeable."

The uniformed cops marched Ludovico out of his room and into the hall, where Duluc gave him a victorious smile.

"Okay," said one of the officers, looking unsure. "So what do you want us to do with this guy?"

"Bring him down to Metro and put him in an interrogation room," Duluc said. "I have some more work to do here. I'll be down there to question him shortly. In a way he won't be able to avoid answering. My way."

Duluc looked towards the camera as he said the last part. Tim knew that this was supposed to be for dramatic effect, but in person, it looked comical.

"I don't believe this," Tim said as he and Carmilla made their way back out through the front door behind Duluc and his crew. "Is Duluc seriously going to charge this kid with murder? He has debilitating PPSD and has spent pretty much the last 20 years locked up in his room!"

Tim watched as Duluc got a quick hair and makeup refresher before making his way down the driveway to address the gaggle of reporters gathered around the gate. The sight was enough to make Tim feel ashamed for ever having watched so much as a commercial for any of Duluc's previous shows.

"Well, it might not be justice, but it sure makes for great ratings," Carmilla said. "I don't know about you, but I'm going to see if I can get myself transferred off this case. I think I'll try to get into the gang unit. Who doesn't want to shove a vampire's head through a stained glass window?"

"I'd like to get off this one too, but I can't," Tim said. "Vol will quite literally torch me if I drop out of it now. Assuming he doesn't fire me, of course."

"How is that ugly old lightning fart?" Carmilla asked. "He still using enough air fresheners to cause rolling blackouts in Morningstar Heights?"

"Pretty much," Tim said. As a demon, Volkerps was exempt from Crimson Seal's scent-free workplace policy, although the multitude of room deodorizers he used to cover his own sulphurous emanations were not really up to the job. "Claims has been trying to muscle in on the investigation, so he's been in an even more thunderous mood than usual."

"Ugh," Carmilla said, shaking her head. "Claims sucks. Ozgoroth's been doing that for as long as SIU has existed."

They watched as Duluc worked the crowd of reporters, his documentary crew filming the news crews as they filmed him.

"That said," Carmilla said. "Claims wants this one? Maybe let them have it."

"It is tempting," Tim admitted. "But I can't give up just yet."

"So what's your plan?" Carmilla asked.

"Well," Tim said. "Everyone I need to talk to keeps getting killed right before I can ask them what I need to know. I've only got one option left now, so I guess I better get to him before this happens again."

17

Tim was positive that Ugarte had met with either Ludwig or Lucretia at the Torn Throat to remove the claims trackers attached to the Puzzle Box. And while he didn't necessarily think the shady former SIU investigator was capable of murder, Ugarte had probably tipped off someone who was.

The window of the Blue Demon was dark when Tim arrived. There was no answer when he tried the bell and no sign of any activity inside. He circled around to check the back entrance, but the door was locked and there was no one around except a couple of large and heavily-tattooed zombies hauling in huge bags of frozen brains through the receiving doors of the nightclub next door. They gave Tim confused and vaguely menacing looks. Tim quickly gave up on the door and beat a hasty retreat back to his car.

Once inside, Tim grabbed his laptop and opened Ugarte's old personnel file. It showed a home address in the Temple District. At one time, that had been one of the most desirable spots in the city. Much of the real estate was considered too cursed for development, so the few buildings that did go up were in high demand. Now it was mostly a home for call centres and tech startups. The address in the file was an old one, but there was a chance that it was still active. Plus, it was only a ten-minute drive from here. If Ugarte wasn't home, Tim had other options for tracking the shifty satyr down.

Tim started the engine and made his way west, cutting a few minutes off his journey by taking the crossroad through Pentacle Park. Some drivers avoided it because cars sometimes entered from one side and briefly vanished before rematerializing in the middle of the main gazebo in the picnic meadow, but that only tended to happen on foggy days.

Tim stopped in front of a four-storey townhouse building on Yidhrra Street. It was an anonymous black lavaglass structure of the type that had been very much in vogue at the time of its construction roughly 30 years ago, but had long since been supplanted by a more recent swing back to the Demonic Revivalist style. There was a zombie fast food restaurant called Braainz on one side and a partially excavated ancient temple and altar mound on the other.

According to the file, Ugarte's unit was on the third floor. The black glass made it impossible to see if there was anyone inside. Tim approached the front door. He could see a worn black label identifying "D Ugorti" as the occupant of 301. It looked like Ugarte wasn't all that bothered about the fact that his name was spelled incorrectly on the front of his own building. Maybe he didn't get enough visitors to notice.

Tim pushed the buzzer for 301 and waited. A couple of young satyrs whizzed by on motorized moonboards on the sidewalk behind him. They were both outfitted in the multicoloured cummerbunds and oversized hoof spur boots that were essential components of this year's hipster uniform dress code. Tim assumed that they worked for one of the big IT companies with offices in the neighbourhood. The headquarters of InfernaChat was just a couple of blocks away. A lot of trolls worked in this part of town, but they tended not to come out in daylight.

Tim tried the buzzer again. Either Ugarte wasn't home, or he was home and just didn't want to come to the door. Given recent events, of course, a third option was also possible. Ugarte might be home, but just too dead to answer.

Tim took a step back onto the sidewalk and weighed up his options. He was extremely familiar with this type of building. Developers had built a lot of them because the materials were cheap and easy to work with. The problem with lavaglass, however, was that it tended to break down after prolonged exposure to direct sunlight. As the glass lost its structural integrity, it released whatever spectral energy had been trapped within at the time it was forged. If it all went at once, the entire building could become possessed, a lesson that residents of the notorious Dark Tower Suites had learned the hard way only the year before.

Lavaglass was no longer allowed under the building code, but existing buildings did not have to completely refit if they installed spectralite emergency escape stairs that were accessible by every individual unit. There was no sign of the stairs on the front and no room for them on the sides, so Tim guessed that they had to be attached to the back.

Tim knew better than to cut through the abandoned construction site and so went down the street and cut around through the alley next to the restaurant instead. As he had expected, the stairs were attached to the back of the apartment building just next to a dumpster on the edge of the tenant parking lot. There was a beat-up looking green Kraken station wagon in the parking spot for unit 301. Tim took a quick look inside and spotted a box of cheap voodoo dolls and a pile of old Curse Burger wrappers and empty drink containers in the back seat.

Ugarte is here, Tim thought. Or at least his car is.

Tim approached the stairs. They were the cheapest type available and had been fitted about as elegantly as a fire hydrant welded to the hood of a luxury car, but they looked like they would at least support his weight. Tim took a quick look around to make sure no one was watching before grabbing hold and starting to climb. Anyone home in either of the first or second floor units might see him go by, but he would have to take that chance. There were no cars in either of those parking spots, so he figured that his odds were good of making it up to three undetected.

Tim reached the third floor landing and stepped over the metal barrier onto the rear balcony. The patio door leading to the unit was open. It was a warm day, so it was entirely possible that somebody might leave the door open to let in some air, but based on the security at his shop, Ugarte did not seem like the kind to be quite so cavalier about accessibility.

Tim peeked inside. He had to be careful here. He couldn't just pull the door open and go strolling in. That might be interpreted as breaking and entering, and Crimson Seal would not look favorably on such an act, especially if one of their employees was caught in the act by the property owner.

It was too dark inside the unit to see much, but he could hear someone or something moving around. He clipped the Spectravision filter onto his glasses and dialled it over to standard IR, which brought things into a sharp but somewhat ghostly clarity. To the right he could see a small dining room table covered with assorted junk. In the middle was a small living room with a couch, a wall-mounted flatscreen TV and some sort of exercise machine that looked like a cross between a stationary bike and a playground swing.

Tim shifted his gaze to the left, where he saw a large closet next to the entrance of what was probably the bedroom. The closet door was open and Tim could see a figure hunched over inside going through a box on the floor. The figure was wearing a dark hooded sweatshirt and jeans. Whoever it was, they were too small to be Ugarte.

Tim hesitated for a moment, trying to decide what to do. Technically, he should call the police to report a potential break and enter, but that would lead to quite legitimate questions about how he came to know that the apartment was being robbed. Plus, by the time the cops arrived, whoever was inside would be long gone. Besides, he needed this lead.

Tim pushed the patio door open and stepped inside, drawing the Devil Stick out of his SIU bag as he went. He was careful to dial the charge down to the lowest setting. No matter what, he didn't want to kill anybody. He moved quietly across the carpet until he was right behind the hunched figure and held the stick out in front of himself, his finger poised on the trigger.

"Hold it right there!" Tim said, struggling to keep his voice level. "Turn around slowly and keep your hands where I can see them!"

The figure stopped rooting through the box and sat back. They did not put their hands in the air.

"You're not Ugarte," the stranger said in a voice that seemed oddly familiar.

"No," Tim said. "And neither are you. So what are you doing in his apartment?"

"The same thing you are, I'm thinking," the stranger said.

"I doubt that," Tim said. "Who are you?"

"Tell you what," the stranger said. "I'll show you mine if you show me yours."

Before Tim could say anything in reply, the figure spun around. Tim could see they were holding something in their left hand, but didn't realize that it was a canister of Demonex until the spray erupted in an arc aimed at his face.

Tim ducked under the jet of pressurized green foam and squeezed the trigger on the Devil Stick. There was a crackling sound and a bright red flash. Tim heard the figure grunt in pain and then saw them fall sideways in a heap. He quickly grabbed the dropped canister of Demonex and backed away until he found a light switch. He flicked on the lights and removed his Spectravision attachment, giving his eyes a moment to adjust to the sudden brightness of the overhead pot lights.

The figure was lying on their side in front of the closet, apparently unconscious. Tim approached them carefully, using his foot to roll them over. Whoever it was was also wearing Spectravision, but the older goggles variety similar to the one Tim had used when he first started at SIU.

Keeping the Devil Stick ready in his right hand, Tim reached down with his left to pull the goggles up, revealing a familiar face.

"Not you again," he said.

Giallo groaned and opened her eyes.

"What the hell are you doing with that thing?" she asked, looking at the Devil Stick. "You could have killed me!"

"It's on the lowest setting," Tim said defensively. "Besides, you tried to Demonex me in the face!"

"What did you expect?" Giallo said, holding her stomach as she moved back up into a sitting position against the closet door. "You sneak up behind a woman in the dark, you get what you deserve."

"What are you even doing in here?" Tim said.

"Same thing you are, probably," Giallo said, grimacing as she took a couple of deep breaths.

"But it's breaking and entering!" Tim said.

"Hello pot?" Giallo said, miming talking on the phone. "I have the kettle on line two. Should I put him through?"

"Okay, fair enough," Tim said. "But this is my investigation!"

"Yes, and you're doing just a bang-up job so far," Giallo said. "Two clients dead and your best lead has just disappeared? If I had my laptop on me, I'd nominate you for employee of the month so fast, your head would spin like an inpatient at the Crowley Clinic."

"You've been following me!" Tim said. "You were the one I spotted spying on me from the alley that afternoon!"

"Relax," Giallo said. "I'm sure you're important enough that you've got lots of people following you. Aside from just your standard debt collectors, process servers and angry ex-girlfriends, of course."

Tim decided to let that one pass.

"You find anything?" he asked, gesturing to the closet.

"Well that depends," Giallo said. "I did find a couple of bags of some very dodgy-looking synthetic blood boosters and a case of even dodgier-looking satyr libido-enhancing pills, which I did not know was a thing that required enhancing. But if you're talking about the Hesselthorn Puzzle Box or anything related to its whereabouts, then the answer is no."

"Why are you still trying to find this thing?" Tim asked. "I mean, to the point where you're breaking into somebody's apartment. Are you really that pissed about SIU taking over the case?"

"None of your business," Giallo said, getting up. "Maybe I'm just sick and tired of you morons always swooping in to grab the credit."

Tim got the feeling that there was more to it than that, but it was evident that Giallo would never admit as much, especially to someone she considered to be one of those swooping morons.

"Fair enough," Tim said. "Next time I see you sneaking up on me in an alley, I'll remember not to use the Devil Stick."

"Spare me," Giallo said, heading for the door. "I've got a way better lead on the box, so don't flatter yourself that I'll be running around after your dumb ass. I'll have it in my hands before the end of the day."

"Sure," Tim said.

"You don't believe me?" Giallo said, stopping.

"Honestly?" Tim said. "No."

"Hundred bucks?" Giallo said, putting her hands on her hips with an air of defiance.

"Okay," Tim said. "It's a bet."

Tim had never bet on the outcome of an investigation before, but this seemed as good a time as any.

"Great," Giallo said. "You better be good for it. I need to get new goggles."

Tim watched as she made her way back out through the patio door. Once she was gone, he completed a quick search of the rest of the apartment. He didn't know how much of a search Giallo had completed before he interrupted her and couldn't afford to take chances. An object like the Hesselthorn Puzzle Box would in theory be powerful enough that it would leave spectrographic traces even if it was removed, but he saw no indications that anything like it had at any time been stored anywhere in Ugarte's place.

Tim completed his search and exited back through the patio door in under five minutes. He wouldn't put it past Giallo to have called the cops to report a break and enter just to slow him down. He didn't know if she was lying about having another lead, but he knew what his next step was going to be.

Tim got back to his car and opened up his laptop. He had planted a claims tracker on Ugarte's cane when he had visited him back at the Blue Demon. It was similar to the units that had been attached to the Puzzle Box, only not quite as advanced. Tim wasn't technically supposed to have them—they were a holdover from his time as an adjuster and he had just forgotten to return them. The units were supposed to be used by Claims staff only, so what he was doing technically qualified as a breach of internal procedure, but he was pretty sure that Volkerps wouldn't care in the least so long as it led them to what they were looking for.

Tim punched in the tag number and waited while the system retrieved the location. Using a claims tag as an improvised surveillance device wasn't exactly ethical, but it was that or go back to Volkerps and admit that he had hit another dead end.

Tim was aware that his justifications were thin, which was why he had waited until he had no other option before going down this route. If it turned out to be just another blind alley, then there was no reason to mention any of it in his final report.

His laptop beeped as a red dot popped up on the map. Tim recognized the location instantly and felt a knot form in his gut.

According to the claims system, Ugarte, or at least his cane, was at 606 Paradise Avenue in the southern Hades district. It was a spot that Tim was quite familiar with, having been assaulted and nearly murdered there while investigating his first case. That was the location of Circle 9, a nightclub that also served as the headquarters of a demon named Az-moda, who was the current head of the city's Hellspawn Triad.

If Ugarte was there, it probably wasn't because he wanted to cut loose with some drinking and dancing in the middle of the day. As Tim's ex-girlfriend had once pointed out, the Hellspawn were disinclined to entertain uninvited guests outside of regular business hours.

Tim closed down the laptop and started the car. He had no idea if Ugarte was still alive, but if the Hellspawn got their claws on the Puzzle Box, then bad things would follow.

18

"I appreciate you stopping by on short notice," Azmoda said, his forked tongue darting between emerald-studded fangs as he sipped on a glass of Red Fairy Absinthe.

The demon had become hooked on the stuff since they started getting it from a Bulgarian supplier the month before. It sometimes caused hallucinations and rage blackouts, but he believed a ganglord needed that kind of an edge to keep his underlings in their place.

"No problem," Ugarte said. Considering that he was chained to a chair in Azmoda's inner sanctum after being kidnapped and forcibly brought here by two massive Triad enforcers, he didn't think there was any point in arguing on the issue of consent.

"How's business, by the way?" Azmoda said, slurring slightly. He was on his tenth cocktail of the afternoon, which was not an unusual number. Normally, he tried to limit himself to eight–more than that and the angry/ wobblies started to kick in–but the last 24 hours had been more eventful than usual, even by his descended standards. "Things are good?"

"Yes, thanks," Ugarte said, nodding to the extent that his restraints would allow. His business would be much better if he wasn't paying 50 percent of his income to the Hellspawn in kickbacks and protection money, but he was far too circumspect to bring up such an impolitic subject in his present circumstances. "Yeah, real good."

"Great," Azmoda said, burping a jet of red flame. "You have any problems, I don't care if it's with those bylaw enforcement jags or the feds, you let me know, okay? That's what I'm here for. To help you solve problems."

"Of course," Ugarte said.

Ugarte had actually been in touch with a federal prosecutor only the week before about setting up a plea deal. In broad terms, he would provide sworn testimony outlining everything he knew about the Hellspawn's operations in exchange for immunity on some outstanding tax charges. The whole thing could get him 10 years if they really pushed it, which they had made clear they were more than willing to do.

Ugarte was morally opposed to incarceration. Particularly his own. The feds were trying to lowball him on the witness relocation part. Ugarte did not want to live in Hellhole Springs. He saw himself as more of a Paradise Point sort of guy. He didn't know if Azmoda had found out about the whole thing and that was the reason for this summons. If it was, he was dead. If not, then there was no reason to mention it.

"Absolutely," Ugarte said. "You'll be the first to hear about it. I swear on my mother's beard!"

"Good," Azmoda said. "Trust is the key to any lasting business relationship, wouldn't you agree?"

"Absolutely," Ugarte said, desperately hoping that he didn't appear to be as sweaty as he felt. Azmoda always kept his office as hot as a blast furnace. "Totally central."

"So anyway," Azmoda said. "The boys here stopped by the Hesselthorn place last night to pick up that little item you tipped us off about."

The gangster gestured to the two enormous Serrabluks standing on either side of Ugarte's chair. The one on the left was green and scaly while the one on the right was red and covered in brands. The green one was using Ugarte's cane as a toothpick. Both of them looked more than capable of crushing the satyr into an unrecognizable mass of hooves and horns. Ugarte could feel malevolent menace radiating off them in waves, which was doing little to help him remain cool and rational.

"Right," Ugarte said, looking around the room for any sign of a hidden microphone. His paranoia hadn't reached heights like this since his first divorce, when he had become convinced that his wife had hired private investigators disguised as mail carriers to spy on him. "Any, uh, problems?"

"Nah," Azmoda said, waving a claw as if casually shooing away a hovering waiter. "Guy tried to play it cute at first. Said he didn't have it. The boys were able to help him refresh his memory."

"I'm sure," Ugarte said. He had seen the breaking news reports of police surrounding the Hesselthorn mansion, but had been in the process of packing to flee the country when Azmoda's goons had broken in and dragged him out through the back door in chains, so he didn't know for sure how many members of the Hesselthorn family were still alive at this point. His best professional estimate was none of them, but he didn't want to jump to legally troublesome conclusions.

"Anyway, after some brief negotiations, yadda yadda whatever, the object in question is finally in my possession," Azmoda said. "Which brings me to why I invited you down for this little tête-a-tête."

Azmoda got up and walked around his chair to a large oil painting of himself that hung on the back wall of his office. It portrayed the mobster as one of the great, all-conquering demon Allfathers of old, albeit one who liked to ride in a custom X2 Inferna supercar surrounded by topless Bacchantae. Azmoda pushed a hidden panel in the picture frame and it slid up to reveal a safe built into the wall behind it. Azmoda placed his left claw against a reader and punched in a code on the keypad. The safe door opened silently.

Azmoda reached inside and pulled out what looked like a red crystal ball roughly the size of a tangerine. The ball glowed from within as strange symbols appeared and disappeared on the surface. Ugarte had seen the thing once before, but it was still impressive enough to make him gasp.

"So here it is," Azmoda said, closing the safe. "The Hesselthorn Puzzle Box."

"Yes," Ugarte said, transfixed.

"Not sure why in Azag's name they call it a box," Ugarte said. "It's a damn ball. Thing looks like an oversized Bloodoak berry."

"It is…something," Ugarte said.

"No doy, hornball," Azmoda said, putting the ball on his desk and leaning down to examine it more closely. "The problem is getting it open, see? There doesn't seem to be any hinge or seam or hole anywhere on this damn thing. I know these symbols that're flashing up are some sort of ancient demonic runes or something, but cast me out if I know what the hell they're supposed to mean! Demon school was a long time ago, you know what I'm saying? And I wasn't exactly the teacher's pet."

"I see," Ugarte said.

"I already had one of my guys try to figure it out," Azmoda said. "All that happened was the ball turned black and then, well, let's just say Zenny had to cancel the rest of his dentist appointments."

Azmoda gestured to a pile of bones and ashes in the corner next to the hot tub. Ugarte craned his neck to see a gold fang glinting in the remains of the charred skull.

"I don't think I would be of much assistance on that point," Ugarte said. He could sense where this conversation was going and desperately wanted to steer it off onto a sideroad before it arrived at a place he wasn't going to like. "Not really my, uh, area of expertise, unfortunately."

"Have some confidence, Ugarte!" Azmoda laughed. "You get it right, you'll be a legend! And if you get it wrong? Well, no sulphur off my tail."

"Yes," Ugarte said. "As much as I would love to be able to unlock such an artefact–and I really would, I mean, the ability to summon up a Djinn that can grant you literally anything you ask for? C'mon, who wouldn't want that? You'd have to be insane to turn down such an opportunity! Anyway, as I was saying. I really don't think, just based on my particular skill set, that I would be the one you would call on to–"

"Let's look at it this way, Ugarte," Azmoda said, leaning forward so that his snout was only inches from the satyr's face. "You got no choice. In fact, you might say that your life depends on it."

Ugarte opened and closed his mouth a couple of times, but no sound came out. Azmoda ordered the green Serrabluk to untie the satyr before tossing him the Puzzle Box. Ugarte was so nervous that he nearly dropped it on the floor.

"Wow!" Ugarte stammered. "Uh, I, um…"

The satyr held the Puzzle Box away from his body, barely able to bring himself to even look at it. The thing felt like a live grenade. The appearance and disappearance of the runes was terrifyingly hypnotic.

"It must be like some sorta combination lock," Azmoda said, scratching behind one of his horns. "Like you gotta pick the right runes in the right order or something."

"Yes…" Ugarte said, trying to make sense of the symbols that were fading in and out between his fingers. Despite his advertised claims to being an expert in supernatural artefacts of all kinds, he had almost no experience with this kind of thing. He had actually majored in sports marketing in college and had only lasted a year before dropping out to work on the direct mail campaign for a synthetic blood-based energy drink. The closest he had come to anything like this was a History of Demonic Civilizations elective in his first year. And he had only taken that because it was popular with first-year exorcism students, 88% of whom were women.

Come on, dammit! Ugarte thought. You've been outsmarting hornheads like this your entire life! Think!

Much to his amazement, an actual idea did occur to him. It wasn't much, but it might just be enough to get him out of this pit un-incinerated. If it worked, he swore that he would never come within a mile of any kind of criminal enterprise for the rest of his days.

"Are you really sure you want *me* to open this?" he asked. "I mean, if I'm the one who gets it open, then technically all resulting wishes would be mine."

Azmoda frowned. He had not thought about this potential technicality.

"As soon as you get it open, you give it to me right away," the gangster said. "As in, immediately. Got it?"

"I don't think it works that way," Ugarte said, reverting back to his loftiest professional tone. "With artefacts like this, all benefits are conferred on the one who breaks the curse or enchantment, not on the one who might happen to be standing next to them at the time it happens."

Azmoda ground his jaws together, making purple sparks.

"Listen to me," he hissed. "You get that thing open, your first and only wish is to transfer all wishes to me, understand?"

"I would be quite happy to do so," Ugarte said, growing in confidence with every passing second. "But based on what we know of Djinn, I don't think that would work, either."

"I think he's right, boss," said the branded Serrabluk.

"Yeah," nodded the green one. "You know what those damn Djinn are like. Remember that one we had on the payroll last year? Kermuxx the Despoiler?"

"I remember that asshole," Azmoda growled. "I don't care if you've got eight dicks! That does not give you the right to jizz all over my priceless collection of celebrity death masks! Spunk was so acidic that it melted half of Kanye's face!"

"I didn't know that guy was dead," said the red Serrabluk. "Didn't he just put out an album last year?"

"Let's just say he was occupied at the time," Azmoda said.

"That actually explains a lot," nodded the green Serrabluk.

"Anyway," Azmoda said after a few minutes of pacing back and forth behind his desk. "Here's what we're gonna do. You're gonna tell me exactly how to open this thing. I get even the slightest hint of a notion that all is not well in Purgatory, I drop the box right in your lap."

"Okay," Ugarte said, barely able to contain his glee. He had always known that Azmoda's greed would one day overcome his sense of self-preservation, but didn't think he would have a front-row seat for the moment that it actually happened.

"However," Azmoda continued. "And I cannot stress this point enough. If something does actually happen that causes even the slightest injury to me–I'm talking so much as a singed horn tip–you know what's gonna happen?"

"I think I can guess," Ugarte said with genuine unease as he glanced at the two massive demons on either side of him.

"Yeah?" said Azmoda. "Well let me make it absolutely clear. Just so there's no confusion between us. Because your wildest, most abominably horrendous nightmare scenario is going to look like a G-rated kiddie cartoon in comparison. Like the one where the cute little werewolf cub and the baby vampire finally overcome their differences and become best buddies in order to save the blood bank from foreclosure and send the lost demon back to its family, you dig?"

"I truly do," Ugarte said, nodding furiously. He had not thought ahead to what he would do when and if Azmoda was vaporized. He only had the capacity to handle one crisis at a time.

"It'll make what happened to the supplicants on the Plains of Gorgaroth look like that episode of Dinky Demon Dashers where Dinky tries to buy ice cream for his human friends," Azmoda said. "You get the picture?"

"Hey, I love that show!" said the branded Serrabluk. "Even if Dinky is kind of an entitled little whiner sometimes."

"It's just 'cause his dad got cast out when he was little," said the green Serrabluk. "You gotta cut the kid some slack."

"Would you two shut up!" Azmoda snapped. "I'm tryin' to make a point, here!"

"Sorry, boss," the Serrabluks rumbled in unison.

"Azag's balls!" Azmoda said, picking up the glowing ball. "This is having a seriously delemental effect on my ability to concentrate!"

"I think you mean 'detrimental,'" said the green Serrabluk.

"Yeah," said the branded one. "Or 'deleterious' maybe."

"Ooh, that's a good one!" said the green Serrabluk.

"Been studying for my high school equivalency," said the branded Serrabluk. "Don't wanna be doin' this muscle work forever."

"Heard that," said the green Serrabluk. "I've been doin' the porn shoots on the side. You know, evenings and weekends and whatever. Think I'll quit, though."

"Makes you feel like an object," nodded the branded Serrabluk. "Hard not to do it without feeling like you're perpetuating a cultural cliché, you know? Just because we have massive–"

"Would you two shut your damn vent holes!" Azmoda yelled. "I don't give a charred werewolf turd about either of your long-term career plans!"

"Sorry, boss," the Serrabluks muttered.

"All right," Azmoda said, taking a deep breath. "Let's open this damn thing. You ready, Ugarte?"

"Ready," Ugarte said.

"Okay," Azmoda said. "So where do I start, here?"

Ugarte cleared his throat and looked closely at the ball. Although he didn't recognize any of the symbols, he could see that the same ones seemed to be repeating as they flashed up on the surface. He counted 13 different symbols before he saw the same one re-appear, although it was hard to be sure as some of the symbols were complex and didn't appear to display in any sort of obvious pattern.

"Okay," Azmoda said, his forked tongue flicking in and out between his fangs. "So which one's first?"

"Afternoon, boys!"

Everyone in the room turned in surprise as a young human female in a dark hoodie came strolling casually through the door and into the office.

"Who the hell are you?" Azmoda barked. He was not used to the sight of people entering his office unannounced. The only humans who came in here were a select few VIP guests of the nightclub upstairs and those whose lives or extremities were about to be permanently shortened for business reasons.

"Good question," the woman said, shooting the red Serrabluk in the back with a Devil Stick she had been carrying close to her leg. She pulled the trigger and the massive security demon exploded in crackling blue bolts of energy, rising up off the floor and letting out a horrible screeching sound.

The green Serrabluk spun around and swiped at her with its massive claws. She ducked under the blow with surprising speed and fired the Devil Stick straight into his groin, giving him a similar jolt to the one experienced by his coworker. Ugarte ducked his head out of the way as the giant demon fell against his chair and collapsed on the floor.

"Now that we've got that out of the way," she said, pointing the Devil Stick straight at the Puzzle Box in Azmoda's claws. "I believe that's mine."

Azmoda looked from the Puzzle Box to Ugarte to the woman, trying to gage if this was some sort of half-assed rescue operation. Ugarte, however, seemed just as surprised as he was by the stranger's appearance.

"She with you?" Azmoda demanded.

"No!" Ugarte said. "I've never seen her before in my life!"

"Shut up and hand it over!" the woman ordered.

"Whoa," Azmoda said, edging sideways to put his desk between himself and the new arrival. "Take it easy with that thing, lady."

"Hand me the box and I won't light your ass up, goblin boy," the woman said.

Azmoda flicked his tongue as red smoke trickled out of his ears. He was sensitive about his appearance, which he was aware was considered less than movie star handsome even by demon standards. He had gotten some plastic surgery to shrink his ears and even out his horns, but the doctors had said there was nothing they could do about his snout without using general anaesthetic, of which the ganglord was paralyzingly afraid. Right now, however, he knew that he had nothing to gain by losing his cool.

"Just chill for a sec!" Azmoda said, taking another step to the left. "Put your little toy there down and maybe you and me can work something out."

"Thanks," the woman said, taking a step forward. "But I think I'll hold onto it for now."

Azmoda eyed the sizzling crackle of blue energy at the tip of her weapon warily. He had been shot with a Devil Stick once before back when he was a street operator. It had happened during a turf war with the Fork Tongues. He and his gang had been on their way back from a drop when they were ambushed by a task force of crooked cops. Three of his guys had been fried and Azmoda had been shot twice in the back, so he was painfully aware of exactly how it would feel to be on the receiving end of such a blast.

"Don't think I've seen you around before," Azmoda said. "You sure you don't work with my horny little friend here?"

"Fortunately, not," the woman said. "The only thing this sicko seems to work with is the blow-up goat doll he keeps in his bedroom closet."

"Hey!" said Ugarte. "What are you doing snooping around in my place? Uh, I mean I have no idea what you're talking about!"

"Figures," Azmoda cackled, taking another step. "Always knew you were a dirty birdie, Ugarte!"

"It's not true!" Ugarte said, reddining. "I'm just storing some items there for my cousin!"

"As enjoyable as our discussion of this pit wiper's social life is, I'm afraid I don't have all day to stand around shooting the shit with you two morons," the woman said. "Now toss me the Puzzle Box before I count to three or I'm going to give you a new brand to go with your Triad one. And I guarantee you're not going to like where I'm going to put it."

"Look," said Azmoda, taking another step. "I'm a reasonable demon. I'm sure we can work something out."

"I'm not reasonable," the woman said. "One."

"I'm just saying," said Azmoda. "I have connections, you know? Whatever you want, I can make it happen."

"What I want is the Puzzle Box," the woman said, holding the Devil Stick out so that the tip was almost under the demon's nose. "Moving from one to two."

"All right!" Azmoda said, holding up the box in apparent surrender. "But don't say I didn't try to negotiate."

Azmoda jumped behind his desk with surprising speed, reaching below the lid to push a button on a control panel mounted underneath. There was a click and a whooshing sound as the safe slid out of the way and was replaced by a whirling vortex of red and black clouds.

Giallo felt herself pulled off her feet and dropped the Devil Stick, grabbing the edge of the desk to prevent herself from being pulled into the raging void. Ugarte had nothing to grab onto and was helpless as both he and the chair rose up off the floor and spun wildly through the air into the maelstrom.

"You like that?" Azmoda shouted over the howling wind and lightning crashes. "Just had it installed!"

Giallo hung on for dear life as the two body guards lifted up off the floor and swept past her. One of them bumped against her left arm as he went, meaning that she was only holding on with her right.

"Pretty cool, huh?" Azmoda yelled. "Latest tech! Doesn't work on me because I'm wearing this!"

The gangster held up his arm to display a glowing green bracelet on his wrist. Giallo assumed that the bracelet offered some sort of immunity to whatever kind of curse had been applied to the area behind the safe. Azmoda evidently didn't think enough of his support staff to grant them the same privilege.

Giallo tried to yell something, but her words were lost in the howling madness. She could feel her grip slipping on the edge of the desk. She tried to reach back to grab it with her left, but the force was too strong.

Azmoda strolled around the desk and bent down to pick up the dropped Devil Stick, which he raised with a smile. She could see that he was still holding the Puzzle Box in his other claw.

"Well, this has been fun," Azmoda said. "But now, I'm afraid that I'm going to have to ask you to leave my club. And once you leave here, I'm sorry to say that all of your re-entry privileges will be cancelled. Permanently."

Azmoda raised the Devil Stick and was about to press it down on the back of Giallo's left hand when he was interrupted by a shout from behind.

"Hey!"

The demon turned around and barely had time to register that someone else had entered the room before he was hit in the eyes with a blast of stinging green foam. Azmoda let out a screech. It felt like he had just been blasted in the face with a pillar of fire–but not like any kind of fire he had ever experienced before. As a demon, he generally liked fire. The only fire he could not tolerate was Hellfire, which he had once burned himself with as a kid because of a stupid dare.

Azmoda dropped the Devil Stick and let go of the Puzzle Box, which flew out of his hand and over his shoulder towards the vortex. Giallo caught it in her free right hand just before it slipped by.

"Nice catch!" Tim said, stepping forward with the can of Demonex in his hand.

Giallo was about to reply when she felt her grip slip on the desk and she was sucked back towards the vortex. Tim jumped forward and grabbed her with both hands, bracing his feet against the front of the desk to keep them both from being pulled in.

"This is new!" Tim said, looking at the wall in disbelief. "He didn't have this the last time I was here!"

"Bracelet!" Giallo yelled.

"What?" Tim yelled back.

"Bracelet!" Giallo screamed, nodding her head in the direction of the fallen gangster.

Tim looked down and saw the glowing bracelet on Azmoda's wrist.

"I get it," he said, measuring the distance. "Okay, this is going to be a little tricky."

Tim grunted as he pulled with all of his might, propping his feet against the desk to get closer to the floor. If he pitched up even a little, he would lose his balance and both of them would be goners.

"Hold on!" he shouted, feeling Giallo lock her fingers around his left wrist. He was going to need to let go of her with his right hand in order to reach down and try and get the bracelet off Azmoda.

"I'm good!" Giallo yelled. "Hurry up!"

Tim let go with his right and reached down to grab the bracelet, but couldn't quite reach it. The gang leader had fallen with his arms splayed out in the opposite direction.

"Damn," Tim grunted.

He grabbed Azmoda by his tailored shirt and pulled him closer. The gangster grunted and came to, swiping wildly with his claws. The Demonex was still leaking out of his eyes, so he couldn't see what he was doing. Tim felt Azmoda's claws swish within inches of his face as the demon attacked blindly.

"Stop messing around!" Giallo shouted.

"Thanks for the tip!" Tim yelled, wincing as Azmoda grazed his side.

The gangster grabbed Tim by the neck and tried to leverage himself up off the floor. Tim elbowed Azmoda in his prominent nose, causing the gangster to raise his arm to cover it up. Tim grabbed Azmoda's wrist and yanked off the bracelet. Tim slid his fingers through the bracelet and gripped it tightly. As soon as he did, he felt the pull of the storm vanish instantly.

"That's mine!" Azmoda screeched.

Tim rolled off the gangster, whose face registered alarm as he was pulled up and into the air.

"Nooooo!" Azmoda yelled, grabbing blindly for something to hold onto. He managed to get one claw into the top of the desk, but it wasn't enough to hold him. The gangster wailed as the claw was ripped out at the root and he sailed past Giallo and into the vortex.

Tim got to his feet and pulled Giallo backwards. It was surprisingly easy–like pulling on a kite. He reached down and grabbed the Devil Stick and backed the two of them out of the room, slamming the door behind them as Giallo dropped back to her feet.

"Whooo," Giallo gasped. "Thanks."

"You're welcome," Tim said. "Even if you did follow me and then knock me out with my own damn Devil Stick."

"Hey, you got me first," Giallo said. "I'd say that makes us even."

They both looked up as they heard grunting coming from the other end of the hall. This was followed by a clattering rumble as dozens of demons started down the stairs at the same time.

"We need to get out of here," Giallo said.

"Follow me," Tim said. "I've escaped from this place before."

"By the way," Giallo smiled, holding up the Puzzle Box. "You owe me a hundred bucks."

19

"I cannot tell you how strongly I advise against this course of action."

As the Metro Police lead exorcist on duty (or EoD, to use the official term), it was Sergeant Elspeth Viraggio's job to assess all suspects, victims, witnesses and anyone else brought into police HQ in an official capacity who was suspected of or showing visible signs of supernatural identity theft. She made the initial assessment on which ones were legit and which ones were faking. Of the ones who were legitimately occupied or recently vacated, she made the determination about whether the occupying entity could or should be, depending on the needs of the open investigation, safely removed. If it could not, she decided what mitigating steps should be taken to ensure said entity did not harm either their host or anyone else in the building.

Having seen firsthand the chaos that could result when a powerful and malevolent entity got loose in a place with a lot of weapons and heavy tactical equipment, it was a responsibility that she took seriously. She had only been working in Metro for a week when another exorcist had confused the scan reports on a pair of identical twins and let the wrong one out of the holding cells by mistake. SCSU technicians had spent three days cleaning up a mess that had made Central Booking look more like the set of *Cannibal Demon Holocaust 3*.

Viraggio had no patience for officers who relied more on intuition than hard science. Cops like that often tried to skip basic processing and screening procedures that they saw as slow and unnecessary, putting lives at risk to satisfy their own egos. She didn't like to stereotype, but it was a group composed almost solely of macho human males, most of whom had seen way too many episodes of *Devil Cops* growing up.

Horatio Duluc was practically the prototype.

"Trust me," Duluc said, posing in a chair by the window. "I know what I'm doing."

Viraggio sighed as the camera swung around to catch her response. The commissioner had signed an order mandating full departmental cooperation to Duluc and his documentary crew. She believed this had happened for numerous reasons.

First, the Hesselthorns had requested Duluc personally and still had some political pull at city hall courtesy of their campaign contributions. Second, the department needed some good publicity to offset the fallout of its stuttering new inclusive hiring program, which was not off to the best start. Third and probably most important of all, the commissioner was going to be prominently featured in the series, which would premiere two weeks before his rumoured senate campaign was scheduled to kick off.

None of this mattered to Viraggio. She hated office politics. She disliked having the cameras around, but accepted that there was nothing she could do about it.

There also wasn't a lot that she could do about the fact that Duluc had arrested Ludovico Hesselthoen and stuck him in an ordinary interrogation room instead of a secured cell in the high-security Spectral Containment Unit. That was where Ludovico should be, based on her professional assessment of his condition. She didn't have the authority to overrule Duluc, but she was damn sure that she was going to get her objections on the record.

"Have you even seen his PSE?" Viraggio said, waving the printout. "His numbers are off the damn charts!"

A PSE was a Psychokinetic Spectral Energy test, a standard procedure performed on all possessed individuals. It would show the supernatural radiation in an individual who either was currently or had recently been possessed by a demon, ghost or other supernatural entity. Trace levels only tended to last 24 to 48 hours, so it was vital that a person was tested as soon after they were vacated as possible in order to gage just how much damage may have been done. Average levels for a possessed individual were usually between 350 to 1,200 psKeu. Someone who had just walked through a haunted house, for example, might register 0.5 to 2.4 psKeu, assuming the place was legit.

Ludovico Hesselthorn's test showed a level of 806,814 psKeu.

Viraggio had never seen a number that high in her entire 12-year career. She had done the test three times and even ordered a diagnostic on the equipment to make sure it wasn't malfunctioning.

Ludivico wasn't just actively possessed, he was occupied by an entity more powerful than anything she had ever seen. And Duluc had stuck him in an ordinary interrogation room only a dozen or so steps away from the tactical secured storage area, which was home to some of the most dangerous weapons in the station.

"I appreciate your concerns," Duluc said, nodding and tapping the side of his forehead at the same time. He had always done this on his past shows to indicate that he was in a state of profound concentration. "But I need to do this my way."

In reality, of course, Duluc was not conflicted in the least. His psychic ability, although it had grown weaker and less reliable with age and lack of use, had given him a strong indication that Ludovico was guilty of something. He had absolute confidence that all he needed to do was march into that interrogation room, apply a little psychic push like he had done in the old days, and Ludovico–or whatever was inside him–would tell him everything he needed to know.

Duluc knew that it wouldn't be the first time he'd needed to give somebody a little supernatural shove to get them to confess. He'd done it to pin the Half Moon Murders on that homeless werewolf. The guy might not have been actually guilty of those specific killings, but Duluc knew he was guilty of at least a couple of wolfsbane clinic robberies, so what difference did it really make? Everybody wanted to see a shifty werewolf locked up and more importantly it made for compelling TV. Besides, solving that case had launched his career.

The same went for the zombie couple who'd gone down for the Savini kidnapping. It was often hard to read zombies because their brains were so messed up, but the flipside was that it made them so much easier to manipulate into confessing to things they hadn't done. Duluc considered zombies to be even less worthy of consideration than werewolves or vampires. They were gross, slow, unintelligible and good only for the kinds of jobs that not even the lowest demons were unwilling to do.

More importantly, their offscreen, hot-mic'd "confession" had been one of the most talked-about TV moments of that year. People still came up to Duluc to ask him how he knew those zombies were going to admit to everything when they did. Duluc always responded in the same way: he would tap his forehead and smile knowingly, just like he had done on the show. People ate it up.

Just like they were going to love this, he thought. The argument with the EoD was so good that he could already picture how it would play in the show. Maybe they would even cut it into the trailer. What was more on-brand for a maverick psychic cop who worked outside the boring and stupid rules than having an argument with some departmental pencil-pusher about the proper protocol for interviewing some evil monster who had wiped out their entire family?

"Your way?" Viraggio said. "That man in there is occupied by someone or something more powerful than any entity that has ever set foot inside this building! If things go bad and it decides to leave, it could easily destroy an entire city block!"

"I understand that," Duluc said, barely able to suppress an ecstatic grin. It would probably be more PC if he was having this discussion with a skinny older man instead of a younger woman, but he also knew that his core viewership would eat this stuff up. "I know this could be extremely dangerous for me personally, but it's a risk I've got to take if we're going to close this case."

Viraggio sighed. She had seen dozens of macho idiots like Duluc come and go over the years. Most of them ended up covered in ectoplasm and floating three feet above their bed in the high security ward of the Crowley Clinic. The one characteristic they all shared was the belief that nothing so horrible could ever possibly happen to them. She called this particular delusion *testosterphasia*. Unfortunately, it was far too common to be formally classified as a disorder in the SDSM.

"Fine," she said. "But civilians are not allowed in that room. Your documentary crew will have to remain outside."

"Wait a minute," said Xetra, the director. "We have an agreement signed by the commissioner that gives us access to everything we want to film."

"Not to Level 5 spectral entities you don't," said Viraggio. "Anything goes wrong in there and they'll be cleaning you off the walls with a sponge."

"My crew can handle it," Xetra said. "We all signed releases. If you want me to get the commissioner on the phone, maybe he can explain that to you."

"You can call whoever you want," Viraggio said. "But the man and the entity occupying that man were booked and processed on my watch, which makes me responsible for their welfare and the welfare of anyone who comes in contact with them during their time in this station. Which means that you and your crew will not enter that room."

Xetra was about to say something in reply when Duluc interrupted.

"Hold up, Xetra," Duluc said, getting up to whisper in the director's ear. "Forget this bitch. We can use the surveillance footage. It'll look more dramatic that way, anyway."

Xetra thought about this for a moment. "Okay. We'll do a re-enactment pickup for anything we don't get."

"Exactly," Duluc said, patting the demon awkwardly on her horned shoulder. He liked working with kids straight out of school because they would do pretty much whatever he told them to do without question. "Trust me. It worked great on the Savini case."

"Right," Xetra nodded. "How many times have I told you that I love all that classic TV stuff? It's why I went into directing in the first place!"

"Yes," said Duluc stiffly. The only drawback about working with a younger crew was being constantly reminded of how old he really was. Some of them hadn't even been born when his first series came out. "Well, I'll just go make sure that some justice is served, shall I?"

Duluc turned and began walking to the door leading to the interrogation room.

"Wait!" Viraggio said. "At least stop by SCTU first and have them fit you up with an SBA suit."

SCTU was short for Spectral Crime Tactical Unit, a special division that responded to the most violent and dangerous supernatural threats. SBA was Spectral Body Armour, which was designed to protect its wearer from most forms of curses, flame (although not Hellfire–nothing was resistant to that), identity theft and other hazards. It probably wouldn't offer much against whatever was inside Ludovico Hesselthorn, but in Viraggio's opinion, it was better than going in there without it. Not going in at all was the smarter option, but that possibility had already been ruled out.

"Thanks again for your concern," Duluc said, pointing to his head. "But I'm going to be just fine. My mind is a stronger defence than any suit could ever offer me."

In reality, Duluc knew that wearing the suit was probably wise, but he could never allow himself to be filmed in such a bulky, unflattering thing. Especially when it would make it practically impossible for the camera to see his face. The suit had only ever been used once on a previous show, and that had been by a stunt performer during a re-enactment of a moment that had never actually occurred in real life.

"Your funeral," Viraggio shrugged. "But whatever you do, do not make physical contact with the subject. Stay on the other side of the desk. Do not touch him under any circumstances. Don't hand him a drink. Don't pat him on the shoulder. If he attempts to make physical contact with you, leave the room immediately. If he falls on the ground or has a seizure, hit the panic button and wait for the techs. Do you understand?"

"Thanks for the tip," Duluc smiled. He turned to the A camera and adopted his serious crimefighter expression, which he had been saving for this very moment. It was a grim set of the eyes with just a twinkle of impending triumph at play in the corners. He knew the A camera would catch it because it was contractually required to be on and pointing at him at all times. When Duluc went to the toilet, the operator was required to hold on the bathroom door until the star re-emerged.

"Time to look the devil in the soul," he said, rubbing his temples with a practiced motion. "Time to cast out evil and replace it with divine justice!"

This was a new catch-phrase that he was trying out. Focus groups had so far expressed a lukewarm response to it, but he was powering through, mostly because he couldn't use the old one. The copyright on that one was held by his previous studio and their lawyers were being complete tools about it.

Xetra smiled and gave Duluc an enthusiastic thumbs-up. She was already imagining how they would shoot the re-enactment of the interrogation scene and drafting a memo in her head to ask for more money for additional special effects. No matter what actually happened in there, it was going to be the biggest scene in the whole series. It had to be.

Duluc had, by arresting Ludovico, stuck all of their dramatic eggs in one basket. If this blew up in their faces, there was a real chance that

DeadFlix could pull the plug and the whole project might get put in turn-around. A disaster like that would follow everyone involved for the rest of their careers. As director, that would mean her career was effectively over before it had even started.

Duluc made his way down the hall, mentally clearing space in his head for what he was about to do. He needed to focus all of his psychic energy to plant the idea in Ludovico's head that Ludovico was himself responsible for the murder of his older brother Ludwig as well as the disappearance of his father, Lucifer, and older sister, Lucretia. Duluc needed to make sure it was clear in his own head before he put the idea in a box and dropped it into Ludovico's consciousness. He needed to keep it simple. He couldn't have Ludovico confess to the muder of his father or sister just yet–that would be awkward if either of them turned up alive and well–but he could start laying the groundwork.

Once he had done that, he would have the leverage he needed to get Ludovico to reveal the location of the missing Puzzle Box. Dead rich people were fine, but Duluc knew that the only reason anyone would be logging on to stream his new show would be because they wanted to see what happened when their favourite detective finally laid his hands on the most famous ancient treasure of all time.

Even finding the box had to be a given. The real question was whether or not he would use his psychic abilities to try to open the box and see if it really was home to an all-powerful, wish-granting Djinn. If he couldn't get to that point, then the show risked being an even bigger failure than the time former game show host Vanza Remoran did an hour-long live special about uncovering Asgaroth's lost temple and found nothing more exotic than a half-empty six-pack of jumbo-sized *Blood Blast* energy drinks. After that, Vanza's career had been reduced to narrating online virtual tours of unbuilt condominiums.

Duluc took a deep breath and grabbed hold of the interrogation room door handle.

This is not your first séance, he told himself. *Now go in there and get those ratings.*

He pulled open the door and stepped inside. Ludovico was sitting handcuffed to the desk in the middle of the room. There were no windows and no two-way mirrors for third-party observers in here, just cameras. Mirrors were not allowed in the interrogation rooms as certain types of entities could escape through them.

"Afternoon, Vic," Duluc said, pulling out the chair to sit down. "I'm Detective Horatio Duluc. You might remember me from back at the house. Wow! What a day, huh? You getting everything you need? You want a soda or some crackers or something?"

Ludovico said nothing. His eyes did not even flicker to acknowledge Duluc's presence. He simply stared ahead. Duluc knew this was common for many victims of possession, as experienced demons and other entities knew that levitation, spontaneous combustion and projectile ectoplasmic regurgitation were all immediate giveaways. Only amateurs and joyriders betrayed signs of their presence so easily.

"I understand that you're not alone in there, Vic," Duluc said. "But I think you might have something you really want to tell me. Am I right?"

Ludovico said nothing.

"I know that you might be having difficulty communicating through the usual channels," Duluc said. "So what I'd like to do is form a psychic bridge with you. Is that okay?"

Ludovico registered no reaction. Duluc knew that, legally speaking, what he was about to do was not okay–at least, not without a lawyer present to give consent–but he didn't have time to wait around for that. Besides, as a star who got results, he was used to doing things however he wanted to do them.

Viraggio was right that it was dangerous for ordinary people to make physical contact with a possessed individual, but Duluc wasn't an ordinary person. His psychic abilities had always been strong enough to protect him from anything he had encountered in the past. Based on his own senses, he was positive that the EoD was either exaggerating or just plain wrong about the threat posed by the youngest Hesselthorn. Duluc could sense that there was something strange in there, but whatever it was, he was confident that he could handle it.

Ludovico was just a brain-damaged kid with lingering PPSD, nothing more. The PPSD made him a bit of a freak, but it also made him weak and thus extremely prone to psychic suggestion.

From Duluc's perspective, an ideal suspect.

"Okay," Duluc said. "Let's see what we can see, shall we?"

Duluc reached out and peeled off the oversized black rubber mitt covering Ludovico's left hand. The gloves were standard protocol to prevent entity transmission while a subject was in custody. They were treated with spectralite powder, which made them smell like stagnant pond water. The gloves only came in three sizes, which meant they didn't fit anyone. The ones Ludovico was wearing were too large for his hands, which made them easy to remove.

Duluc felt a surge of excitement. This had always been his favourite part of the whole process. He took a deep breath and blew on his fingertips before reaching out and taking Ludovico's pale and clawlike left hand in his own.

Duluc closed his eyes and mentally reached out to take hold of Ludovico's consciousness. This was always the tricky part. He needed to assert control quickly before the subject or any occupying entity knew he was in there and tried to fight back. Some of them had given him quite a run for his money over the years and it wasn't always the ones you expected. The production assistant on the set of his first ever series had been surprisingly resistant to not only his charms but his ability to make her forget the whole thing had ever happened. Duluc had brought her around in the end, though. He always did. It was his one real talent.

In his mind's eye, Duluc sensed that he was standing in a great entrance hall. As the psychic fog dissipated, he recognized it as the front hall of the Hesselthorn mansion. He could hear crying from somewhere overhead. He climbed the stairs and followed the sound down a familiar corridor to Ludovico's room. The door was open. Duluc stepped through it and entered the cell.

Duluc could see Ludovico floating just in front of him. He pushed forward through the darkness and approached a small, frightened child cowering in the corner. The child was bent over and appeared to be crying.

"There, there," Duluc whispered, approaching slowly and putting his hand on the child's bare back. "Nothing to worry about. I'm here to help you."

The child stopped crying and turned to look at him. The face was not Ludovico's. The face was not like anything that Duluc had ever seen before. The floor suddenly erupted in a bright green flame that Duluc felt searing through every cell in his body at once. He tried to let go of the child, but his hand was melted in place. He opened his mouth to scream, but all that came out was fire.

Duluc watched as the child slowly transformed into something that was not a child. The detective had seen a Djinn before. They were horrifically powerful creatures that made regular demons seem like cuddly stuffed animals in comparison. Some of them were so monstrous that their very appearance could turn other demons to charcoal.

This creature made the other Djinn that Duluc had seen look like a kitten in a humane society adoption video.

"Oh, detective," the Djinn said. "You have no idea how long I have waited for someone like you to come along."

20

Tim and Giallo made their way across town to a derelict-looking apartment building in an area of the city known as the Devil's Playground. It had gotten the name courtesy of a nearby amusement park that had closed after more than a dozen customers had gotten on the Ghost Train and never been seen again.

"What is this place?" Tim asked as they approached the front door. The building did not match the mailing address listed in Giallo's personnel file.

"What do you mean?" Giallo asked, looking insulted. "This is where I live."

"Oh," Tim said, not wanting to start an argument. "Okay."

Giallo paused and gave him a knowing look. "You looked up my file, didn't you?"

"Yes," Tim said, deciding that there was no point in pretending otherwise.

"Unbelievable," Giallo laughed, shaking her head.

"I needed to know more about who was horning in on my investigation!" Tim said.

"Oh, really?" Giallo said. "See anything interesting while you were in there violating my privacy?"

"It wasn't a violation," Tim said. "SIU has the right to investigate anybody associated with a case, inside or outside the company."

"Of course," Giallo said. "I had a feeling I was going to regret letting you get involved in this."

"*Letting* me get involved?" Tim said. "This is *my* case!"

"So you keep saying," Giallo said. "But I need you to do me a favour and not tell anybody at Crimson Seal about this. SIU or otherwise."

"About what?" Tim asked. "The fact that you don't live where you say you live?"

"Yes," Giallo said.

"Okay," Tim said after a moment's thought. He wouldn't be able to avoid referencing Giallo's involvement in the case report, but at the moment he saw no reason why he needed to include the discrepancy in her address.

"I'm serious," Giallo said. "You breathe one word of this to anybody in that building and both of our lives won't be worth a dynamite suppository, you understand?"

"Charming thought," Tim said. "Why all the secrecy?"

Instead of answering, Giallo unlocked the door and headed inside. The elevator did not appear to be working, so they took the stairs up to the fourth floor. Tim followed her down a damp hallway lit by flickering fluorescent lights. The place smelled like the dumpster behind a synthetic blood clinic, but lacked some of the charm.

What in the hell is she doing here? Tim wondered. He had worked as a claims adjuster for a while. The pay wasn't great, but it was still good enough that she could afford a better place than this.

Giallo unlocked a dented metal door at the end of the hall and motioned Tim inside. The apartment was numbered 409, but the last digit had fallen off years ago and was only detectable by the outline of faded paint where it had once been.

Tim stepped inside, expecting the worst. The apartment was actually nicer than he expected, although it was short on certain refinements. There was no TV or couch that he could see. Sitting rather incongruously in the middle of the room, however, was an old and ornately carved wooden desk that looked like it belonged in a museum.

Tim walked over to have a closer look. There was an anachronistically modern office chair with a groove worn into the top of the right armrest that looked like it had been carved out by years of repetitive motion. On the desk was a laptop, printer, scanner, and a set of Sectragoggles similar to the ones Tim had used before upgrading to the more modern clip-on variety. The laptop, he was impressed to see, was the latest model MicroDemon 6600, which was about three generations more advanced than the ones Crimson Seal issued to its employees.

The most striking thing, however, was a framed photo sitting at the corner. It featured an image of a younger Giallo smiling and standing next to…herself.

"Who is this?" Tim asked, picking the picture up to examine it more closely. "You have a *twin*?"

Giallo took the picture out of his hand and put it back on the desk. "That's my sister."

Tim was about to ask something else when Giallo turned on the light, illuminating the wall opposite the desk, at which point Tim's question died in his throat.

Instead of artwork or shelves, the entire wall was covered with what looked like an extensive network of photos, printouts, drawings and scribbles, each one connected by an intricate web of zigzagging lines. Tim had seen similar things many times in SIU and had even drawn up a few himself. It was a visual representation of some sort of investigation. Based on its size and the level of detail, it was obvious that Giallo had been working on it for months, if not years.

"What on earth?" Tim said, stepping forward for a closer look. The layout was almost impossible to follow, containing dozens of references to people and places that he had never heard of. The outer ring was made up of temples for entities named the Silent One, the Magikal One, the Kindly One and others. Tim had never heard of those. Were they real or was this all just part of some paranoid delusion? It occurred to him that maybe Giallo, although probably dangerous, might also be crazy. Had she brought him here just to murder him and take the Puzzle Box for herself?

He was considering this when he saw a face on the board that he recognized: Lilith Warwick.

"I know her," Tim said.

"I imagine there might be one or two faces on that board that you recognize," Giallo said.

"Uh, yeah," Tim said, pointing to Warwick. "What is she doing up here? What is this?"

Giallo took a deep breath and sat down in the chair behind the desk.

"All this," she said. "Is the reason that I came to work for Crimson Seal in the first place."

"Say what?" Tim said.

"The woman in the picture is my twin sister, Gwen," Giallo said. "It was taken when we were 16. We had both just got our driver's licences on the same day, which is why we both look so happy. Well, she looks slightly happier because she scored four points higher than I did, which she never let me forget. Until she disappeared."

"Disappeared?" Tim said.

"It was right at the end of our first year at university," Giallo said. "We went to different schools. She had always been really into supernatural history and demonology. We thought she might become a professor or maybe write a book on the subject. But during her first year, she got *really* into it. Started hanging around in these private InfernaChat groups. Seemed harmless at first. But then it started to get less harmless."

"How so?" Tim asked.

"Started getting into some really bonkers conspiracy theories," Giallo said. "Like how tech company CEOs were using DRE technology to cross-breed humans and demons in order to make themselves live forever. Or how vampires were kidnapping newborns to drain their blood for weird resurrection rituals. Stuff like that."

"I've heard some of those," Tim said. The tech CEO thing was, he knew from experience, not complete fantasy.

"When Gwen didn't come home at the end of her first year, we thought all kinds of crazy things might have happened," Giallo said. "That she'd been kidnapped or murdered or who knows what. My parents went insane with worry. They called the cops, the feds, the media. Anybody they could get to try and find out what had happened. Turns out what had really happened was much worse."

"And what was that?" Tim asked.

"About a month after she had disappeared, my parents got a call," Giallo said. "It was Gwen. She told them to stop looking for her. That she was fine, but she wasn't coming home or going back to school ever again."

"Why?" Tim asked.

"She wouldn't say," Giallo said. "All she would say was that she had found her purpose. She said that she was on a path to enlightenment. A path that rose up out of the darkness."

"That sounds familiar," Tim said.

"I thought you might recognize it," Giallo said. "Having run into them once before."

"You're saying that she joined the Sons of Darkness," Tim said.

"Right," Giallo nodded.

"But they're not that old!" Tim said. "I only ran into them just over a year ago and nobody I talked to had ever heard of them before that!"

Giallo laughed. "They're a lot older than that. They're just better at keeping a low profile than the Hellspawn or the Blood Brothers."

"You don't understand," Tim said. "My girlfriend at the time had never heard of them either and she was in charge of the Metro Supernatural Organized Crime Task Force Unit!"

"The Sons of Darkness is just a small part of a much larger organization," Giallo said. "The Sons were the ones tasked with finding and opening the Temple of the Holy One."

"Holy One?" Tim said. "You mean Belial?"

"Right," Giallo said. "Legend says that there are six demon Allfathers: the Magikal One, the Kindly One, the Dark One, the Righteous One, the SIlent One, and the Holy One. The goal of this organization is to resurrect them all."

Tim remembered some of the names from demonology studies in university, but it had been a while since he had examined the subject in any detail.

"Wait," he said. "You're saying that the Sons of Darkness were just a part of something even bigger?"

"Right," Giallo said. "The organization calls itself the Infernium."

"I've never heard of them, either," Tim said.

"Well, they've been around for thousands of years and perpetrated more evil than any other single organization in history," Giallo said. "So in one sense, that's kind of on you. On the other hand, they're pretty serious about keeping a low profile, so I guess your complete ignorance is understandable."

Tim turned to look back at the chart on the wall. Written at the top was "The Nameless One", whom Tim assumed was in charge.

"The Nameless One," Tim said, pointing. "Who is that? Another one of the Allfathers?"

"No, that's their leader," Giallo said. "And before you ask, I have no idea who it is in real life. All I have is the title. I don't know if it's been the same person all along or if they have elections or what."

"Right," Tim nodded. "Most demon worshippers don't usually have an org chart."

"Although it would make things easier if they did," Giallo admitted.

Tim's mind was spinning as he tried to make sense of what Giallo was telling him.

"Okay," Tim said. "So you said this is the reason you started working at Crimson Seal. Why?"

"Each one of the temples has an ancient artefact associated with finding and opening it," Giallo said. "The Hammer of Belial was one. I believe the Hesselthorn Puzzle Box is another."

Tim took the glowing red ball out of his SIU bag and looked at it closely. He could see the images of the runes flickering on the walls as they appeared and disappeared on the surface.

"Wait," Tim said. "So you started working at Crimson Seal because we insure some of these things?"

"Correct," Giallo said. "But I'm not the only one. Why do you think Warwick was a VP?"

"You're saying that there are still members of the Sons of Darkness working for the company today?" Tim said.

"They're everywhere," Giallo said. "Sure, they caught a few after your little stunt, but certainly not all of them."

"Whoever murdered Lucretia Hesselthorn was definitely dressed like one of them," Tim said.

"You were there?" Giallo asked, raising her eyebrows.

"Yeah," Tim nodded. "We snuck into thVrst to try to talk to her, but we got there too late."

"We?" Giallo said.

"Me and my brother," Tim said. "And my brother's agent."

"Your brother's what?" Giallo asked.

"My brother's a vampire," Tim said. "He's trying to break into movies and TV, so he's got this agent who wants to be turned into a vampire because he's dying. Although I think he might have been lying about that. And maybe about being an agent. It's complicated."

"Yeah, I get that impression," Giallo said.

"When I talked to Ugarte, he hinted that Lucretia was the one who stole the Puzzle Box out of the vault," Tim said.

"Lucretia?" Giallo said.

"Yeah," Tim said. "He let it slip out. Like it was something he gave away by accident. But he was just trying to throw me off. I'm sure that he met with Ludwig to remove the tracking tags. He probably offered to help sell the thing."

"That follows," Giallo agreed.

"Either that fell through or it was taking too long," Tim said. "Whoever killed Lucretia was wearing a black robe just like the ones the Sons of Darkness used."

"They must have thought she had the Puzzle Box," Giallo said. "Or that she knew where it was. Either she didn't know or wouldn't say, so they killed her."

"Most likely," Tim said. "I think Ludwig got the box, although I don't know how. He couldn't really do anything with it until he got rid of the tracking tags, though, so he went to Ugarte."

"Right," Giallo nodded. "That night they met up at the Torn Throat. They probably made some deal that got Ugarte a piece of the proceeds if Ludwig figured out how to open the box."

"I'm guessing Ugarte was probably in debt to the Hellspawn," Tim said. "Being the classic middle man that he is, he cut a deal and told Azmoda that Ludwig had the Puzzle Box."

"Right," Giallo said. "But the Hellspawn have no idea how to open it, either."

"Nope," Tim said, holding up the box. "Unfortunately, neither do we. Unless you discovered something over the course of your investigation?"

"Nope," Giallo said, shaking her head.

"So what are we supposed to do with this thing?" Tim asked. "Technically, it's the property of the Hesselthorn family, but that's problematic. Lucifer is missing. Ozymandia is in a PPSD coma. Ludwig and Lucretia are dead. And Ludovico is in jail."

"Do you think Ludwig killed his father to get his hands on the box?" Giallo asked.

"It's possible," Tim said. "The Hesselthorn house is an omniportal, so there are literally an infinite number of places he could have hidden the body."

"Or he could've just dropped it in a hole in the backyard," Giallo said.

"Yeah," Tim said. "But Ludwig doesn't strike me as a guy who's enthusiastic about manual labour. Besides, the grounds are covered with Bloodoak trees. It's not unusual for those things to loop their branches around nearby mammals and try to drain their blood."

"True," Giallo said. "He couldn't just feed Lucifer to the trees because the body would show up a few days later after the tree spat it back out again. Do we know for sure that it was Ludwig in the Torn Throat? Maybe Lucifer was behind the whole thing."

"Maybe," Tim said. "But why go to all the hassle? Lucifer already had access to the safe and probably even knew how to remove the tracker tags. He could have just taken it out anytime he pleased."

"True," Giallo admitted. "Maybe his disappearance wasn't planned. I bet he caught Ludwig in the act and Ludwig had no choice but to bump him off."

"You're probably right," Tim said. "Whatever happened, Ludwig didn't have the box for long."

"And now we've got it," Giallo said. "We can't just hand it in to Crimson Seal. The Infernium would have it before the end of the workday."

"Are you sure?" Tim said.

"You of all people should know that's true," Giallo said. "Didn't they try to have you killed by sending you into a house with a Djinn in the basement before the Hazardous Entity and Materials Team had cleared it?"

"That's true," Tim admitted. He had narrowly avoided being fatally cursed by a Djinn, although a former tenant of the home who had returned to retrieve some personal belongings had not been quite so fortunate. "They had control of someone inside SIU who altered the file."

"We need to figure this out on our own," Giallo said. "Everyone and their familiar is going to be looking for this thing. And some of them won't think twice about killing us to get it."

Tim's phone beeped. He pulled it out of his pocket and saw an email from Crimson Seal IT. They had decoded the raw security data from the Hesselthorn safe. As the file contained privileged and confidential internal material, the email stated that they could not transmit it to him electronically. He would need to come to the Information Technology Secured Data Centre in person to view it for himself.

"Interesting," Tim said.

"What?" Giallo asked.

"Looks like we might not have to figure this out all on our own after all," Tim said. "IT has decoded the raw security data from the Hesselthorn safe."

"What does it show?" Giallo said.

"I don't know," Tim said. "The file's too high security for them to email it to me. We're going to have to go down there in person to find out."

"Seriously?" Giallo said.

"Looks that way," Tim said.

"Okay," Giallo said, grabbing her jacket. "I hope you've got some nose plugs in that bag. I hate those damn trolls."

21

Duluc emerged from the interrogation room looking slightly less triumphant than Xetra had been expecting.

"So?" she said, standing up as Duluc entered the room. "Did you get it?"

Duluc appeared to have no idea what the producer was talking about. In fact, he appeared to give no indication of even knowing who any of them were.

"Sorry?" Duluc said in an oddly distant voice.

Xetra reminded herself that Duluc had a reputation for emerging from psychic interrogations in a highly dissociative state. She had seen it in almost every one of Duluc's previous shows. She had always assumed it was just for dramatic effect, but the detective truly seemed to have no idea where he was.

"So what did the kid say?" Xetra said. "Did he confess?"

"Oh," Duluc said, glancing back over his shoulder and then turning back to them. "Right. Yes."

"Did he confess to all of the killings?" Xetra said, already visualizing how they would shoot this for the recreations. They would need to get an actor who looked like Lucretia, as she was the only member of the family who had not consented to being filmed. Well, that wasn't strictly true. She had refused unless the network paid her enough money to get the surgery she wanted. The surgery cost way more than DeadFlix was willing to pay for her participation, however, and so she had locked herself in her vault in a sulk. Xetra knew of a couple of people who might be available on short notice, although one of them was supposed to be doing a commercial for a new brain-flavoured diet yogurt for obese zombies.

"Yes," Duluc nodded.

"That's great!" Xetra said, crossing the room to shake Duluc's hand.

Duluc held up a hand to stop Xetra in her tracks. "No contact, please."

"Sorry!" Xetra said. In her excitement, she had momentarily forgotten that Duluc had a rider in his contract that specified no one on the crew was allowed to make any physical contact with him. This, Duluc had insisted, was as much for their protection as his own, as he would be able to see all of their deepest and darkest secrets in an instant.

"What about the Puzzle Box?" Xetra said. "Did he tell you where it is?"

"Not exactly," Duluc said. "But I think I might have an idea where to start looking for it."

"Excellent!" Xetra said. "See? I told you this show was gonna be a hit!"

They were interrupted by Viraggio, who stormed into the room and right up to the detective.

"What did you do to him?" Viraggio demanded.

"Excuse me?" Duluc said.

"Ludovico," Viraggio said. "As soon as you walked out of the room, he collapsed on the floor!"

"I have no idea what you're talking about," said Duluc.

"I watched your entire conversation on the monitors," Viraggio said. "I told you not to make physical contact! He didn't say anything! And certainly nothing that could be used in court!"

"Perhaps nothing your microphones could pick up," Duluc said. "But I heard it all courtesy of our psychic connection."

"After you left, his heart rate and respiration flatlined!" Viraggio said. "We had to call in SEMT! We're going to have to move him into the SICU at the Crowley Clinic. He could die!"

"Sacrifices must be made," Duluc said. "I have a greater responsibility than you could possibly understand."

"Are you kidding?" Viraggio said. "We ran another PKS on him. His number's suddenly down to 22."

"Perhaps you should check your equipment," Duluc said. "It appears to be faulty."

"There's nothing wrong with our equipment!" Viraggio said. "I told you, I tested it to make sure it was working!"

"Well then," Duluc said. "Maybe the problem is with the people running the equipment."

"What the hell are you suggesting?" Viraggio said, taking a step closer. "Are you saying that I don't know how to do my job?"

They were interrupted by a uniformed officer who ran into the room and spotted Duluc.

"Yes?" said Duluc.

"Sorry detective," the officer said. "Commissioner asked me to find you right away. There's been some sort of explosion at Circle 9!"

"Explosion?" Duluc said.

"Yeah," she said. "Or, more like an implosion, actually. The whole place appears to be getting sucked into an inter-dimensional void!"

"Whoa," Xetra said. "That's not something you see every day."

"Commissioner thought it might be connected to the Hesselthorn murder," the officer said. "Thought you might want to check it out."

"I certainly will," Duluc said. "Thank you."

The officer turned and ran back out of the room. Xetra motioned to the crew.

"Let's get ready to roll!" she said as they began a scramble to pack up their gear. "We gotta get this on tape pronto!"

"Wait a minute!" Viraggio said, stepping in front of Duluc. "You're not going anywhere until I find out what you did to my patient!"

"Nothing," said Duluc, trying to step around the insistent exorcist. "I set him free."

Viraggio stepped sideways to block the detective and grabbed him by the shirt.

"I don't care who you think you are! I'm-"

Viraggio's voice died as she felt something strange start to happen to the hand pushing back on Duluc. She had been working in the job for long enough to know something was very wrong. Duluc supposedly had psychic powers, but this was different. The person she was making contact with wasn't a person at all.

"What the hell?" Viraggio gasped, trying to pull her hand away, but Duluc had taken hold of it.

"You should have listened," Duluc said. "I was telling the truth. The kid is free. He probably won't live to enjoy it, but then, who does?"

"Let me go!" Viraggio hissed.

"Yeah, come on!" Xetra said. "We've got what we need, let's get out of here."

"Oh I will free you," said Duluc. "I will free you all."

There was a series of cracking sounds. Viraggio shrieked as Duluc crushed every bone in her hand.

"What the?" Xetra said, turning around to see what all the commotion was. "Hey, what the hell are you doing?"

Duluc reached up with his other hand and grabbed Viraggio by the top of the head. As soon as he did, his hand burst into a raging blue flame.

Xetra had only seen real Hellfire once before in her life, but that was just a tiny flicker in a studio executive's backyard fire pit. This was a raging, crackling, swirling inferno of fury the likes of which he had never imagined was possible. She stumbled backwards and tripped over one of the gear bags, landing heavily on the floor.

Duluc's face remained strangely impassive as he melted Viraggio's skull and pushed her headless body aside. In a few quick movements, he reached into the chest of Torgun, the camera operator, and pulled out his heart. The organ was still pulsing when Duluc opened his mouth–which was now full of long black fangs–and took a bite. Blood spurted across the front of Duluc's suit and some of it got on Torgun's shoes, causing him to flinch like he'd been sprayed by acid.

"Gugg!" Torgun gagged, collapsing on the wet tile.

Kayleigh, the sound recordist, tried to turn and run, but Duluc simply reached out and touched her shoulder, at which point she erupted in blue flame and turned almost instantly to ash. Xetra watched in horrified disbelief as the ashes began to float up into the air and settle on the ground like snow.

"Sorry, Xetra," Duluc said, walking towards the prone director. "But I think this is a wrap."

Xetra scrambled to her feet and ran for the door. Her mind was no longer processing rational thought. The only thing she was aware of was the need to get as far away from her former subject as possible.

"Help!" Xetra yelled, sprinting out into the hall.

Xetra raced down the hallway past a puzzled pair of uniformed officers and ran through the first door she came to, which happened to be the staircase. She jumped down the first flight and almost face planted on the landing, somehow managing to stay upright as she rounded the corner and exploded through the door leading to the bullpen.

"Help me!" Xetra yelled, catching the attention of more than a dozen cops, suspects and other uniformed personnel.

"Stop that demon!" siad Duluc, emerging through the doors right behind her. "She just killed an entire film crew along with the EoD!"

Xetra saw an entire room full of armed people reach for weapons. She yelled that it wasn't true–that Duluc was the one responsible. But no one was listening. No one would believe her. Not over the most celebrated detective that the department had ever produced. She realized that her only hope was to get the hell out of here.

Her eyes fixated on the security checkpoint leading to the main reception area. If she could just get through the gate, maybe she could get outside. If she could get outside, maybe she could get away.

"Freeze!" yelled a dozen cops at once as Xetra raced desperately towards the door. She was dimly aware that they were pointing weapons in her direction, but her legs were no longer listening to the part of her brain that was telling her to stop.

"Nooooo!" Xetra screamed, focused only on putting one foot in front of the other as quickly as possible.

She made it two steps before she felt the first Devil Stick blast hit her just below the ribs on her right side. The pain was much more intense than she had been expecting, lifting her off the ground. Her vision narrowed to pinpricks. Compared to the next eight hits, however, it wasn't so bad. She was completely unconscious by the time both her wrists and ankles were secured with flex cuffs.

"Good job," Duluc said, nodding to the three uniformed officers that had climbed on Xetra's back in order to secure her.

"No problem, sir," the first one said. "What happened?"

"She escaped interrogation and killed some civilians upstairs," Duluc said. "Also got the EoD."

"Damn it," said the second uniform. "What do you want us to do with her?"

"Better put her in secured spectral containment," Duluc said. "She's definitely possessed. Don't let anyone near her until I get back."

"Yes sir," the first uniform said as they pulled the unconscious Xetra to her feet and began to hustle her out of the room.

"We better get SCSI upstairs, stat," said the second uniform. "Was she alone? Do we need TAC? Do we need to lock down the building?"

"Good idea," Duluc said. "She may not be."

The other uniformed officers in the room sprang into action. Duluc heard an alarm begin to sound as he headed for the front door.

"Sir!" came a voice over his shoulder.

"Yes?" Duluc said, turning.

"Where are you going?" asked the second uniform, looking confused.

"I'm going to round up some of her associates," Duluc said.

"Wait!" the uniform said. "Do you need backup?"

"No," Duluc said, smiling. "I'm pretty sure I can handle this by myself."

rimson Seal's IT department was located in an office underneath the Cushing Viaduct. The old rail bridge spanned a notorious sinkhole that at one time had served as a waste dump for a long-defunct synthetic blood manufacturer.

An ambitious developer had built condos on the site in an attempt to cash in on the short-lived craze for converted industrial spaces. Those didn't sell, largely because the overpowering smell of death and decay was more than even the slickest slideshow or complimentary upgrades could overcome. Now the place was home to a ghoul law firm (Corpulent, Necrosis & Bloat), a vampire-owned concert promoter (ExsanguiNation), and a satyr charcuterie (Horn2Tail).

The IT department was in the basement. Like Giallo, Tim did not enjoy being around trolls, who tended to conform to every unpleasant stereotype about their kind. They were cranky, ugly, foul-smelling and pedantic as hell. You couldn't spend more than five minutes with one before they started troll-splaining about everything from risk selection algorithms to which zombie bands could be officially categorized as braincore and which could not.

Trolls were also oblivious to whether or not you were interested in what they had to say. You could fall asleep or even die in the middle of one of their lectures and they wouldn't notice. Despite holding some of the most lucrative jobs in the tech and gaming industries, they also considered themselves the most socially marginalized of supernatural groups. According to them, vampires, werewolves, demons and even zombies were all treated like first-class citizens while they were forced to live in dank, dark holes. The fact that trolls seemed to *want* to live in dank, dark holes was apparently irrelevant.

Some of their views were so extreme that they had started their own social network called T-Chan, where they believed they could say the kinds of things that had gotten them banned from InfernaChat and other services. T-Chan's servers were reportedly located in the 9th circle, where the regular laws concerning libel and hate speech did not apply. You didn't have to be a troll to join, but nobody else seemed to want to.

Tim and Giallo crossed the lobby and made their way to the special sub-basement elevators. Since they averaged eight and a half feet tall, most trolls did not fit in the standard passenger units and so the company had installed customized ones. No non-troll employees wanted to be trapped in a box with a being who smelled like a goat carcass pulled from a vat of industrial waste, so this was considered a necessary accommodation.

"I wish I'd brought my respirator," Giallo said, breathing into her sleeve.

"It wouldn't help much," Tim said, pushing the greasy down button with the corner of his ID badge so as to avoid physical contact. "It's not so much a smell as it is a presence."

No sooner had he said this than the doors opened and the smell, which until then had seemed like a lingering suggestion, erupted like a warehouse fire backdraft. Tim rocked back on his heels and staggered against the wall while Giallo took her jacket off and wrapped it around her face.

"Come on," Tim said. "Let's get this over with."

The two of them stepped out of the elevator and entered the sub-basement, which had once been part of an ancient temple complex. The only part of the original site that still remained was the stone floor, which had been sectioned off into dozens of drab gray cubicles organized in groups of four. Ethernet and power cables snaked over and around everything, including the foundations of the old rail bridge high above. The space was lit by flickering green fluorescent lights that gave the room the same cheerful aura as a mortuary.

Tim and Giallo made their way down between the cubicles, each one home to a troll hunched over a keyboard, typing away in front of a wall of monitors. Some had personalized their workspace with an animal carcass or poster. No manager above the associate VP level ever came down here, so it was not unusual to see decorative touches that would never be allowed anywhere else in the company. Tim spotted at least five signed pictures of famed adult troll actress Fugma Puzz in poses that he knew he would not easily be able to forget no matter how hard he tried.

They had almost reached the end of the row when Tim spotted the name of the employee who had emailed him the update: Thraxx Sludd. Thraxx, however, did not appear to be at his desk.

"Do you know where I can find Thraxx?" Tim asked the troll in the neighbouring cubicle, a massive grey lump wearing an Ultimate Were-wolf Fighting Championship branded bucket hat and sucking on a soda the size of an oil drum. Tim had to shout to be heard over the troll metal blasting from a pair of wall-mounted speakers.

"Think he said he was going to squeeze one out," the troll said.

"Charming," muttered Giallo.

"Or maybe the kitchen," the troll shrugged. "You'll have to check with his personal events secretary if you want to know for sure."

"Thanks," Tim muttered. The two of them left the cubicle and headed for the break room, where they found three trolls standing around an open box of animal bones.

"So I take her out to that new sludge pit down in central Hades, right?" said the troll in the middle, picking a bone out of the box and crunching it between his mossy yellow teeth. "And five minutes after we get into the slop, she just casually mentions that her boyfriend is working on a Kraken boat that's due back to port in like, three days."

"I hate it when they just drop that in there," said the second troll, drinking what looked like tar from a large mug with the words "I'm not ignoring you, I'm multitasking" printed on the side.

"Wait, she didn't mention this before?" asked the third troll, his right hand buried deep in his shorts and scratching with what Tim found to be unnerving intensity.

"Not a word!" said the first troll as goopy grey clumps of marrow dripped on his shirt. "You believe that?"

"Hi," Tim said, waving. "I—"

"You think she was making it up?" asked the second troll.

"I bet she was," said the third. "Bet he doesn't work a Kraken boat. They're not allowed to fish for Kraken out beyond the Fork anymore. It's a protected species."

"I'm not saying she was making the Kraken part up," said the second troll.

"Excuse me!" said Tim, trying a second time to insert himself into the proceedings. "I'm—"

"Then what?" asked the third troll.

"I'm saying she was making up the boyfriend part," said the second troll.

"Oh," said the third troll, nodding. "As in, in his entirety? As in, the boyfriend was a total fabrication in order to avoid her obligation to fulfill the carnal requirements of our colleague?"

"Exactly," said the second troll.

"Damn," the third troll said. "That's cold. I've been there. I once took out this super mossy chick from my gym. I tell you, she loved the mud.

Couldn't get enough of it, she said. And then we arrive at my place. And keep in mind I just got this custom upgrade on my Bog Vortex, right? I mean–"

"Shut up!" Giallo screamed at the top of her lungs, making everyone including Tim jump.

"The hell?" muttered the second troll, looking at Giallo.

"Which one of you troglodytes is Thraxx?" Giallo demanded.

The first troll slowly raised his meaty green hand, which appeared to be stained with mustard. Or what Tim hoped was mustard. There was an open jar of Bone Jelly on the counter, so that was also a possibility.

"Great," Giallo said. "You recently emailed a notification to this man, Tim Lovecraft, that you had decoded some raw security data from the Hesselthorn safe?"

"Uh, yeah?" said the troll.

"Good job," Giallo said. "We need to see it."

"Uh, okay?" said the troll.

"Right now," Giallo said.

"Okay," said the troll. "I just need to finish my lunch and then I've got a platform support meeting, but if you come back in, like, three–"

"Now!" Giallo said.

"Listen, lady," the troll said, shaking his head and smiling in a condescending manner. "Just because it's an emergency to you doesn't mean–"

Giallo grabbed the Devil Stick out of Tim's SIU bag and held it directly under the troll's chin.

"It is an emergency for me," said Giallo. "Which means it's an emergency for you, too. After all, we're all on the same team, right?"

"Whoa!" the troll said, taking a step back. "Take it easy with that thing!"

"I am taking it easy," Giallo said. "If I wasn't taking it easy, I might have shoved it all the way up the other end of your disgusting food processing pipe and squeezed the trigger until the battery died. Now let's go!"

Thraxx shot a martyred look at his coworkers and turned towards the door. The two of them followed the recalcitrant troll out of the break room and back to his desk, Thraxx keeping one wary eye on Giallo the entire way.

"That was intense," Tim whispered.

"It's the only way to get anything done with these walking fungus farms," Giallo muttered. "Give me ghouls any day. Even a golem. They're slow, but at least they don't take two weeks to get around to something as simple as a friggin' password change."

Thraxx sat down and began typing, looking nervously over his shoulder to make sure Giallo wasn't about to shock him when he wasn't looking.

"It was actually pretty easy," he said, pointing to a screen at the top right. "I'm surprised they don't give SIU access to SSML files decoders."

"Uh huh," Tim said, leaning closer to the screen as the file appeared. He had seen these kinds of data dumps in the past when handling claims for secure storage sites and auction houses, which used similar systems. "How far back does it go?"

"Only to the last software update," Thraxx said. "They're supposed to go all the way back to activation, but it looks like the file got corrupted somehow."

The software used to run the Hesselthorn safe recorded every time the safe was opened, who opened it, and what was added or removed. That record was supposed to go back all the way to when the safe was first installed. Some of the newer models had a feature that allowed a new user to clear the activity history in the event the safe underwent a transfer of ownership.

The change had been instituted for data privacy reasons, but In Tim's opinion, it was pointless. Safes this big almost never changed hands. And the kind of people who bought one did not tend to go looking for a secondhand unit to save a few bucks.

"How far back is that?" Tim asked.

"Only a month," Thraxx said.

"Still far enough back to cover the time period of the theft," Giallo said, standing next to Tim and squinting over his shoulder.

"Yeah," Tim said. "But maybe not far enough back to know if the box was still in there."

"I brought up the timestamp for the last time the safe was opened," Thraxx said. "Should be coming up now."

Tim watched as the dense lines of machine code began to scroll past on the screen.

"Ugh," Giallo said. "You know what any of this means?"

"A little," Tim said.

Most of the code was, for his purposes, meaningless data. Room temperature. Seismic activity reading. Psychokinetic radiation level. Power backup system charge percentage. The system tracked almost 120,000 individual data points on a second-by-second basis. The slightest change in any of them would be recorded and timestamped.

Tim needed to look for only two things: who had opened the safe and what had been taken out.

Tim waited until he saw the first piece of information that he was looking for. The file showed that the safe had registered a room temperature change of 0.05 degrees four minutes and 13 seconds before the safe was opened. That was consistent with the change in temperature that would be registered when somebody entered the room, except...

"That's weird," he said.

"What?" Giallo asked.

"Well," Tim said. "The room temperature went up just before the safe was opened, which you would expect to happen when somebody walked into the room."

"Okay?" said Giallo. "So how is that weird?"

"The temperature went up too much too fast for it to have been a single person," Tim said.

"Hmmm," said Giallo. "So maybe there was more than one person."

"The data also shows the audiometer picked up a major increase in ambient room noise," Tim said.

"How major?" Giallo asked.

"Loud," Tim said.

"Maybe it was just whoever opened the safe talking on a phone or something," Giallo suggested.

"I doubt it," Tim said, pointing at the data on the screen. "Regular ambient room noise level is about 3.2dB. That's not even enough for the human ear to pick up."

"I could pick that up," Thraxx sniffed. "My ears are hyper-receptive."

"That's great," Tim said. "Just before the safe was opened, the noise level in the room shot up to 125dB. That's rock concert level."

"That's weird," Giallo said. "What in the hell was making so much noise?"

"No idea," Tim said. "The system only tracks how loud it is in the room, it doesn't actually record the sounds themselves."

"And there are no cameras in the safe room, either," Giallo noted.

"Nope," Tim said. "The only cameras cover the outside of the house. Lucifer was paranoid about privacy. Didn't want to take any chances that anyone could spy on him or his family."

"That's understandable," Giallo said. "Did the front cameras happen to record the tour bus for Mega Dead pulling up out front?"

"Nope," Tim smiled. "The exterior cameras don't really work, anyway. Too much spectral interference from the house itself."

"Why?" Giallo asked. "Because it's an omniportal?"

"Most likely," Tim said. "Or maybe the ground's just haunted. Who knows?"

"I'm guessing that whoever opened the vault knew that, too," Giallo said.

Tim kept his eyes glued to the screen as the next piece of information he was waiting for appeared. It showed that the safe had been opened by <adminsecureidencr_0002>.

"What the hell?" he muttered.

"Now what?" Giallo asked.

"According to the file," Tim said. "The safe was opened with somebody using Admin ID number two."

"So?" said Giallo.

"So there is no Admin ID number two," Tim said. "According to the policy file, Lucifer Hesselthorn is the only person with security access to open or close the safe."

"So maybe Ludwig added himself on," Giallo said.

"He couldn't have," Tim said, shaking his head.

"Why?" Giallo asked.

"A couple of reasons," Tim said. "One, only Lucifer would have been able to set it up. And two, the creation time stamp on the ID is more than 20 years old. Ludwig would have had to set it up when he was like, six years old."

"Maybe Lucifer set up one for each hand," Giallo said. "You know, just in case he got in some sort of accident and lost his right. He could still use his left to open it."

"Nope," Tim said. "That's a very creative guess, but they would both be under the same biometric ID number. This is somebody else."

Tim watched as the data scrolled up to reveal the moment the safe was opened. He could see that item numbers <ssid_1077936TXCS>, <ssid_std_099878777> and <ssid_std_099878776> were removed. He knew from the case file that the last two numbers belonged to the claims tags that had been later removed by Ugarte. That meant that the first number almost certainly belonged to the Puzzle Box.

"Okay," he said, pointing to the screen. "This is where the Puzzle Box is removed."

"You're sure?" Giallo said.

"Yeah," Tim said. "And then…okay, this just keeps getting weirder."

"What?" Giallo said, grabbing his shoulder.

"Well," Tim said. "The safe registers another small increase in the room temperature."

"Meaning what?" Giallo said. "Maybe they just got closer to the sensor when they opened the vault."

"No," Tim said. "It doesn't use a single sensor to measure that."

"So what does it mean?" Giallo asked.

"I think it means that somebody else entered the vault room," Tim said.

"Who?" Giallo asked.

"No idea," Tim said.

"Okay," Giallo said. "So somebody else walks into the room. Then what happened?"

"Then it registers a minor increase in seismic activity," Tim said.

"Seismic activity?" Giallo said. "Like an earthquake?"

"Not quite that much," Tim said. "This was more like…"

Tim's voice trailed off. A sudden connection had just been made in his brain.

"What?" Giallo said, shaking his arm. "More like what?"

"Oh man," Tim said, shaking his head. "I have been such an idiot!"

"I know that!" Giallo said, gripping his arm tightly enough to cut off the blood flow to his hand. "But you better tell me what you're thinking before I rip your arm off and beat you with it!"

"Just a sec," Tim said. He focused his attention back on the screen, his eyes practically bulging out of their sockets as he looked for the one piece of data he was waiting for. When it came up, he let out a whoop of disbelief that caused Thraxx to drop his giant mug of tar in his lap.

"What?" Giallo yelled. "Why are you so excited?"

"I think I know what happened," Tim said, pulling Giallo back towards the elevator. "Come on, I'll explain on the way."

23

The front gate at Hesselthorn Manor had been taken off its hinges and tossed in the garden, where it was leaning awkwardly against a statue depicting the demon god Xaxuss being pulled back into the underworld by his angry followers. His anguished expression looked, given his present circumstances, like it was more connected to the way his head was stuck between the railings than the prospect of eternal torment, but Tim was in a hurry and had no time to ponder the matter.

"Are you sure about this?" Giallo asked as they screeched to a halt in front of the stairs and got out of the car.

"Actually, more than I am about most things," Tim said, jogging up the steps.

"Even if it is bigger on the inside than it is on the outside, it's weird that a family like the Hesselthorns would live in a place like this," Giallo said, looking up at the house.

"From what I've seen of this family, the house is one of the most normal things about them," Tim said as the door was opened by Ugathia a moment later. "Hi Ugathia. I need to speak with Mrs. Hesselthorn."

Ugathia groaned and staggered back, motioning them in through the door. Tim stepped through into the hall, where he heard the familiar strains of the *Necronomicon* coming from the speaker system. He saw Ozymandia dancing energetically at the bottom of the stairs, her body spiralling up into graceful pirouettes in time with the music.

"Unbelievable," Giallo said as she entered the hall and caught sight of the bouncing Hesselthorn matriarch. "I thought you *had* to be making this up."

"Nope," Tim said, shaking his head.

"She does this every day?" Giallo asked.

"Yep," Tim said. "And that's only the half of it."

Tim crossed the hall and approached the control box on the wall at the bottom of the stairs. He studied it for a moment before reaching up to switch the music from the galloping arpeggios of the dance opera to the grinding guitar hellscape he had cued up the last time.

"Hey, I know these guys!" Giallo said. "Hammer of Hell! I saw them live at the Altar Pit last year. They had to cut the show short because two people spontaneously combusted in the front row."

"Uh huh," Tim said. He was not a fan of demon death metal and, in his experience, those who were tended to take it personally when you didn't share their enthusiasm.

"What am I looking for?" Giallo said.

"Just watch," Tim said as Ozymandia stopped dancing and approached Giallo in the same submissive pose as Tim had seen before.

"What is she doing?" Giallo asked, taking a nervous step back. Ozymandia took a step forward in response, which caused Giallo to step back again. "Make her stop! This is freaking me out!"

"Stay where you are!" Tim said. If Giallo took one more step, she would be back outside on the front porch. Tim jogged back across the hall to stand next to Giallo, who looked ready to bolt. "Hello, Mrs. Hesselthorn!"

"She can hear you?" Giallo said, peering at the old woman.

"She can do more than that," Tim said. He wasn't sure what he was about to try was remotely going to work, but he figured that it was worth a shot. "Ozymandia, I need you to open the safe!"

"Are you kidding?" Giallo said. "The woman's a zombie! She can't–"

Giallo's word died in her throat as the old woman turned around and started walking purposefully towards the elevator.

"Come on!" Tim said, waving Giallo to follow as he took off after Ozymandia. He reached into his pocket and pulled out his phone, opening the music app. He needed to be ready for when the elevator doors closed.

"What in the hell is going on?" Giallo asked.

"I did some research on this," Tim said. "Some exorcists use music therapy to treat people with extreme cases of PPSD. Different music can trigger different responses. She used to dance to the *Necronomicon*, so there must be some deeply buried part of her brain that still responds to it. When she's exposed to demon music, that seems to trigger obedience. Speaking of which…"

Tim cued up *Organ Eater*, the first single off Hammer of Hell's most recent album, and hit play. He tried to time it so that the song started as the elevator doors closed, cutting off the music from the hall. He was working on the assumption that Ozymandia would only remain compliant for as long as she was exposed to the music. He hadn't been able to get the exact version that she had been listening to in the hall because it was only available as an import and not available on DevilStream, but it was the best he could do. To his relief, Ozymandia showed no change of expression or position.

"So that's why there was a jump in the noise level right before the safe was opened!" Giallo said.

"I think so," Tim nodded. His phone didn't put out anywhere near 120dB, even at full volume. Ludwig must have been carrying some sort of personal stereo system.

"You like them too?" Giallo asked, nodding her head in time with the music.

"Uh, not really," Tim said. He resented the fact that he'd been forced to spend his own money to buy the album, especially since the ghouls in accounting would ask a million questions if he tried to expense it. "I was just playing a hunch."

"You should have told me," Giallo said, taking out her own phone and opening up the music app, which Tim noted was full of similar artists. "I have their whole catalogue."

"Good to know," Tim said.

"I wonder when Ludwig figured this out?" Giallo said. "It would be a great trick to get your parents to buy booze for you when you're underage."

"That's a good question," Tim said. "I'm guessing he only figured it out recently, or he would have used it to steal the Puzzle Box ages ago."

The doors opened and they stepped out into the vault room. Ozymandia strode purposefully across the floor and held her hand up to the reader, which blinked green.

"Unbelievable!" Giallo said. "How did you know?"

"Best guess," Tim said. "There was only one access ID listed on the policy, but the safe data showed two. Lucifer must have added Ozymandia as a backup without telling anyone."

"How did you know it wasn't one of the kids?" Giallo asked.

"It was added too long ago," Tim said. "Besides, would you have trusted either Ludwig or Lucretia with access to this?"

"Good point," Giallo said. "So if we've got the box, what *is* in there?"

"We're about to find out," Tim said as the demon clawed its way to the top of the well on the other side of the glass and regarded them menacingly.

"Holy shit!" Giallo gasped. "Is that an Akumamizu? I've never seen one in real life before!"

"It is," Tim nodded. "They're extremely powerful and hard to contain, which is why you only find them as guardians in the absolute top-end secured storage units."

"I can understand why," Giallo said. "It's creepy as hell. What's it going to do to us?"

"Hopefully, it's going to help us get some answers," Tim said. He stepped forward and looked directly at the demon, which looked straight back with its lidless black eyes. It raised both claws and opened them to reveal two pulsating jaws in the middle of each palm.

Tim swallowed. He needed to be careful how he did this. An Akumamizu was extremely particular about how commands needed to be worded. The slightest ambiguity could lead to him being skinned alive and hung up as a decoration. Normally, they only responded to a listed security administrator, but since Ozymandia couldn't talk, that option was out. All safes had a master backup in the event that all listed administrators became incapacitated, however, and it was listed in the raw data that Tim had scanned and downloaded from IT. He just needed to hope that the code had not been changed in the time since.

"Get ready to catch her," Tim said, motioning Giallo towards Ozymandia. "I'm not sure what she'll do when I turn off the music."

"Got it," Giallo said, stepping up beside the old woman.

"Now!" Tim said, stopping the song.

Ozymandia seemed to faint as soon as the song ended. Giallo caught her and moved her over to the side to lean against the wall.

"Whoa!" Giallo said. "For a ballet dancer, she's heavier than she looks!"

Tim brought up the file he had copied from Thraxx's computer and studied it closely. He didn't want to make any mistakes with this.

"Okay," Tim said, clearing his throat and looking at his phone. "I've got the master override code."

"What does that do?" Giallo asked.

"It allows me to control the demon," Tim said. "I hope."

"And what if it doesn't work?" Giallo said, her voice dropping to a near whisper.

"Well," Tim said. "If it doesn't, we'll end up looking like the photos attached to the case file for the Cormyn theft from two years ago. If you're feeling curious and want to look it up."

"I don't think I am," Giallo said.

"Here goes," Tim said. "Master override code 41LOH6699337DN."

To Tim's immense relief, the demon closed its claws and lowered its arms.

"Is that good?" Giallo asked.

"We're still alive," Tim said.

"I'd really prefer it if you could be more definite," Giallo said.

Tim ignored this and looked back at the demon. "Bring up all the contents of Vault One," he said. "Intact."

The demon disappeared back down into the well.

"What is it bringing back?" Giallo said.

"Well," Tim said. "If my hunch is right, some answers."

Giallo cursed under her breath. "Could you be any more obtuse? Answer my damn question or I'll shoot you with the Devil Stick again."

"Wait," Tim said. He could hear the demon making its way back up the inside of the well. "It's coming back."

Giallo was about to say something when the demon clawed its way to the top of the well carrying a strange black and grey shape in its claws. It took her a moment to realize that the shape was a person, more specifically, a man who looked to be in his late 60s or early 70s.

"What the hell?" Giallo gasped.

The demon lifted the man over the edge of the well and put him on the floor. He looked unconscious and extremely pale, which Tim thought made sense considering the guy had probably just spent the last week inside a high security vault. Tim couldn't tell if the man was breathing. The safe was airtight, but was also of indeterminate size, so there was no way to tell just how long the oxygen supply might last in there.

"Good," Tim said to the demon. "Return to lockdown."

The demon climbed back into the well and started to climb back down. Tim waited until he saw the vault indicator flip back to the red "Sealed" position before he rushed forward.

"Who in the hell is this?" Giallo asked, rushing up next to him.

"It's Lucifer Hesselthorn," Tim said. "I only hope that he's still alive."

"Get back!" Giallo ordered, shoving Tim out of the way. She immediately checked the elder Hesselthorn for a pulse. Failing to find one, she started chest compressions with practiced urgency. A moment later, the old man let out a groan and sucked in a large breath.

"Nice job!" Tim said.

"I got stuck on the health and safety committee in my first year," Giallo said. "So I had to get first aid certified. Nobody else wanted the job and I was lowest on the pole. Do you have any water?"

Tim scrambled in his SIU bag and found a bottle of water, which he handed over.

"Help me get him up," Giallo said as they lifted the old man into a sitting position and propped him up against the bottom of the well. She took the bottle from Tim, unscrewed the lid and held it up to Hesselthorn's lips for him to drink. Once he was aware that the bottle was there, the old man grabbed it and tried to suck all the contents out at once. Giallo held the bottle back and restrained him gently. "Whoa! Slow down there, guy! I don't want you barfing all over my shoes, okay?"

The old man took a few more gulps of water and then opened his eyes, looking up at them in confusion.

"Who are you?" he gasped.

"My name is Tim Lovecraft, Mr. Hesselthorn," Tim said. "And this is…" he turned to Giallo. "What is your first name?"

"I'm Giallo," she said. "You may refer to me as Ms Giallo if you feel the need to go for greater formality."

"Why won't you tell anyone your first name?" Tim asked.

"None of your damn business," Giallo said.

"I don't get it," Tim said. "Are you named after a demon or something? It's not even in your employee file. What's the big deal?"

"You don't need to know," Giallo said.

"But–" Tim started.

"Excuse me," interrupted the old man. "But do you think I might have some more of that water?"

"Of course," Giallo said, handing him back the bottle. "Just go easy."

"Sorry, Mr. Hesselthorn," Tim said. "As I was saying. I'm Tim Lovecraft and this is Ms. Giallo. We work for Crimson Seal Insurance."

"Insurance?" said the old man.

"Yes, sir," Tim said. "Your Puzzle Box was stolen. We were working to try and locate it."

"Indeed," said the old man. "Well I can save you some time and effort there. Ludwig stole it."

"Yes," Tim said. "We were able to determine that."

"I was in my office when the vault notification was triggered," Hesselthorn said. "He didn't know that I had a secondary monitoring system activated. But he did know that his mother's handprint would open the vault. How he managed to get her down here to do it, I have no idea."

"It seems she responds to certain kinds of spectro-musical suggestion," Tim said, motioning to Ozymandia. "In much the same way that she dances to one piece, he figured out that he can use others to control her."

"Ozzy!" Hesselthorn said, struggling to get to his feet and failing.

"She's fine!" Giallo said, restraining the old man as gently as possible. "She opened the vault door so we could get you out."

"Yes," the old man said. "When I rushed downstairs to confront Ludwig, he overpowered me and locked me in my own vault. At first I thought it was just common thieves who had broken in. Some of them have made it that far in the past. But it was my own son. How did you know I was in there?"

"We downloaded the raw data feed from the safe," Tim said. "When we looked at it, it showed that the ID number of the item locked in the vault was the same as the ID number of the primary admin."

"So that's how you knew," Giallo said. "Why didn't you just tell me?"

"Sorry," Tim said. "I thought I might be wrong."

"Where is Ludwig now?" the old man asked. "Does he still have the box?"

Tim and Giallo looked at each other uneasily. Neither of them wanted to be the one to break the bad news.

"I'm afraid not, Mr. Hesselthorn," Tim said. "He had the box briefly. Then it seems he consulted with a satyr named Damien Ugarte on how to remove the tracking units that were attached to it."

"Ugarte," the old man muttered, shaking his head with evident distaste. "A thoroughly disreputable individual. He approached me many years ago about acting as an intermediary should I wish to sell the Puzzle Box on the black market. I turned him out of my home so quickly that his hooves barely touched the ground."

"Yes," Tim said. "Well, ah, it looks like he never gave up on that idea. It seems he let the Hellspawn know that Ludwig had the box and, uh…"

"They killed him," the old man said.

"I'm afraid so, sir," Tim said.

The old man closed his eyes and shook his head. "Oh, Ludwig. My son never did a minute's work if he thought a minute's graft would earn him even half as much money."

"They got your daughter, too," Tim said. He decided not to get into the question about who was specifically responsible for Lucretia's death, partly because he didn't know for sure and partly because now did not seem like the best time to dig into that question.

"Poor Lucretia," Hesselthorn said, his already weak voice breaking. "It seems that all we did was fight. I didn't agree with her wish to turn herself into a bloodsucking creature of the night and wouldn't finance the surgery she wanted to make it happen. It was madness, I thought. And such a waste. I told myself I was doing it for her own good. But as I get older, I have realized that most of my certainties are just prejudices that got mixed up in some misguided sense of righteousness."

"I haven't known you long," Giallo said. "But you do kind of strike me as a stubborn bastard."

Tim wasn't sure how Hesselthorn would react to that, but the old man looked at Giallo and smiled.

"You remind me of my daughter," he said. "She used to hurl the most amazing insults at me during our fights. Unfortunately, I tended to give as well as I got."

"The police arrested Ludovico," Tim said.

Lucifer's eyes went wide. "They did what?"

"Well, Horatio Duluc did that," Giallo said. "He seemed convinced that Ludovico had something to do with the theft."

"They should never have removed him from his room!" Lucifer said, clutching his face in disbelief. "They have no idea what they will unleash!"

"And what is that, exactly?" Tim asked.

"That goes back many years," Lucifer said. "Back to when Harry and I first found the box."

"Harry as in Harrison Ackroyd-Jones?" Giallo said. "Your expedition partner?"

"Correct," Lucifer said. "We knew we had to get our hands on the box before the Infernium, who were desperate to find it. They were convinced that it would lead them to the temple of one of their former masters."

Now it was Giallo's turn to look shocked. "You know about the Infernium?"

"Of course I do," Lucifer said. "My brother Lucius was one of their members. They believed the box contained information crucial to locating the temple of Maefisto."

"The Magikal One," Giallo said.

"According to some sources," Lucifer nodded. "Others refer to her as the Ethereal One. Or the Mystikal One. It depends on which line of scholarship you choose to follow."

"But you found the box first," Tim said.

"Yes," Lucifer said. "Harry was convinced that the box could be found in the Crypt of Corinth, which many believed to be located in a cave network in the Upper Styx Valley. I thought it was more likely to be somewhere beneath Flayer's Palace."

"Flayer's Palace?" Tim said. "You mean the casino that got shut down after part of it collapsed into a Hellhole?"

"The same," Lucifer said. "Of course, it was still standing in those days. I believed it was built on top of a much older sacrificial altar or temple complex, which turned out to be the case. As it turned out, we were both wrong about the Puzzle Box, which we found almost by accident. Not that it mattered. We tried to keep it secret, but word of the discovery naturally leaked out and drew more attention than we could have possibly dreamed."

"I can imagine," Tim said.

"Unfortunately, our troubles were just beginning," Lucifer said. "Harry and I disagreed from the beginning on what to do with the box. We couldn't destroy it, naturally–there is no known way to destroy such a powerful object–but I believed it should be locked away, buried as far out of the reach of those who would seek to use it as possible."

"But your partner thought differently?" Giallo said.

"Yes," said Lucifer. "He believed that the Puzzle Box might be used for good. That we could control it or bend it to our will. I told him that the box was an artefact of pure evil and that no good could ever come from it. In the end, we came to something of a compromise. We would lock the box away, but continue to study it. Like all compromises, it led only to disaster."

"What happened?" Tim asked.

"What happened was that Harry deduced how to open the box," Lucifer said. "And in so doing, unleashed the evil within. The Djinn attacked the first person it saw, which happened to be my wife, Ozymandia. She was pregnant with Ludovico at the time."

"I guess that explains why she is the way she is," Giallo said, looking at Ozymandia, who was standing staring at the control panel.

"The demon took control of her, but was too weak after thousands of years of imprisonment to be able to survive on its own," Lucifer said. "We went to all the best exorcists in the country. None of them were able to help. When Ludovico was born, it was evident that the demon had somehow transferred itself to him. Possibly as some kind of bizarre attempt to escape. No one knew what to do."

Tim nodded. The case literature on possession related to pregnant victims was not extensive as it was extremely rare.

"Ludovico had to be locked away from birth," Lucifer said. "For his safety as much as everyone else's. And my wife became a shell of herself. Although the demon was gone, people would still attempt to break in and steal the box. That's why we moved into this house."

"What do you mean?" Giallo asked.

"As I'm sure you've seen, this house is a Trans-Dimensional Omni-iPortal," Lucifer said. "Much larger on the inside than it appears on the outside, which rather makes it the opposite of almost every other house in Ravensloft. But it does have one other key advantage. Anyone who tries to enter the premises by any means other than through the front door will find themselves stepping directly into non-dimensional space."

"Of course!" Tim said, slapping his forehead. "You just deactivate the other entry points!"

"Precisely," Lucifer said. "Converting it from an OmniPortal into rather more of a UniPortal, but the end result is the same. Anyone who tried to gain entry through an open window or an unlocked back door would suddenly find themselves floating in a state of limbo, very much like a demon cast out to the 9th circle or beyond."

"So as long as you come in through the front door, you're fine," Giallo said. "But if you don't, the house spits you out into the middle of nowhere?"

"Correct," Lucifer said. "I cannot tell you how many would-be thieves ended up that way. We have a filter system that clears them out. We run it roughly once a month. Some of them actually tried more than once."

"I wonder if I could get something like that for my apartment?" Giallo wondered.

"I would advise against it," Lucifer said. "Sometimes the filter would get blocked and we had to call in a company to clean it out. The results were, shall we say, not pretty."

"I believe you," Tim said. As a claims adjuster, he had seen some of the rehabilitation files for injuries sustained as a result of portal accidents. Sudden dimensional shifts were not things that biological entities handled well.

"I prepared for every possible scenario involving someone attempting to break into the house in order to steal the box," Lucifer said. "I should have given more consideration to the possibility that somebody would try to steal it from within."

"Meaning Ludwig," Giallo said.

"Yes," Lucifer said. "My older son tried his hand at many businesses over the years. Rare artefacts. Property development. Finance. He even called himself a movie producer at one point. This despite failing to produce anything more than he did at any of his other failed careers, which is to say massive debts and a long list of angry former associates."

"It looks like some of those associates were a little more aggressive about recouping their losses than the others," Tim said.

"Yes," Lucifer said. "He did tell me at one point that he was in debt to gangsters, although he never mentioned the Hellspawn specifically. I told him that he was going to have to solve the problem on his own. He had already used far more than his share of the family fortune in pursuit of his own vainglorious ends. I never imagined that he would use his own mother as a puppet to undermine everything I had tried to build."

"Well, he wasn't entirely successful on that front," Tim said, reaching into his SIU bag and pulling out the glowing red globe. "We were able to recover the Puzzle Box."

The old man looked at the flicker ball like it was a frozen chunk of radioactive waste.

"That thing has been nothing but a curse on my family ever since the day I discovered it," he said. "My time as its keeper is done."

"Uh, okay," Tim said uncertainly. "I was just assigned to recover it. I can't keep it, either on my behalf or the company's. If you want to sell it—"

Lucifer laughed. "Sell it? It's worthless! The demon is out. And if Ludovico has been removed from his cell, then the beast is almost certainly roaming free. It has but one goal, now. To find the temple of its mistress and free her."

"Are you talking about the Magikal One?" Giallo asked. "Maefisto?"

"Yes," Lucifer said. "The creature who was trapped in the box was named Enfaxizbel. Well, that was one of its names. High priest of the temple of the Magikal One. Enfaxizbel's only loyalty is to its mistress. It will use any and all means at its disposal to free her."

"How do we stop it?" Giallo asked.

"I have no idea," Lucifer said. "I suppose since it was trapped in the Puzzle Box once, it is conceivable that it could be trapped in there again."

"Right," Giallo nodded. "But how do we do that?"

"Well," Lucifer said. "You would, I presume, need to be able to open the box. And only one person has ever figured out how to do that."

"You mean your former partner," Tim said.

"Yes," said Lucifer.

"But he's been dead for years!" Giallo said.

"Quite so," said Lucifer.

"So that's no good to us at all!" Giallo said. "Did he leave any kind of journal or diary or any other record of his work?"

"Not that I am aware of," Lucifer said, shaking his head.

"So we're totally screwed!" Giallo said, throwing her hands up in the air.

"Maybe not," Tim said.

Giallo looked at him like he was crazy.

"What?" she said.

"We might not be entirely screwed," Tim said.

"What are you talking about?" Giallo said. "The only guy who knows how to open that thing is dead! He isn't talking!"

"Maybe," Tim said.

"What the hell are you talking about?" Giallo said.

"It's a long shot," Tim said, stuffing the Puzzle Box back in his SIU bag. "But I think I might actually know somebody who can help us."

24

Looking at the remains of Circle 9, Carmilla realized that she had only seen such damage once before, and that was when liquid Hell-fire bombs had destroyed the old Crimson Seal archives building.

The sight that greeted her as she pulled up in her cruiser was slightly different in terms of the probable cause, but similar in the sheer scale of the destruction. The entire centre of the building had collapsed in on itself. The grand crystal dome where half naked succubi would dance under a spinning black mirror ball was now partially buried in a crater two stories below street level. A booming subterranean thrum was causing the ground to shake as flickers of red light shot out from under the debris and into the sky.

Carmilla paused for a moment to take it in. She had worked as a waitress at Circle 9 back when she was in university. As a half-succubus, she had made a lot of money in tips, but not enough to make the constant sexual harassment from the owner, the staff and most of the customers tolerable. Seeing it like this gave her a grim sense of satisfaction. As the first uniformed officer on the scene, however, she also had a job to do.

"What the hell is that?" asked her partner as he got out of the passenger seat of their cruiser and stared at the building with his jaw hanging open.

Her partner's name was Domenic Trentino. He was in his early 50s and had been a beat cop for the entirety of his unexceptional career in law enforcement. Officer Trentino had spent the last eight years in the traffic division, where he had earned the dubious distinction of causing more collisions and pedestrian injuries at his assigned intersection than it had seen before he arrived. He had even managed to somehow run himself over with his own patrol car. He had six months to go before he would be eligible to retire with 75 percent pension, which everyone in the department was desperately hoping that he was going to take. A few people had even started up a collection to try and make up the funding shortfall as an inducement.

"Looks like they opened up some sort of portal in the basement," Carmilla said, reaching back in through her window to grab the radio mic.

"Portal?" said her partner.

"Yeah," said Carmilla. "Place is run by a Hellspawn boss named Azmoda. He has a portal built into a hot tub in his office. Looks like it malfunctioned."

"Hot tub?" said her partner, looking even more confused. "Why in the hell would you do that?"

"He's a gangster," Carmilla said. "It's a good way to get rid of people you'd rather not have around."

Carmilla used the radio to call in for backup. They were definitely going to need the Spectral Containment Unit as well as the EoD and probably the city engineers, since the damage looked like it might go all the way down to the utility and subway lines. The dispatcher told her to sit tight and secure the scene as units were already inbound. The plan was to secure a three-block radius and evacuate all buildings within the danger zone until the full extent of the damage could be assessed.

302 • CRAIG McLAY

"Roger that," Carmilla said, tossing the radio back in the car. She told her partner to stay in position and did a quick circuit of the building to check for any trapped or wounded civilians. The only ones she spotted were a couple of terrified satyrs who said they had been cleaning the kitchen when some sort of explosion went off in the next room, putting a hole in the wall and sucking out two of the line cooks, who had come in early to start prep work.

Carmilla helped them climb out and told them to make their way two blocks north to Pentangle Park, which was where Metro would be setting up a temporary mobile command centre. There they would be able to give a statement and get checked by SEMTs before leaving the scene. The satyrs nodded and took off down the alley.

By the time Carmilla completed her sweep and got back to the front of the building, her partner had been joined by somebody else. Carmilla was about to warn the new arrival to move back beyond the three block restriction zone when she noticed that it wasn't a Circle 9 employee or other civilian–it was Horatio Duluc.

"Hello, detective," she said warily. "Can I help you?"

What in the hell was Duluc doing here? Carmilla wondered. As far as she knew, he was supposed to be interviewing the Hesselthorn suspect at Metro HQ.

"What happened here?" Duluc asked, looking past her at the remains of Circle 9. His voice was different from the last time she had met him. He had lost his phony-baloney dramatic TV intonation. His expression was oddly flat as well.

Something is wrong here, Carmilla thought.

"We don't know yet," Carmilla said, surreptitiously unclipping the hasp on the Demon Charger attached to her right hip. "We're locking off a three-block radius while we wait for SEMT. Should be here any minute."

"Say, you're Harry Duluc!" said Trentino, coming around from the other side of the cruiser to get a better look. "My wife loves your show! I saw you back at the house, but we didn't get a chance to talk."

Duluc gave no indication of having heard. Instead, he was crouching down to study the ground intently.

Something is definitely weird here, Carmilla thought. The Duluc she knew would not ignore a chance to self-aggrandize in front of a slobbering fan.

"Something we can help you with, detective?" Carmilla asked, moving a few steps closer to see what Duluc was staring at. Aside from the glowing destruction right next to it, the sidewalk looked perfectly normal as far as she could tell.

Duluc continued to stare at the ground for a minute before standing up and reaching into his jacket. Carmilla tightened her grip on the charger. Instead of pulling out a weapon, the detective pulled out his cellphone and scrolled through it for a moment before holding it out so that she could see the screen.

"Have you seen this man?" Duluc asked.

Carmilla looked at the image, which she recognized instantly.

"That's Tim Lovecraft," she said. "He's working the Hesselthorn case for the insurance company."

"Yes," said Duluc. "Have you seen him?"

"The last time I saw him was when you arrested the Hesselthorn kid," Carmilla said. "Why are you looking for him?"

"I believe he is in possession of something that I need," Duluc said.

"Say, where's your crew?" Trentino said, looking around. "Don't they follow you everywhere?"

"Something you need?" Carmilla said, ignoring her partner. "Are you saying Lovecraft is a suspect in the Hesselthorn case?"

"Yes," Duluc said, putting the phone back in his pocket. "I need an alert put out immediately. It is imperative that I find him."

"This guy Lovecraft," said Trentino, getting excited. "Is he dangerous?"

"Extremely," said Duluc. "He just massacred my entire documentary crew and several officers back at Metro HQ. The man is a maniac."

"No shit?" Trentino said, eyes wide. "Well don't worry, detective! We're on it!"

Trentino leaned into the cruiser and grabbed the radio mic as Duluc turned and began walking down the street, following some trail that only he appeared to be able to see.

"Dispatch, this is H665," Trentino said into the mic. "Be advised we are issuing an APB on T–"

"Hold off," Carmilla said, grabbing the microphone out of her partner's hand.

"Hey!" said Trentino, trying to grab the mic back. "The hell are you doing?"

Carmilla reached up and shoved her partner back up onto the sidewalk.

"Don't call that in," she said.

"The hell are you talking about?" Trentino said, looking wounded. He reached up to rub his chest despite the fact that she had not pushed him that hard.

"Something doesn't feel right," Carmilla said.

"Doesn't feel right?" Trentino said. "The detective just told us to call in an APB! Said the guy was a crazy murderer and a cop killer, to boot!"

"I know Tim Lovecraft," Carmilla said. "One thing he is not is crazy. Or a murderer."

"Look," Trentino said. "You can't always tell with people. Maybe he got so bored working in insurance that he finally snapped and went on a rampage!"

"I doubt it," Carmilla said, putting the mic back on the radio unit. "But until we confirm the details, we are *not* calling in that APB! Got it?"

"But Duluc's on TV!" Trentino whined. "Have you seen his show? He's the psychic detective for cryin' out loud! That guy *never* gets things wrong!"

"Maybe so," Carmilla said. "But if you touch that radio before I get back, there's going to be one more name added to the missing persons report for this Circle 9 implosion. You understand, Trentino?"

"Jeez, relax!" said Trentino, holding up his hands in surrender. "Whaddya mean when you get back? Where ya going?"

Carmilla jogged around and opened up the trunk of the cruiser. She rooted around for a moment before grabbing a tactical helmet.

"What the hell are you doin' with that?" Trentino asked as Carmilla put the helmet on.

"Stay here," Carmilla said, flipping the visor down and activating the built-in Spectravision heads-up display. "I'll be right back. And do not touch the radio! If you do, I'll shove that parking meter so far up your ass that people will be feeding you quarters for the rest of your career."

Carmilla jogged down the sidewalk in the same direction Duluc had gone, turning right to follow him into the alley next to the building. She could see a strong red spectral trail and the remains of Duluc's footprints on the ground, neither of which should have been there. Humans did not leave such signs of their passing.

Carmilla reached the next corner. She stuck her head around to see Duluc crouching at the back of the building next to a spot that she knew from experience was a secret back door entrance into the club. Carmilla crouched down behind a dumpster and peered carefully around to observe the detective at work. He appeared to be focused on a faint purple spectral trail that led out from the back of the building and down the alley in the opposite direction towards Milton Street.

What drew Carmilla's attention, however, was the detective himself. Viewed through a spectral radiation filter, most humans looked like photonegative black blobs. A rare few–usually powerful psychics or seers–might register a slight, flickering aura of pink.

Duluc, in contrast, was as bright as an atomic bomb blast. So bright, in fact, that Carmilla had to dial down the exposure on the visor to keep herself from being blinded. The helmets were supposed to have automatic dampeners built in that prevented overexposure, but the units were glitchy and didn't always work.

She knew that Duluc was supposed to be a powerful psychic, but even the president of the seer's union didn't light up like that. Besides, she had always secretly suspected that Duluc's so-called abilities were just a load of marketing hype to sell his shows and books.

Carmilla knew what she was seeing was not hype. Something was very wrong with Metro's most famous detective. He was either a demon or possessed by the most powerful demon that Carmilla had ever encountered. But what in the hell was Duluc doing here? And why was he so interested in Tim?

It had to have something to do with the Hesselthorn thing, she figured. Duluc was probably looking for the Puzzle Box just like everyone else. Could that have been what had left the purple spectral trail behind the club? She knew practically nothing about it. She needed to talk to Tim immediately. But first, she needed to figure out how she was going to handle Duluc. There was no way she could take him in on her own. She hadn't heard anything through the regular comm channels about any issues at Metro HQ, so Duluc might be lying about that. Even if he wasn't, she had no doubt that Tim had nothing to do with it.

Duluc stood back up and turned to walk back in Carmilla's direction. She quickly ducked behind the wall and jogged back to the cruiser, where her partner was leaning against the rear fender whistling the theme from a popular TV game show.

"Something's wrong," she said, tossing the helmet in the passenger seat and grabbing the Devil Stick off the special mount on the front dash. She checked the battery light to make sure it was fully charged.

"What?" said her partner, looking confused. "You mean, other than the building blowing up?"

"It's Duluc," Carmilla said. "He isn't who he says he is."

"Huh?" Trentino's confusion only deepened. "If he isn't who he is, then who is he?"

"I don't know," Carmilla said. "But I think–"

She stopped as she saw Duluc round the corner.

"I'm going to need your cruiser," Duluc said as he approached.

"You are?" said Trentino, looking honored that the great detective was asking to sit in his seat. "Hey, man, It's yours!"

"Hold it!" said Carmilla, stepping in front of Duluc and raising the Devil Stick. "The cruiser stays where it is."

"What the hell are you doing?" Trentino said.

"I'm going to need you to get on the ground and put your hands behind your head," Carmilla said. "Now!"

Duluc didn't move. Instead, he narrowed his eyes and smiled in a way that Carmilla found extremely unnerving.

"Are you crazy?" Trentino said, trying to step in between Carmilla and Duluc. "This is Horatio Duluc you're talking to! This guy solved the Butcher Block murders before you was even born!"

"Get out of the way!" Carmilla said. "That's not Duluc! Like I was trying to tell you. It might look like him, but it's something else!"

"That's nuts!" said Trentino, taking the keys out of his pocket and holding them out to Duluc. "Here, man. Just take the car! My partner's just a stupid rookie who doesn't know eggplant from ectoplasm. Wouldn't even have got the job if she wasn't a demon. Stupid hippie-dippie equity bullshit, am I right?"

"Back off, Trentino!" Carmilla said. "We are not giving this thing our cruiser! Get down on the ground! Now!"

"Be careful, officer," Duluc said. "Otherwise I may have to file an official complaint with the department of professional oversight."

"She's just kidding," Trentino said. "Just forget about it and t–"

Trentino stopped talking as Duluc reached up with lightning speed and grabbed him by the throat, lifting him up off the ground. Trentino's body began to twitch and spasm as bolts of red lightning crackled down his arms and arced wildly into the air.

"Let him go!" Carmilla said, taking a step back and dropping to one knee. "Drop him or I'll shoot!'

"Drop the weapon," Duluc said calmly. "Do it now and maybe I'll leave enough of your partner behind for his widow to identify."

"Half the cops in the city are headed here right now as we speak!" Carmilla said. "You've got nowhere to run! Now let him go! On the count of three!"

"Half the cops in the city, huh?" Duluc said, cocking an ear for the distant sound of approaching sirens.

"Here they come now!" Carmilla said. "One!"

"Well," Duluc said. "As it appears that our time together is limited…"

"Last warning!" Carmilla said. "Two!"

"Very well, then," Duluc said, shooting out a massive bolt of spectral energy that knocked Carmilla off her feet. She flew nearly 20 feet through the air and landed unconscious on the sidewalk with a thud. The Devil Stick flew out of her hand and rolled across the concrete into the gutter. Duluc dropped Trentino on the ground just as the first cruiser rounded the corner and screeched to a halt. Two uniformed officers jumped up and ran up to the detective, their sidearms drawn but pointed at the ground.

"What happened?" yelled the first officer, looking quizzically at the two unconscious cops.

"I'm not sure," Duluc said, pointing first at Carmilla and then Trentino. "I had just arrived on the scene when I saw that one shoot this one."

"She shot him?" said the second officer, running over to Carmilla, who was lying on her back.

"Yes," Duluc said. "And then the weapon appeared to backfire and blew up in her face."

"I got no pulse," the first officer said, kneeling down to feel Trentino's throat. He grabbed his shoulder mic. "We've got an officer down in front of Circle 9. Correction. Two officers down. One with no vitals. We need SEMT on scene pronto!"

"This one's alive!" the second officer said, checking Carmilla.

"Cuff her!" said the first, kneeling down to start CPR on Trentino. "If she shot him, we can't take any chances!"

The second officer rolled Carmilla onto her side and attached a pair of flex cuffs to her wrists.

"Knew we shoulda never let these damn demons into the department," he muttered under his breath as he finished binding Carmilla's hands.

"Excuse me, gentlemen," Duluc said, bending down to grab the keys that Trentino had dropped on the ground. "I need to take this vehicle in order to pursue another suspect that I observed leaving the scene."

"Yes, sir," the first detective said. "What do you need us to do?"

"Just make sure that no one enters or exits that building," Duluc said. "The suspect's name is Tim Lovecraft. We need to locate him as soon as possible."

"Roger that, sir," said the second officer, grabbing his shoulder mic to report this information to dispatch.

Duluc got into the cruiser, started the engine and peeled away from the scene. He had never been behind the wheel of a car before, but like most human technology, its primitive simplicity was laughably easy to master. He smiled to himself as he pushed down on the pedal and activated the siren, watching as other cars scrambled to get out of his way. He had waited a long time for this. He believed that he was entitled to enjoy it as much as possible.

25

It had been a long time since Tim had set foot in one of his mother's salons. The last time he could remember was when he was still in high school and she had conscripted him and his brother Keef to help with the overnight job of the yearly inventory count, which she naturally expected them to do for free.

Keef had snuck out with one of his mother's staffers–some girl named Sherezade (Sherry for short)–and hadn't returned until seven o'clock the following morning. That had left Tim to count hundreds of power crystals, spectral ointments, psychic balms, totemic jewellery and other dubious merchandise all on his lonesome. This was before Keef had been turned into a vampire, but long after he had demonstrated his chronic aversion to labour.

As he stepped through the door, Tim heard the familiar tinkling of the electronic chime and inhaled the smoky whiff of incense designed to make visitors feel that they had stepped into a highly-exclusive new spiritual realm. The absurdly high levels of Essence of Mercan certainly explained the 500 percent markups on everything in sight.

"Welcome to Seer!" said the woman behind the counter. Like all of his mother's employees, she was young, attractive and dressed like a fortune teller at a carnival, albeit one who shopped at only the most exclusive Italian designer fashion houses. "How may we transport you today?"

Tim did not recognize her, but that was to be expected. His mother had notoriously high staff turnover in all of her locations because she was extremely demanding and disinclined to reward loyalty with raises, increased benefits or incentives of any kind. Regina believed that psychics were essentially a dime a dozen and paid accordingly.

"Hi," Tim said. "I actually need to talk to Madeline. If she's here."

"Do you have an appointment?" asked the woman. Tim noticed that the nametag partially hidden by her stylish black scarf identified her as Cleo.

"I actually don't," Tim said. "But my mother Regina owns the salon. I'm Tim. Tim Lovecraft."

"Oh, hi!" said Cleo, her smile becoming wider but more rigidly set. "Sorry, I didn't recognize you!"

"No reason you should," Tim said. His mother had tried to set him up with a woman named Cleo around 18 months ago, but he was pretty sure this was a different Cleo. At least, he hoped it was. He had gotten out of it at the time by claiming that he had become unexpectedly possessed by the ghost of a former sea captain and needed to go for an emergency exorcism.

"I think she's just finishing up with another client," Cleo said. "I'll just go and check to see when she might be free."

"Thanks so much," Tim said as Cleo disappeared behind the silver satin curtain behind the register.

"Did you say your mother owns this place?" Giallo said, picking up an apricot-scented tube of Spiritual Energy face cream and looking at it distastefully.

"Six locations in the greater metropolitan area," Tim said. "With three more planned to open next year."

"Really?" Giallo said, unimpressed. "I didn't know you were the heir to a whole empire of supernatural snake oil. Doesn't this stuff give people sebaceous curses?"

"My mother insists that the lab results were contaminated and never properly verified by an impartial third party in a certified, peer-reviewed journal," Tim said. "Which is her way of saying that she buys it for two dollars a tube and sells it for 40."

"Well then, I'm sure it's fine," Giallo said, putting the face cream back on the shelf. "So why'd you get a job in insurance instead of going to work in the family business? People didn't buy your fake channeling of their dear departed Aunt Shirley?"

"Something like that," Tim muttered.

"And what about your dad?" Giallo said. "Does he work here, too?"

"He runs his own supernatural pest control business," Tim said. "I actually did work there in high school and a few summers when I was at university, but I didn't want to spend the rest of my life covered in Demonex and crawling through old ventilation shafts."

"What a wuss," Giallo said, shaking her head.

Tim was about to ask Giallo about exactly what kinds of jobs she'd had before working at Crimson Seal when the curtains parted and Madeline stepped through. When she saw Tim, she quickly adopted a smile that was even more pained-looking than Cleo's.

"Tim!" she said stiffly. "Hi."

"Hi Madeline," Tim said, dropping his voice and stepping up to the counter so that Giallo couldn't hear. "Look, I know you're going out with Stake and that's fine. I'm not here to make things weird. I just need your help. In a professional capacity."

"What?" Madeline said, looking totally flummoxed. "I, uh…"

"I need you to help us summon somebody up from the dead," Tim said. "It's for an investigation we're working on." He turned sideways and gestured to Giallo, who waved.

"I'm sorry," Madeline said, looking from Tim to Giallo and back again. "You're here because you need my help to talk to a dead person?"

"Correct," Tim said.

"Who is it?" Madeline said. "A family member? Wouldn't your mother–"

"It's not a family member," Tim said, cutting her off. "And between you and me, my mother couldn't summon up a deleted email if she tried. She has almost no ability for it whatsoever. Her talents really lie more in branding and upselling than fortune telling or necromancy these days."

"I don't understand," Madeline said.

"It'll just take five minutes," Tim said. "I'll pay you for the time. Don't worry about giving me any kind of family discount. I'll work that out with my mother later. But we're in kind of a hurry."

Madeline looked confused for a moment before waving the two of them to follow her behind the silver curtain and into the back. They walked past the spa area, where Tim could see a couple of women floating above deluxe leather recliners while staffers waved glowing sticks of his mother's trademark "supernatural essence" around their faces. The smoke was supposed to make anyone inhaling it relive past life experiences in a way designed to cure present-life ailments, like joint pain or migraines. One of the women appeared to be enthusiastically engaged in the exercise and was shouting at the top of her lungs.

"Don't open that basement door, Ralphie!" she yelled. "Mama told you not to go down there! The demons got into the water tank again!"

"What the actual hell?" Giallo muttered.

"Just ignore it," Tim advised. "People say some crazy shit in those chairs."

"Ralphie! That ain't grandma! Don't eat that, Ralphie!"

"You've gotta be kidding me," Giallo said.

"Believe me, you do not want to be here when they're hosting a pre-wedding party," Tim said. "Things get weird."

"Thanks for the tip," Giallo said. "I already regret being here in any capacity."

"I warned you it would melt your face, Ralphie! You never listen to me, you little turd! Mama's gonna kill me!"

They continued down the hall to a door on the left. Madeline motioned them through into a small space that Tim recognized as one of his mother's basic psychic consultation rooms. It had three fairly simple office chairs organized around a circular table with a crystal ball sitting in the middle. There was a flat screen TV mounted on the wall opposite the door that was controlled by a special touch screen app built into the ball. The app also controlled the smoke, lighting, room temperature, holographic cameras and the speaker units that were hidden in the walls.

Tim's mother wasn't a faker–she was licensed and certified–but, like all psychics, she appreciated the value of a few high-tech frills. When she had opened her first salon, she had opposed all the bells and whistles. Tim figured her qualms had more to do with the expense than with their role in diluting the so-called purity of the psychic's art, but as the dollars rolled in she had quickly gotten on board. Her psychic ability might have diminished, but Regina's capitalistic instincts were razor sharp.

"Look," Madeline said. "I'm really sorry about the whole thing with Stake. It's just, I sensed a powerful psychic connection with him right from the get-go and I think your mother picked up on it, too. I was going to call you, but it was awkward, what with you helping to get me this job and everything."

"Wait a minute," Giallo said. "You two used to go out?"

"No!" Tim said. "Well, we went on one date, but that was it."

"Wow!' Giallo laughed. "This just keeps getting better and better! So one date and you dumped him for another guy? Let me tell you, having spent a not insignificant amount of time with him, I totally get it."

"Can we just focus on why we're here?" Tim said.

"Let me guess," Giallo said. "You went to a restaurant. Just after you leave, he grabs your boobs and claims he can't help himself because he's possessed."

"No!" Madeline said, shocked.

"I didn't grope anyone!" Tim said.

"Sure," Giallo said. "Or maybe he insists you just half to see this adorable baby Kappa picture he's got on his phone and when you lean over to look, he flashes a curse app in your face. Next thing you know, you're waking up 24 hours later in the alley behind a synthetic blood clinic with no memory of what happened except for a strange burning sensation where your self worth used to be. Sound familiar?"

"Say what?" Tim said. "You must have been on some terrible dates. There are very specific details in there that make me think this is more than just anecdotal."

"No," Madeline said, frowning. "Nothing like that happened, either."

"I don't date," Giallo said. "For exactly those reasons."

"As I was saying," Tim said, eager to get the conversation back on track. "All I need you to do is summon up one dead person one time. After that, we never have to see each other again."

"Okay," Madeline said, sitting down and motioning them to do likewise. "I'll try. Who do you want me to bring forth?"

"His name is Harrison Ackroyd-Jones the third," Tim said, sitting down.

"Okay," Madeline said. "And do you have an object that once belonged to this person?"

"I do," Tim said, reaching into his SIU bag and bringing out the Puzzle Box.

"What is this?" Madeline said, picking up the ball and looking at it closely.

"It's the Hesselthorn Puzzle Box," Giallo said.

"Didn't I hear about that somewhere?" Madeline said. "Wasn't somebody selling it on InfernaChat or something?"

"Are you kidding?" Giallo said.

"We just need some help figuring out how it works," Tim said, cutting in. "And the only person who might be able to do that is dead."

"Okay," Madeline said. "I'll do my best."

Madeline reached out and grabbed Tim and Giallo's hands, nodding that they should also join hands to complete the circle.

"This is stupid," Giallo muttered, reluctantly grabbing Tim's hand.

"We must banish all negative thoughts!" Madeline said.

"All of them?" Giallo said. "What if I can only reduce them by, say, five percent? Will that do?"

"We must offer only welcoming psychic vibrations!" Madeline continued, ignoring this.

"Shhh!" Tim hissed. "This might be our only shot!"

"Fine," Giallo grunted. "I'll try to picture a rainbow unicorn boning a sugar plum fairy in a candy store. Is that happy and welcoming enough?"

"What's the spirit's name again?" Madeline asked.

"Harrison Ackroyd-Jones," Tim said. "The third, if that matters."

"Oh mystical orb of enlightenment," Madeline said, leaning forward to speak clearly to the crystal ball in the middle of the table. "We seek an audience with Harrison Ackroyd-Jones the third!"

The crystal ball appeared to fill up with smoke, which swirled for a moment before a black and white image of a face emerged. The image also popped up on the TV screen next to them. Tim recognized it as one that had come from a newspaper story written about the Puzzle Box shortly after its discovery.

"Is this the man you seek?" Madeline asked.

"Uh, I think so," Tim said. He had only ever seen a couple of photos of Ackroyd-Jones and would not have felt confident picking him out of a police lineup. He was, however, impressed with the new voice-activated crystal balls his mother had installed in her salons. The older models were strictly touchscreen control, which tended to detract from the overall effect.

"Very well," Madeline said, dropping her voice an octave. She was still new to the business, so her customer service skills were a little rough around the edges. "We hereby call upon the spirit of Harrison Ackroyd-Jones the third! Arise, arise, arise! We the living wish to speak with a member of the numbered dead! We call to you to rise from your place in the neverland of the spirits and cross the ethereal plane to answer our call! Arise!"

The lights in the room dimmed and the crystal ball began to glow brighter, swirling through flashes of purple and green and red and yellow. Tim felt a blast of cold air as the climate control system kicked in.

"Uh, we don't really need the light show," Tim said, his breath suddenly visible in the freezing air.

"Agreed," Giallo said. "I would also prefer not to freeze my ass off."

"Sorry," Madeline said. "It's automated. I only started yesterday and I'm not exactly sure how to turn it off."

"That's okay," Tim said, wishing he'd worn a thicker shirt. None of this was necessary when it came to summoning ghosts, but his mother knew that she was only able to charge premium rates by giving her customers a show.

"I mean, I could ask Cleo if it's really bothering you," Madeline said. "She's the day manager, so she probably knows."

"No, it's fine," Tim said. He didn't want to risk breaking Madeline's concentration and ruining their chances entirely. "Don't worry about it."

"Okay," Madeline said. "Now where was I? Oh yeah. This Jones guy. Did he die near here? Does he speak English?"

"I'm not sure about the first question," Tim said. "But yes on the second one."

"You don't know how he died?" Giallo asked.

"No," said Tim. "Do you?"

"No," Giallo said. "Does it matter?"

"It can be a sticking point for some," Madeline whispered. "Especially if they died in a, you know, embarrassing way."

"I guess I can understand that," Giallo said. "If I got electrocuted by my vibrator, I probably wouldn't want to talk about it with a bunch of total strangers, either."

"I'm sensing strong resistance from this one," Madeline said, closing her eyes.

"Is that common?" Tim asked.

"Not usually," Madeline said. "Depends on the circumstances, but with most of the ones I summon, all it takes is the slightest hint of hello and they come charging through the door immediately. The hard part is getting them to leave."

"I don't much care to talk to the living, either," Giallo said. "So I get it."

"He's really fighting me," Madeline said, frowning. "Any idea why he might not want to talk to us?"

"Maybe," Tim said, thinking. "Would it help if you told him that this is his chance to atone for letting the demon out of the box in the first place? To make up for what he did to Ozymandia and Ludovico?"

"I'll try," Madeline said. "But I'll warn you, they don't often jump at the chance to revisit mistakes they made when they were alive."

Madeline began humming to herself. It started out as medium-pitched and quickly turned into more of a growl. Tim had only been present at a few summonings, but knew from listening to his mother that no two of them were the same. This was largely because no two ghosts generated the same kind of energy. A lot depended on what kind of person they had been when they were alive. How they died was also a factor. Somebody who had died quietly of old age did not enter a room the same way as a rock star who had seized the wheel of their own tour bus after inhaling half a kilo of Narlune and driving off the road into a Hellhole.

"He's coming!" Madeline said in a thundering voice. "Get ready!"

Tim felt the floor begin to shake and watched the Puzzle Box vibrate on the table. His mother had not installed seismic simulators in any of her salons, so he knew this had to be the real thing. The crystal ball became brighter and brighter until he had to close his eyes and turn his head to avoid the glare. A moment later, the lights went out and there was a crackling sound. Tim opened his eyes to see a spectral head and partial torso rise up through the table and float just above them.

"Not again!" boomed a voice. "Who the hell are you jackasses?"

The floating head and body appeared to belong to a man in his early 40s. He was bald and wearing thick glasses that made his eyes appear twice as large as they were. His most striking feature, however, was definitely the five-foot-long pitchfork stuck in the middle of his forehead.

"I'm Tim Lovecraft," Tim said quickly. "And this is Giallo and Madeline. We need your help."

"Let me guess," said the apparition. "You want me to tell you how to get your hands on the Puzzle Box. The one I discovered before I died. Am I getting warm?"

"No!" Tim said. "We already found it. We need your help to figure out how to open it!"

"Well, forget it!" said the ghost. "Do you have any idea how many morons have tried to summon me over the years because they thought I would tell them how to find and open that thing? Let me give you a hint, okay? I've been pulled into more séances than you have brain cells in your head. Granted, I'm not dealing with Fulci Scholars here, but I think you get what I'm trying to say."

"It's not like that!" Giallo said. "We–"

"Of course it's like that!" the ghost bellowed, spinning around to look back at Tim. "You idiots think it's the ticket to eternal life and wealth and whatever else your greedy little imaginations might conjure up! Well, I'm not your ticket to a lifetime of consequence-free sex parties and all-you-can-eat Kappa buffets, get it?"

"Gross," Giallo said. "Why would you think those two things go together?"

"That isn't what we're looking for!" Tim said. "We already have the box! We know you let the demon out and it got into Ozymandia and then Ludovico! We're trying to get it back in!"

The ghost looked down at the Puzzle Box sitting on the table, causing the handle to go straight through Giallo's arm. She clenched her teeth and shivered as the cold, dead sensation ran up through her shoulder and into the rest of her body.

"How the hell did you get that?" the ghost demanded. "You broke into Lucifer's vault?"

"No!" Tim said.

"Actually," Giallo mumbled. "We kind of did, when you think about it. I mean, using the music to get the old lady to unlock it like that."

"We work for Crimson Seal," Tim said. "Ludwig stole the box out of the vault, but he couldn't figure out how to open it. Long story short, the Hellspawn stole it from him and we got it back."

"Ludwig?" said the ghost. "I never liked that little bastard. Even when he was five, the twerp walked around like he thought he was the prince of the universe."

"You know, you don't really sound like a scientist," Giallo said.

"That's because I'm not," the ghost said. "Lucifer was the book guy. I was the get things done guy. Lucifer would never have left his own library if it wasn't for me!"

"But you're the one who solved the box," Tim said.

"Me?" said the ghost. "No. I wasn't the one who figured out how to open the box."

"What?" Giallo said, confused. "But Lucifer told us that you were the one who figured out how to open it."

"He would say that," the ghost said. "The dumb cuck."

Tim and Giallo looked at each other. Lucifer's former expedition partner was not remotely like the character they had been expecting. So much so that Tim was tempted to ask Madeline if she had summoned the wrong person.

"You are Harrison Ackroyd-Jones the third, right?" Tim asked.

"I prefer Harry," said the ghost.

"Okay, Harry," Giallo said. "So if you didn't open the box, then who did?"

The ghost smiled. "That was Ozzy."

"Ozzy?" Tim repeated. "As in Ozymandia Hesselthorn?"

"Yep," said the ghost. "Ho boy, that woman was flexible. All that ballet, I guess."

"You were sleeping with your partner's wife?" Giallo said.

"What can I say?" the ghost said. "When I was alive, women just couldn't get enough of me. I had this real air of devil-may-care adventure about me that they just couldn't resist. And Ozzy was no exception. Especially being stuck with that miserable old bastard."

"Seriously?" Tim said in disbelief.

"Don't get me wrong," the ghost said. "Old Lucifer was absolutely second-to-none when it came to research. Top notch. I'll give him that. But take him out in the field? The man couldn't even pitch a tent without a dozen porters to help him. And Ozzy was the kind of woman who liked to camp, if you know what I mean."

"I think I'm starting to understand why this partnership broke down," Giallo said.

"Me, too," Tim agreed. "How did Ozymandia end up opening the box?"

"I don't know," the ghost said, shaking his head.

"How could you not know?" Giallo asked. "What happened? Weren't you there?"

"Oh, I was there," the ghost said. "But she had her back to me at the time."

"What did she say?" Tim said. "She must have said something!"

"No," the ghost said, then paused. "Well, she did almost say something, but then her words were cut off."

"What did she say?" Giallo said.

"It was strange," the ghost said. "She was humming and then she said: *'Harry! It's just like the ober!'* And that was the last thing she ever said."

"Just like the ober?" Giallo said. "What the hell does that mean?"

"No idea," said the ghost. "Even now, I wonder."

"You said she was humming," Tim said. "What was she humming?"

"That I did recognize," the ghost said. "Although I can never put a name to it."

"Also helpful," Giallo grumbled.

"Why did you recognize it?" Tim asked.

"I'd heard it before," the ghost said. "It was one of the pieces she used to dance all the time for the ballet. I remember because she had a grand solo she used to perform for me. Had danced it that very afternoon, in fact. Right after we had, uh…"

"Boned?" Giallo offered.

"Is that the modern expression?" the ghost said. "In my day, we used to say shanked."

"Yes," Giallo said. "Yours is much classier."

"The thing she was humming," Tim said. "Was it the *Necronomicon*?"

"Could have been," said the ghost. "I just remember there was this point near the end where she did several of those midair splits things in a row. Yowza. That woman liked to move."

"She still does," Tim muttered. "Do you remember anything else?"

"Sadly, no," the ghost said. "All I remember was this bright flash and a loud bang, as if lightning had struck right where we stood. The next thing I knew, I was lying on the floor."

"Wait a minute," Tim said. "You said that was the last thing she said?"

"Correct," said the ghost. "After that, she lapsed into a coma. A state in which I believe she remains to this day."

"That was when she was pregnant with Ludovico," Tim said. "So you were having this affair with her while she was pregnant with your partner's child?"

"Er, not exactly," the ghost said, looking uncomfortable.

"Oh no, I get it!" Giallo said, her eyes going wide. "Ludovico isn't Lucifer's kid–he's *your* kid!"

The ghost flickered a couple of times and adjusted his cufflinks. "Ahem."

"He is!" Giallo said, bouncing in her chair. "He totally is!"

"That might explain why Lucifer had so few qualms about locking the kid away in a cell for his entire life," Tim said.

"I tried to see him a few times, but Lucifer wouldn't let me anywhere near the house," the ghost said.

"That's a shocker," Giallo said. "You banged his wife and she ended up in a coma before giving birth to a demon child that wasn't his? I can see how he might be a little miffed about that."

"Look," Tim said. "We're not here to dredge all that history back up. The cops have arrested Ludovico. Chances are good that whatever is possessing him has already escaped. We need to know how to get the demon back into the Puzzle Box."

"That's tricky," the ghost said. "The demon's been imprisoned so long that it can only survive inside a host. You'll have to get it to abandon whoever it's inhabiting and revert back to its natural form. Otherwise you'll trap the person in the box with it."

"And how do we do that?" Tim asked.

"The only place it'll abandon its host and assume its natural form is on top of the temple mount," the ghost said. "At the entrance to the Mausolopticon."

"Mauso-what?" said Giallo.

"The Mausolopticon," the ghost repeated. "Also referred to as the Temple of the Mystikal One. It's where Maefisto was locked away in when the Allfathers were originally imprisoned many thousands of years ago."

"Wait," Tim said. "I think I've seen one of those before. Does it look like a giant door?"

"No one really knows," the ghost said. "It might. No record or image survives."

"Where have you seen one of those?" Giallo asked.

"I saw it when I was working on my first case in SIU," Tim said. "When the Sons of Darkness tried to free Belial."

Tim remembered how large that door had been and didn't want to think too hard about what might have been on the other side of it.

"The demon in the box was Maefisto's high priest," the ghost said. "He was trapped at the same time as his boss, only he got stuck in a Puzzle Box instead of a vault. Over the years, the true story got lost and mixed up with legend. People thought the box was some sort of Aladdin's lamp. They thought that if they opened it, they'd release a genie that would grant them whatever they wished for. Lucifer had done the research and knew the truth. He wanted to drop it down the nearest Hellhole, but I thought it was far too valuable to just throw away. I should have listened to him."

"Agreed," Giallo said.

"Ozzy would sneak the box out so that I could study it," the ghost continued. "She was the only other person who Lucifer trusted to access the vault. He would never trust me with such a thing. When the box was opened and the demon got free, it went straight into her."

"Where is the temple?" Tim asked.

"I don't know," the ghost said. "The location is said to be hidden within the box, but the box was closed again almost as soon as the demon escaped, so I didn't get to check."

"Okay," Giallo said. "So just to recap. You don't know how to open the box and you don't know where the temple is. Is there anything useful that you do know?"

"Well," said the ghost. " I do know that if the high priest does manage to locate the temple and free the Mystikal One, then it's only a matter of time before she frees the others. And if that happens, then the three of you are going to wish you were in my position."

"As in, dead?" Giallo muttered. "Yeah. Thanks. That is helpful. Maybe I should have asked for advice on how to nail lots of vulnerable women. I bet you have a lot to say on that subject."

The light began to flicker as the mist in the crystal ball began to swirl again.

"I'm losing him!" Madeline said.

"Wait!" Giallo yelled as the ghost began to flicker and shrink. "What else can you tell us?"

"Nothing!" the ghost said as his voice began to echo and fade. "But if you see Ozzy, do give her my regards! And tell Lucifer from me that he can go fu–"

Before he could finish, the ghost was sucked down like a whirlpool into the crystal ball and disappeared. Giallo dropped Tim and Madeline's hands like they were grenades and stood up.

"Great," she said. "Well that was a total waste of time."

"Maybe not," Tim said, looking thoughtful.

"What are you talking about?" Giallo said.

"It's a long shot," Tim said, picking up the puzzle box. "But I think I might have figured out how to open this thing."

"Seriously?" Giallo said. "How?"

"Not here," Tim said, motioning for Giallo to follow him out. "Thanks for all your help, Madeline!"

"No problem," Madeline said, looking groggy. "Say, what was all that stuff he was saying about demons rising up and us wishing we were dead? Was he serious about that?"

"Probably," Tim said. "But I wouldn't worry about it too much. You know what ghosts are like."

"Yeah," Madeline said, rubbing her forehead. "They're always spouting crazy shit. I had one tell me yesterday that there's an orthodontist buried under the floorboards of my childhood bedroom, for crying out loud! Although, that would explain why I used to have so many weird dreams about my teeth falling out."

"I'm sure that's it," Giallo said, heading for the door. "Let us know if you ever decide to dig them up."

"Probably better to leave the bones where they are," Tim said as they made their way out. "I've heard that dental exorcisms are extremely expensive."

26

Tim didn't want to try opening the box in his mother's salon, so they decided to drive back to his apartment. They were halfway there when his phone rang. Tim hit the button on the dash to pick up and was so surprised to hear his brother's voice that he almost ran a red light.

"Keef?" Tim said, screeching to a stop. "What are you doing up?"

Keef never rose from his coffin during the day. They had blackout curtains over all the windows in the apartment, so he could technically move around when the sun was out, but Keef was not exactly an early riser.

"Cops were just here," Keef said.

"Cops?" Tim said. "What'd you do?"

"Me?" Keef said, sounding insulted. "Nothing!"

"All right," Tim said. "Then what did Killian do?"

"Also nothing!" Keef said. "They were looking for you!"

"Cops were looking for me?" Tim said, looking at Giallo in confusion.

"Yeah," Keef grunted. "They stormed into the place and dragged me and Killian out of our coffins. He was so freaked out he almost bit one of them. He's still working through his transition."

"You turned him?" Tim asked.

"No choice," Keef said. "Those Triad guys at thVrst sucked too much out of him. He would've died otherwise."

"But what if he doesn't come through on his end of the bargain to make you a star?" Tim asked.

"He will," Keef said. "Don't you worry. I had to pull him off the cops before they used a sun gun on the guy."

"Maybe they just had the wrong address or something," Tim said.

"Nope," Keef said. "They were looking for you specifically. Said they had a warrant and everything."

"Why in the hell would the cops be after me?" Tim said.

"They said they were working for some detective named Duluc," Keef said. "Said you killed a documentary crew in a police station? And then blew up a nightclub?"

"Documentary crew?" Tim said, confused. "Police station? I wasn't even at the police station!"

"No," Giallo said. "But that's where they took Ludovico, right?"

"That's right," Tim nodded. "Duluc had him arrested and carted downtown to Metro HQ."

"Looks like the demon inside Ludovico escaped," Giallo said.

"That makes sense," Tim said. "But why would they be looking for me?"

"Think about it," Giallo said. "The demon probably jumped out of Ludovico and into somebody else. And what was always Duluc's signature move to get confessions on his show?"

"He would take their hand," Tim said. "Although sometimes he grabbed other things."

"Right," Giallo said. "And what is literally the first thing you should never do with a possessed person?"

"Touch them," Tim admitted.

"Exactly," Giallo said. "I bet that putz walked right in and tried to use his so-called psychic power to get Ludovico to confess. The demon saw its chance and jumped out of Ludovico and straight into Metro's most famous detective."

"And then kills a whole documentary crew?" Tim said.

"We're talking about a Djinn that's been locked away for a long time," Giallo said. "First in the box, then in this kid. I'm guessing it's super pissed and looking for payback on whoever happens to get in its way. Besides, it doesn't want a film crew following it around."

"True," Tim agreed.

"And who better to take control of than a police detective?" Giallo said. "It can go anywhere and do anything it wants and no one will give it a second thought."

"You're right," Tim said. "But why in the hell is it after me?"

"We have the Puzzle Box," Giallo said. "Maybe the demon still needs it for something."

"Did you really melt a documentary crew?" Keef asked.

"No!" Tim said.

"Okay," Keef said, sounding disappointed. "Well, did you at least blow up a nightclub?"

"I didn't do that, either!" Tim said. "Well, I didn't cause it, but I was kind of there when it happened."

"Well, I guess that's something," Keef said. "They asked me where you were. I said, I dunno, man. It's the middle of the day. Guy's probably at work."

"We can't go back to your apartment," Giallo said. "They're probably still watching the place in case you come back."

"You're right," Tim said. He was trying to figure out what to do next when a police cruiser went screaming through the intersection ahead of them with its lights flashing and siren blaring. Both Tim and Giallo crouched down in their seats to avoid being seen.

"We need to get off the street," Giallo said, looking over her shoulder.

"Yeah," Tim said, making up his mind. He checked the road and swung the car into a U-turn.

"Where are we going?" Giallo asked.

"The office," Tim said.

"We can't go there!" Giallo said. "Your roommate just told the cops that's where you were going!"

"Yes," Tim said. "But the only address they have is the head office on Sixth Street. The SIU isn't in the main building. Its address is secret."

"Oooh!" Giallo said. "So you're going to take me to your secret headquarters?"

"Yes," Tim said. "But no one else is supposed to know about it, so I am going to have to insist that you keep the location to yourself. You can't tell anybody about it. Inside or outside the company."

"Somebody at HQ has to know where it is," Giallo said. "The cops are bound to find it eventually."

"Maybe," Tim said, making a sharp right. "But right now it's pretty much the only option we've got."

"So if they come back, what d'you want me to say?" Keef said.

"Nothing!" Tim said. "Just go back to sleep!"

Tim stabbed the button to hang up the phone.

"So what's it like living with a vampire?" Giallo asked. "He seems pretty oblivious."

"Oblivious and messy," Tim said. "He had a party a few weeks ago. When I got up, the living room looked like they just finished filming the slaughterhouse scene from *Blood House II*."

"Is that why you and this Madeline chick broke up?" Giallo asked.

"No," Tim said. "We only went on one date. Actually, it was technically only one half of a date because I had to run out to the Torn Throat in the middle of dinner."

"Oh yeah," Giallo said. "Sorry about leaving you in the lurch back there."

"Yeah," Tim said. "Maybe I should've just let you get sucked into that vortex back in Azmoda's office. Then we'd be even."

"Nah," Giallo said, shaking her head. "You wouldn't do that."

"Oh no?" Tim said. "Why not?"

"Because you're too much of a straight arrow, Lovecraft," Giallo said, grinning. "I bet you don't even jaywalk."

"I jaywalk!" Tim said. "I break all kinds of rules!"

"Sure thing, bad boy," Giallo snorted. "Don't forget to signal your turn."

Tim turned into the SIU staff parking lot behind Ashtaroth's Relics and Ritual Supply. He didn't see anything strange or out of place as he pulled into his usual spot next to Volkerps's rusty black Altar Master SL minivan and shut off the engine.

The two of them got out of the car and headed for the entrance. Tim poked his head around the corner of the building to check for police. This stretch of Sixth Avenue was mostly made up of downmarket reliquary stores and custom coffin shops, which meant that it was not exactly in the beating heart of the city's commercial zone. The only beings he saw were a couple of zombies pushing a shopping cart full of empty Blood Blast bottles. The cart had only three wheels, which meant they were moving in a slowly advancing series of grinding circles.

"Okay," Tim said. "Follow me."

The two of them jogged down the sidewalk. Tim tried the front door and found it locked. He pulled out his ID and waved it in front of the reader. The lock beeped and flipped to green. Tim pulled the door open and motioned for Giallo to follow him inside. They moved quickly through the store. They were just moving past the cash desk when a kid wearing a wizard's hat and glittering purple robe that was at least two sizes too large for him rose up from behind the counter with a surprised look on his face.

"Oh, hello seekers of the mystical!" he said. "Sorry, but the portal to the supernatural realm is closed for inventory right now and–"

"Crimson Seal," Tim barked, flashing his SIU badge. He had never seen this guy before and assumed he was Madeline's replacement.

"Oh right," the wizard said. "They told me about you guys. Kind of like some cool, top-secret crime-solving unit, right?"

"Exactly," Tim said, punching the elevator button.

"Well, I'm Garrett!" the wizard said, waving. "If you ever need a psychic consultant to tag along on one of your cases? You know, to read the invisible spectral traces at the scene and tell you exactly what went down? I am seriously, like, one of the best. When my aunt Bernice got attacked by a werewolf? Well, it turned out it wasn't exactly a werewolf, it was just a really pissy Weimaraner that probably ate some zombie brains? Anyway, I was the one who figured out that–"

"Thanks, Garrett!" Tim said, stepping into the elevator and pulling Giallo in with him. "I'll be sure to mention your name to the ghouls in HR."

The doors opened and they stepped inside SIU. The main office appeared to be empty, but Tim could hear the low rumble of voices in conversation. He crossed the room and saw the door to Volkerps's office was open. Standing inside was Lonnie Fuhrman, the werewolf senior investigator who was supposed to be on stress leave, and a squid-like demon he had never seen before.

"Lonnie?" Tim said, looking surprised.

"Lovecraft?" boomed Volkerps. "Get in here!"

Tim and Giallo stepped cautiously into the office.

"Uh, hi," Tim said. "This is Giallo. She works in Claims. This is Volkerps, my boss. And Lonnie Fuhrman, who also works in SIU. I'm afraid I don't know–"

"Hey Oz," Giallo nodded to the demon. "This is Ozgoroth, my boss."

"The director of Claims?" Tim said, looking from the swirling mass of tentacles to Volkerps. "But I thought you two hated each other? What's going on?"

"Before we get into that," Volkerps said. "What's happening with the Puzzle Box?"

"I've got it right here," Tim said, reaching in and pulling it out of his SIU bag. He gave a quick summary of the investigation to that point, eliding over some of the less legal parts. "I think we might have figured out how to open it, but now it seems the cops are after me."

"It's not the police," Volkerps said. "It's Enfaxizbel. The high priest of the Temple of Maefisto. The demon who was trapped in the box."

"Why does he need the Puzzle Box?" Giallo asked. "Wouldn't that be the last thing it would want to see after having been trapped in there for so long?"

"The Puzzle Box contains the location of the temple," Ozgoroth said. "He needs that in order to free his old master."

"Wait," Tim said. "So you knew that was what was in this box all along and you didn't tell me?"

"Yes," Volkerps said.

"Why?" Tim demanded. "I almost got killed! So many times!"

"That's a long story," Volkerps said.

"How about you sum it up?" Giallo said.

"Fine," Volkerps rumbled. "As you can tell by the fact that he's standing here, Lonnie is not on administrative leave."

"I was wondering what was happening there," Tim said, nodding. "Good to see you again."

"And you," Lonnie said, nodding.

"So if you're not on admin leave, what have you been up to?" Tim asked.

"Lonnie's been working on a top-secret assignment to find out how and where the Infernium has infiltrated Crimson Seal," Volkerps said.

"What?" Tim said.

"I knew it!" said Giallo, pumping the air with her fist.

"Yes," Volkerps said. "No doubt you remember the Sons of Darkness?"

"The name does ring a bell," Tim said.

"Just one of their many subgroups," Volkerps said. "The Sons of Darkness were worshippers of Belial. That's why they were trying to get their hands on the hammer to break him out of his cell. In which they very nearly succeeded."

"I remember," Tim said. "It was the first case I worked in SIU."

"Then I'm sure you'll remember that one of our own vice presidents was working against us from the inside," Volkerps said.

Tim did remember that, too. Lilith Warwick had kidnapped Stake to use as a human sacrifice to complete the ritual, but had gotten the top of her head chopped off by her own elaborate execution device. On the flip-side, she had also introduced the diversity hiring initiative that had gotten him the job in SIU, which had never previously hired a human.

"I do," Tim said. "But what do you mean by '*working against*'? We're not the police or anything like that. We're just an insurance company."

Volkerps and Ozgoroth exchanged a look.

"Crimson Seal did not originally start out as an insurance company," Volkerps said. "Even today, that is only a part of our main function. Although granted, it is a moderately profitable one."

"Say what?" Tim said.

"It's our public face," Ozgoroth said. "That's what people *think* we do. Something to provide cover for our main purpose."

"Which is?" Tim said.

"The Order of the Crimson Seal was responsible for hunting down and imprisoning the demon Allfathers thousands of years ago," Volkerps said. "I know it must seem like a long time to you, but to Oz and me, it's just something that happened in our grandfather's time."

"Yes," said Ozgoroth. "We maintain the illusion that we despise each other in order to avoid suspicion. In reality, Vol and I are third cousins. His brother is actually married to my sister-in-law."

"The followers of the various Allfathers were pretty scattered in the beginning," Volkerps said. "But over time, they organized themselves into something of a coalition."

"It's complicated by the fact that not all of the individual Allfathers had similar aims or methods," Ozgoroth said. "So although they all operate under the same umbrella, technically, some of them still break off from time to time to act on their own. That's where the Sons of Darkness came from."

"The Infernium has infiltrated every aspect and level of society," Volkerps said. "Government, media, business...you name it. They've been there since the beginning. And, despite our best efforts, that includes Crimson Seal itself."

"Who is it?" Giallo asked. "I bet it goes right up to the CEO! Does it include the CEO?"

The CEO of Crimson Seal was a 760-year-old Dybbuk named Lothnar Czanthaa, whom Tim had never met and had never even been in the same room with. This was not unusual, as Lothnar was rumored to be a hyper-manic germaphobe who never went within six feet of anyone else and conducted all meetings, interviews and town hall seminars via videoconference.

"Not that we know of," Ozgoroth said. "As of this moment, we are aware of only 13 employees who we have either confirmed to be members or who have been in suspicious contact with those we know to be members of the Infernium."

"Wow," Tim said, wondering who the 13 were. Was it anybody he knew? "Anyone inside SIU?"

"No," Volkerps said. "Unless there's something you'd like to tell us."

"Nope," Tim said. "Why?"

"It's the main reason that we didn't hire any humans into the department for more than three thousand years," Volkerps said. "No offence, but your species doesn't have the best track record for trustworthiness."

"No offence taken," Tim said. "I think."

"What about the 13 you mentioned?" Giallo said, tapping the Devil Stick against her palm. "When do we grab them?"

"We don't," Volkerps said.

"Why?" Giallo asked.

"Because," Ozgoroth said. "We need them."

"Need them?" Giallo said. "For what?"

"We need them to lead us to the others," Volkerps said. "After centuries of relative silence, the Infernium has become increasingly active of late. We think it's because they have a new high priest."

"Exactly," said Ozgoroth. "And whoever the new Nameless One is, they've lit some serious Hellfire under the asses of their followers."

"I'm sorry," Tim said, holding up a hand. "I'm still trying to get my head around the fact that five minutes ago, I thought I worked for an insurance company."

"We are an insurance company," Volkerps said. "When the Allfathers fell, we became the guardians of the sacred objects that were the keys to their continued imprisonment. It was our responsibility to ensure those objects were protected and didn't fall into the wrong hands. You could say that we became so good at it over thousands of years that the insurance business part just sort of grew from there."

"So what about this Nameless One?" Giallo asked. "Who do we think it might be?"

"We don't know," Volkerps said.

"We think it's probably somebody who rose to power after the fiasco with the Sons of Darkness at the temple of Belial," Ozgoroth said.

"Maybe," Volkerps said. "But we're also pretty sure it isn't any of the 13 employees that we know about."

"And what about the other objects?" Tim said.

"Objects?" Volkerps said.

"Yes," Tim said. "You said there were sacred objects associated with each of the temples. You said the Hammer of Belial was one. The Hesselthorn Puzzle Box is another. If there are four other temples, then there must be four other objects."

"Yes," Volkerps said. "The Hammer was stored in the Crimson Seal deep secured storage archive. Until, of course, an employee who shall remain nameless completely destroyed the building."

"That was you?" Giallo said, turning to Tim.

"Not just me!" Tim said. "Besides, we didn't have any choice! Those liquid Hellfire canisters were going to detonate no matter what!"

"You detonated *multiple* liquid Hellfire canisters inside the archives building?" Giallo said with a note of awe in her voice. "Okay, Lovecraft. I take back some of the things I said about you."

"Since then, we've had to move the Hammer to our new, top-secret high-security storage facility," Volkerps said.

"I didn't know we had one of those," Tim said.

"Maybe you weren't listening to the first part of the description there, genius," Giallo said.

"At the time, we didn't know if you were clean or not," Volkerps said.

"You didn't know?" Tim said. "But I was the one who busted the Sons of Darkness in the first place!"

"True," Volkerps said. "But we had reasonable grounds for suspicion. And your bringing them down didn't mean you weren't working for another group within the Infernium."

"Reasonable grounds?" Tim said. "What reasonable grounds?"

"Your girlfriend at the time," Ozgoroth said.

"Tabitha?" Tim said, stunned.

"Yes," Ozgoroth said, checking his tablet. "Her current fiancé. The one she was still in communication with while you were dating."

"She was?" Tim said. He had always suspected as much, but had never been able to prove anything conclusively.

"Ouch," said Giallo. "I am so embarrassed for you right now."

"Yes," said Ozgoroth. "Sorry to be the one to break that bit of news. Jared Toccini has had several contacts with known members of the Infernium in the last 18 months."

"Son of a bitch!" Tim growled. "I knew it!"

"Based on your reaction, I'm not convinced that you did," Giallo said. "Who else have you identified?"

"We haven't found your sister, if that's what you're wondering," Ozgoroth said.

"How do you know about that?" Giallo demanded.

"If it's related to the Infernium, it's our business to know," Volkerps said. "Although we don't know anywhere near as much as we'd like."

"That makes two of us," Tim muttered.

"But we were able to establish that you were clean," Volkerps said, turning to Tim. "That was the reason you got this assignment."

"Great," Tim said. "But back to my original question."

"Yes," Volkerps said. "A lot of time has passed. As you can imagine, a few records have been misplaced over the years."

"Misplaced?" Tim said. "You're saying we lost the other objects?"

"Only insofar as their present precise locations are unknown," Volkerps said.

"I'm pretty sure that means the same thing," Giallo said.

"Regardless," Volkerps said irritably. "Our main priority at this time is to make sure that Enfaxizbel doesn't get his hands on the Puzzle Box and open the temple. The only way to do that is to trap him back in the box. Which means we need to work out how to open it."

"How can we be guarding this box for thousands of years and not know how to open it?" Giallo asked.

"Like I said, records get lost," Volkerps shrugged, looking at Tim. "And sometimes unexpectedly incinerated."

"That wasn't entirely my fault!" Tim said.

"So you mentioned," Volkerps said. "Now what was that thing you said about knowing how to open the box?"

"Okay," Tim said, taking out the Puzzle Box and holding it up. "The ghost of Hesselthorn's partner told us that Ozymandia was the one who figured out how to open it."

"Also that he was boning her on the side," Giallo added. "Ludovico was his kid. So he was a pretty lousy expedition partner, all things considered."

"Right," Tim said. "She opened it and let the demon out, which jumped into her when she was pregnant with Ludovico. The demon got trapped in Ludovico, whom Hesslethorn felt compelled to lock up in a high security jail cell partly for safety and partly out of spite because of the whole not being his kid thing. Anyway, it seems the last thing Ozymandia said just before she opened the box was that it was '*just like the ober*'."

"Which makes no sense," Giallo said.

"No, it doesn't," Tim agreed. "Because I don't think that was what she said. I think what she said was '*over*' and not '*ober*'. I think Jones misheard."

"But *over* doesn't make any more sense than *ober*," Giallo said.

"No, but I think she was cut off," Tim said. "I think what she wanted to say was *overture*."

"Overture?" Giallo said.

"Yes!" Tim said. "Specifically, the overture to the *Necronomicon*. The same song she danced to as part of her bizarre daily physical therapy sessions."

"I don't understand," Ozgoroth said. "You're saying the key to opening the Puzzle Box is a piece of *music*?"

"Sort of," Tim said. "Well, I think the music was inspired by the same story that the whole legend of the Puzzle Box was based on."

"Okay," Volkerps said, scratching behind one of his horns. "Let's hear this theory."

"All right," Tim said, taking a deep breath. "Is everyone familiar with the original opera?"

"Of course," Giallo said. "But it's been a couple of years since I forgot to renew my season tickets. I'm in the platinum circle patron's group, you know. Box seats. Fancy as hell. But why don't you give me a quick refresher?"

"Okay," Tim said, ignoring the sarcasm. "The *Necronomicon* is the story of Thordal, a human prince who's actually a bit of a letch, especially by modern standards. When he isn't out raping and pillaging, he likes to sneak down to the waterfall behind his castle to spy on the nymphs frolicking in the nude."

"That's not hard to believe," Giallo said. "I had a high school gym teacher who was fired for basically the same thing."

"So one day, Thordal sees this particularly beautiful water nymph named Mineera," Tim continued. "He decides he has to have her, but she's also caught the eye of Thanatos, the lord of the underworld, who wants her for himself."

"And Mineera gets no say in this whatsoever, naturally," Giallo said.

"Not really," Tim said. "She gets a couple of arias about cruel fate and how all she wants to do is swim, but I think that's about it."

"Of course," Giallo nodded.

"Get to the point, Lovecraft!" Volkerps said.

"Right," Tim said. "Well, after some hemming and hawing, Thordal and Thanatos come to an agreement. Thanatos says he'll let Thordal have Mineera, but only if Thordal tracks down and brings him six enchanted items that he needs for some war with his brother, whose name escapes me at the moment. Anyway, Thordal's quest to recover the items provides the basic structure for the rest of the opera. Each one has its own theme, but all of those themes are woven together into the overture, which is something like 16 minutes long."

"And so you're saying you think those six objects correspond to the symbols flashing up on the Puzzle Box?" Giallo said.

"Yes," Tim nodded.

"Incredible!" Ozgoroth said. "What are the items?"

"Uh, I'm a little fuzzy on that part," Tim said. "I only took one arts elective in university and Demonic Symbolism in the 19th Century Musical Epic was the only class left that still had space by the time I got around to signing up. I'm pretty sure there was a sword–"

"Shut up!" Giallo barked, holding up her phone. "I just searched it up. You ready? It looks like the six items in order are a spear, a torch, a pitchfork, a key, a jawbone and a heart. Sound right?"

"Where did you find that?" Tim asked, suspiciously.

"SpectraPedia!" Giallo said, showing him the screen. "Where else?"

SpectraPedia was a notoriously unreliable source of information, especially since werewolves and vampires were so fond of propagating false and embarrassing "facts" about each other. These claims were usually easy to spot, as they were often written by bored teenagers who thought it was funny to suggest that werewolves were known to hump fire hydrants or that vampires could be destroyed by exposure to zombie country music. Having heard it himself, Tim could certify that *any* sentient being would be destroyed by zombie country music.

"Hmmm," said Tim doubtfully.

"What do you care?" Giallo said, stepping closer to look at the ball. "Let's just get this damn thing open. Anyone know demonic runes?"

"Don't look at me," Volkerps said. "I haven't been inside a classroom in over 900 years."

"I might be able to help with some of them," Ozgoroth said, also stepping closer. "I took a course in policy wording as part of my chartered spectral risk management certification. Many of the modern symbols are derived from their ancient counterparts."

"Brag," Volkerps muttered.

"You're just angry that I got the honours certificate and you had to settle for the associate one," Ozgoroth said.

"Like that matters to anybody," Volkerps said. "Add yet another cluster of pointless letters to the signature line on your emails, why don't you?"

"Let's try to focus, here!" Tim said, getting the sense that although Volkerps and Ozgoroth might be technically on the same side, their mutual enmity was not entirely a clever ruse. "This one looks like a spear to me."

Tim pointed at an image on the Puzzle Box that looked like a stick with a diamond on the end.

"That's it!" Giallo said. "Push it!"

"But—" Tim said.

"Just do it, before it disappears again!" Giallo said.

Tim put a finger over what he thought was the spear symbol. The Puzzle Box flickered blue for a moment.

"That's it!" Giallo said, actually jumping up with excitement.

"Yeah," Tim said. "More importantly, it didn't vaporize me."

"I think the one with the circle and the three spikes is the torch," Ozgoroth said, pointing.

Tim covered that one with a second finger, which also caused the box to flash blue.

"Did you see that!" Giallo said. "It's working! Okay, the pitchfork is next."

"That one's easy," Tim said. "It's the stick with four spikes on the end."

He covered that one. Another blue flash.

"Guys, we're getting it!" Giallo said. "Next is the key."

"Is it this one?" Tim asked, pointing to an image of a wavy line with perpendicular spikes running down one side.

"No!" Ozgoroth said. "That's the jawbone! The key should look like a hand,"

Tim waited until he saw an image pop up that looked like a six-sided star. "That one, maybe?"

"I think so," Ozgoroth said.

Tim touched the star. The ball flashed blue again.

"Okay," he said, covering the wavy line with the spikes. "And this is the jaw bone. Just one left."

"That looks like a heart!" Giallo said, pointing at a circle with a triangular indent at the top.

"No!" Ozgoroth said, pulling her hand away. "That's the eye of Orath!"

"The what?" Giallo said.

"It's the symbol for divine vengeance," Ozgoroth said. "I have also seen it used to describe a pillar of Hellfire large enough to destroy the entire world."

"Okay, so maybe don't touch that one," Giallo said.

"I think that's the one," Tim said, nodding at an image of three concentric circles.

"Are you sure?" Giallo said. "It looks like an eye."

"I think so," Tim said. "The ancient glyphs used to show the eye in the centre of the chest. It was supposed to represent all-seeing wisdom, since demons didn't believe they actually had hearts."

"He could be right," Ozgoroth shrugged.

"You're really sure?" Giallo said.

"Let's say pretty sure," Tim said. "But I can't reach it." Tim had five other fingers attached to different points on the box and couldn't twist his hands to reach the final symbol without taking one of those fingers off.

"Okay then," Giallo said, taking a deep breath. "Here goes nothing."

Giallo reached down and touched the symbol. The Puzzle Box turned a brilliant blue and then white. The symbols on the outside were replaced with an image that projected out like a 3D hologram of a black pyramid with what looked like a large clamp on the top. This image quickly dissolved and was replaced with a map. The map showed rivers and mountains and canyons with a glowing red dot at a point in the middle. There were no buildings or roads, but there was still something about the image that Tim recognized. He was trying to figure out what that was when Lonnie reached out and put a hand on Giallo's shoulder.

"Nice work," Lonnie said. "But my master is going to need this."

Tim looked up to see Lonnie reaching for the Puzzle Box. He could tell from the expression on his face that something was wrong. Lonnie's eyes were glowing red and he was smiling in a way that could only be described as predatory. Tim could see that Lonnie's bared teeth were growing longer and sharper. His nose was extending into a muzzle and fur was growing out in dark patches all over his face. The nails on Lonnie's hands were growing out into razor-sharp points as the joints extended to form claws.

Lonnie was transforming into his werewolf form, which Tim knew his coworker had never done before inside the office.

"What?" Giallo said, pulling the ball away as Lonnie reached for it. This broke Tim's connection with the symbols and the holographic map immediately vanished.

"Give it to me!" Lonnie roared, swiping at Giallo's head.

"Watch out!" Giallo yelled, bumping into Tim and knocking him to the floor.

Lonnie's swipe missed Giallo by inches and caught Ozgoroth full in the face, sending him flying backwards over the desk. Giallo rolled sideways and grabbed the Devil Stick out of Tim's SIU bag, firing it at the charging Lonnie at point blank range. The blast caught the werewolf in the hip. Lonnie staggered slightly but kept coming.

There's no way, Tim thought. Even in werewolf form, a blast like that should have knocked him across the room. Something strange was going on here. Based on the red eyes and sudden boost of superspectral strength, there was only one possible explanation.

"He's possessed!" Tim shouted.

"Stand clear!" Volkerps boomed, sending a blast of blue lightning at the charging werewolf. The bolts seemed to curve through the air and roll right off the beast, who turned and sent a blast of red light in response. The beam hit Volkerps in the arm, knocking him backwards and sending him flying into the wall, shattering many of his framed professional certifications.

The Puzzle Box rolled across the floor. Giallo grabbed it before Lonnie did and scrambled to get to her feet and make a run for the door.

"We need to get out of here!" Giallo yelled. "Now!"

Tim grabbed the first thing he could find in his SIU bag, which happened to be the sun gun. He aimed it straight at Lonnie's face, hoping he might be able to at least temporarily blind his coworker for long enough that they could make their escape. Lonnie, however, just laughed and knocked it out of Tim's hand.

"You don't understand!" Lonnie said. "The box is mine."

Lonnie reached down and grabbed Giallo by the ankle. There was a flash and cracking sound. A moment later, Lonnie's body crumpled to the ground and Giallo stood up. Now her eyes were blazing red.

"Excuse me," she said in a voice that was very much not her own.

"No!" Tim said, scrambling to grab his Demon Charger. "Let her go!"

"Oh I will," Giallo growled. "But not quite yet."

Giallo raised the Devil Stick and pulled the trigger. Tim dived behind a chair as the blast hit it. The force was enough to send him crashing head first into the wall.

As he struggled to get back up, Tim was dimly aware that he desperately needed to make a phone call. He knew exactly where the temple was. He had seen a similar map only a few days earlier. He needed to warn the people in the area that something extremely dangerous was coming their way. They needed to get out of there. Fast.

Tim pulled his phone out of his pocket and tried to open his contacts, but it slid through his fingers and clattered to the floor. He reached for it, but the lights in the room seemed to be dimming and his hands didn't appear to be working properly.

"Come on!" he mumbled. His voice sounded like he was underwater.

The last thing he saw before he blacked out was Giallo reach down to pick up the Puzzle Box, blow him a kiss, and run out of the office.

27

Stake lowered himself down on the rope that extended from the edge of the concrete service tunnel. This section at the far northern end of the Crypt Network connected to a system of caves that extended for several miles under the city. He could dimly make out the entrance to one of the caves about 30 yards away on the other side of a shallow ravine.

There were thousands of caves down here. Some of them had Hellfire vents or subterranean lakes. The more dangerous ones contained reverse-gravity chambers, which could send the unwary explorer flying towards a ceiling covered in jagged stalactites as quickly as if they had stepped off a cliff. Some of them were home to large colonies of flesh-eating Hemodytes, a terrifying cross between a zombie and a werewolf that would bite the top of your skull off and eat your brain. Not much was known about them because the only group of spectrobiologists who had mounted an expedition to study the creatures had never returned. And that was not even counting all the different types of demons, water monsters, feral vampires, homeless werewolves and other creatures that lived down here. It was easily one of the most dangerous places in the world.

Stake loved it.

He had never been more enthusiastic about any job he'd ever had before joining Thad's supernatural removal service. Sure, he'd had some good times working in private security, but rousting the occasional blood bagger or garlic-blasting a trespassing teenage vampire just couldn't compete with the thrill of confronting the enemy on their home turf on a daily basis. Especially not when he had the tools to do it. As he saw it, he was making a real difference in people's lives.

On top of that, Thad had been dropping hints about handing the business off to Stake when he retired. His own kids weren't much interested in assuming the family legacy, he said. Tim was stuck in an office all day working for an insurance company. Sure, the guy did some investigating every once in a while, but Stake couldn't imagine working in the financial sector, not with all its archaic rules and procedures. And as for Keef? As far as Stake was concerned, Keef was just like all vampires: a lazy, bloodsucking parasite who did nothing but drain hardworking humans of their precious lifeforce. According to Thad, Keef had never managed to hold down any job for more than a week, including his time working for the family business, so that oversized mosquito certainly wasn't about to step up, either.

Stake reached the bottom of the ravine where Thad was waiting for him. It was awkward climbing in the spectral hazmat suit, but he didn't mind. It was part of the new equipment they'd purchased for the job. Wearing it made him feel almost like a superhero. He had dabbled in extracurricular hero work when he'd been a security guard, but this felt like the real thing. How else could you define being out on the literal front line of the war between humanity and the forces of darkness?

"You believe this?" Thad said, grinning as he surveyed the vast dark cavern in front of them. "I never thought I would ever land a job like this."

"Get used to it," Stake said. "This is what the future is going to look like."

Stake craned his neck to see the crumbling foundations of the old Cravensloft Institute for the Criminally Possessed sticking out through the rock ceiling on their left. Most of the building had collapsed a century earlier after a Hellhole had opened up underneath the south wing, taking more than 80 patients and staff down with it. Many of their ghosts were probably still wandering around somewhere in this labyrinthine network of caverns.

"All thanks to you," Thad said. "Believe me, I'm not gonna forget it. I love my boys, but they've never really had any interest in this stuff. But you do. You talk about the future? Someday, it'll be your name on the trucks, buddy."

"Oh no," Stake said. "It's gonna be Thad's, no matter what."

"Nah," Thad said. "I'm not gonna be doin' this forever. Reg hates it when I'm on call. Phone ringin' in the middle of the night 'cause some vampire punks broke into a blood bank or a bunch of zombies are sneakin' brains out of the morgue again. She hates the smell of Demonex. Doesn't matter how many decontamination showers I take. It's always there. Probably just because she spends all day breathing in that incense at the spa. Messes with her brain. In the early days, it used to make her do so much online shopping that we nearly went broke."

"My uncle had the same problem," Stake said. "Only he was betting on Chupacabra fights. Ended up owing a ton of money to the Blood Moon Riders."

"Those furry bastards are dangerous," Thad said.

"When he couldn't pay, they made him work as a Narlune mule," Stake said. "One night, he went out to do a drop for them at the docks and just never came back. My aunt was on disability 'cause she'd been possessed. At least, she said she was possessed. I always kind of thought she was just making it up to milk the insurance, you know? But after my parents were killed by that vampire, she was pretty much the only family I had left."

"Well, we're your family now," Thad said, patting him on the shoulder. "Besides, you're getting to the age where a man needs to start thinking about starting a family of his own, am I right?"

"I guess," Stake said, smiling awkwardly.

"That Madeline's okay, huh?" Thad said, elbowing him in the ribs.

"Yeah," Stake said, glad that Thad couldn't see him blushing in the dark. "It's a little awkward, though. I mean, I think Tim asked her out first."

"Don't you worry about that," Thad said, shaking his head. "Reg has a sixth sense about you two. Besides, Tim's still all hung up on that police sergeant who left him in the lurch. Damn shame, too. I liked that one. She got me VIP passes to SpectraCon last year."

"Well, this year you won't need any insider help," Stake said. "Not now that we're on the preferred vendor list."

"Damn straight!" Thad said, rubbing his hands together. "So what are we lookin' at down here?"

Stake pulled a map out of one of his many velcro-sealed pockets and unfolded it in his left hand, illuminating the surface with a flashlight that he unclipped from a voluminously stocked utility belt.

"It looks like the main tunnel for the new crypt extension is supposed to go northwest at roughly 265 magnetic," Stake said, using the flashlight to outline the projected path on the map. "That means we'll need to clear the big cavern in the middle and those two smaller ones on either side."

"Right," Thad nodded. "And what's our intel say about those caves?"

"Nothing," Stake said. "At least, not in the package we got. If they ever did any spectral impact studies back in the day, they were either lost or never got included with the final report before the project was put on hold."

"So we're on our own," Thad said.

"Pretty much," Stake said. "But I can tell you from experience of the time when I used to patrol near this end of the tunnels that shit gets weird out here on the fringes. I've seen things that would make even a Serrabluk turn tail and run."

In reality, Stake had never been this far out before, even in his most adventurous amateur nightly patrols. The closest he had come was the time he had accidentally stumbled into a demon brothel in the Lower Pitchfork neighbourhood. A tattooed succubus had set fire to his pants and laughed like hell as he had been forced to jump into a mud wrestling pit to try to put them out.

"Okay then," Thad said, pulling a Devil Stick out of a custom holster on his back. "Then I guess we need to be ready for anything."

"Roger that," Stake said, putting away the map and grabbing his own weapon. He checked to ensure it was fully charged. "You wanna take point?"

"All yours," Thad said, shaking his head and motioning for Stake to take the lead. "You've earned it."

The two of them moved down the hill and across the rocky ground to the main cave entrance. The ground sloped down steeply to the remains of what looked like a dried river bed. Up close, they could see that what at first glance appeared to be smooth rocks were actually human skulls half buried in the dried mud. Thad crouched down to pry one of them loose and lifted it up for closer inspection. A large hole had been drilled through the middle of the forehead, making it look like this long-deceased individual had three eyes.

"Check this out," Thad said, feeling the edge of the puncture with a gloved finger.

"Looks like they all got the same treatment," Stake said, examining the dozens of other skulls closely. "I wonder if they came from a sacrificial altar somewhere upriver?"

"Nah," Thad said, shaking his head. "Patients."

"Patients?" Stake said, confused.

"From the asylum," Thad said, pointing up at the remains of the building foundations jutting out high overhead. "This was how they used to treat identity theft in the old days. Good old trepanning. Cut a hole in the skull to let the demon out."

"Gnarly!" Stake whispered.

"And effective," Thad said, placing the skull back on the ground. "Every single patient died, but the demons usually left, too. They probably just buried them out back in a mass grave or piled them up in a cellar for incineration. Once the ground gave way, they all ended up down here."

"Spectral radiation levels are pretty low," Stake said, adjusting the controls on his visor to scan the area. "Well below the upper range listed in the project specs."

"Based on the stories I used to hear about that place as a kid, this is probably the least of what we'll find," Thad said.

"What kind of stories?" Stake asked.

"Let's just say that exorcisms were not the only kind of procedure that they experimented with," Thad said. "Keep your eyes open. And whatever you do, don't touch anything with horns."

"Roger that," Stake said.

They crossed the river bed, being careful to avoid stepping on the skulls. Thad had seen plenty of mass grave sites in his time and knew that nothing brought angry spirits out faster than desecrating their remains, whether intentionally or not. Once they were across, they began making their way up the hill on the other side.

"I wonder why the city is expanding the network way out here?" Stake wondered. "It's so far from the city centre. There's nothing much out here for anybody to see."

"Not yet," Thad said. "New mayor is really ambitious, though. I guess she figured this was the easiest way to get a lot done in a short time."

"You think it'll work?" Stake asked.

"Probably not," Thad shrugged. "But it's sure as hell good for my business, so I ain't complaining."

"True that," Stake said.

They reached the entrance to the central cave, which was roughly the same size as a subway tunnel. The plan was to extend the existing

N2 Crypt Network line straight through for a further five kilometres before building a new N7 line that would run on a perpendicular east-west
course between the city zoo to the airport. Before any of that could happen, however, a full survey and spectral remediation would be required to
make sure that the project did not become irretrievably cursed.

"I bet nobody's been down here in at least a hundred years," Stake
said, peering down into the cave.

"You kidding?" said Thad. "There's a good chance that nobody's been
down here before *ever*. You think the crews working the last half mile of
the line were gonna come wandering down here for a smoke?"

"Good point," Stake admitted.

"Okay," Thad said, stepping between a couple of jagged stalagmites.
"Let's go. Once we're inside, we stay together and stay on the radio. You
see anything weird, you blast first and ask questions later. Understood?"

"Roger that," Stake nodded. "Let's kick some ass!"

"Just don't get too trigger happy and fry mine," Thad laughed. "You
melt my cheeks together and I may feel compelled to seek retribution.
You know what I mean? As in, you and Madeline may need to look into
adoption on account of the fact that you'll need to carry your nuts around
in a little glass jar."

"Understood," Stake laughed.

The two of them made their way into the cave, which descended at
a shallow 10 degree slope, their path winding around large boulders and
ominous, seemingly bottomless pits. Stake made sure that the spectral IR
on his visor was dialled all the way up to make sure that he didn't step into
an unseen Hellhole and disappear from the map permanently. They had
only been walking for about five minutes when Thad put out an arm to
stop Stake in his tracks.

"You see that?" Thad breathed.

"See what?" Stake said. His visor kept fogging up. He wiped it with
the sleeve of his suit and saw a massive pyramid-like structure rising up
in the distance. "Whoa! What is that?"

"No idea," Thad said. "But it is definitely not on the map."

The structure, whatever it was, appeared to sit in the middle of a large opening in the centre of the cave. It was hard to tell exactly how big it was, but to Stake, the tower looked like it was at least 10 stories tall.

"Looks like some sort of temple," Thad said.

"Yeah," Stake nodded. Whatever it was, it was lighting up on his scope like a radioactive amusement park. This place was positively pulsating with spectral energy. Not only that, it was giving off a very particular kind of supernatural power. It was of a kind that Stake had felt only once before, and that had not been a very pleasant experience.

"It feels…" Thad started.

"Evil," Stake finished.

"Yeah," Thad said. "What say we bring some of the boys down here with some survey gear before we get any closer to that thing?"

"I think that's an excellent idea," Stake said.

The two of them turned around and started heading back to the entrance. It was surprisingly hot down here and they both flipped their visors back up to be able to see through the fog of their own exhalations. They were about to climb over the stalagmites and start making their way back to the ravine when they stopped in their tracks.

A woman was walking up the hill towards them. She appeared to be in her mid-twenties and was wearing green combat pants and a black hoodie. The detail that caught both of their eyes was the glowing red ball she was carrying in her left hand.

"What the hell is a civilian doing down here?" Stake wondered.

"She musta snuck in past the barrier," Thad said. "Happens on job-sites all the time. Nobody pays any attention to warning signs in this town."

The two of them moved quickly to intercept the woman as she approached the cave entrance.

"Sorry young lady," Thad said, holding out a hand as she approached. "But you can't be down here. This is a restricted area. It's not safe."

"That's true," the woman smiled. "It isn't safe. For you."

"Who are you?" Stake said.

"I am but a humble servant," the woman said, smiling.

"A what?" Thad said, looking confused. "Look here, little lady. This ain't no place to go wandering around alone, you understand? There's dangerous entities down here. You need to head back above ground."

"You're right," the woman said, smiling. "There are dangerous entities in this place."

"She's crazy," Thad said, shrugging his shoulders.

Something strange was going on here, Stake thought. He flipped his visor back down just in time to see that the woman was glowing even more brightly than the temple.

"Look out!" he yelled, taking a step back and raising the Devil Stick. He got off a blast that hit the woman in the middle of her chest. It should have been enough to knock her flat on her back, but she just laughed.

"Actually," she said, stepping forward. "I think you might be useful after all."

28

Tim opened his eyes and groaned. He was dimly aware that he was lying on the floor and that he was pinned under something heavy. He raised his head and saw that the heavy thing was actually two heavy things, as both Lonnie and Ozgoroth seemed to have landed on top of him.

He remembered the look in Lonnie's eye and the explosion when he had reached for the Puzzle Box. Lonnie had not looked like himself. Specifically, Lonnie had looked like he had somebody or something else in control when he did that, which would suggest that Lonnie was not really Lonnie.

Tim pulled himself out from under the heap and grabbed for his SIU bag. He could see Volkerps rematerializing over his black clouds on the other side of his overturned desk. Neither Giallo nor the Puzzle Box were anywhere to be seen.

"What the hell?" Lonnie groaned, rubbing his head. "Where am I?"

Tim found his SIU bag and grabbed the Demon Charger, pointing it at Lonnie.

"What the hell was that?" Tim yelled. "Who else is in there?"

"What?" Lonnie said, sitting up.

"You're possessed!" Tim said.

"I'm what?" Lonnie said.

"We opened the Puzzle Box and you grabbed for it!" Tim said.

"The what?" Lonnie said. "What did I grab?"

"Where's Giallo?" Tim demanded.

"Who?" Lonnie said.

Tim grabbed his SpectraVision attachment and clipped it to his glasses. He dialled quickly through the frequencies, but the Lonnie in front of him showed only trace spectral energy. Whatever had occupied him appeared to be gone.

"It's Enfaxizbel," Ozgoroth said, sitting up and rubbing his tentacles. "He took possession of Giallo and beat it with the Puzzle Box."

"The last thing I remember is going into the parking garage of my building," Lonnie said. "There was this guy waiting next to my car. I recognized him from someplace."

"It must have been Duluc," Tim said. "You ever watch the Psychic Detective?"

"Yeah!" Lonnie said. "I remember he said he was a cop! Had the badge and everything."

"He must have known I would be coming back here," Tim said. "He knew I couldn't go back to my apartment, so his best bet was to find another SIU employee and possess you to sneak inside."

"Probably used your phone's known locations to find it," Volkerps said, coughing out a small volley of thunderbolts and blinking dozens of eyes to clear his vision.

"Now he's taken control of Giallo," Ozgoroth said. "And he has the Puzzle Box."

"More than that," Tim said. "He knows where the temple is. He's probably on his way there as we speak."

"I didn't happen to see where that was," Ozgoroth said. "Anybody else?"

"I did," Tim said. "I think I know where he's going."

"Where?" Volkerps asked.

"It's in some caves," Tim said. "Way up at the north end of the Crypt Network. In the Pitchfork District. My father's company landed the contract for the spectral remediation before the next phase of construction kicks off."

"We need to stop him," Ozgoroth said, getting up. "We can't let him re-open the temple."

"I'll come with you," Lonnie said, getting to his feet before staggering and falling back down again.

"I don't think you're going anywhere except maybe in an ambulance to the Crowley Clinic," Ozgoroth said, helping Lonnie into one of the chairs.

"He's right," Volkerps said. "You were just occupied by a powerful supernatural entity. It may have melted part of your brain."

Lonnie tried to get out of the chair and almost slid onto the floor. "You can't go by yourself!"

"I'll go," Ozgoroth said.

"We should call the cops," Lonnie said.

"We can't!" Tim said. "They all think I'm a homicidal lunatic."

"He's right," Volkerps said. "But you can't go out there with nothing."

Volkerps floated over to the wall and removed a framed photograph of his family on vacation at the Orloth Hellfire Pits. Behind the picture was a keypad. Volkerps quickly tapped out the 13-digit code with one of his claws and a panel opened. Volkerps reached inside and removed an object that he handed to Tim.

Tim took the object, which was a black metal spear. It was about as long as his arm and had a pointed blade on one end and three curved spikes sticking out of the other. There were runes carved into the handle, but he had no idea what they represented. It weighed at least 30 pounds and looked extremely old.

"What is this?" Tim asked, trying not to sound ungrateful without betraying the sense that he secretly thought this might be some sort of practical joke.

"It's the Spear of the Unnamed," Volkerps said. "It might be the only thing that'll kill Enfaxizbel."

"Why are you keeping something like this in your office safe?" Tim asked, not entirely sure that he actually wanted to know the answer.

"I told you," Volkerps said. "Crimson Seal is not just an insurance company. Our primary mission is to ensure that the Allfathers never rise again. Like it or not, your employment contract technically binds you to fulfill that duty."

"Okay," Tim said, deciding to set that matter to one side while he processed the implications. "So how does it work?"

"It's a spear," Volkerps said. "It's not exactly theoretical spectraphysics. You walk up and stab the bastard in the throat."

"But it's in Giallo!" Tim said. "I can't just stab a coworker!"

"I'm afraid we probably won't have a choice," Ozgoroth said, putting a tentacle on Tim's shoulder. "Enfaxizbel can't survive without a host. It'll be extremely reluctant to leave."

"So we're supposed to *impale* it out?" Tim said.

"We cannot allow the Magikal One to be freed," Volkerps said. "If that happens, bad things will follow."

"I get the apocalyptic implications," Tim said. "Believe me, I do. But there has to be another way."

"The longer we stand here and talk, the closer Enfaxizbel gets to its goal," Ozgoroth said. "Come on! We can discuss this on the way."

"Wait!" Tim said, grabbing his phone off the ground. "I need to warn them!"

Tim dialled his father's number, but there was no answer. That wasn't surprising. If Thad was down in the tunnels, his cellphone reception would be nonexistent.

"Damn!" Tim grunted. "No answer!"

"Come on!" Ozgoroth said, grabbing Tim by the arm. "We can try again on the way!"

Tim grabbed his SIU bag and the two of them raced out of the office, up the stairs and out into the parking lot. They jumped into Tim's car and screeched out onto the road, Ozgoroth doing his best to adapt to the human dimensions of the seat as he pulled on the safety belt.

"Haven't been in a human car for a while," he said, adjusting his tentacles to avoid pinning them in place. "Smells kind of like Demonex in here."

"Sorry," Tim said. "I spilled a canister on the backseat a few months ago. I had it detailed, but the smell never really goes away."

Tim figured the easiest way to get to the temple site was to take the Devil's Expressway, but it was usually jammed at this time of day. Besides, there were traffic cameras all over it. If the cops were really looking for him, there were fewer things he could do to make himself easier to catch than pull on to a busy highway at rush hour. He elected to take Lower Beelzebub Avenue instead. It was mostly underground and in lousy repair, so it wasn't used much. From the top end, he could cut across on 666th to the old asylum, where his father had set up the worksite for access to the planned Crypt Network expansion.

Tim was just congratulating himself on the wisdom of his plan when he heard a siren. He looked in the rearview mirror and saw flashing red and blue lights on the roof of a police car that had appeared out of nowhere as he entered the part of town known as Hell's Pantry. It had at one time been the home of almost every knockoff and discount electronics and appliance store in the city. Nowadays many of the shop fronts were empty, having been muscled out by cheaper online competition.

"Shit!" Tim said.

"I think you ran a stop light back at Price and Karloff," Ozgoroth said, turning his head to look through the back window.

"We're screwed!" Tim said.

"Relax!" Ozgoroth said.

"I'll try," Tim said. "But I'm not promising anything."

"Just get ready to make the next right onto Cauldron Street," Ozgoroth said.

"Okay," Tim said, checking his mirror and reaching for the signal.

"Don't signal the turn!" Ozgoroth shouted. "This is a car chase!"

"Right!" Tim said, grabbing the wheel and speeding back up. "Sorry!"

Ozgoroth unbuckled his seatbelt, rolled down the window and leaned his head out, tilting his body around to face back towards the pursuing cruiser. "Get ready!"

Tim tightened his grip and gritted his teeth. He was acutely aware that, if he wrecked his car while trying to make a high-speed turn into a narrow alleyway whilst being pursued by law enforcement, the ensuing damage would definitely not be covered by insurance. He was also aware of the fact that if he lost control and drove through a dry cleaners during business hours that his liability exposure would not be his most pressing concern.

"Now!" Ozgoroth yelled.

Tim slammed the brakes and spun the wheel, feeling the car's tires lift off the road as they fishtailed around the corner. Ozgoroth opened his mouth and spewed a projectile stream of bluish-black fluid onto the road, spraying it across the intersection as the car swung in an arc over the pavement.

Tim felt the car come back down with a bump and the tires grip as he squeezed between a delivery van and a parked scooter to race down the alley. As soon as the cruiser hit the blue-black puddle, its tires lost all grip and it spun clockwise, sailing right past the intersection. Tim glanced at the rearview mirror and saw the cruiser smash into a fire hydrant, sending a jet of water three stories into the air.

"I know they were chasing us, but I still feel vaguely responsible for that," Tim gasped.

"Ah, I missed this," Ozgoroth said, pulling himself back inside.

"You've done this before?" Tim asked. "When?"

"Vol and I used to get into all kinds of crazy shit back in the day," Ozgoroth said.

"You did?" Tim said. He could not imagine his boss getting up to anything as bonkers as a high-speed police chase.

"Oh, hell yeah!" said Ozgoroth. "He got his ass fried so many times! Why else do you think his lower half is hidden in all those clouds?"

"I never thought about it," Tim said. "I just kind of assumed that was his natural form."

"Ha!" Ozgoroth laughed. "Nothing natural about it. Next time you see him, make sure to ask him about the Vorloth exorcism. That was fun."

"Okay," Tim said, although he wasn't sure that he would.

"Just make the next left," Ozgoroth said, pointing. "We're almost there."

They reached the worksite. Tim parked behind one of his father's trucks, grabbed his SIU bag and the spear, and got out of the car. Ozgoroth followed him across the gravel driveway and around the orange construction barricades. Tim couldn't see any sign of his father or Stake or any other employees. He had been desperately hoping that they hadn't already gone down into the site already, but he knew that was a longshot. One thing Thad and Stake had in common was an overpowering urge to march right into the middle of the kinds of spectral hot zones that sensible people would avoid like a reactor accident.

Tim tried his father's cell phone again and got another automated message telling him that the customer he was trying to reach was not currently available.

"No answer," Tim said. "They're probably already down there."

"Yep," Ozgoroth said. "Just keep in mind–this thing can take control of anyone. We need to be ready."

"Right," Tim nodded. The spear felt like it weighed a ton. "Let's go."

29

Tim and Ozgoroth stepped around the barricade with the large red DANGER—SPECTRAL REMEDIATION IN PROGRESS sign and entered the tunnel, following the string of 2,000 kilowatt lights to the edge of the ravine. There were no lights beyond the edge, so it was impossible to tell how deep it was.

Tim clipped his SR filter onto his glasses and waited for a moment for it to activate and pair to his cellphone. He dialled them into low range IR and peered over the edge, where he could see the ravine was only about 20 feet deep. He could also see that there were two shapes near the bottom that looked distinctly like bodies.

"Hurry!" he said, grabbing the nylon rope in his free hand and starting down. He almost lost his grip a couple of times and had to grab on with both hands, tucking the spear awkwardly under his arm as he went. He reached the bottom and ran across the rocky ground to the first body. It was Thad.

"Dad!" Tim yelled, dropping the spear on the ground and kneeling down. Thad appeared to be alive, but unconscious. There were no obvious injuries aside from a small cut on his forehead and a few scrapes on his right cheek that he appeared to have sustained when he fell down.

"He's alive," Ozgoroth said, crouching down next to Tim and wrapping a tentacle gently around Thad's wrist to check for a pulse. "But only barely. Looks like he took a pretty good hit."

"The demon must have beat us here," Tim said, rushing to the other body. He grabbed it to roll it over and received a shock that went all the way up his arm and nearly caused his knees to buckle. "Gah!"

"Careful!" Ozgoroth said. "They're still hot!"

Tim shook the stars out of his eyes and used the side of the spear to roll the body over. It was Giallo. She appeared to have come off less well than Thad, as she was bleeding from the eyes and her skin was on fire. The latter condition wasn't fatal, but only if it was treated quickly.

"Looks like it jumped out of her," Ozgoroth said.

"Yeah," Tim nodded. "That means the demon is now running around using another host, and I have a horrible feeling that I know who it is."

"We need to get them out of here," Ozgoroth said. "The first guy isn't too bad, but she needs immediate treatment or she'll end up much worse than dead."

Tim checked his cell phone. Not surprisingly, he had no signal whatsoever. No one was coming to rescue them. He took a sharp breath and made a quick decision.

"You get them out," Tim said.

"No," Ozgoroth said. "You can't face that thing by yourself."

"No choice," Tim said. "We can't call anyone. We have to get them out of here. Especially Giallo. I can't even touch her because of the subdermal Hellfire, but you can. Get them above ground and call SEMT. The Holcroft Clinic isn't far from here. They might be able to save her. I'll head into the cave and try to stop our friend from reaching the temple."

"But–" Ozgoroth said.

"Just do it!" Tim said, jumping back to his feet and running up the hill. A thought occurred to him and he stopped. "Wait, you're her boss, right?"

"Yes," Ozgoroth said.

"What's her first name?" Tim asked.

"Her what?" Ozgoroth said, not sure he had heard correctly.

"Her first name!" Tim repeated. "What is it?" He figured there was a better than average chance that he wasn't going to make it out of this and, although he was conscious of how strange the impulse was, he didn't want to die with the question still nagging at him.

"I don't know," Ozgoroth said. "She wouldn't tell anyone and it wasn't in her file. I don't know how you humans think, so I let it go. Why?"

"Damn!" Tim grunted. "Okay, thanks anyway."

Tim turned and continued running up the hill to the mouth of the cave. Stepping inside, he jogged into the darkness. Through the filter, he could see a trail of bright red footprints on the ground that had been left by his quarry.

After a few minutes, the cave began to widen. Tim came to a ledge where he could see the outline of a massive pyramid-shaped complex looming up in the distance. He stepped down and made his way carefully between the sharp, fang-like rocks, which felt like stepping inside the jaws of some giant and horrible beast.

The weight of the spear, which had previously been a hindrance, now felt distinctly more reassuring, even though he had no idea how on earth to use it. The last time he had even held a spear was in Grade 8 gym. That was back before javelin toss had been dropped from the curriculum because of the unfortunate impalement of Mr. Hernandez, whose career as a substitute PE teacher did not get off to a glorious start.

Tim picked up the pace a little as the uneven cave floor gave way to perfectly smooth black lavastone. He could see lights flashing and someone moving on a circular stone platform that jutted out near the top of the pyramid. That had to be the demon, he thought. He wasn't sure what it was doing up there, but he had a feeling that it had already started the ritual designed to resurrect the Allfather known as the Magikal One.

And the only one who can stop it is me, Tim thought. But how?

He stopped at the base of the structure. It looked like a standard lavastone step pyramid. It was roughly 100 feet tall, with a stone platform that jutted out just below the top. Climbing it wouldn't really be a problem. The problem would be what to do when he reached the top.

Do I just try to take it by surprise? Tim wondered. Run straight up the building, wait until it's not looking and then run up from behind and stab it in the back?

He tried desperately to form an actual plan in his head, but nothing was taking shape. He was alone. In a strange place. With a weapon he had never used before and didn't even know if it would be effective against his enemy. And most importantly, he was running out of time. By the time he did think of an actual plan, it would probably be too late.

Screw it, Tim thought, gritting his teeth and starting to climb. There was no time to overthink things.

He gripped the spear tightly as he made his way up, pausing a couple of times to catch his breath.

I need to start going back to the gym, he thought. This is embarrassing.

Tim reached the platform and peered over the top, where he saw the most extraordinary sight. Stake was standing in the middle of the circle. As Tim watched, Stake pulled off his supernatural hazmat suit, stained white T shirt, shorts, and everything else. As he removed each piece of clothing, he tossed it over the side of the platform where it disappeared into the darkness. Tim flipped the filter on his goggles to SIR and had to dial it almost immediately down, as Stake was glowing so brightly.

Stake reached up to make two searing red gashes in his chest with the nails of both hands. Blood began to pour out of the wounds immediately. Stake leaned forward so that the blood was caught in some sort of circular stone bowl in the middle of the platform.

Ouch, Tim thought, cringing at the sight of the wounds. Although the possessed Stake gave no indication that he felt any pain, he certainly would as soon as the demon decided to leave.

Stake leaned over the bowl until enough blood had pooled in it and then reached down and placed the Puzzle Box in the middle. As soon as it touched the blood, the Puzzle Box lit up with swirling red light and began to spin like a glittering disco ball, sending flickering images of glowing runes in every direction. Stake stepped back, holding his arms up in the air as blood continued to pour down his belly and over his legs. He appeared to be saying something, but Tim couldn't make out the words over the low rumble of the earth shaking.

He could feel the tremor move up through his legs and all the way to the tips of his fingers. Was it an actual earthquake? Was the cave about to collapse on them? He had no time to consider the matter as his attention was pulled back to the platform, where the Puzzle Box suddenly became dimmer and what had been a multitude of flashing lights narrowed to a single beam that focused on a stone pillar on the edge of the platform. The pillar was one of six identical stone columns, each roughly six feet in height and about as wide as a telephone pole.

The light moved from the base of the pillar and worked its way up, illuminating a series of carved runes as it went. The beam got about three quarters of the way up before settling on one particular image. Tim was too far away to see what it was.

As soon as the beam stopped, Stake crossed to the pillar and touched the carving, which retreated back into the stone. Tim heard a crumbling sound and looked up just in time to see the stone on top of the pyramid explode, sending shattered chunks of rock careening down the side of the structure like boulders in an avalanche.

Tim ducked down just in time to avoid having a piece of rock the size of a bowling ball move through the space where his head had been. He stayed in a crouch, choking on dust, until he was sure nothing else was coming before peeking back up over the edge.

A ghostly white glow had begun to emanate from the top of the pyramid. It was faint, but it definitely gave the impression that there was something inside that was getting ready to come out.

Tim looked back at the platform, where the beam from the Puzzle Box had already settled on another pillar. Stake stepped forward and touched the second rune, which also vanished into the stone.

Tim ducked and pressed himself against the stone just as the second, larger section of the pyramid also exploded, sending even more debris raining down the side. As the dust cleared, he could see that the light emanating from within had become brighter. He looked back at the platform. The beam was already heading up the third pillar.

Okay, he thought. No time to just sit around on my ass. Plan or no plan, it was game time.

Tim jumped up onto the platform just as the third section of the pyramid blew out. At least, being on the platform, he was no longer directly in the path of the falling debris. He stayed behind Stake and tiptoed up behind him just as Stake was making his way towards the fourth pillar, apparently oblivious to Tim's presence.

Tim tightened his grip on the spear and picked up speed. His plan was to just charge at Stake and try to stab him somewhere in the leg. Hopefully that would be enough to expel the demon without causing a fatal injury.

He leaned forward to plant the tip of the spear in Stake's right leg when his target shifted suddenly out of the way and spun sideways, swinging his arm to connect with the side of Tim's head. Tim felt the blow land like a hammer and lost his footing, staggering sideways and crashing into the first pillar. He staggered quickly back to his feet and raised the spear again just as the fourth level of the pyramid blew up.

"Get out of him!" Tim yelled, choking on the dust as the cloud of powdered rock gradually cleared. He could see that the beam was already heading for the next pillar. He needed to stop Stake from getting there somehow. If he could do that, maybe he could halt this whole process in its tracks.

"I'll be happy to!" Stake said in a voice that was not his. "You have no idea how disgusting humans are. This one more than most."

"Stop right there!" Tim said, waving the spear.

"Or what?" Stake said, walking towards the fifth pillar. "Are you willing to kill your friend to stop me?"

"We're not really friends!" Tim said. "We're more like casual acquaintances. He works for my father. Who you attacked down in the ravine! Along with somebody I work with who shot me with a Devil Stick!"

"Wow," Stake said. "You're a popular guy. Ever considered that maybe you're on the wrong side?"

Tim saw the beam begin to make its way up the pillar and looked back at the Puzzle Box, floating in the pool of blood in the stone bowl. An idea occurred to him. He began backing away from Stake and heading to the centre of the platform.

"Ah, wouldn't do that if I were you," Stake said, seeming to sense Tim's intentions.

"Well, you're not me," Tim said. "In fact, you're not even you. So I don't think what you believe matters."

Tim reached the centre of the platform and reached out to grab the Puzzle Box. His hand only got within a foot of it before he was hit with a bolt of red lightning that blasted him all the way across the stone and nearly sent him flying off the platform. He only managed to avoid falling by dropping the spear and grabbing onto the final pillar. As he was pulling himself up, Stake pressed the fifth rune and the next level of the pyramid disappeared in a blast of rock.

Tim pulled himself back up. He felt around for the spear, but as the dust cleared, he could see that it had fallen on the other side of the platform. He lunged for it, but Stake got to it first, picking it up and looking at it admiringly.

"Haven't seen this thing in a while," Stake said, before tossing it away. "Won't ask you where you got it."

Stake smiled and began walking towards him. Tim backed up against the sixth pillar. He could already see the beam from the Puzzle Box was working its way over. He needed to find a way to stop the Stake demon from reaching the final pillar, but he had nothing except his SIU bag. There was nothing in there, however, that would have any kind of an effect on this thing.

"You can't stop this!" Stake said. "Now get out of the way and maybe my master will grant you the honour of eating your heart. The first meal after such a long sleep is a pretty big deal, you see."

Tim was about to say something when he heard an odd chirping sound. There were no birds up here, though. It took him a moment to realize that the sound was coming from his bag. He opened it up to see a tiny demon flutter out and hover over his head.

"Clawfist?" Tim said in disbelief.

"Murg Mag," Clawfist said, looking around with evident curiosity.

Stake stopped momentarily in his tracks.

"What in Ashtaroth's name is that thing?" Stake said, unable to suppress a laugh. "Your pet?"

"Not exactly," Tim said.

"Tim Trub," Clawfist said, narrowing his eyes at Stake.

"Nothing wrong with a little snack before the main meal," Stake said, smiling to reveal a mouth full of blackened fangs. "C'mere squirt."

Stake charged straight at them. Clawfist flew up into the air, dodging around Stake's outstretched claws, opened his mouth and sent a jet of blue fire straight at Stake's face.

"Yeaaarrrgh!" Stake roared as his hair caught fire. He swatted at Clawfist, who simply fluttered up and out of reach. When he was unable to get the Gogrub, he charged at Tim, who pulled out the only thing he had left in his bag, which was his canister of Demonex, and sprayed it straight in Stake's face. The spray seemed to react with the flames and cause an explosion, which sent Stake tumbling across the platform.

Tim ran forward to grab the spear. He turned to face Stake, whose head looked like a flaming skull. This was his chance. Despite his head being on fire, Stake was still reaching for the sixth pillar, where Tim could see that the beam had settled on a rune that was only inches away from Stake's outstretched finger.

Tim raised the spear over his head and, aiming as carefully as he could under the circumstances, drove it down into the shoulder of Stake's outstretched arm.

There was a flash of red light and a scream as Stake and the demon were separated. The demon remained on the ground while Stake flew backwards through the air, landing on the stone next to the Puzzle Box. The demon erupted in bright green flames that gave off withering heat. Tim pulled the spear out and staggered back, holding it up just in case the demon moved, but it appeared to be dead. Tim watched it for a moment more and then turned and ran over to Stake, whose eyebrows had been burned off but whose head was otherwise unmarked.

"Where the hell am I?" Stake said, sitting up.

"Take it easy!" Tim said, bending down to help Stake up. "You were possessed."

"Why am I naked?" Stake asked. "And yeow! What the hell happened to my chest?"

"The demon took you over to complete a ritual," Tim said. He realized that he didn't have a first aid kit in his SIU bag to help Stake with his wounds. He made a mental note to write an email to Volkerps about that. A small medical kit really should be part of the minimum standard equipment list.

"How did I get these cuts?" Stake said. "Did the demon do this?"

"The demon made you do it," Tim said. "It needed your blood."

"Damn it! Stake said. "I am sick and tired of these assholes using me for their stupid rituals!"

"Can you walk?" Tim asked. "We need to get out of here."

Tim hoped that Ozgoroth had managed to get help after exiting the tunnel. The cops would probably arrest him as soon as he showed his face, but he would deal with that later.

"I think so," Stake said as Tim helped him to his feet. "Where am I? The last thing I remember is getting out of the truck with your dad. What is this place?"

"This is the Temple of the Magikal One," hissed a voice that was not human.

Tim stopped and turned to see that the demon had pulled itself up to its knees. It was half-melted in a flaming pool of its own liquefied flesh, but it wasn't quite dead. And it was reaching for the final rune.

"No!" Tim said, taking a step towards the creature and raising the spear.

"The time…of the resurrection…is at hand!" the demon said, poking the rune with what was left of one of its claws.

The rune disappeared. Tim tried to move Stake off the platform, but it was too late. The final level of the temple exploded with an eardrum-shattering boom, sending debris flying in every direction. Tim and Stake managed to duck behind one of the pillars as stones the size of SUVs rolled past them and flew off into the darkness. One of them landed on what was left of the demon, obliterating it in a flash of green flame.

Tim and Stake remained huddled behind the pillar until the last of the reverberations died. Tim poked his head out and saw brilliant white light shooting out of the remains of the pyramid. He thought he could hear a high-pitched howling sound—like the cry of a large, wounded animal—but it was hard to tell with all the echoing buzz in his ears.

"What in the hell was that?" Stake said, crawling back to his feet.

Tim thought he saw something move in the light. It was hard to tell because he couldn't look straight at it for more than a few seconds without being blinded. He squinted and looked back. He wasn't sure, but he thought he saw a head rise up on a long, slender body. In the middle of the head were two large, glowing red eyes.

"Let's go!" he said, grabbing the spear and pulling Stake to the edge of the platform.

"What is that?" Stake gasped, catching sight of the figure.

"I'll explain later!" Tim said. "We need to leave! Now!"

"I've never seen anything like it!" Stake said, dazed.

"And if you don't move your ass, neither of us will ever see anything again!" Tim said, pulling Stake down off the platform and onto the pyramid. They had to step carefully because the surface was covered in debris from the multiple explosions. "Climb down! Follow me!"

"Zun Run!" Clawfist said, fluttering past them and heading for the ravine.

"What is that thing?" Stake asked. "Did it just tell me to run?"

"Yes!" Tim said. "And you need to listen to both of us! Come on!"

"Can I just go back and at least get my pants?" Stake asked. "I think I saw them back there on that platform thing."

"No!" Tim barked. "Just keep moving! When we get out of here, I'm sure you can expense an entire new wardrobe through work! Tax deductible!"

"Including cargo pants?" Stake asked. "I get them custom made by a guy in Little Carpathia. He sews special pockets for my holy water canisters and garlic bombs."

"Sure thing," Tim said. "We'll call him just as soon as we get out of here. Now run!"

The three of them made their way quickly down the side of the pyramid and back to the ravine. Tim didn't know a lot about the logistics of the resurrection of ancient demons, but he was pretty sure that it was preferable not to be in the immediate vicinity when they happened.

30

"Apologies," Volkerps said as Tim sat down in his office a few days later. "I should have told you about all of this back when you started."

"Yeah," Tim said, pulling his SIU bag off his shoulder and dropping it on the floor. It was a new one and the shoulder strap wasn't as long as he liked, which made it difficult to retrieve items without taking it off. His old one had been partially melted by a fireball during the escape from the underground temple. "Why didn't you?"

"Oh, you know," Volkerps said, waving one of his claws absently. "Wanted to wait until your probationary period was over I suppose."

"Isn't that supposed to only last 90 days?" Tim asked.

"This isn't like other departments," Volkerps said.

"So it wouldn't have anything to do with the fact that I was a human, then?" Tim asked.

"Officially, no," Volkerps said. "But, off the record–between you and me and the gravestone–probably. Yes. There's a reason that we've never hired a non-spectral in over 3,000 years. No offence, but your species does have something of a reputation for causing a shit-ton of chaos."

"None taken," Tim said. Although he was slightly offended, he couldn't really argue the point on any kind of evidentiary basis. "But still, you hired me."

"Yeah," Volkerps said. "Don't get too high on your own gas, there, though. We were the last department in the company with no humans on staff. Pressure was mounting. Besides, if we continued to hold out, it would start to look suspicious."

"To whom?" Tim said. "The Infernium or the Sons of Darkness or whatever this group is calling itself that has infiltrated the company again?"

"We know they're out there," Volkerps said, looking suspiciously at the walls. "We just don't know who they are. Not all of them, anyway. Not yet."

"Right," Tim said. "So Crimson Seal was responsible for locking all of the demon Allfathers up in the first place?"

"Yes," Volkerps said. "It wasn't an insurance company back then. It was just a group of like-minded individuals who got together to try to stop some all-powerful demons and their followers from destroying the world. That required the safeguarding of certain places and objects. Over time, that became costly. They needed to find a way to finance the operation, I guess you could say. And so the insurance business sort of grew out of that."

"Wow," Tim shook his head. "That's not the version of the story they teach in the Supernatural Chartered Insurance Professional certification courses."

"Of course not," Volkerps said. "If you want to keep something secret, turning it into a module in an industry-wide diploma program is not a smart idea. Crimson Seal isn't the biggest, but we were the first."

"I should have realized there was a connection when I saw the red seal on Belial's vault," Tim said.

"Yes, that was us," Volkerps said. "Although the logo has gone through a few rebrands over time. I never would have given you the Zoudini case as a first assignment had I known about the Belial connection. As far as I knew, it was just another routine identity theft."

"The Hesselthorn case certainly wasn't routine," Tim said.

"No," said Volkerps. "Based on what you saw and heard in the cave, it seems that they have succeeded in resurrecting Maefisto, also known as the Magikal One. The cave collapsed on what was left of the temple site shortly after you got out, so there's no way for us to get in there to know for sure. But if Enfaxizbel completed the ritual, then it's a done deal."

"Maybe all that rubble sealed it in," Tim suggested. "I mean, the explosion brought down half a city block."

Volkerps laughed, which was actually a more frightening sound than when he yelled.

"I'm afraid not," he said. "If the temple is unsealed, then you could drop the moon on her head and it wouldn't matter."

"Her?" Tim said. "The Magikal One is a she?"

"Yes," Volkerps said. "Insofar as you can call her anything. She will appear that way to human eyes, at least. I've only seen brimstone etchings, myself. Whole thing was a bit before my time. She's a shapeshifter. Some human scholars have said she's considered quite attractive by your standards. When in human form, that is. Personally, I think all humans look like chum leeches. Again, no offence."

"None taken," Tim said, although he actually kind of was. "So why are we still here? Isn't she supposed to start some great and horrible end of days in motion? Shouldn't we all be on fire right about now?"

"That's the plan," Volkerps said. "But she needs to raise the others to complete the circle."

"What about the others?" Tim asked. "There are five more, right?"

"Correct," Volkerps said. "The Dark One, the Kindly One, the Holy One, the Righteous One and the Silent One. The Holy One, you already have some experience with."

"Belial, right," Tim said. "The Sons of Darkness almost let him out. What do we do about that? They already know where the temple is."

"They do," Volkerps said. "But they still need the hammer. And it has been relocated to a more secure location."

"Do I need to know where that is?" Tim asked. "I have a feeling the answer is no. In fact, I'd kind of prefer it if the answer was no."

"Good instincts," Volkerps nodded.

"So what do we do now?" Tim asked.

"Now?" Volkerps said, snorting blue flame. "Now things get tricky. Maefisto has been out of it for a while, but it probably won't take her long to return to full power. Not if she has disciples out there willing to get her what she needs."

"What can she do?" Tim asked.

"A variety of things," Volkerps said. "She can move things telepathically. As well as conjure certain items out of thin air. That's why they call her the Magikal One, I guess. Now that she's out, she's going to concentrate all of her energies into freeing her mate."

"Her mate?" Tim said.

"Yes," Volkerps continued. "The six Allfathers are actually three pairs. Maefisto's other half is the Dark One, Azazel. He has control over the sun and stars. So the story goes, anyway. By themselves, they are extremely bad news. In their pairs, they're a disaster. And if all six of them are able to rise up to combine their powers? That's what the actuaries would call an Armageddon-level event."

"Sounds about right," Tim swallowed. "So what do we do? Track her down and try to lock her back up again?"

"Containment is probably impossible at this point," Volkerps said. "She's out. We're probably not going to get her back in."

"Then what?" Tim asked, not sure he wanted to know the answer.

"Now?" Volkerps said. "Now we're going to have to get the board involved."

"The board?" Tim said, confused. "What board?"

"Our board," Volkerps said, looking at Tim like he was dense.

"You mean the board of directors?" Tim asked. "As in, the Crimson Seal company board of directors? That board?"

"Correct," Volkerps said.

"Are you kidding?" Tim said. "They're just executives, right? They approve five-year plans and meet every once in a while to vote on how big a bonus they should give themselves for doing next to nothing! What possible help could they be with something like this?"

In reality, Tim was aware of the fact that he could not actually name a single member of the Crimson Seal board of directors and had only a vague idea of how much involvement they might have in the day-to-day business of running the company, but that was his general understanding of what most boards did with their time.

"Maybe that's what human boards do," Volkerps rumbled. "Ours is a little different."

"Sorry," Tim said. "I'm sure they are. I'm just not sure I understand how a bunch of high-paid executives are going to be able to help with something like this."

"The board has been around since the beginning of the company," Volkerps said. "Many of them were responsible for locking the Allfathers up in the first place. I met with them yesterday to bring them up to speed on where we were at with the investigation. They will probably be in touch with you shortly."

"They will what?" Tim said. "You're saying that the board of directors is going to be coming…for me?"

"Yes," Volkerps said. "Don't know if we can trust them all. Some of them only got elected a thousand years ago, but there's nothing we can do about it at this point. This is beyond the scope of just the audit committee."

"What are they going to do?" Tim asked nervously. "And what do they want with me?"

"Don't worry about that for the time being," Volkerps said. "Our primary concern is rooting out any members of the Infernium who have infiltrated the company already. I've got Lonnie working on that, but he's going to need help, especially in light of recent events."

"Right," Tim said.

"On top of that, we still actually have to do the day-to-day SIU stuff," Volkerps said. "We have to continue to function like a working division. Or at least appear to. All this fraud and malfeasance doesn't just suddenly go away because we find ourselves facing the return of a major supernatural threat. That puts us in kind of a bind. We need more staff, but we have to be incredibly careful about who we hire. No matter how much investigation we do, we might end up bringing a member of the Infernium right into the middle of our operation, which we can't afford."

"Right," Tim agreed.

"That means we're all going to be doing double duty from her on out," Volkerps said. "Things are going to get complicated. And dangerous. This is probably not what you thought you were signing up for."

"That's okay," Tim said. "If I wanted a nice, quiet life, I would have taken a job in underwriting."

"That's the spirit," Volkerps grinned. "Now you better get out of here. We're going to need to secure the rest of the artefacts. Quickly. That's partly where your next assignment comes in."

"Next assignment?" Tim said. "What is it?"

"I can't give it to you through the usual channels," Volkerps said. "That could be seen by too many other eyes and we don't know who we can trust and who we can't at this point. You'll get the info shortly."

"Okay," Tim said.

"From this point out, trust no one," Volkerps said. "Certainly no one who works outside this department. Got it?"

"Got it," Tim nodded.

"Back at the start of this Hesselthorn thing, I said that it was the kind of case that should normally go to a senior investigator," Volkerps said. "So I guess, since you completed the job and you're not dead, that makes you a senior investigator."

"Seriously?" Tim said. "Did you just give me a promotion?"

Tim wasn't expecting a promotion. Based on his informal research, staffers didn't move up from junior to senior SIU investigator roles for periods ranging from 10 to 200 years.

"No joke," Volkerps said. "Not much more money, but at least everyone will have to stop calling you 'junior' at the staff meetings."

"I'm not gonna lie," Tim said. "I won't miss that."

"You've earned it," Volkerps said. "Besides, under the circumstances, it's necessary."

"Necessary?" Tim said. "What do you mean?"

"Well," Volkerps shifted uneasily. "Only senior investigators have access to all of the, er, tools that will be required to execute certain aspects of the job."

"I'm not following," Tim said. "You mean like, certain internal databases or record systems or something like that?"

"Not exactly," Volkerps said.

"Then what?" Tim asked.

"All right," Volkerps sighed. "You'd have to find out eventually anyway. Under the terms of the original covenant that Crimson Seal was founded on, which were later included in the redacted draft of the subsequent articles of incorporation in subsection six, it officially makes you a...ummmm..."

"A what?" Tim asked.

"It sounds more elaborate than it is," Volkerps said.

"What is it?" Tim said. "If I'm being promoted to something elaborate, I think I'd kind of like to know what I'm being turned into."

"The official title is Paladin," Volkerps said.

"I'm a what?" Tim said, not sure he had heard correctly.

"It's an old title," Volkerps said. "The job description was only amended to senior special investigator about 400 years ago."

"So does that mean I'm a knight?" Tim said. "Can I call myself Sir Tim? Do I get a horse?"

"I knew I should never have hired a human," Volkerps muttered, shaking both his heads.

"What about a sword?" Tim said. "You can keep the suit of armour, though. Wearing a tie every day is bad enough without having to clank around in one of those. Not to mention what it would do to the upholstery in my car. Assuming I could even get into my car. Maybe–"

"Enough!" Volkerps thundered, sending red lightning bolts shooting up through the suspended ceiling tiles, which were already blackened from many previous outbursts.

"Sorry," Tim shrugged. "Got carried away."

"It just means that you will have access to additional SIU resources," Volkerps said. "Ones that, up until this point, for reasons that will become evident, have been forced to remain secret."

"Secret resources?" Tim said. "Like what?"

"You'll find out," Volkerps said. "Now get out of my office. I need to make some calls."

"Wait," Tim said. "Isn't there somebody else we should tell about this? Like the cops or the army or somebody?"

"Go ahead and tell them if you like." Volkerps said. "They'll probably stick you straight in the Level 9 secured spectral containment unit at Xanadu."

Xanadu was the name of the high-security psychiatric facility for the criminally possessed east of the city on the shore of the Alph River. Those who were admitted rarely walked out again–at least not without leaving a significant portion of their old selves behind.

"Maybe," Tim said. "But this has implications that extend well beyond Crimson Seal! A lot of people could die!"

"The last time this happened was so long ago that everyone has either forgotten about it or thinks it's a myth," Volkerps said. "Even if they didn't lock you up, you'd never get them to take you seriously."

"That part is true," Tim said. "I majored in Demonology at university and even there they talked about the Allfathers like they were imaginary comic book supervillains."

"Believe me," Volkerps said. "For now, this is the way to go. If it gets to the point where other people need to know, they will."

"Okay," Tim said. "By the way, Ozgoroth told me that I should ask you about the Vorloth exorcism."

"The what?" Volkerps asked. The clouds under his torso turned dark and lightning bolts began to spark in the swirling mass.

"Actually," Tim said, standing up. "Maybe we can talk about that some other time."

Tim made his way quickly out of the office and across town to the hospital, where he found his father and Stake lying in adjoining beds eating lunch.

"There's the guy!" Thad said, his mouth full of microwaved spaghetti. Aside from the green hospital gown, he looked more or less back to normal.

"How are you feeling, dad?" Tim asked.

"Fantastic," his father said, continuing to chew. "They said I can get outta here this afternoon. Just as soon as the doctor comes around to sign my discharge. Hate being stuck in this damn bed all day with nothin' to do except watch old *Psychic Detective* reruns on TV. Speakin' of which, I heard he's in here someplace, too! The main guy in that show! Horatio Duluc! You believe that?"

Tim had heard that Duluc had also been admitted to hospital due to an unspecified "supernatural trauma" of some kind, but official statements from both the police department and DeadFlix had refused to provide any additional details. Duluc's new documentary was on indefinite hold due to production delays related to the deaths of almost the entire crew. Ludovico had been transferred to the Crowley Clinic, where Tim had heard he was responding so well to treatment that he had regained nearly full function. Exorcists were even talking about releasing him.

"I heard that Duluc was in hospital, but I didn't know it was this one," Tim said. "How are you doing, Stake?"

Stake did not look quite as recovered as Thad. His entire upper torso was wrapped in bandages and he still had an IV line plugged into his arm.

"Better," Stake said. "But I don't remember anything that happened in the tunnel. First thing I remember was waking up right here."

"He was kinda rough for a bit," Thad said. "But he'll be up and right back at it before you know it. At least, if I know anything about this guy. Couldn't keep him away from the jobsite with a Devil Stick!"

"What about you, dad?" Tim asked. "Do you remember anything?"

"Me?" said Thad. "Not really. Cops told me it was some whacko who was possessed. Musta wandered down into the site somehow. They said the cave collapsed, so it's a good thing we got outta there when we did."

"It is," Tim agreed. Tim had been briefly taken into custody before security footage from Metro HQ had shown he had nothing to do with the deaths of Duluc's crew, the EoD, or anyone else at the scene.

"I've been talkin' with the city site supervisor," Thad said. "He said they're gonna divert west instead of digging out the original route. Too expensive, I guess. Plus the ground obviously wasn't stable. Good news is they're not gonna abandon the project, so we're still in business!"

"Great," Tim said. "That is good news."

"I heard you were there too," Thad said.

"Yeah," Tim nodded.

"What were you doin' there?" Thad asked. "Got sick of bein' cooped up in an office and decided to get out and watch us guys do some real work for a change?"

"I was just in the area and thought I'd stop by to see how things were going," Tim said. He saw no reason to get into all of the details.

"Musta taken you back, huh?" Thad grinned, dribbling spaghetti sauce on his gown.

"Back?" Tim said.

"Yeah," Thad said. "To when you used to work with me on the job sites. Bet you miss it sometimes, eh? Beats pushin' numbers around in a spreadsheet."

"Sometimes my job is like that," Tim said. "But I would say it has its eventful moments, too."

They were interrupted as Tim's mother Regina and Madeline arrived carrying food bags and balloons.

"Our poor injured men!" Regina called.

"Hey girls!" Thad said, sitting up as Regina picked a piece of dried pasta off his chin.

"Hello, Timothy," Regina said, looking at Tim with a pained expression. "Whatever brings you by? Aren't you supposed to be at work?"

"Just wanted to see how everyone was doing," Tim said, alert to the fact that his mother had not expected him to be there and clearly wasn't happy to see him in light of the fact that she had brought Madeline along. "But I was just heading out."

"Hi Tim," Madeline said, giving him a quick nod before making her way quickly over to Stake's bedside.

"Hi Madeline," Tim said.

"Were you able to figure out what that ghost was talking about?" Madeline asked.

"We did," Tim nodded. "Thanks again for your help on that one."

"Ghost?" Regina asked, looking suspicious. "What ghost?"

"Just a work thing," Tim said. "Madeline did some consulting for a case I was working on."

"Well, we brought food," Regina said, holding up one of the bags. "You're never going to recover on a diet of this reheated hospital swill. I swear, their food is designed to keep people sick so that they stay longer so hospitals can bill them straight into bankruptcy!"

"Great!" Thad said, setting his tray aside and rubbing his hands together. "I'm starving!"

Tim was well aware that Thad not only ate a lot, but also that he tended to scarf his food faster than a Kappa swallowing a school of water nymphs. In restaurants, it was not unusual for Thad to have cleared his plate before the server stopped by to do the 60-second quality check.

"How is my big brave warrior?" Madeline asked, pinching Stake's cheek. "Nurse Maddy is here to make everything better!"

"Uh, I'm feeling a bit better," Stake said nervously.

"You're so brave!" Madeline said. "Making sure everyone got out of that dangerous cave before it fell down and crushed everything!"

"I guess," Stake said, grinning sheepishly. "I don't really remember much."

"Don't you worry," Madeline said, reaching into her bag and pulling out a large green tube. "I brought this special skin salve from work. It specializes in treating supernatural burns and things like that. Once we get these bandages off, I'll apply it myself. It's good to have a professional around for these things, don't you think?"

"Uh, sure?" Stake said, looking slightly terrified.

"All right," Tim said, taking that as his cue to leave. "I'll um, see you all later."

Tim's next stop was the Holcroft Clinic, where he had planned to stop in to check on Giallo. When he asked at the front desk, however, they said that they had no record of a patient with that name.

"What?" said Tim, confused. Ozgoroth had specifically said that Giallo had been brought here. "Are you sure?"

"What's the first name?" asked the clerk. A large satyr with a nose ring whose name tag identified him as Zek.

"Uh, I don't actually know," Tim said.

"I thought you said you were a friend?" Zek said, eyeing Tim suspiciously.

"We work together," Tim said.

"Well, we've had nobody checked in here in the last 24 hours under that name," Zek said. "Is there something else I can help you with?"

"No thanks," Tim said. He had been in a similar position in the past and knew there was no point in pushing it. Clinics like the Holcroft were sticky about security, as they often played host to high-profile celebrity clients.

Tim headed back to his apartment, where he was surprised to find a small army of personal assistants coming and going through the door carrying heavy objects. This time, however, they appeared to be moving things out of the apartment instead of into it. Tim made his way inside and found Keef, who was busy texting on his phone.

"What's going on?" Tim asked as two young men in fashionably tight white button-down shirts stumbled past him carrying a gold lamé coffin.

"I got the part!" Keef said, looking up from his phone.

"The part?" Tim said, distracted by a crash as one of the young men lost his grip on the coffin and dropped it on his foot with a loud curse.

"In the new BloodStalker!" Keef said.

Tim blinked and tried to process what his brother was saying. "Wait," he said. "You're telling me that you're going to be the new BloodStalker?"

"Yes!" Keef said. "Well, I'm not the main guy. But I got the role of Grimaldi!"

"Grimaldi?" Tim said. "Who's Grimaldi?"

"Are you kidding?" Keef said. "BloodStalker's archnemesis is Count Ragnar von Vein."

"Okay," Tim said, trying to follow along.

"The Count's right hand guy is Grimaldi the Putrescent," Keef said. "That's me!"

"You're putrescent?" Tim said.

"Exactly!" Keef said. "It's like, the best role in the whole damn movie! I'm the main comic relief, man! I get all the best lines! Plus, I get this super-awesome death scene where BloodStalker throws me into this giant particle accelerator machine. My body gets stretched out at the speed of light under half of Transylvania before the whole thing blows up!"

"Wow," Tim said, trying to picture how such a thing might work. "That sounds pretty…uh…"

"It sounds pretty damn epic is how it sounds!" Keef said. "I went in there to read for one of the smaller parts, but the casting director liked me so much that they wanted me to do this one, instead!"

"Wow," Tim said. "That's great."

"Plus, Killian's moving into his new office down in the Neck," Keef said. "He told me I can have his old apartment while he looks for a new one."

"So you're…moving out?" Tim asked, almost unable to actually say it.

"You're damn right I am!" Keef said. "I'm a movie star, man! I can't live in my little brother's dumpy spare room any more!"

Tim decided to overlook the dumpy remark and focus on practicalities. Keef had made promises about hitting the big time and moving out many times in the past.

"So you've signed an actual contract to do this?" Tim asked.

"Killian's looking over it now," Keef said, waving his phone. "By this time next week, everything'll be signed and I'll be on my way! Principal photography starts in Paris before we head over to do some location shooting in the Carpathians."

"You're going to Europe?" Tim said.

"Bet your ass!" Keef said. "Once that wraps, we're coming back here for another two months of shooting at Necromancer Studios. You know that new complex out by the docks? Used to be warehouses. Now they make movies there. Movies in which I will star!"

"Congratulations!" Tim said, still not entirely sure he believed it. "Did you tell mom and dad about this yet?"

"Not yet," Keef said. "Maybe I'll wait until the trailer drops. Man, I cannot wait to just rub this in their fat, stupid faces! Thought I'd never amount to anything, huh? Well, suck on this, you judgmental blood bags!"

"Make sure and mention that in the commentary track," Tim suggested.

"Don't worry, buddy," Keef said, putting a hand on Tim's shoulder. "There'll be a nice slice for you. I won't forget everything you've done for me over the years."

"That's okay," Tim said. He didn't need any reward. Getting the apartment to himself again was more than enough.

"Now it's your turn to be the underachieving one!" Keef said, laughing. "Since they won't have old Keef to kick around any more."

"I think I'm already there," Tim said. "They set Madeline up with Stake behind my back. Plus, I'll bet even money the old man leaves the business to him when he retires. They treat him like the son they never had. And they have two of us already!"

"Welcome to the club," Keef said, sourly. "They may look normal, but the sad truth of the matter is that our parents are monsters. They played us off each other our whole lives, comparing me to you or vice versa. They can't function unless somebody's competing for their attention. That's why I knew I had to get out."

"Wait," Tim said. "Are you saying that's why you became a vampire in the first place?"

"Maybe," Keef shrugged. "As you know, self-analysis isn't really my bag. I'm more of a go-with-the-flow type guy. My advice? Get as far away from them as you can, buddy."

"Thanks," Tim said. He was surprised to realize that he was actually going to miss his brother when he left, although that might just be residual stress from the incident in the tunnel. "Good luck."

"Thanks," Keef said. "Oh, that reminds me. There's somebody here to see you."

"Somebody to see me?" Tim said. "Who?"

"No idea," Keef said, once again texting furiously on his phone. "One of the interns let them in. Think it's somebody from work. They're waiting in your room."

"They just let somebody walk into my room and you didn't even find out who it was?" Tim asked, suddenly uneasy.

Keef's phone rang and he answered it immediately, ignoring Tim's question. "Hey Killian! Yeah! Wait, is that normal? Okay. No. Yeah. I don't mind drinking artificial blood on camera. Do I get paid extra for that?"

Keef wandered off to continue his conversation in the kitchen to avoid the interns, who were in the process of trying to dismantle Killian's exercise machine. Tim waffled for a moment, trying to decide what to do. Should he just walk into his room and see who it was? What if it was a trap? Maybe it was Giallo. Maybe she had checked herself out of the clinic early and had something important to tell him.

Then again, maybe it wasn't.

He opened his SIU bag and took out his Demon Charger. It was low on battery, but it was all he had. He didn't want to use Demonex in the apartment because it would stain the upholstery and it took ages to get the smell out. He considered taking his laptop out and leaving it on the dining table, but he didn't want to take the chance that one of the interns might think it was Killian's and grab it.

No point in standing around out here, he thought. If somebody wanted to get me, they wouldn't announce themselves. They would just sneak up behind me in the parking garage.

Keeping a tight grip on the Demon Charger, Tim crossed the room and opened his bedroom door.

A massive red demon was standing on the other side of the room looking out the window. It turned as Tim entered and stared at him with burning yellow eyes. It was at least seven feet tall, with long curving black horns that made it a couple of feet taller still. It was wearing a suit of black Demonite armour with the letters "SV" emblazoned on the chest plates.

Tim gasped. He recognized the shield logo behind each of the letters as an extremely old version of his own company's logo. He guessed that "SV" was short for SIgillum Vermiculo, the original latin name of Crimson Seal.

The demon was holding a large silver pitchfork, the tines of which were flickering with bubbling green flame. It also appeared to have a long sword strapped to its back.

"Who are you?" Tim croaked. His mouth had suddenly gone bone dry.

"My name is Athlazar," the demon rumbled in a voice that seemed to come straight from the centre of the earth. "I'm head of corporate security for the board."

"Oh, hi," Tim squeaked. The Demon Charger he was holding seemed like a squirt gun in the face of a raging inferno. He dropped it on the ground. "I'm, uh, Tim. Lovecraft. From SIU."

"I know who you are," the demon said. "You're the one who set the Magikal One free."

"Actually," Tim said, finding his voice. "That wasn't my intent, strictly speaking! I was trying to stop that from happening! You see, there was this–"

"Silence!" roared the demon with a voice that shook the walls and made Tim shut his mouth so quickly that he nearly bit off the tip of his tongue. "I am not here to assign blame."

"Oh," Tim whispered. "Okay."

"Events have been set in motion," the demon said. "You had better sit down. There is much to discuss."

THE END